A STRING OF BEADS

Also by Thomas Perry

The Butcher's Boy

Metzger's Dog

Big Fish

Island

Sleeping Dogs

Vanishing Act

Dance for the Dead

Shadow Woman

The Face-Changers

Blood Money

Death Benefits

Pursuit

Dead Aim

Nightlife

Silence

Fidelity

Runner

Strip

The Informant

Poison Flower

The Boyfriend

Forty Thieves

A STRING OF BEADS

A Jane Whitefield Novel

Thomas Perry

The Mysterious Press
New York

Published simultaneously in Canada
Printed in the United States of America

ISBN 978-0-8021-2444-9
eISBN 978-0-8021-9204-2

The Mysterious Press
an imprint of Grove Atlantic
154 West 14th Street
New York, NY 10011

Distributed by Publishers Group West

groveatlantic.com

15 16 17 18   10 9 8 7 6 5 4 3 2 1

To Jo, as always,
with thanks to Otto Penzler and to Paul Williams

A STRING OF BEADS

1

Nick Bauermeister sat in the stained, threadbare arm-chair in the front room. Chelsea's mother had dragged the chair out to the curb because it wasn't brand-new, but he had taken it home because it was much better than any other place he had to sit, and he couldn't do much better than free. He aimed the remote control at the television set, and saw that Chelsea had left it on the channel where they always showed girls buying wedding dresses.

For a girl who hardly ever wanted anything to do with a guy anymore, she sure was interested in stuff about weddings and honeymoons or some woman getting to pick one from a bunch of bachelors. He had to click the channel button several times to get to the basketball game. He adjusted the sound, but kept his thumb on the little Mute button.

Nick was mostly pretending to watch the game. What he was really watching was Chelsea. Usually he liked watching Chelsea because she was the perfect embodiment of what a girl was supposed to look like. Even now, as she walked around in the kitchen picking up plates from the table and taking them to the sink, he couldn't help thinking about how incredible she was. She seemed unaware of the way she looked—couldn't see the way her shorts neatly hugged her thin waist and, in the back, defined her ass nearly as well as if she were naked. Her blouse had worked another button open since they'd finished dinner and she'd begun scrubbing dishes. The femaleness of her body was a force of nature too strong for her clothes.

But tonight he wasn't watching her in a friendly way. He was just watching. Nick was pretty sure that Chelsea had been cheating on him. He had no idea who the guy was, because anybody would sleep with her if she wanted him to. That information might not be available until he caught her at it.

He had noticed that she had begun sitting far away from him in the evenings lately, rapidly texting back and forth with somebody. "Who's that?" he had asked. She would answer, "My mom." Her mother was a woman who would never have had the patience to sit around sending texts. She liked to talk, and when she called she always used the chance to tell everybody what she thought of everything they were doing or weren't doing. You couldn't do that with a text message. And sometimes Chelsea would just pull a name out of the air. The last two times he'd asked her she had said she was texting Carrie or Chloe. Both of them worked as waitresses in the evening, and probably would have been fired for standing around texting their friends.

The only times he'd actually seen her talking on the phone lately was when he walked in unexpectedly and she was lying on the couch talking on her cell phone, laughing and playing with her long, blond hair. As soon as she saw him her voice would go flat. "Got to go," and she'd stand up, put her phone in her pants pocket, and get moving. She'd do something to distract him, to force him to think about something besides her phone call. She'd offer him a beer, go to the kitchen to get it, and come back already talking about something that was wrong with the car or the sink. Two days ago he had gone into her computer and noticed that she had erased about a month of e-mails.

Everything had changed on the night when he had been in the fight with the big Indian in Akron. She had been quiet for a couple of days after that, and pretended to be busy all the time—busier than anyone could possibly be. Then, when she would come home, she would always be too tired. She didn't show any signs of caring how bad he had been hurt in the fight, in spite of the fact that he had been unconscious and woke up with a broken nose and four cracked ribs.

The fight might have been his own fault, like she'd said, but losing so badly hadn't been his fault. He'd been drunk, and the Indian wasn't drunk at all. How was that a fair fight? Ever since then, Chelsea had been cold and distant, so cold that he was sure she was getting ready to leave him. But in order to do that, she would need two things—a place to live, and a new guy. Women were like frogs, jumping from one lily pad to another. Before Chelsea jumped, she would have to be sure the next lily pad was going to be there. She was nearly ready. He could feel it.

He kept his face turned toward the television set, but his eyes moved with her. Wherever she stepped, he watched. At some point there would be that peculiar twinkly sound her phone made when she got a text message, and he would be up in a second like a big cat, snatch it out of her hand, and read it. If he heard instead the buzz it made for a ring, he'd take it and say, "Who's calling?" If the man hung up instead of answering, he'd find out his name from her. Once he'd caught her like that, she couldn't deny it. If he had to, he'd beat the name out of her.

She walked across the front room without even glancing in his direction. He muted the TV so he could hear her. He heard her go down the hall, and then heard a door close quietly.

He turned the television up again to cover his movements, and stood to follow her down the hall. He would
fling open the door and grab the phone. All he had to do
was keep the sound of his steps quieter than the television
set. He began to walk very slowly. One step seemed quiet
enough, so he began the next.

The metal-jacketed 180 grain bullet that was already
spinning through the night air at 2,800 feet per second
smashed through the glass of the front window, pounded
into the back of his skull, and burst out the front, taking
with it bits of bone, blood, brain, and thirty-four years of
accumulated jealousy, disappointment, and anger. Nick was
dead before his knees released their tension and his body
toppled to the floor.

Chelsea ran out of the hallway yelling, "Nick! What
the heck are you—" before she saw his body and the window pane behind him. She cut off her mother's phone call,
dropped to her belly, and dialed 911.

2

Jane McKinnon jogged along the shoulder of the road toward home. Every morning after her husband, Carey, went off to the hospital to prep for surgery at six, she did tai chi and then went out to run. Sometimes she drove from the big old stone house in Amherst to the Niagara River near the house where she'd grown up, and then ran the three miles along the river to the South Grand Island Bridge and back. That was the run she had always made as a teenager—three miles each way with the wide blue-gray river beside her flowing steadily northward toward the Falls. Sometimes she would drive over the bridge to Grand Island and run along West River Road, looking across the west branch of the river at Navy Island and Canada. Sometimes she ran on one of the college campuses, or in Delaware Park in Buffalo.

Today she ran along the roads near the house she shared with her husband. The house had been here for a long time, the original structure a building made of fieldstones mortared over logs a foot and a half thick around 1760. Carey's ancestors had done some farming and some trading with her Seneca ancestors who made up most of the population at the time. For the past few generations the McKinnons had been doctors.

When she was a child there had still been thousands of acres of farmland along here, mostly lying fallow and waiting for the developers. Now the developers had been at work for many years, and she ran past deep green golf courses and huge, low houses set far back from the highway and surrounded by enough remnants of old forests to provide shaded yards in the summer and windbreaks against the storms that blew off the Great Lakes in the winter.

Jane seldom ran the same route two days in a row. She never permitted a pattern to develop or ran in a predictable place on a predictable day. Random changes were one of the habits she had nurtured since she was in college. Before she had been Jane McKinnon she had been Jane Whitefield. Now, like other suburban housewives, she bought groceries at supermarkets, but unlike them, she had a list of fourteen markets, and she shopped in them randomly, often at odd hours.

Life was usually quiet for Jane McKinnon, much of it taken up by various kinds of volunteer work—benefits and fund-raising for the hospital, teaching two classes a week in the Seneca language for junior high and high school children at the Tonawanda Reservation during the winter, and helping to elect political candidates in the fall. Jane avoided being chairwoman of any public events, never had her name on stationery, and never identified herself on phone calls for causes except as "Jane."

Jane still kept bug out kits in the McKinnon house in Amherst and in the house where she had grown up. Each one consisted of a packet with ten thousand dollars in cash and a collection of valid identification cards, credit cards, and licenses. The pictures on the cards were hers and Carey's, but the names were not. Over the years she had learned to grow identities, using a set of forged papers to obtain real ones, buying things with the credit cards and paying the bills so other companies would offer more credit. As soon as she had a few valid forms of identification for herself and Carey under new names, she had obtained passports in those names. Each kit also included a 9 mm pistol and two extra loaded magazines.

Jane had persuaded Carey to accept her precautions as a part of their lives. He was tall, strong, and athletic, and had no enemies of his own, so it had taken a few new experiences for him to understand that he needed to take the steps she asked of him. The most powerful had happened only a year ago. Jane had gone to Los Angeles and sneaked an innocent man serving a murder sentence out of a courthouse. Jane's runner had driven off as she'd planned, but she had been captured by his enemies, shot, beaten, and tortured for several days before she had escaped. Now Carey drove to work at the hospital on one of five different routes she had plotted for him, each with a cutoff where he could circle back and come out in the opposite direction if he was followed. But more important, she had taught him to *look*. He was aware of the people, the cars, the changes around him, and that was the one precaution that mattered most.

As Jane ran, she could still feel the effects of the damage the bullet had done to her right thigh a year ago, and she listened to the rhythm of her steps to be sure she was not favoring that side or developing a limp. She also kept her eyes moving all the time. She watched cars coming and going, studied each person she could see in a window, noted anything that looked different in any yard. Today almost everything was exactly as it had been last time she had passed. The few things that were different she memorized for the next time.

She was coming up the final stretch of road before the old stone house, building up speed because she was coming to the end, when she saw two unfamiliar cars parked in front of it.

Jane reduced her speed while she studied the cars. They were both relatively new full-size cars. The front one was a Lincoln, and the second something like it, perhaps a Cadillac. They were both plain even under scrutiny, without any of the aftermarket equipment like floodlights or antennas that plain-wrap police vehicles usually had.

She maintained her speed, ran on toward her house, and saw that both cars had people in them. There were two women in the front and two in the back of each car— eight in all. The ones she could see were elderly and a bit overweight. She didn't want to stare any harder. They were probably in the neighborhood for some charity meeting or other. One woman looked a bit like Ellen Dickerson.

All at once she realized who had come, and it made her knees feel weak. This was a visit from the eight clan mothers. They were important dignitaries in the Seneca culture. In the old times they had been simply the oldest, wisest, and most trusted women of each clan. When the Senecas in New York State had been divided into several reservations, Jane's band, the Tonawanda band, had overwhelmingly retained the old religion and codified the old form of government, including the clan mothers.

But the clan mothers were stronger and older than law. Since the day in prehistory when the Senecas had first appeared on the great hill at the foot of Canandaigua Lake, the women of each clan—Snipe, Hawk, Heron, Deer, Wolf, Beaver, Bear, and Turtle—owned a longhouse, and all of them together owned the village and the land where they raised the three sisters—corn, beans, and squash—and brought up the children. Because the women knew each child best, the clan mothers had always chosen the chiefs, and could remove them if they were disappointed.

And now, here they were, the eight clan mothers, not much different from the eight who had signed the letter to President John Tyler in 1841 to inform him that every Seneca chief had refused to sign the despicable and fraudulent 1838 Treaty of Buffalo Creek, and so the Senecas refused to be forced off the Tonawanda Reservation. The eight were also not so different from the women a thousand years before that, who had decided whether a captive should be adopted to take the place of a dead Seneca, or be killed to avenge him.

Even though she'd been running for miles, Jane felt her heart actually speeding up as she walked to the driver's side of the nearest car. She smiled. "Hello, Dorothy. Hi, Sarah. Hi, Mae. Hi, Emma. What are you all doing here in Amherst?"

Dorothy Stone said, "We came to see you, Jane. I hope you don't mind. We called ahead early this morning, but you were out already. We took a chance. Are you free, or should we come back tomorrow?"

"Come on in," said Jane. "Don't sit out here in a car."

The car doors all opened, and Jane hurried to the next car and said, "Hi, Natalie. Hi Daisy. Hi Susan. Hi Alma. Come on in. I'm so sorry I didn't know you were coming."

She trotted ahead to the front door, her mind already scrambling from place to place in her mental image of the house, picking things up, straightening others, or in desperation, hiding them. Another part of her mind was in the kitchen opening the refrigerator and searching for appropriate food and drink. It was a tradition that Seneca wives keep food ready for unexpected visitors. In the old times people from any of the Haudenosaunee nations might arrive unexpectedly after a journey along the great trail that ran from the Hudson River to the Niagara. If she had lived then she might have served soup made with corn, beans, squash, and a little deer or bear in it for flavor. Jane swung the front door open and rushed into the kitchen.

Jane pulled some berries from the freezer. She defrosted strawberries, raspberries, and blueberries in the microwave and found some angel's food cake to pour them over. She started a pot of coffee, made lemonade and put the pitcher and glasses on a tray, then piled everything on the biggest tray she had and carried it out so she could serve it as soon as the ladies had settled into seats near the big stone fireplace in the living room.

As Jane poured lemonade and brought in a tray of cookies, she surreptitiously looked around the living room. These eight formidable women looked like any gaggle of matronly ladies in spring dresses with flowered patterns, middle-aged and older, who might have come out for a game of bridge or a club meeting. But the clan mothers held great power. They were a governmental council that had been functioning the same way in the same region for many centuries longer than the British Parliament. In the old times they'd called for war by reminding the chiefs that there was a Seneca who had been killed but not yet avenged. When they didn't want war they would say that the women weren't inclined to make the moccasins for warriors to wear as they made their way to the distant countries of enemies.

As Jane occupied herself serving the cake and berries she felt the muscles in her shoulders relax a little. The women were all very cordial to Jane. "You have such a beautiful house." "I love the flowers you've got in that bed along the side. My grandmother had tulips like that when I was a little girl."

Jane accepted their compliments, and felt an almost childish sense of validation, but she could not ignore the unusual nature of this visit. This wasn't just Jane's own clan mother stopping by for a chat. This wasn't even a delegation made up of her *moitie*—Wolf, Bear, Beaver, and Turtle. It was the mothers of all eight clans assembled here together—something that couldn't be meaningless, any more than the arrival of all nine Supreme Court justices could.

She held Ellen Dickerson in the corner of her eye. She was a tall, straight woman about fifty-five or sixty years old, with deep brown skin and long, gray hair gathered into a loose ponytail that hung down her back. She sat on the edge of her chair with her back perfectly straight, and yet managed to look comfortable. Jane knew that it would be Ellen Dickerson who spoke first because she was clan mother of the Wolf clan, Jane's own clan.

Jane's father, Henry, had been a Snipe. Her mother had been a young woman he brought home from New York City who had milk-white skin and eyes so blue they looked like pieces of the sky. In order to marry Henry Whitefield she should have been a Seneca and come from a clan of the opposite *moitie* from the Snipes. The women of the Wolf clan had insisted on adopting her, just as they had taken in captive women, runaways, or refugees hundreds of years earlier. In Seneca life, children were members of their mother's clan, so a couple of years later when Jane was born, she was a Wolf.

They all talked for a while about topics of polite conversation—the early thaw this year, the beautiful spring they'd been having. Daisy Hewitt said, "I've been trying to figure out when to plant my corn. The sycamore leaves aren't the size of a squirrel's ear yet, but it's like midsummer."

"I've got a nursery catalog that divides the country into zones," said Mae. "This year I'll just go by the zone south of ours."

Then the random conversation faded, and they all looked at Jane. Ellen Dickerson said, "Jane, do you remember Jimmy Sanders?"

"Sure," she said. "He and I used to play together when we were kids. During the summer, when my father was away working, my mother and I would go out to the reservation to live."

"That's right," said Alma Rivers, of the Snipe clan. "I used to see the two of you running around in the woods. You were pretty cute together."

Ellen frowned. "He's in some real trouble right now."

"He is? Jimmy? Is he sick?"

"No. The police are looking for him."

"What for?"

"He got in a fight in a bar in Akron about two months ago. He won, so he got charged with assault I think it was. But before his trial, the man he'd fought with died." She frowned again. "He was shot. Jimmy hasn't been seen since."

Jane said, "That's horrible. I can hardly imagine Jimmy in a bar, let alone hurting somebody in a fight. And he'd certainly never shoot anybody. His mother must be going insane with worry."

"She is."

Jane looked closely at Ellen, who was sitting across the coffee table from her. Ellen's eyes were unmoving, holding her there. Jane said, "I haven't seen him in twenty years, when he was at my father's Condolence Council. No, it had to be my mother's funeral, when I was in college. Still a long time."

"We want you to find him and bring him back."

Jane's eyes never moved from Ellen's. "What makes you think I can do something like that?"

"We know it's something you can do. I'll leave it at that."

"You know that about me?"

"We've never had a good enough reason to speak. Sometimes when a person has a secret, just whispering it to yourself can risk her life."

"All this time, you've been watching me?"

"We watch and we listen. Years go by, and the sights and sounds add up," said Ellen. "Don't you think we wanted to see how you turned out? Your mother was an important member of the Wolf clan. She gave me the dress I wore to my senior prom, and helped me cut it down to fit. She drove me to Bennett High School in Buffalo so I could take the SATs and get into college." Ellen paused. "Then she took me to lunch at the restaurant in AM and A's. She was so beautiful. I can still see her."

"Thank you."

"For what?"

"For not making her sound different because she wasn't born Seneca."

"Some people are born where they belong, and some have to find their way there," said Alma Rivers. "There's no difference after that."

Ellen said, "Jimmy needs to be found and persuaded to turn himself in before the police find him. They think he's a murderer, someone who killed a man with a rifle. They'll be afraid of him, and if he resists, they'll kill him too."

"I knew him, and he was a close friend when we were kids," said Jane. "But that doesn't give me—"

"We think the one most likely to find him is you."

"That can't be true."

"Who, then?" asked Ellen. The eight women stared at her, waiting.

Jane kept her head up, her eyes meeting Ellen's, but there was no answer.

Ellen stood up. "All right, then." In her hand was a single string of shell beads. Each shell was tubular, about a quarter inch long and an eighth of an inch thick, some white and some purple, made from the round shell of the quahog, a coastal clam.

Jane's eyes widened. The Seneca term was *ote-ko-a*. The rest of the world called it wampum, its name in the Algonquin languages. Ellen placed the string in Jane's hand. Jane stared at it—two white, two purple, two white, two purple, the encoded pattern signifying the Seneca people as a nation. Ote-ko-a was often mistaken by the outsiders as a form of money, but ote-ko-a had nothing to do with monetary exchange. It was a sacred commemoration, often of a treaty or important agreement. Giving a person a single string of ote-ko-a was also the traditional way for the clan mothers to appoint him to an office or give him an important task. "Come see us soon."

"I really don't know where Jimmy is." She fingered the single string of shell beads, feeling its weight—like a chain.

"Of course not," said Alma Rivers. "I'll let his mother know to expect you. You were always a great favorite of hers."

Dorothy, Daisy, Alma, and the others all stood up too. One by one, they thanked Jane for her hospitality and hugged her. They were all softness and warmth, and together they gave off the smells of a whole garden of flowers, some mild and subtle and others spicy or boisterous. Senecas were tall people. Most of the older generation of women were shorter than Jane, but when the eight clan mothers hugged her they seemed to grow and become huge, like the heroes of myths, who only revealed their true size at special times.

In minutes they were gone, driving off in the two cars to the east toward the reservation. Jane stood alone in her living room looking down at the single strand of ote-ko-a she held in her hand. She tried to set it on the mantel, but that seemed wrong, almost a sacrilege. She put it into her pocket, where she couldn't help feeling the weight of it as she went about collecting the cups and dishes.

WHEN CAREY CAME HOME AT eight, Jane was already preparing. He came in the front door, and she called, "I'm in here."

He came into the kitchen dressed in the white shirt and tie he changed into after his morning surgeries and wore until he'd made his hospital rounds. He kissed her and said, "Something smells good. Is that dinner?"

"I'm sorry, Carey. When I came home from my run, the clan mothers were here waiting for me. I had to start hauling things out of the freezer so I wouldn't seem to be a terrible wife. As it was, I looked like a madwoman, all sweaty with my hair all over the place. Dinner is one of the things I pulled out but forgot about, so it started to thaw. It's some stew."

"I remember that stew. I liked it."

"You're such a liar." She poked his stomach with her finger. "But I made you a pie as an apology. It was the best I could do, up to my armpits in clan mothers."

"Clan mothers? Not just Ellen Dickerson?"

"All of them."

"Is that normal?"

"No." She slipped by him, plucked pieces of silverware out of the drawer, then two plates, and went into the dining room. She returned and got two water glasses and two wineglasses.

"So what was it about?"

"What?"

"The visit. All eight clan mothers coming to see you, all in a bunch."

"That's another story. I'll get to it. Meanwhile, I'd rather hear about your day."

"As surgeries go, they were all good, with no sad stories waiting to be acted out afterward when the anesthesia wore off. Everybody will be alive on Christmas if they look both ways before crossing the street for the next few months."

"Great," she said. She slipped past him again carrying two plates of salad, then came back and brought the bowl of stew. "Open a bottle of wine."

They came to the table, Carey poured the red wine, and Jane ladled the stew into bowls. They each sat down and took a sip of wine. Carey said, "So stop evading. What did they want?"

"You know that when I was a kid, my mother and I used to move out to the reservation every summer. My grandparents had left my father a little house there, and the idea was that I wouldn't lose my connection with the tribe, and I'd be better at the language, and I'd have the fun of running around loose in the woods with the other kids. My father was always gone in the summer, off in some other state building a bridge or a skyscraper or something. On the reservation my mother always had a lot of other women to hang out with."

"You were lucky. Other kids just got to go to camp and pretend to be Indians."

"I liked it, and I suppose it gave my father peace of mind to know that she and I were safe surrounded by a few hundred friends and relatives. I got to spend summers running around in the woods and hearing people speak Seneca. But I found out today that the clan mothers were watching me then, and never stopped. They knew things I didn't think they knew."

"Such as?"

"Yes. That. They knew what I was doing for all the years from college until I married you."

"How?"

"I don't know. Maybe I made a careless mistake one time, or somebody I helped told them. For all I know, one of them found out in a dream."

"Have they told anybody else?"

"No. They don't tell people things. They just know, and maybe they never use what they know. Or maybe years later they use it when they have to make a decision or solve a problem."

"You sound as though you're afraid of them."

"I don't know," she said. "Maybe I am, a little. They're eight ladies, most of them old, and a little chubby, but they have power—the regular political kind, but something else, too. When you and I are here in the house together, with the lights on, I believe in quantum mechanics and the big bang and relativity, and everything else is crap. But there's the power of history. When your ancestors built this house, they had to get the permission, or at least benign acquiescence, of eight clan mothers, who could just as easily have had them disemboweled and roasted. But I feel something else in those women. And there's a ready-made explanation that's been waiting in the back of my mind since before I was born, if I let myself pay attention to it. They're drenched in *orenda*, the power of good in the world that fights against *otgont*, all the darkness and evil."

Carey said, "Sounds like a lot of responsibility."

"Thanks for not laughing at me until I leave the room. What they said was that a little boy they saw me playing with on the reservation twenty-five or thirty years ago has grown up, and he's in trouble. He got into a fight, and a short time later the man he fought was murdered. He took off and hasn't turned up."

"What are you supposed to do about that?"

"They asked me to find him and bring him back."

"What are you going to do?"

"Find him and bring him back."

Carey stopped eating and sat back in his chair. His eyes were staring, and he took several deep breaths. "Really?"

"I know."

His face was tense with dismay and growing anger. "It's hardly a year since you came in the kitchen door barely able to walk. The burns on your back have hardly had time to heal even now. Tell me—when you go out running, don't you ever feel a twinge on your right side and remember what caused it?"

"Of course I do," she said. "I know this sounds to you as though I'm out of my mind. But I'm not going off with some stranger who's got people chasing him down to kill him. They want me to find an old friend and tell him that coming back is for his own good."

"I can't believe that you'd even consider getting involved in something like this. We have police. We have courts. In spite of everything, most of the time they do their jobs and get things right. It almost never makes sense to run away from them. This is just madness. For a long time you told me this part of your life was over."

"I'm sorry, Carey. I know this is difficult for you to understand. I don't want to go. I especially don't want to spend any time away from you. But this time I have to."

He stared at her for a moment. "If you honestly believe that's true, then I guess I have to accept your judgment. I can have my people postpone my appointments and go with you."

She shook her head. "They're not just appointments. They're surgeries. People could die if you don't help them. And what I have to do might be possible if I do it alone. It won't be if anyone goes with me. That's why the clan mothers came to me."

"You know that if you shelter him from the police, even for a day, you can be arrested and charged with a crime."

"I know."

He sat unmoving. He looked as though he was about to give in to the anger, but she could tell he was fighting it to keep his composure. "I think you're making a mistake. That's for the record. But I can see you're going to do it anyway."

"I'll try to make it as quick and painless as I can."

"I hope you succeed." Dinner was over. He got up, tossed his napkin on the table, and walked to the staircase.

When Jane finished clearing the table, loading the dishwasher, and cleaning the counters, she went upstairs. Carey had gone to bed.

3

Jane drove away from the McKinnon house early the next morning. The traffic on the New York State Thruway going eastward away from Buffalo was light, even though the incoming traffic was heavy.

The Tonawanda Reservation was about three miles north of the Thruway, just northeast of Akron. After the Revolutionary War, George Washington had signed the treaty letting the Senecas retain roughly two hundred thousand acres of land in this single plot. During the next half century, a cabal of prominent New York businessmen formed a land company and stole legal ownership of the reservation with the help of federal Indian agents who were openly on their payroll. The Tonawanda Senecas, led by the clan mothers, could only repurchase eight thousand acres. What was left was mainly swampy lowlands and second-growth forest, but various parts had been farmed as long as the land had been occupied.

Jane drove through Akron to Bloomingdale Road, then to Hopkins Road. The houses she passed were all ones she had known since she was born. She knew the people who owned them, and knew the complicated network of kinship that connected one family with another throughout the reservation, and even some of the connections with people from other Haudenosaunee reservations in New York and Canada. Jane turned and drove up to the house on Sand Hill Road that belonged to the Sanders family. She stopped her white Volvo beside the road and studied the place for a few seconds. There had always, for Jane, been a profound feeling of calm in the silence of the reservation. The thruway and major highways were too many miles away to be heard. The roads on the reservation didn't allow for much traffic, and didn't lead anywhere that big trucks wanted to go. Today the only sounds were birdsongs and the wind in the tall trees.

The Sanders house was old, but it had a fresh coat of white paint on it, and Jane was glad to see the shingle roof was recent too. Jane got out and headed for the wooden steps to the porch. She had always loved the thick, ancient oak that dominated the yard and shaded the house, so she patted its trunk as she passed. She remembered how she and Jimmy had made up stories about it when they played together as children. They agreed that a great sachem had been buried on this spot thousands of years ago, and an acorn planted above his heart had sprouted into this tree. They decided that the buried sachem's power inhabited the tree, and so the tree had always protected the family from harm.

The front door of the house opened while Jane was still climbing the steps, and Mattie Sanders came out. "Jane?" she said. "You're looking wonderful."

"So are you, Mattie. All I did was grow taller."

Mattie Sanders hugged Jane tightly. She was about five feet nine inches tall, with long, thick hair that had been jet black when Jane had come here as a child. Now it was hanging down her back in a loose silver ponytail, the way

Jane wore hers to do housework. "If you came to see Jimmy, I'm afraid I have bad news for you."

"I heard about his troubles yesterday," Jane said. "I came to see you."

"Well, then, come on inside." Mattie looked up and around her at the sky and the trees. "Or we could sit out here if you'd like."

"Out here would be nice," Jane said. "It's such a spectacular day."

"Yes," said Mattie. "Of course, I see a day like this, and I hope that Jimmy's somewhere getting the benefit of it. It could still get cold and wet even at this time of year."

They went to a small round table on the porch under the roof, and Jane sat in one of the four chairs. She thought about how pleasant this spot was during a late spring or summer rain, and felt sorry for Jimmy.

Mattie went through the screen door into the small kitchen. She would feel compelled to observe the ancient customs, so Jane knew she would be back with food and drinks, just as Jigonsasee had, six or seven hundred years ago when Deganawida and Hiawatha—the historical one, not the Ojibway hero Longfellow later used in a poem and gave Hiawatha's name—had stopped at her dwelling beside the trail. Jane sat alone and listened to the chickadees and finches calling to each other in the big old trees. Mattie returned with a plate of brownies and a pot of tea, and resumed the conversation. "So you heard about Jimmy's problems."

Jane took a brownie and nibbled it. "These are wonderful, just as I remembered them. Thank you."

Mattie nodded.

Jane said, "I got a visit from some of my mother's old friends, and somebody remembered that Jimmy and I were close friends when we were kids, and thought I'd want to know."

Mattie looked at Jane's face for a second, and in that second, Jane knew that she had already seen through what Jane said to what she hadn't said.

Jane braved the look, like swimming against a current. "Since I heard, I've been worried. What happened?"

Mattie looked at the surface of the table for a second, then up. "Jimmy isn't the boy that you knew, any more than you're the little girl he knew. You both grew up. You're like the woman I thought you would be. Maybe girls are more predictable. He fooled me. When boys are little you can't imagine them getting into fights in bars. Or some of the other things they do either. Jimmy is a good person, a good son, but he's all man."

"Where is he?" asked Jane.

"I don't know," said Mattie. "He didn't say he was leaving. After he was gone he didn't call or write to say where he was going or when he'd get there."

"Do you think he needs help?"

Mattie sighed. "Anyone who's alone and running needs help, whether he knows it or not. I just don't know where he went. And I assume the police are watching me to see if I get into a car and drive."

Jane said, "I think I can find him."

Mattie said, "You can only get in trouble, and that would be twice as bad."

Jane said, "South?"

Mattie sat motionless for a second, then nodded. "Maybe like you two went south that time when you were teenagers."

Jane said, "And how about you, Mattie? Are you getting along okay here?"

Mattie shrugged. "I always have. I have my Social Security, and a pension from the school system." Jane remembered Mattie had worked as a janitor in the Akron schools at night. "I also work four mornings a week at Crazy Jake's.

It gives me a few bucks to save." Crazy Jake sold tax-free cigarettes and gasoline just outside the reservation.

Jane said, "If Jimmy gets in touch, please tell him I'd like to help. I know some good lawyers."

"We probably wouldn't have what they charge."

"I'll get him a deal." Jane heard the sound of a car engine, and then the squeak of springs and shock absorbers as a police car bounced up the road toward them. The car stopped, a tall state trooper got out and reached for his Smokey Bear hat, put it on, and walked toward the porch. A second car, this one a black unmarked car, pulled up behind. The driver sat there staring frankly out the window at the women on the porch. Jane and Mattie sat motionless as the state trooper climbed the steps to the porch. "Good morning, Mrs. Sanders," he said. He nodded to Jane and said, "Ma'am." He turned to Mattie. "I came by because I was wondering if you had heard from Jimmy yet."

"I haven't," said Mattie.

"Sorry about that," said the trooper. "If he calls or writes, please let him know we'd like to talk to him. Thanks, ladies." He got into his car and drove up the road.

Mattie said, "They drive by my house day and night, hoping they'll see Jimmy. They must have seen your car and hoped it was him."

"I suppose that's to be expected," Jane said. "I'm surprised they're so obvious, though. I guess they thought they couldn't fool you anyway." She took another sip of her tea and finished her brownie. Then she stood and hugged Mattie. "It's been great to see you again. I wish it hadn't been at such a bad time."

"Me too," said Mattie.

"I'll come and see you when things are better." She bent to kiss Mattie's cheek. Then she got into her car and drove. The reservation had only a few roads, and they all met. She went up Parker Road past Sundown Road to Council House Road.

She took Allegheny Road to Java, where it became Cattaraugus Road. She drove south to the mechanic's shop that was owned by the Snows. She pulled close to the garage doorway, got out, and walked to the front of her car.

"Janie?"

Jane turned her head and saw a dark-skinned man about her age wearing blue work pants, steel-toed boots, and a gray work shirt with an embroidered patch above the pocket that said RAY. Jane stepped up and hugged him. "It's great to see you, Ray. I was afraid you would be on vacation or something."

"No, the guys who work for me get vacations. I'm always here, like the doorknob. Got a car problem?"

"I wondered if you could do the scheduled maintenance on my car—you know, oil, filter, lube, check and replace belts and hoses—and then keep it here safe for at least a week or so."

"I'd be glad to. You staying around here?"

"I thought I'd go on a hike, like we used to when we were kids."

Ray Snow's brows knitted. "You trying to find Jimmy?"

Jane looked around to see if anyone else was in earshot. She smiled and said, "Not me. That's the police's job. I wouldn't want to get involved."

"Well, that's good. A person would have to be stupid to do that." He whispered, "Give him my regards."

4

Jane pulled her backpack up over her shoulders, adjusted the waist strap, and began to walk. She had known from the visit of the clan mothers that it might come to this, but she had not been sure until she talked with Mattie. She had not been able to tell Jane where Jimmy was—had not known, specifically—so what she did was let Jane know that maybe the answer was already there, inside Jane's memory.

Jane wasn't in doubt about how to get there. When Jane and Jimmy were fourteen, they'd saved money all spring. They had spent a few days collecting road maps, hoarding clean socks and underwear from the laundry, and planning. On the third morning after school let out in June, they set off toward the south.

Today, as Jane walked out of town away from Ray Snow's mechanic shop, she made a hundred-yard detour so she could walk in the footsteps of the fourteen-year-old Jane. She and Jimmy had begun their journey on the reservation and walked to the south. The first big moment for Jane was when they crossed Route 5. It was an old road, one that white people had made by paving the Wa-a-gwenneyu. Underneath the pavement was the trail that ran the length of the longhouse-shaped region that was Iroquois territory, from Mohawk country at the Hudson River to Seneca country at the Niagara River.

The reason for their trip was personal and complicated. They told other people they wanted to explore a bit of the region. But what they were looking for was themselves. Jane and Jimmy had lost their fathers when they were eleven and twelve. Later, after Jane had become an adult, she realized that this coincidence must have been what drew them together and launched them on their trip. Without their fathers they had lost part of their link to the past, to the long history that had produced them. Changes that had taken place before they were born left them as two lonely Senecas, survivors among countless millions of other people in a world that sometimes bore no resemblance to the one that had formed their culture. Jane had been especially lost without her father, because her mother was white and didn't speak Seneca even as well as Jane did, and they lived in a city miles from the reservation. Jane and Jimmy had seen nothing in junior high school that made them want to be part of the wider world, learned no point of view that gave them an acceptable place or a purpose in it.

When they talked about this during their thirteenth summer, they had made a pact to go on a trip the following summer, when they would be fourteen. They would travel as the old people had, speak only Onondawaga, and visit places that had not been changed, deforested, tamed, or demolished. Maybe they would learn something about who they were. In their fourteenth summer, they went.

Jane and Jimmy had hiked only a few miles by the time they reached Route 5, but when they crossed the highway they became travelers, not kids going for a walk. They were going back to the indeterminate time before the arrival of white people, when the eastern woodlands still extended from the Atlantic to the Mississippi, and from James Bay to the Gulf of Mexico. Whenever Jane and Jimmy stepped a hundred yards into the woods between the roads it could have been two hundred or ten thousand years ago.

A couple of miles farther on would be the New York State Thruway. Jane looked at her watch when she reached it, and remembered. It had been noon by the time Jane and

Jimmy had arrived on this spot. The thruway was a serious barrier. There was a high chain link fence, then a weedy margin about two hundred feet wide, and then a two-lane strip of highway full of cars driving sixty or seventy miles an hour toward the west. Next came a central island of grass and trees, and then the two-lane strip going east, and another weedy margin before the next fence. Kids from the reservation knew that the thruway was a fearsome barrier that kept deer, foxes, and other animals captive on one side or the other. The thruway was a toll road, so it had few exits a pedestrian could use for crossing. Some were thirty miles apart.

Jane and Jimmy had stopped to eat their sandwiches and study the traffic on the thruway. Their maps said they'd have to go east as far as Le Roy to reach the next exit, or chance a quick run across the pavement. They had begun their journey already knowing which it would be, but they took their time sitting side by side in a bushy area outside the first chain link fence and watching the cars go by, the nearer ones from left to right and the farther from right to left. Jane knew a car going sixty covered eighty-eight feet per second. If they could start right at the moment when a car passed, they could be across the pavement before the next arrived, but there was a problem of visibility. If a state police car came by at the wrong moment, they'd be picked up and suffer serious but nonspecific consequences far beyond the anger of their mothers. In the end they climbed the fence, crawled close to the pavement, pushing their backpacks ahead of them, and waited. They watched cars coming, evaluating each one, and finally saw a break in traffic that was inexplicable but welcome, and dashed across the two westbound lanes into the stand of trees in the center margin. They sat and laughed, not because there was anything funny, but because their fear had made them giddy. A state police car passed on the side they had just crossed, and it was twenty minutes before they dared to make the second crossing.

Grown-up Jane climbed the fence at a post, swung a leg over and set her toe in a link on the far side, lowered herself to the ground, then trotted across the field to the center strip and began to look to the right, barely pausing in the trees before she crossed the last two lanes. When she got to the second fence she dropped her backpack on the other side and stepped on the top of the fence to vault over. As she walked on, she thought about how easy it had been this time. Had she and Jimmy been smaller at fourteen? Probably Jimmy had, but he was fast, strong, and wiry, and could climb a tree like a squirrel. She guessed the fear of doing something they knew was illegal and dangerous must have weighed them down.

Jane faded into a stand of hardwood trees on the other side and kept walking south. She remembered the trip as fully as she could, bringing back details and finding others in the landscape as she went. She and Jimmy had stayed away from big north-south routes because they'd wanted to be in the woods and not on a road. In the old days, Senecas used to travel south on foot to the countries of the Cherokees and Catawbas to fight. They took canoes down the rivers and streams that ran south from Seneca country into Pennsylvania, and she had read in old sources after she'd grown up that they had also used a route along the crests of the Appalachian mountain ranges to strike as far south as Georgia. A number of times in the early 1700s the sudden appearances of Iroquois war parties in the high country had raised formal protests from the governors of the colonies of Pennsylvania, Maryland, and Virginia.

While Jimmy and Jane had walked, they spoke Onondawaga by advance agreement, forcing themselves to avoid blurting out something in English. But as the time passed, they spoke more comfortably, thinking less and less about it. Jane's vocabulary was good, but a bit formal and archaic. Much of it had come from her grandfather and grandmother, who had taken over the job of teaching her after her father died when she was eleven. But Jimmy had always lived on the reservation, and his language was more flexible and functional, replete with borrowings from English.

Now, as Jane retraced the route over twenty years later, she thought about the two fourteen-year-olds and their relationship. They had been very close at six, closer still at eight or nine, but then they had reached that strange age around ten when Jimmy stopped playing with her. She had gone back to her parents' house for school at the end of one summer, and when she came back to the reservation in the spring, Jimmy and his friends had refused to have anything to do with her. At first she searched her memory for the crime she must have committed, but came up with nothing. Eventually her mother had asked her why she was alone all the time, and heard Jane's story with sympathy. She explained it as "the way boys are. A time comes when they go away from us for a while. They fight a lot. It's the last time in their lives they can do it without killing each other, so it's probably okay. They play rough sports, they have secrets, they compete. There seems to be an agreement that girls don't exist. It lasts two or three years, and then around seventh or eighth grade, they admit girls to the world again. It's as though they couldn't see us for a while, and then they can again."

Just as her mother had predicted, when Jane came back to the reservation in the summer of her thirteenth year, not only Jimmy but the other boys too were friendly again. Jane and Jimmy became close, but forever after there was a slight reserve between them. They had each discovered things during the break that made using the different pronouns "he" and "she" seem not nearly large enough to reflect the real differences between the sexes.

Jane knew she was coming to a bad place as she walked today. The first night she had camped, just as she and Jimmy had twenty years ago, under the stars in an old apple orchard at the back of a farm. The second was so warm and still that they lay in a field under the stars, and she did the same on her second night. But on the third night the weather had changed. When they had decided to take a summer hiking trip, they hadn't thought hard enough about rain. She remembered one of them saying, "We should set aside extra time in case it rains," and the other replying, "The old people didn't hide under roofs when it rained. They just kept going. Skin is waterproof." She was pretty sure the stupid one was the fourteen-year-old Jane Whitefield.

The rain began before first light on Jane and Jimmy's third day and didn't stop. They walked southward under a ceiling of gray clouds that produced a steady summer downpour as though the sky were draining onto the earth. The pair walked all day in soaked clothing. They were cold at the start, and kept telling each other the rain would end in the afternoon. In the afternoon the rain was heavier. They both agreed that rainstorms in Western New York blew through from somewhere on the Canadian plains across the lakes and eastward, and since they were walking south, the rain clouds shouldn't stay with them this long. They should just pass over them to the east and be gone. But the rain went on all day, and as night fell, the rain picked up strength.

They trudged along the edge of an alfalfa field where a farmer's ancestors had left a windbreak of chestnuts and maples that had long ago grown too tall to stop the wind. A more recent owner had planted a set of six-foot-tall evergreens as a hedge, so if they stayed beside it they didn't feel the full force of the northwest wind. They were approaching the second major highway, the Southern Tier Expressway, just as the dim glow from the invisible sun gave out.

To them the expressway looked almost exactly like the much-older New York State Thruway. It was illegal to climb over the fence to the margin of the big road, and dangerous to cross the lanes to the other side. Now that it was dark, the traffic seemed to be mostly giant tractor trailers carrying cargo across the southern edge of the state. Commuters had already made it to safe, dry homes, and vacationers were somewhere waiting for the weather to improve. Jane and Jimmy watched a few high, long trucks coming along the highway like trains, their headlights appearing in the near lanes somewhere a mile or so to the left, where the road curved gradually, and their taillights blinking out a few miles to the right at the crest of a low ridge. The map in Jane's pack told them they were near the exit for the Seneca Nation Allegany Reservation.

Jane said, "See across on the other side?"

"It's a rest stop," said Jimmy. "The building might be closed at night. I don't see a lot of cars."

"It won't hurt to check," Jane said.

As Jane remembered their conversation now, she'd had no sense of concern, no reluctance or foreboding. The rest stop was just an unoccupied place that might be dry inside.

They got a sense of the speed of the trucks, the average distance between them, and a measure of how far in front the beams of their headlights extended. They clambered over the chain link fence, moved closer, and waited for the right moment.

It came. They scooped up their packs, ran hard, and came across to the wooded center strip before the next truck's headlights could reach them. They squatted in a thicket for a few minutes before they chose a time to run again, and this run was successful, too. They made it all the way to the opposite fence before the glare of the next set of headlights appeared.

They used the next period of darkness to climb the fence and trot into the long parking lot of the rest stop. Jane remembered that she felt hopeful for the first time in hours. Her sneakers were so wet they squished as she walked on the pavement. She said, "I only see two cars, and they're way down there by the entrance. That building is probably bathrooms, and this one too." She pointed to a low building like a cinderblock box with a roof.

As they approached she saw a small sign that said MEN and let Jimmy peer inside while she walked around the building to the door that said WOMEN. She held her breath as she reached out to the doorknob. It turned and she breathed again.

She slipped into the restroom and felt the rain stop pounding on her head and shoulders. Suddenly the water was reduced to a thrumming sound on the roof, and a noise as it trickled down off the eaves. The room was a single concrete-and-cinderblock box with three toilets in small stalls, three sinks, and a big plastic trash barrel. The mirror above the sinks was scratched with initials. She couldn't imagine why some woman would make use of a diamond that way.

Jane used the farthest stall and thought about the luxury of it after three days on the trail. She came out the door and sidestepped along under the eaves, where there was a curtain of water coming down. She stopped at the men's room door and knocked. "Jimmy?"

"Coming." She heard a flush.

She waited until he opened the door a few inches. "Come on in."

She said, "No, it smells like pee. Let's wait it out in the ladies' room." She remembered thinking that men and boys' anatomies gave them the option of missing, but didn't want to say anything that would start that kind of discussion.

"Okay," he said. They sidestepped to the ladies' side and entered.

There was a switch on the wall like the ones in hallways at school that kids weren't supposed to be able to operate because only teachers had keys. But the girls Jane knew had discovered by second grade that a bobby pin was just as good as the principal's light key. She had a couple of pins in her jeans pocket, so she took one out and stepped to the switch.

"We don't want light," said Jimmy. "It'll attract attention."

When they started out they'd both been convinced that they had a perfect right to be exploring a part of the Seneca homeland on foot. They also believed that if the state police came along they'd be arrested and their mothers forced to drive to a remote police barracks to bail them out. "Yeah, you're right," Jane said, and put away the pin. There was light coming through the small, high window from a streetlamp lighting the parking lot, so they could see well enough.

They sat down on the concrete floor together and listened to the rain. "It's raining harder," she said. "We're lucky we found this place. We'd better plan to sleep here."

Jimmy shrugged. "When we get home let's not tell people we slept a night in a bathroom."

Jane imitated the shrug. "In the old days the warriors would have loved a nice, dry girls' bathroom to stay in."

Jimmy laughed. "But one of them would have said, 'Let's not tell anybody.'"

They unrolled their sleeping bags and found that they were only soaked around the edges, where their covers had left an end exposed. Then they took out a few items to see if they had also stayed dry. Jane was already thinking about the awkwardness of changing clothes in the restroom, but she was pretty sure she was going to try. She had packed fairly well, with her clean clothes in a couple of plastic trash bags, and her snacks in another. The maps and other papers had been in a pocket on the side of her backpack, but even they seemed salvageable.

She opened the road map they had used the most because there were details besides roads, and held the paper under the hand dryer on the wall for a couple of minutes, until it was crinkly but dry. At the same time she surreptitiously moved her lower body under the dryer too, and found that the hot blast of air helped. She turned around to look at her friend. "Jimmy," she said. "What's that?"

In his left hand was the frame of a small gun-blued revolver, with the cylinder pulled out and to the side. He was wiping it carefully with a rag made from a torn-apart cotton undershirt. He had emptied the cylinder onto his sleeping bag, and Jane could see nine .22 long rifle rounds. "I've got to wipe it down so it doesn't rust."

"Where did you get a gun?"

"It was my dad's," he said. "I guess that makes it my mother's now. It's only a twenty-two, but it holds nine rounds. He was going to take me out shooting cans and things, but I didn't get old enough in time." Since Jimmy and Jane had both lost their fathers, she was familiar with the feeling that she hadn't grown up fast enough to do things with her father that she would never do now.

"Can I see it?"

She could tell he was reluctant, but he knew he had to acquiesce because Jane was his friend, and he could hardly bring out a gun and then refuse her. As he held the revolver out, he turned the barrel downward toward the concrete floor and left the cylinder open. "See?" he said. "You always look to be sure the cylinder is empty." His right to state the rules was all he insisted on keeping for himself.

Jane took the pistol. Engraved on the barrel was EU-REKA SPORTSMAN MODEL 196. She swung the cylinder in and aimed the gun at the Tampax dispenser mounted on the wall across the room. Then she slowly turned the cylinder and appreciated the clicks as it reseated each of its chambers between the hammer and barrel. "It's cool," she said. "If my mother knew you had this, she wouldn't have let me out of the house." She gave the gun back to him, her carefulness displayed as respect for its powerful magic.

"I wasn't planning to take my gun out, so nobody would ever know unless I needed it."

"For what? Are you suddenly afraid of bears?"

"This wouldn't kill a bear," he said. "But it might sting him enough to make him leave us alone."

Jane smiled. "Or maybe you could just bravely hold him off while I run two or three miles to the next town."

Jimmy laughed. He finished wiping the gun down, used a separate rag from a plastic sandwich bag that smelled like oil, and then reloaded it and put it into its own pocket inside his pack. Jane couldn't help memorizing its exact position, because knowing was power too.

They sat in the dim light, listening to the rain.

Jane couldn't remember when she first became aware that there was trouble. Afterward she thought that she had heard trouble in the sound of the car coasting off the highway into the rest area. The engine was too loud, a burbling sound that meant it had a rusted-through muffler. There were deep puddles in the rest stop lot, and when the car went through them she could hear the spray whishing up against the thin sheet metal, and an occasional squeak of springs. The headlights were bright, stabbing through the small, high window and lighting the women's restroom.

They saw the light go out, then heard the car door creak as it opened and then slammed, and then a man's footsteps splashing a few steps to the shelter. They heard him enter the men's room, and then there was silence for a time as he was, she imagined, relieving himself.

Jane and Jimmy didn't need to tell each other to remain still and silent. There had been only one set of footsteps heading into the men's room. That was good. In a minute or two maybe they would hear him leave. They listened, but it didn't happen. Instead, the door of the women's restroom swung open, and the spring pulled it shut.

"Well, well." A man's voice, not young. It sounded slightly raspy and cracked, and they could smell cigarettes. There was a slightly Southern elongation of the two words that told Jane he was from the Pennsylvania side of the road, a few miles south. "Where did you two come from?"

Jimmy said, "If you need to use the bathroom, we can go next door and give you privacy."

"Me?" The man laughed. "No. I just did that, and I'm not shy." He took out a cigarette and flicked his lighter. The flame cast an eerie wavering light like a weak candle, but the glow made his eyes gleam. He was about forty, but he had long hair that was longer in the back, and a tattoo on his left hand. "Oh, my Lord," he said. "A girl too. And you're both all wet." His lighter snapped shut, throwing the room back into darkness. "You two run away from home?"

"No," said Jane. "We were just walking and the rain got worse. We don't live too far from here."

The man said, "Yes you do. Nobody who lived close by would choose to spend the night in a shit house." There was no rancor in his voice, but no kindness either. It was simply an observation, a fact.

"We figured the rain will stop before long," she said.

"You're probably right," the man said. "Tell you what. I'll hang out for a while, so you'll be safe, and when it stops, I'll give you a ride."

"We're fine," Jimmy said. "We don't really need a ride."

The man chuckled. "Hell, the two of you sitting in here shivering wet, you need some adult supervision. First thing you got to do is get some dry clothes. That hand dryer over there work?"

"Yes," said Jimmy. "But we're fine."

"I wasn't thinking of you so much as her," said the man. He kept talking as though nothing they said mattered, looking straight at Jane. "A young girl like you could catch her death sitting all night in wet clothes." He leaned forward to look at her. "I've seen that happen. What's your name?"

Jimmy said to Jane, "I think the rain's slowing down. Let's go." He began rolling his sleeping bag.

"Okay," the man said to Jane. "I'll give you a name, then. How about Jenny? Or Jill. Or—"

"Thanks for the offer, but we're leaving," Jane said. She began to pack her things hurriedly.

"If you're too shy to change among friends, I'll help you," the man said, and stepped toward her.

Jimmy lunged and collided with the man in a football tackle that pushed him into the wall, but the man wasn't entirely taken by surprise. When Jimmy tried to disentangle himself and fight, the man held him in a headlock and punched him in the face three times, then brought his knee up into Jimmy's face. Then the man tossed him to the concrete floor, where he lay unmoving.

"Your playmate's plan seems to have slipped his mind," said the man as he took his next step toward her. "If you'd like to take your clothes off yourself, get started."

Jane's hand was already in Jimmy's backpack feeling for the gun. She closed her fingers around the handgrips just as the man clutched her arm. He yanked her arm up out of the backpack, but with it came the gun, and Jane pulled the trigger.

The shot was a bright flash of spitting sparks, and the small caliber charge gave a loud, reverberating report in the tiny concrete room. The man completed his tug and pulled Jane to her feet, but she didn't release the gun. Instead, she squeezed the trigger and the bright light and loud noise ripped the air again. It was then that the man realized he had been hit by the first round. "Bitch."

Jane kicked her foot toward his groin, and probably missed, but she kicked his thigh where he had been shot, and he pushed off backward and retreated toward the door.

"Wait," Jane yelled. "Take out your car keys and drop them on the floor."

"Are you kidding?"

She gripped the gun with both hands to keep it from shaking. "Do it."

The man began to fumble in his pocket.

"Pull a knife," she said. "Please try it."

He changed hands and pockets, and then dropped the keys at his feet.

Jane said, "That's it then. I'm not the only one with a gun. When he wakes up, he's going to be mad. If you're not gone, he might kill you. So get going."

"How am I supposed to walk out there after you shot me in the leg?"

"It's not my problem, but you'd better get as far as you can, because if either of us ever sees you again anywhere, we'll kill you."

The man went out through the door, and she heard the spring pull it shut. Jane moved to stand along the wall at the hinge side of the door, the gun in her hand, watching the door for the next half hour before Jimmy came back into consciousness. Now as the grown-up Jane approached the rest area in daylight, she thought about the fourteen-year-old boy who had taken that terrible beating to protect her. It was unlikely he could have grown into a man who would do something as cowardly as ambush and murder a witness against him. People changed, but she was sure Jimmy hadn't changed that much. And as she allowed herself to repeat the feelings of that horrible night, she knew a second reason why she had come. It was her turn.

5

Jane felt trepidation as she came from the brush on the side of the Southern Tier Expressway. She stood perfectly still for a full minute as she studied the cars in the lanes close to her. She looked in each direction and reassured herself that all the threats were simple and visible. She walked onto the parking lot. Nothing had changed in this place since she'd been here twenty years ago. She kept looking ahead for signs of Jimmy. She had guessed that when he decided to escape, he would think of the path they had taken the summer when they were fourteen. Maybe she'd been wrong.

She looked at the small building at the end of the parking lot as she approached, and her stomach tightened. She hadn't imagined she would ever return to this rest stop. She walked directly to the ladies' room door on the small, lonely building. She pushed the door so it opened against its spring, and then closed as she came in. She looked around her. The initials scratched in the mirror over the sinks were gone. Probably someone had gone all the way and broken the mirror at some point, so it had been replaced. Today there was graffiti on the walls. Had there been twenty years ago? No. If Jimmy came here and saw the writing, he might have left a message to her here. When she had the thought she realized that was what she had been searching for—not Jimmy himself, but a message only for her, to tell her where he was hiding. Jimmy wasn't somebody you could just track down and find at the end of a trail. He had to invite her, allow her to find him.

Jane stepped to the spot away from the door where she and Jimmy had sat that night and tried to get their sleeping bags to dry. There were the same three sinks on the right, the three stalls beyond them, and the same hand dryer on the opposite wall. She took out a hairpin like the one she hadn't used twenty years ago and walked toward the switch plate for the lights. She stopped. Last time, when they were fourteen, Jimmy had stopped her. Keeping the lights off hadn't kept that horrible man from finding them, but the darkness had probably saved her from being raped. This time she used the pin to turn on the lights, then stepped to the wall and began to read.

She knew his message wouldn't be any of the big, bold marker lines. His would be one of the small pencil messages that a person had to look for. "They're cute when they're little, but don't bring one home," some woman had written. "They grow up stupid." She kept reading the small handwriting on the wall. "Kylie, Mona, and Zoe were here, but wish they were somewhere else." Somebody had replied, "We wish you'd never come back." There it was. "J. If you're here to help me out, I'm heading for the oldest place. J."

Jane knew what Jimmy meant by the oldest place. When they had come this way twenty years ago they had been on a summer camping trip. But they had also been trying to go back in time. They had wanted to feel the way they would have felt if they'd been an Onondawaga boy and girl long ago. For them the easiest way to do that was to turn away from everything that had happened since the 1600s, and that meant entering the forest. In the second-growth woods between the Tonawanda Reservation and the southwestern part of Pennsylvania, they felt like *ong-we-on-weh*, "the real people." They were on parts of the land that had not been damaged much. They were where the past still was.

Jane found the pencil in her backpack, took it out, put her face close to the wall, and erased Jimmy's message. She checked it from several angles to be sure it couldn't be read or brought back, then wrote in the same tiny space, "J., I'm going to the oldest place to find you. If I miss you come see me. J.," put the pencil away, turned off the lights, and went into the cleanest stall to use the toilet, then headed to the door, pushed it open, and looked in both directions. It was at that moment that she realized she wasn't alone.

She saw the man on the north side of the divided expressway. He was tall and thin, with blond hair, a reddish face, and big hands. She watched him emerge from the trees beyond the expressway. He began to trot toward the highway. He ran at about half speed and looked comfortable loping along, even though he was in the high weeds and uneven ground of the margin. As he neared the chain link fence, he sped up slightly, ran up the fence high enough to get his toes into some links at midpoint and his hands at the top at a vertical post, and hoisted himself up and over. As his feet hit the ground, his knees bent to absorb the shock. He popped up and resumed his trot.

Jane noticed a mechanical, trained quality to his movements, like a soldier on an obstacle course. He ran to the road and crossed without pausing to look, timing the cars without effort and stepping out of the way of one into the slipstream of the next and on to the grass stripe in the middle. "Cop," Jane thought. He ran the way cops did when they wanted to reach a car that had stalled in the left lane.

Jane stepped back inside the restroom, closed the door, and climbed on one of the toilets to look out the window. She heard the men's room door open and close, so she knew he had made the stop. She waited a few minutes, and then heard it again. Through the window she watched him stride across the parking lot. He was in a hurry and she knew he was in that moment of heightened alertness when he was rushing to catch up with her, hoping that she had not just turned off on another path or stopped to sleep for an hour so he would run on ahead and lose her.

The man gradually worked his way up from a long stride to a jog. She could see he was a habitual runner, a man who was comfortable going long distances on foot. As she slipped out the door and started after him, his strength and steadiness worried her.

The man crossed the narrow road that ran parallel to the expressway. The road still had a string of decrepit businesses left behind when the highway had bypassed them. She sensed that he was about to look behind him to see if he had over-run her position, so she altered her course and ducked into a small convenience store and bought some bottles of water, apples, nuts, and protein bars. Then she came out and looked southeast to southwest to spot the tallest hill along the path. That was where he would ultimately have to go to spot her. As Jane moved south she sped up, testing herself against the man.

It was already late in the day and he would be getting around to admitting that he had lost her and would have to climb to higher ground. He would be reduced to looking down from the top of the high hill and see if he could spot her on one of the trails beneath the trees. That was the most effective thing he had left to do. Ten or fifteen thousand years ago, when the ice age glaciers still covered the land a few miles north of here, Paleo-Indians used to live on the heights and watch for the migrating herds of caribou they hunted and for approaching enemies.

Jane couldn't yet allow herself to be sure what this man was. He looked like a policeman, but he still could be almost anything—the real killer of the man Jimmy had fought in the bar, a private detective hired by the victim's family, or a friend of the victim. Or he could be a long-distance hiker who had simply come along behind her on the trail, but had nothing to do with her or Jimmy.

She checked the level of the sun, estimated that it would be down in an hour, and decided to head up the east side of the highest hill, where it would be dark soonest, and prepare to start out before sunup.

She climbed the hill quickly, stopping only a few seconds at a time on the thickly forested slope to listen for his footsteps, or for an abrupt silencing of the birdsongs that would warn her of another interloper in the woods. The way up was steep, but it would take her to the top faster, and test her legs and her wind. In the year since she had been shot in the right thigh, she had gone harder and longer and steeper every time she felt uncertain about her strength. She had to make up for the months when she had barely been able to stand.

As Jane was approaching the summit she began to smell the pungent, perfumed scent of a pine fire. The fire was small, probably a few sappy pine twigs as kindling to start a piece of hardwood that would give off less smoke and more heat.

She moved off the path into the wooded terrain. She followed the smell and after another two hundred yards she found him. He had set up camp in a small copse a bit higher than the surrounding ground, and hidden from view by trees and brush. Jane dropped down and crawled closer to watch him. He was camped on the east side of the hill, just as she had planned to. He had unrolled a mat to pad his sleeping spot. He had a plastic tarp with brass grommets that he'd hung as a lean-to, and then spread a lightweight sleeping bag on the mat.

His simple preparations made Jane wary. He was not some fat, soft cop who spent his weeks in a patrol car and then went out on weekends to drink beer and pretend to fish. He poured water in a small pot, added some dry soup from a packet, and set it above his tiny fire to warm.

Jane considered leaving immediately, but staying might give her a chance to gain an advantage that she might not get again, so she waited. She watched the man make his dinner, and she watched him eat. He was a slow, thoughtful eater who looked at the trees and listened to the calls of birds and the chattering of squirrels in the limbs above. He was alert but at ease in the woods, and had soon finished his dinner, wiped the pot clean, and put it away. He stood up carrying a folding entrenching tool from his pack and a roll of toilet paper, and disappeared into the woods.

Jane waited a minute until she heard the entrenching tool digging into the ground fifty yards off. She kept the sound in her ears as she moved into his camp, quickly examining everything. She found a box of 9 mm pistol ammunition in his backpack, but he must have taken the pistol with him. Next she found a little black leather wallet. There was a badge that said NEW YORK STATE POLICE, and an identification card that said he was Isaac Lloyd, Technical Sergeant, Bureau of Criminal Investigation. He was based in Rochester.

When the state police had seen Jane visit Jimmy's mother, this one must have decided to follow her. Jane thought about taking the bullets, badge, and ID, but dismissed the idea. She didn't want to taunt this man, and alarming him would be the fastest way to turn one cop into fifty cops.

She heard the crunch of footsteps on leaves, ducked down, and moved off into the woods. When she descended again to the level of the long trail south it was already getting dark. Deep, gloomy shadows painted the east sides of the wooded hills. Jane plotted the route she would have to take to stay out of Isaac Lloyd's sight. She thought about the name as she began to move south. Isaac was almost certainly "Ike." Yes, he was definitely an Ike.

She reached a trail on the far side of the next hill with the sun sinking quickly, and then followed it to a north-south road. She moved along the sparsely traveled road at a strong pace for a time, and periodically stopped to verify she was still alone. She stayed on the shoulder of the road, and then began to trot. Jane let her eyes get used to the darkness and then picked up speed. She was glad she had checked his identity. She didn't want harm to come to him, but she also didn't want to answer the questions he might ask if he caught up with her.

At the first public trash can she took apart her cell phone and threw the battery in. At each spot where she could dispose of another part of the phone, she did. She didn't think the police had followed her this far using her cell phone's GPS, but she was certain they could if they knew her number, and they could get that if they knew her name. She was running for Jimmy's life, and if they were going to overtake her, they would have to work harder than that.

6

Jane traveled for several hours that night. Once she had divested herself of her cell phone, she began to change her course. Until the rest stop she had followed the exact route that she and Jimmy had followed at fourteen. It had led them to the Juniata River in eastern Pennsylvania, because that was the place where archaeological finds had placed the Iroquoian speakers before most of them had migrated north to the land that became New York State. That had been an old place. But it had not been the *oldest* place. The one they'd called the oldest place, one of the oldest sites in North America, was the Meadowcroft Rockshelter near Avella, Pennsylvania, southwest of Pittsburgh. Carbon dating on baskets and animal remains in the shelter showed that people had been there sixteen thousand years ago.

The Meadowcroft shelter was an overhang in the side of a sandstone cliff where small groups of Paleo-Indians had stayed for short periods of time, probably following the caribou herds at first. But others in later millennia stopped to wait out a storm, rest from a journey, hunt for meat in the surrounding woods, or fish in Cross Creek. Many groups had stopped at Meadowcroft, including Senecas, who regularly traveled though the upper Ohio valley until at least the 1780s.

To reach the shelter Jane headed south. All night long as she alternately ran and walked, she thought about her husband, Carey. They had known each other since sophomore year at college. She had not been a guide in those days, had never taken a person away from his troubles—never even thought of it until she was a junior and a friend needed that kind of help. But years later when Carey had reappeared in her life and they'd fallen in love, she had told him all about her past before she'd agreed to marry him. In fact, at first she had told him to explain why she wouldn't marry him, but he had kept after her until she had agreed. When they married, she stopped taking on runners and their troubles, and concentrated on being a good wife, a doctor's wife. But people still came sometimes. Runners she had made to disappear and who were living new lives met other people in the same kinds of trouble, and sent them to Jane. Usually she had resisted and found other ways to help, but now and again she'd made exceptions and gone on the road again. This was one of the exceptions. She had discussed the reasons with Carey, and she had thought about them over and over while she'd been traveling on foot down deserted Pennsylvania roads. Now Carey was angry, and disappointed, and acted as though he'd been betrayed.

She reached into the pocket of her jeans and took out the ote-ko-a, running her thumb along the strand, feeling each of the polished shell beads in the dark. Two white, two purple, two white, two purple, and on down to the end. The string of shell beads was one of the things Carey couldn't possibly understand. The string of beads was an appointment to act as the agent of her people. It was a license, an assignment, a contract, a physical symbol of an agreement.

It was all of these and none of them, but having it gave her a responsibility she couldn't duck or amend. She put it back in the pocket where she had been carrying it since she'd started her journey. A small part of her brain reminded her that she had never shown it to Carey, never tried to explain to him what it meant. The ote-ko-a was a burden, but at the same time, it was a proof of her acceptance by the women, people whose opinions mattered. The time had come when the tribe needed the specialized kind of help that she could give. How could she have refused?

Jane thought about what she wished she had said to Carey, how she should frame her sentences when she talked to him again. At last she fell asleep in a cornfield, and slept uninterruptedly until afternoon when the heat of the sun woke her. She got up, rolled up her sleeping bag, shouldered her pack, and began to walk.

She kept moving south. Each night she wished she could call Carey, but as cell phones had become nearly universal, it had gotten harder and harder to find a pay phone. But one night she came to a diner in a small village along the road. She ate, and then found a pay phone on the wall outside the diner by the parking lot. Carey didn't answer, so she left a message. "Hi, honey. I'm still on the trip, but I'm not anywhere I can call very often. I don't have my cell phone anymore, so don't try that." She paused for a second. "I'm afraid I've got nothing to say but I love you, so here it comes. I love you." She hung up.

She kept moving south, mostly at night. Sometimes her road ran through small towns, where it was transformed into a main street, and ran past churches and schools. At times she would go up on a sidewalk and jog along beside the display windows of stores, and then the road left the town behind and became rural again.

She wished she had gotten to talk to Carey on the phone, and not just leave him a message. The anger she felt at his lack of understanding had faded, and now when she thought about him she simply missed him.

Late on the fifth night of hard travel Jane reached the Meadowcroft Rockshelter. Since she and Jimmy had been here long ago the state of Pennsylvania or some institution had built a sturdy-looking wooden shelter to put a roof over the ancient outcropping of rock. There were platforms and steps to the shelter now. She stopped in the woods a hundred yards from the wooden structure, staying far enough away so that the security cameras in or on the building wouldn't pick up more than a slight thickening of the darkness at the edge of the woods for a moment, and then nothing. She continued into the woods above the building, went another hundred yards to a suitable thicket made of sprouts and saplings of a vanished maple tree, and spread her sleeping bag in the center of it.

She woke a few hours later already aware that she wasn't alone. She carefully rolled out of her sleeping bag and squatted to be ready to spring if she needed to. Jimmy? No, he wouldn't sneak up on her. But it could be a Pennsylvania park ranger looking around to be sure she wasn't somebody dangerous. She waited a few minutes in motionless silence, and then saw the source of the movement. It was five deer, two bucks and three does, moving along outside the edge of the woods where the foraging was best. In a few more minutes they faded back into the forest, up some narrow trail that she had not seen.

Jane packed up and walked toward the creek, but then realized that she hadn't been intended to go that way. She was supposed to think the way she and Jimmy had thought when they were fourteen.

She took the path that had been marked and cleared above the creek, and then climbed a bit to the broad opening of the wooden structure over the rock shelter. There sat Jimmy Sanders in the mouth of it, smiling like a jovial stone god in a forest shrine. He wore a gray-green T-shirt that showed his bulging biceps and a pair of cargo pants with a zippered leg that could change the pants to shorts. His legs hung off the platform at the cavernous entrance to the shelter, kicking happily. On his head was an olive drab watch cap of the sort that Jane had brought to keep warm when she camped at night, but she could see enough above his hairline to see his hair was cut very short. His shoes were brown hiking boots made of netting and rubber like high-top sneakers. His skin was like Jane's, but it had been darkened by the sun to look like Jane's father's—like a worn copper penny. His face was still handsome and a little boyish with the same amusement showing in his black eyes.

"Hey, Janie," Jimmy said, his cheerful smile growing. He looked down at her from the platform and then stared up at the sky and took in a deep breath of morning air. Then he looked down at her again. "I knew that if anybody would come and find me it would be you." He closed his eyes to the sunshine and then opened one eye. "I had hoped for your sake that you'd look about that way at our present age."

"You look pretty chipper yourself, Jimmy."

"I wasn't talking about chipper."

"I know you weren't," she said. "I'm married. Happily."

"I'd heard that. Good for you. It takes character. Another sign that you grew up just the way I thought. He's a doctor, right?"

"Yes, and a good man. How about you? Get married yet?"

"No," he said. "I'll bet you stopped off at my mom's before you came, and she would have said so if I had."

"Probably," said Jane. "But we didn't get to talk much this time."

"I would have been a better husband in the old times I think. I'd go off up the trail with my friends to fight whoever we were fighting that month and the little woman would stay in her clan's longhouse and raise crops and babies with her friends. When I came back we'd make her section of the longhouse a happy place for a while, and then I'd go off again."

"Very romantic. But I'll hold on to some hope that you find a regular modern girl and live a dull life." She climbed the steps to the platform where he sat. She sat down beside him and let her legs dangle from the edge of the platform.

"Maybe I'll give it a try if I live."

At last, she thought. "Tell me why the police are after you."

"It started, as a lot of stupid stories do, in a bar. I was there, and so was a guy named Nick Bauermeister. I didn't know his name at the time, but I noticed him. He was about thirty I'd say, maybe a little older. He was drunk and loud. It was around midnight and I was getting ready to go home, because I always figure if you haven't met somebody who will change your life by midnight, she isn't coming."

"Good policy," said Jane.

"I thought it was fairly practical," he said. "I was heading for the door and this guy stepped in my way."

"Why?"

"Stupid and drunk."

"How big was this guy?"

"Slightly bigger than me."

"Bigger than you? Wow."

"Slightly. He looked like a bleary-eyed Viking. He took a poke at me and I sidestepped and dropped him. He was one of those hopeless guys who does that, and then gets up. It's the getting up that hurts you."

"I can see how that might be," said Jane.

"Well, sure. I'm just going home. All he has to do is lie there for less than ten seconds while he thinks about why I might not have been his best choice. But he's not a thinking man. He's the 'back up in your face' guy. So when he came for me again, I knew I'd have to hit him a little harder and faster. I did. Maybe five times. Then I went home."

"And?"

"And the next day the police came to my house after work to say that they'd picked this Nick guy up off the floor and taken him to the hospital last night. They were considering charging me with assault."

"And you said . . ."

"I said, 'I hope you won't waste your time doing that, because the bar was full of regulars who saw him take a swing at me out of drunken belligerence. That's probably why nobody helped him up before you got there. They didn't want to have to knock him back down themselves.'"

"I take it the police decided to waste their time."

"They did. They made it misdemeanor assault. I pleaded self-defense, and they set a hearing. It was supposed to be May third. I got a public defender and lined up a dozen witnesses. Then, on April twenty-fifth, the cops came to my place again. They said this Nick Bauermeister had gotten murdered, and they liked me as the suspect."

"How was he killed?"

"He was shot with something on the order of a thirty-aught-six rifle from a moderate distance—maybe a hundred yards. He lived in the country with a girlfriend, and they shot him through a lighted window at night. This was not great, because in the western half of the state there are probably six people who couldn't have made that shot, and I don't know any of them. But because I'd been in the army and gone to Iraq and Afghanistan, I made a great sniper suspect. Prosecutors love it when you've served your country."

"So they just assumed you killed him because of that fight?"

"Well, you know how we are."

"Who? Veterans?"

"Indians."

"Wily," she said. "Skulking around in the woods, tracking and hunting people."

"Yep."

"In other words, they didn't have any real suspects?"

"Apparently not."

"Do you have an alibi for the night of the murder?"

"I was at my mother's house until nine, and then went home and got to bed around ten. I had to be at work on a construction job at six the next morning."

"You had witnesses to the fight in the bar, and I assume the police didn't have a murder weapon or anybody to place you at the crime scene."

"Right. No evidence."

"So why did you take off?"

"Because evidence was starting to appear."

"What kind?"

"Somebody who said he sold me a thirty-aught-six rifle for cash at a garage sale. Not just sold some guy a rifle. Sold one to me, picked my picture out of a stack of pictures, and remembered my name."

"Interesting. Did you know him?"

"Never seen him; never heard his name before. I'll bet I haven't gone to a garage sale since my mother took me at the age of fifteen. Right about then I used to outgrow my clothes in a couple of hours, so she bought some of them secondhand."

"What is his name?"

"Slawicky," said Jimmy. "Walter Slawicky."

"That's progress. We know the name of the man who is trying to frame you. Or one of them, if there are more."

"Not enough progress."

"It wasn't a good idea to take off."

"Wasn't it?" he said.

"They're looking hard for you, Jimmy."

"How hard?"

"They're watching your mother's house. As soon as I drove up and sat down on the porch, two state policemen drove up, probably to see if the car that had just arrived had brought you home. And there's a state cop who's a regular tracker a few miles behind me. I looked in his wallet to be sure that's what he was. His name is Isaac Lloyd, and he's a sergeant."

"They sent one state trooper after me? One?"

Jane shook her head. "There's no such thing as one state trooper. He's just the guy out running point. If he finds a gum wrapper that you leave somewhere, he'll call it in and there will be a hundred of them, five dogs, and a chopper."

"Good thing I don't leave trash around."

"Your feet leave big footprints, and you have to buy food, and people see you from a distance, even if you don't see them."

"So what am I supposed to do about that, Janie?"

"Since you're smart enough to ask, I'll tell you what I'm going to do for you."

"What?"

"Remember the helicopters that used to come to get you out of tight spots in Afghanistan?"

"Very well."

"That's me. That's what I'm doing here. I've come to help you get back home before they catch you. Having a woman with you might help you look a lot less like a fugitive, and it might even make the state police a little hesitant if they see us."

"Why would you do this for me?"

She looked at him as though she hadn't thought about having to tell him. She hesitated, then said, "This isn't just me that you see here. The clan mothers—all eight of them—came to my house one morning and told me to go find you. This is our people coming to take you out of trouble."

"The clan mothers sent you? I can hardly believe it."

"Believe it." She took the single strand of shell beads out of her pocket and dangled it before his face. "They knew we were close when we were kids, so they asked me to do it. Here's their ote-ko-a."

He took the wampum string into his hand, looked closely at it, and then handed it back. "So it's official. You're working for them."

"You know who they are," she said. "What it means is, if I get put down, there will be somebody else—maybe another rescuer, maybe an avenger. But it doesn't end with me."

For the first time Jimmy seemed serious, almost chastened. "I really don't think going back is such a good idea, or I would have stayed there."

"Your chances are much better if you turn yourself in. I told you there's already a state policeman out here trying to track us."

"You know what?" Jimmy said. "I think I see him."

"Who? The cop?" asked Jane.

"Is he tall, thin like a heron, with khaki pants and a blue jacket?"

Jane was up in a second, kneeling to see where Jimmy was pointing. "Get off the platform, but stay low," she whispered. "We've got to move."

Jimmy slid off the platform, held on to the edge for a moment, and then dropped to the ground. Jane watched for the trooper. He was trotting along the crest of the hill beyond the creek that separated him from the rock shelter. He was about five hundred yards away, but moving back and forth on a trail to make his way down to level ground. Jane lowered herself off the platform, hung for a second, and then dropped.

Jane and Jimmy slung their packs over their shoulders and began to make their way deeper into the woods. "Do you think he saw us?" Jimmy asked.

"It almost doesn't matter," Jane said. "He's a cop, and he's obviously done this kind of thing before, and he seems to know this part of the world. He doesn't need to see you to know where you must be. I've been traveling hard for five days. He must have tracked me for a while, then realized where I must be headed, and called for a ride to be here first. Come on, we've got to speed things up."

Jane moved ahead on the trail and worked herself up to a trot, and then to a half-speed run, watching the spaces between the trees for protruding roots or stones that could trip her. She could hear Jimmy behind her by about ten feet, giving her the chance to plot a course, stop to look, or change directions without crashing into her or stepping on her heels. Jane chose surfaces that wouldn't leave a readable track—stone surfaces, openings in the middle of groves where the leaves had piled up. After a few minutes she found the bed of a small stream that flowed from an unseen spring near the top of the ridge, and led him down by the water so they could run along the pebbly bank, giving them a bit of invisibility.

She could hear Jimmy's heavier steps as he ran, and she listened to his breathing. He had been a good athlete when they were young. He had probably stopped playing games at some point—they were both in their midthirties now— but he had obviously stayed active. He was more muscular, but other than that, not much heavier than he'd been in high school. His breathing was even and unlabored so far. If they could both keep up the pace for a while, and avoid twisting an ankle, they might make it through the day. That cop back there was a worry, but he thought he was chasing a killer, so he would be second-guessing himself, looking harder and longer at each thicket, each rise in the ground ahead, to be sure it wasn't an ambush, or at least a hiding place. That would slow him down.

Jane's biggest worry was that there was no such thing as one cop. If this one had seen them on the rock, if she had led him to Jimmy, then he didn't need to catch up with them.

All he had to do was use his cell phone to call more cops and send them to block the way ahead. As soon as she'd thought about it, she caught herself listening for the throbbing sound of a helicopter's rotors in the distance.

In time the stream bed became steeper and the banks disappeared. The trickle of water was running over bare rock. She altered her course to keep from having to travel in the open, bringing them instead among the pines that dominated the heights near the crest of the ridge. The ground under the pines was thick with needles, and it soothed her feet. She turned to check on Jimmy, and found he was still the same ten feet back, still not ready to collapse after the quick climb. His T-shirt had a dark streak where sweat had soaked the shoulders and neck, then run down to his belly, but he didn't seem to be in distress. When Jane stopped, she squatted in the shade under the pines, and he did too. They both looked back down the high hillside in the direction they'd come from, trying to see if they were being followed.

If the cop was on his way up, the full green foliage of the trees was shielding him from their view. Jane was sure that if he had called for reinforcements she or Jimmy would be able to see them or hear them. There were no roads nearby for police cars to travel, and nothing was in the air but a couple of red-tailed hawks circling on thermals very high up and calling to each other now and then. She said, "I don't see him, or anybody else. Do you?"

Jimmy slowly shook his head. "No. But if I was tracking somebody, I'd try to be sure they didn't see me, too."

"So would I," she said. "We'd better keep going."

Jane got up and headed for the top of the ridge, and heard Jimmy follow. When they had almost reached the crest, she moved along just below it, trying to keep from being visible to the man following them. She looked ahead, trying to find a notch or a grove of trees that was thick enough to hide them all the way to the top, so they could slip over to the downslope on the other side without being silhouetted against the bright sky.

After a short time she came to a spot where the pine trees seemed to spill down from the crest to the beginning of the deciduous forest. She entered the pines and led Jimmy to the crest and over to the far side. Immediately she saw the reason the vegetation grew so thickly to the top. A spring had formed a pool up there, and water seeped downward on both sides of the ridge. On the new side, she could see that the water had formed the beginning of a stream, and that farther down, the width and depth of the stream grew. The stream provided another clear path downward without fighting underbrush. As each section of the stream bed became wider and deeper, she and Jimmy could trot along it without being seen.

The climb they had just completed had put strain on the muscles along the backs of Jane's legs, and now going downward put stress on the muscles in the front. The bullet wound in her thigh was old now—it had happened over a year ago—and she had come to think of herself as fully recovered, but as she descended, she felt a twinge, a sudden weakness in her right thigh that startled her and made her wonder for an instant whether her leg would give way under her. From time to time she felt the twinge again, but the leg held.

"We seem to be heading south," Jimmy said. "That's not toward home."

"We don't have much choice. The direction we've been taking is just *away*."

"Then what? Circle back at night?"

"Maybe. Somehow we've got to lose this cop and get you back up to the reservation."

"So I can surrender to a different cop."

"Yes. That's what it amounts to, but running makes you seem guilty. And being a fugitive in a murder case is highly risky. Any cops you meet will almost certainly draw their sidearms, and sometimes a nervous cop will misinterpret any movement as hostile. When we're home we'll get you a great defense lawyer, and get some private detectives going on investigating your case. While we're out here running through the woods nobody's doing anything to clear you."

Jimmy said, "Clearing me sounds like it costs a lot of money."

"Enough will be available," Jane said.

"The clan mothers set aside money for this kind of thing?"

Jane didn't bother to correct his impression.

They moved along the stream bed, careful not to step on the mossy rocks right near the water because they were slippery. "To tell you the truth, I wouldn't have thought that you'd do something like this."

"Then why did you leave me a message in the ladies' room by the expressway?"

"I don't know," he said. "I guess being there again brought that trip back to me, and I had been feeling sorry for myself. I didn't really expect you to find it."

"Just because I don't live on the reservation I'm not suddenly a stranger. I never lived there anyway, except in the summer when my father was working far away."

"That's part of it," he said. "And the other part is that you can be Indian or not whenever you want."

"That's not how it works. I don't get to pick, and never did. My mother had eyes so blue they looked like the sky reflected in ice water, and skin like cream. She's the one who chose, and she wanted to be Seneca because she loved my father. After the Wolf clan women adopted her, she was never anything else. And I've never been anything else."

"You have blue eyes just like hers."

She laughed. "Don't sound like that. I didn't steal them."

"I meant you can pick."

"If I wanted to, I could pass as something besides Seneca, and so could you—at least outside New York, where everyone's used to seeing Haudenosaunee people. Having black hair and a dark complexion opens up a lot of possible ethnic identities. But I don't forget who I am. And when the clan mothers say I'm the one to do something, I know who they are too."

"Janie, you're not still a true believer in the old religion, are you?"

"What I believe in these days is pretty much dominated by what I learned in science classes. But I sometimes like remembering that I'm not just one person. I'm part of a group of people like me. And I've never heard anything to make me think the old people were stupid."

"I get you," he said.

They kept trotting along the stream bed for a time, and then they both heard a faint hoot of a train's horn, then another. They moved on, making their way downhill. As the stream bed flattened and no longer kept them hidden, Jane altered her course a little. The train horn sounded again, this time a long wail, then another hoot.

"There must be a town down there," she said.

"How do you know?"

"They're blowing their horn for a crossing—two short, one long, one short. They're warning the vehicles that might not see them coming."

They ran on for a few minutes and then saw, stretched across the bottom of the valley below, the train tracks. The double line of steel rails was coming out of a small town to their right. Jane stopped running and walked through a stand of trees, keeping herself in the foliage.

She followed the tracks with her eyes, moving her gaze from the spot where they emerged from the cluster of buildings at the edge of a grid of streets, stretched across a level field that looked like wheat, and then reached the hillside where they began to wind and go upward. She pointed. "Right over there—where the tracks turn and climb—I'll bet a train would have to slow down to practically a walk."

"Are you planning to jump a train?"

"I'm considering it," she said, and watched Jimmy for a reaction. He said nothing.

She said, "Thank you for not mentioning Skip Walker." Skip was a harsh nickname for a boy they had both known when they were young. At some point in early childhood he had decided to hop a train. He had run along beside it, then either tripped or been unable to hang on to a handhold after he'd made his leap. The train wheel had rolled over his leg and amputated it. "Skip" was a reference to the way he walked on his prosthetic leg, with a limp and a little hop. He had been one of those boys that everyone's mother cited to scare them out of taking risks.

Jimmy shrugged. "Skip was seven or eight when he did that. We ought to be able to keep from being hurt that bad."

Jane was still tracing the tracks with her eyes, walking along the hillside to see where the tracks went after the first turn. "It looks to me as though the tracks go mostly north," she said. "If we jumped the train, our trip home might be a whole lot quicker."

Jimmy said, "Let's head for that place right over there, where it takes another turn and climbs at the same time. If they have people watching at the front and the back, they won't see us if we pop out in the middle and climb aboard."

They trotted along the hillside, staying among the trees but heading for the spot where the tracks turned and disappeared into thick woods. It took them a few minutes to run from their hill to the one where the tracks were. When they arrived they could look down above the tracks to see a place where the rails bisected the town. On one side they could see four church steeples, a row of long, flat-topped buildings that were probably stores and offices, and farther out, dozens of small houses with pitched gray roofs. On the other side of the tracks were a number of old brick buildings with rows of dirty, barely translucent windows, smokestacks, and railroad sidings. Beyond them there were metal Quonset huts that were either warehouses or garages.

A train snaked around the hill on the far side of the valley and sounded its horn as it came into town at the first intersection—two short, one long, one short blare, still somewhat faint. At each spot where the tracks crossed a road, they could see red lights begin to flash, and then a black-and-white barrier came down, and the train came through. Now they could see that the train had a big yellow engine in front and one right behind, and more and more freight cars appeared behind them from around the hill.

"It's a big train," said Jimmy. "I'll bet it's a hundred cars."

"That's got to be good for us," Jane said. "Let's get closer."

They came down through the trees just as the front of the train passed, moving along at a slow, steady rate. There were hoppers, tank cars, boxcars, flatbeds laden with big loads of pipes or thick packs of flat material like wallboard or plywood, all strapped down tightly. There were gondolas full of coal or slag. The names blazoned on the cars were familiar from their childhood—Canadian National, Georgia Central, Chicago and North Western, Erie Lackawanna.

Jane stopped beside the tracks. The engines were at least twenty-five cars ahead of them now. Jane looked ahead toward the place where the tracks turned and climbed upward, and looked back to the curve where the next part of the train was still to appear, rolling toward them. She looked back up the hillside through the trees. She said, "I'm ready. Are you up to this?"

"Yep," he said.

"Stay low. When we see the one we want, we'll run for it. You get aboard, and then I will."

He looked at her. "Are you sure you don't want to go first?"

"I'm being sensible. If you get up there first, you'll be able to pull me up. If I'm there first, I won't be strong enough to pull you up."

"What you're really afraid of is that you'll make it and I won't," he said. "But that's okay. We'd better get going before that cop catches up and sees us."

They watched the cars coming past, and then Jane said, "I see one coming. It's a hopper with an open top. Black. See it?"

"I see it." Jimmy began to trot, then sped up a little to match the speed of the car, jumped to grasp a vertical bar at the back that formed part of a ladder, and then stepped onto the small level space just before the rear coupling.

Jane ran in right behind him, grasped the bar, and pulled herself up. She clung there for a few seconds, and then they looked at each other and smiled as the engines pulled them around the first curve into deeper woods. "Let's see if we can get up there on top," Jane said, and sidestepped to the ladder. She climbed up, stepped over the rim of the hopper, and disappeared.

Jimmy climbed up after her, looked over the rim into the hopper, and climbed in beside her. The hopper was loaded with tiny, coarse stones like the gravel under the railroad ties. It was mounded in the center and shallower along the sides, so if they stayed near the outer areas, they were well hidden. Jimmy gave her a high five, and then lay back to look up at the sky. There were a few wispy white clouds very high up, each like a single brushstroke, but most of the sky was a pure blue.

The train stopped. A moment later, it began to back up. It went about twenty feet, and then stopped with a jolt, as though something had collided with the rear of the train. "They must be adding more cars," said Jimmy. In a moment, the train started moving ahead again, very slowly overcoming its inertia and immense weight, and making its way up the first hill.

Jimmy started to sit up, but Jane put her hand on his chest. "Please don't sit up yet. Let's wait until we're at least a few miles farther on, where there's zero chance Tech Sergeant Isaac Lloyd will see us."

Jimmy smiled. "You certainly have gotten cautious as a grown-up."

Jane didn't smile. "Sometimes the difference between sort of safe and absolutely safe is pretty unpleasant, so I lean toward absolutely safe."

The train climbed the hill slowly, tugging its long string of cars up the gradual incline until it reached a gap in the hillside and sped up to twenty-five, then about thirty-five miles an hour.

Jane and Jimmy both unrolled their bedrolls and spread them on the gravel, their heads slightly inclined toward the mound. They used their packs as pillows and rested from their long, hard run. They passed through areas where the tall trees and the cuts through the hillsides kept them in shade much of the time, and then through rolling farmland. After a half hour they were both asleep, rocked gently in their hopper, hearing only the constant clacking of the wheels and feeling the fresh breeze passing over them.

They woke when the train blew its whistle to signal its approach to the first crossing at the next town, and they remained alert but out of sight until it regained its full speed on the way out of town.

As Jane lay on the gravel bed she decided riding the train was like lying in a boat. The hopper was open to the sky, and traveled at a nearly uniform slow speed, almost never stopping. Even twenty miles an hour felt like a huge luxury after so many days of traveling on foot.

Jane had been trying to keep herself persuaded that her wounded leg had recovered completely from the gunshot. She had certainly proven that it was strong enough to do what she had needed to do. Over a year of hard, steady training had brought back enough strength to travel on foot for two hundred miles or more in hilly country. But she wasn't so sure the injuries nobody could see had healed.

The four men who had captured her in California had wanted desperately to find out where she had sent James Shelby, the man she had rescued from the courthouse. She would not tell them. For years, whenever she had taken on a new runner, she had promised, "I will die before I reveal where you are to anyone." To make sure her promise would never be a lie, she had always carried in her purse a cut-glass perfume bottle containing the distilled and concentrated juice of the roots of *Cicuta maculata*, the water hemlock plant. Swallowing two bites of hemlock root was the traditional Seneca method of committing suicide. The common name for water hemlock in Western New York was cowbane, because now and then a foraging cow would try some. A single root would kill a fifteen-hundred-pound Holstein. But Jane had lost her purse in the fight before she'd been captured.

She'd had no way to kill herself, and so they had gotten the chance to torment her, to inflict enough suffering to make her want to trade James Shelby's life, not for hers— she'd known they would kill her anyway—but for simple relief, the chance to make the pain stop. She had not told them. She had been preparing for death when her captors realized that Jane had helped victims to escape many times before, and so she had enemies who would pay millions to interrogate her themselves.

The four men who held her were all dead now. But in her dreams sometimes they would come back, and she would have to kill them again. It was as though she hadn't yet been able to make their deaths final. She knew that the dream meant something. It meant that what had happened to her was not over. This afternoon, if she stretched and ran her own hand up her back from the waist to the shoulder blade, she could still feel the rows of horizontal scars. They had heated steel barbecue skewers with a propane torch and laid them on her back. She knew that in a few years the scars might be level with the rest of her skin, or even be hard to see, but they would never be gone. The puckered scar on her thigh from the bullet would never be smooth again.

She was not able to forget any of it, and that was the part that she felt most. From the time she was a child she had been strong, physically confident, and occasionally even reckless. She had gotten hurt, even hurt badly, but she had always known that bruises would fade, pain would go away, and she would be fit and strong again. She didn't know that anymore.

Jane was feeling something that she had never felt before her capture, the suspicion that she was harboring an inner weakness, like a virus, that had begun to attack her during those awful days and nights. Now that she had felt the sensation of being utterly powerless, and the knowledge that somebody had really hurt her—not just caused her pain, but disfigured her, changed her so she would never be the same—she was sure she was the worse for it internally too. Would she be able to face the risk of going through such pain again?

Jane had learned to accept death fifteen years ago, when she started carrying poison with her every day. She had become accustomed to rising from her bed with the knowledge that she might have to die that day—die quickly, a few minutes of sharp pain and then darkness. This new condition was worse, a threat that she could not control by thinking about it. It was a reflex. She had been hurt once, so would she flinch each time after that? If Jimmy needed her, would she be quick and decisive, or would she hesitate?

When the clan mothers came to her she had not felt ready to take on Jimmy Sanders and his problems. She had wanted to agree with Carey and stay home. But having all eight clan mothers waiting on her doorstep had simply not permitted her to make excuses or even tell them that she was not the person they thought she was. They were modern American women like her, but they were something else too. They had inherited the powers of eight women who had lived some-where deep in prehistory, in the times when the names of matrilineal families were first represented by wolves or bears or herons. In those days the world was a deep, endless forest, and being a lone person was always fatal.

Jane glanced at Jimmy. He was asleep again. Maybe things would be all right. Maybe she had completed this er-rand without having to test her courage or her confidence. She watched the utility poles going by. Thirty miles an hour, she thought. As long as the train kept going, they might get through this without trouble.

After a time, her own exhaustion caught up with her again. She had been on the trail, moving at high speed, for nearly a week. Her energy was depleted. She remembered there was a bottle of water and a protein bar or two in her pack. When she opened it and looked, she saw there were two of each. She set aside some for Jimmy, and opened hers. She ate and drank, and then slept again.

Next time she awoke, it was dark. The train was slowing down, and when she looked up she could see tall buildings with hundreds of tiny windows in rows. She crouched to look out over the side of the hopper. They were on tracks that had been joined by others, so there were at least five sets in a row. She gave Jimmy's foot a kick.

He sat up, and then knelt beside Jane to see what she saw. "Do you know where we are?" he asked.

"No idea," she said. "I'm looking for some sign, or something I recognize."

"If you've been here, you probably didn't ride in on a load of gravel."

"No. But it occurs to me that what we're doing is illegal, and we're coming to a place where there will be more people to catch us at it. There seems to be a big train yard up ahead. Let's collect our belongings and get ready to bail out." She knelt, rolled up her bedroll, arranged everything in her pack, and craned her neck to look ahead while Jimmy packed up his gear.

The train began to slow markedly. Jimmy said, "Ready to go?"

"Yes," Jane said. She put on her baseball cap, hid her hair under it, hoisted herself up on the back rim of the hopper, found the first rung of the ladder with her foot, and climbed down. The train was slowing more and more. Jimmy was beside her now, so she dropped her pack, jumped, and ran for a stretch to slow her momentum. Jimmy jumped a few yards on, and then they both went back and retrieved their backpacks. Jane slung her backpack over one shoulder. "Carry it this way, so you look like a worker with a tool bag, and not a train jumper." Jimmy imitated her, and they looked ahead. The train was moving into a huge freight yard, with fences and buildings and lots of lights, so they walked briskly away from it, toward the back of the train. They didn't walk so briskly that they seemed to be running from something.

When they were in a darker, more deserted area, they crossed several sets of tracks, walked across a weedy plot of land that had been paved once but now had plants thriving in each crack, and came to a street. It was dark, and the old brick buildings seemed to be abandoned with the doors and windows boarded. The next street had a few neon lights, and cars passed now and then.

Jane stopped and said, "Let's dust ourselves off and straighten up before we get into the light. That gravel wasn't exactly clean." They spent a few minutes getting themselves freed of dust, buttoned up, and looking a bit better. The evening was cool, so Jane took her jacket out of her pack and put it on, and then turned around so Jimmy could see. "What do you think?"

"Very respectable, and dust-free. How about me?"

"Much better."

Jimmy put on a light jacket too. "Are you hungry?"

"Sure," she said. "Maybe there will be a restaurant on one of the next streets, where there are lights." She looked at her watch. "It's only eight."

They walked for another couple of blocks, and when they came to a trash basket, Jane looked into it, then reached down and pulled up a newspaper. "The *Syracuse Post-Standard*."

"What's the date?"

"Today's. I guess we're in Syracuse."

"Okay," Jimmy said. "Let's see about that food."

They walked toward the streets with bright lights, and passed a small pizzeria. They looked in the window and saw a few people at tables wearing jeans and casual shirts. "What do you think?" she asked.

"Just the smell makes me want to break down the door."

"Give me a few seconds." Jane stepped into the doorway, then stood still for a two count while Jimmy was still outside, partially shielded from view behind her. She scanned the people inside, saw nobody she knew, or whose face held an expression of recognition, and nobody who looked hostile. She saw a few women, which was good, because the presence of women usually discouraged the more extreme forms of male misbehavior. She saw a hallway at the back of the restaurant that led to restrooms, and another on the left leading to the kitchen. If they had to they could slip out through the exit that was sure to be at the rear of the kitchen. Jane stepped in, and Jimmy followed.

A sign said they should seat themselves, so Jane went to a table by the wall and they sat down. Jane sat so she could face the front window and door, and Jimmy could face the back. The side location of the table meant that no matter how rough things got in the place, they couldn't be surrounded, and nobody could approach unseen.

They set their backpacks on empty seats by the wall and looked at the printed menus that had been left at every table. In a few minutes a middle-aged waitress emerged from the kitchen with a tray in each hand—the plates on the left and the drinks, which were heavier, on the right. Jane studied her. She had a weary but alert look as she maneuvered between tables. She showed relief when she set down her heavy trays on an empty table and served two couples at the table beside it. Over the years Jane had learned to check the faces of the waiters and waitresses. If there were some kind of trouble, they would see it first, and show it.

The waitress stopped at their table and took their order, then went off to the kitchen with her trays. She returned immediately with their pitcher of cola and glasses.

They poured some and drank, and Jimmy spoke to her quietly in Seneca. "I haven't bothered to thank you for coming to help me. I know you were asked, but we both know you could have found a way out of it if you tried."

"I suppose I could have," she said in Seneca. "They knew I wouldn't."

He raised his glass of cola and clinked it against hers. "You're more old-fashioned than my grandmother, and it's a good thing for me."

"They said you were innocent," Jane said. "But I didn't have to take anything they said on faith. I knew what kind of man you were the same way they did—by knowing you as a boy. I climbed trees with you. And in case you've forgotten it, you once saved me from getting raped. I didn't forget. Now let's talk English." She moved her eyes to be sure nobody nearby had overheard them speaking another language.

"Certainly," he said. "Everybody else's food looks so good. I can hardly wait for ours."

"Neither can I," said Jane. "I guess we've both been living on protein bars and candy for too long."

While she sat in the restaurant, Jane couldn't help thinking about what Jimmy had said about her—that she was old-fashioned. What he meant was her attachment to old customs. She hardly ever thought about herself that way, but at times something reminded her that the Seneca ways of looking at the world were part of the structure of her mind. And she knew that one reason she had clung to Seneca traditions was to maintain the connection with her parents and grandparents—especially her father since he'd died.

She was eleven that summer, and she and her mother had been staying at the reservation because he had been away working on a bridge in the state of Washington. One day he had been standing on a steel beam as a crane lowered it into place. The cable snapped, and Henry Whitefield and the beam fell to the bottom of the gorge below. She sometimes dreamed about his fall.

In the dream, her father was wearing his bright red flannel shirt and blue jeans, his yellow hard hat and his leather tool belt. As he fell, the beam stayed beside him. He turned as he fell, doing a slow somersault, so his tools spilled from his belt pouch. His hard hat left his head and his black hair fluttered in the wind as he came right again. He spread his arms and legs and faced downward, his shirt flapping violently. In the dream the disembodied Jane was beside him. He and Jane could both see the bottom of the canyon, the thin ribbon of water winding down the gorge like a silvery snake—the water not wide enough to catch him or deep enough to do anything for him but wash his body after he hit. The white buttons of his red shirt gave way, and it opened and flew off him. But as he fell, his fluttering black hair grew longer, and seemed to spread down his back and arms, first like fringe, and then widening and flattening like feathers. And soon his arms were revealed to be wings.

His head and shoulders dipped forward and he swooped downward. As he did, he changed more, and when his swoop arced upward again she could see her father was a crow. He circled once and looked back at Jane with his black, shiny crow eyes—so much like his own bright obsidian eyes—and she felt the deep, painful love he was sending to her, all of it now because there would never be another time. When the circle was complete he began to fly straight across the open canyon to the other side.

Waking from that dream each time was like learning that he had died again. Years later, after Jane's mother died, she became part of the feeling Jane had that her parents and her childhood were inextricable from the old ways. It was mainly the celebrations that brought her mother back—the women all bringing big bowls of soup and hot casserole dishes and setting them out on the long tables for everyone to share. They were like Jane's mother—like the woman she had chosen to become out of love. And later, there were the dances. There were the drums and the rising voices of the singers, sometimes making her imagine she heard her father's voice among them. Jane's mother had been a graceful, effortless dancer. She had worn her hair long, and for these occasions she put on a traditional outfit, a long black dress with embroidered flowers, an untucked blouse, and an embroidered shawl. When she danced with the other women, she didn't look different in any important way. There were women old enough to have white hair, which was a shade lighter than her blond hair. She was tall and thin, but there were others taller, and some just as thin. They were all beautiful together.

Their food arrived and Jimmy and Jane ate happily. Jane could feel the way the food renewed their energy and restored their spirits. When the waitress returned with the check, Jane paid with cash. Before the waitress left, Jane asked, "Do you know where the bus station is?"

"Erie. It's on Erie, which is right down that way, south from here. I forget the number, but it must be in the eight hundreds or so."

When they were alone outside, Jimmy said, "Bus station, huh? I hope I can get on a bus without being spotted."

"I'll check the place out before you go in, and make sure there aren't police watching for you." She paused. "Or you could turn yourself in right here in Syracuse. We're in New York State again. I'm pretty sure they would give you a ride to Buffalo."

Jimmy thought for a moment. "If I turn myself in to the cops where I'm wanted, won't it seem better for me?"

"I think it might," she said. "But if we get caught on the way, you'll look like you're still running away."

"Let's head for Buffalo." He began to walk.

Jane hurried to keep up. "That's fine. But if we get into a situation where it makes more sense not to try to go on, I hope you won't be stubborn. As long as you go in voluntarily, it will help."

"Fine," he said.

As they walked, they moved out of the area where there were lights and restaurants and businesses into a stretch that was darker and consisted of larger buildings that were all shut down during the hours of darkness—office buildings, parking lots, and other structures that seemed to be deserted. Between them there were dark alleys and driveways for deliveries.

Jane caught a quick motion in the corner of her right eye, but as she turned her head she was already hearing the sound of the two-by-four against the back of Jimmy's skull.

As Jimmy fell forward, Jane could see the man completing his swing, holding the two-by-four in both hands like a bat. The two-by-four was about five feet long and heavy, so its momentum brought his arms all the way around, leaving his face unguarded.

Jane jabbed, hitting his nose with the heel of her right hand. The man staggered backward, his nose gushing blood, and brought his hands to his nose while the two-by-four fell to the pavement. As the second man bent over to pick it up, Jane took a step and pushed his head downward while she brought her knee up to meet his face.

The third man retained some vague conviction that the only real threat must be Jimmy, the big, muscular man who lay on the pavement. The man stepped to Jimmy's side and kicked him in the ribs, then brought his right leg backward to prepare to deliver a kick to Jimmy's head. Jane saw he had shifted all his weight to his left leg, so she ran at him and delivered a hard stomp kick to the side of his left knee. She felt his knee give and heard the pop as she dislocated it. He went down as though he'd been shot and clutched at his knee and rocked back and forth, yelling.

Jane had always been aware that it was stupid to try to fight a man for the space between them, and even worse to let him grapple with her. Men were much bigger and stronger than she was, and most of them had been fighting since they were toddlers. If she was cornered, her strategy was to take advantage of the man's assumption that she was helpless, use any means to hurt him as badly as she could, and run. This time she had to stand her ground to keep the men from killing Jimmy while he was unconscious.

She danced back and forth over him for a moment, and used an instant to glance down at him. It crossed her mind that he could already be dead, but she had no time to think because the first two attackers were recovering. Jane snatched up the two-by-four and held it like a staff. As the first man lunged toward her, she left the lower end of the two-by-four planted on the pavement and pushed the upper end forward so it hit his sternum hard, rocking him back, then lifted the two-by-four straight up so the upper end of it came up to hit his chin, and brought it down hard in the middle of his left instep. As he lifted his injured foot in pain, she brought the end of the two-by-four down on his other instep.

The man's howls were not as loud as those of the man with the dislocated knee, but they were loud enough to confirm her hope that she had broken some of the small, narrow bones in his feet. He staggered stiffly on his heels, as though his legs were made of wood.

Jane raised the two-by-four with both hands, clutching it like a harpoon, but instead of jabbing the man again, she pivoted and aimed her stab at the chest of his partner. The man's attempt to duck her attack by crouching brought the butt of the two-by-four to the level of his collarbone. It hit the bone hard and slipped upward into his trachea. He grasped his throat with both hands and bent over, trying to protect it and breathe at the same time. Jane swung the two-by-four down hard on his head and he collapsed forward onto the pavement, dazed but conscious.

The three men were badly hurt, and as she swept her eyes to survey them, they began to edge away from her. She took out her lock-blade knife and flicked open the blade with her right thumb. She said, "In ten seconds I start cutting."

The two men who could walk began to hobble away down the alley they had come from. The man with the broken leg shouted, "Wait! Help me. Please!"

The man bent over holding his trachea kept going, but the one with the injured feet and the broken, bloody nose relented. He stopped and limped back, pulled his friend up so he could stand on his one good leg, and took his arm over his shoulder to help him hop off along the alley.

Jane was left with Jimmy's prone and unmoving body. She set the two-by-four beside him and knelt to feel his pulse. It was strong and steady. She patted his cheek, and then patted it harder. "Wake up, Jimmy," she whispered. "We've got to get out of here before their friends show up." She looked closely at the wound where the two-by-four had hit his head. The blood was already beginning to glue his hair in hard tufts, but his skull was not misshapen. The wound had bled a lot at first, but appeared to have nearly stopped. Jane kept raising her eyes to look farther into the alley, then to see if anyone was coming on the street. "Come on, Jimmy," she whispered. "You're going to be okay. You've got to be." She saw her pack lying on the ground, pulled it to her, and searched for the half bottle of water she'd saved. She took a kerchief, made it wet, and dabbed at his wound. She poured some of the water on it, and he began to stir.

"It's me, Jimmy," she said. "Wake up."

After another try, he opened his eyes. His hand went to his head.

"It's probably better not to touch it," she said.

"Wha—wow," he moaned. "I know somebody hit me."

"That's right," she said. "You could have a concussion. Just lie there for a minute and get your bearings, if you can."

"What happened?"

"You got knocked on the head." It sounded worse to her, because that was the way the old Senecas used to refer to death in battle—getting knocked on the head. "Don't worry, though. They were trying to rob us, but they didn't."

Jimmy felt for his wallet, and confirmed that it was still there. The movement seemed to bring him more awareness. "I feel awful." He sat up.

"Take it slow. Just sit for a few minutes." She wanted to say exactly the opposite, but moving too soon might be a mistake.

Jimmy stood up and leaned against the wall of the building on that side of the alley. Now that he was standing, he saw the pavement, the two-by-four, the wall on the opposite side. "Lots of blood." He looked down the alley and saw the three men, still trying to hop or hobble away. One of them turned, and Jimmy could see the blood covering the front of him.

"It's mostly nosebleeds," she said. "Let's try walking." She helped him out of the alley to the street. He was still wearing his pack, and she reached into it. "Here, let me put this knitted cap on you. It'll help stop the bleeding, or anyway, hide it."

They walked on, and before long they reached Erie Street. There were many cars, businesses with lights on, and pedestrians. When they were a block away from the station, she stopped him under a streetlamp. "Look into my eyes."

He did. "How do I look?"

"Your pupils aren't dilated. That's a very good sign."

"I'll take anything that's not a very bad sign."

"Good policy. Can you just hang around here by yourself for about five minutes? I'll go see when the next bus leaves, and if we can get tickets, I'll buy some."

"Okay."

In a few minutes she came trotting back, smiling. "We're in luck. There's a bus that came in from Albany a few minutes ago, and it leaves for Buffalo in about five minutes." She held up two tickets. "I also looked everywhere, and there's not a cop in sight."

They began to walk toward the station. "I've been thinking," Jimmy said. "What are you, really?"

"What are you talking about?"

"You tell me you're just this doctor's wife, but after those guys coldcocked me, you beat the shit out of them. Three men, and they all looked half dead."

"Don't be silly," Jane said. "How could I do that?"

"I don't know. How?"

"Sh. You're disoriented and confused. Just keep as quiet as you can, and once we're on the bus I'll make you comfortable so you can rest."

7

Jane took another look at Jimmy's head wound after the bus was on the thruway moving west. They sat at the back, where they had some privacy. The light was dim, but she could see Jimmy well enough. She had some alcohol-based hand sanitizer in her pack, and she used it to sterilize Jimmy's wound. In her first aid kit she had Band-Aids and a large gauze pad, which she stuck over the wound. His knitted wool cap was soaked with blood so she put hers over his head to cover the bandages, and then went into the bathroom to wash his with the antibacterial soap in the dispenser over the little sink. She wrung out the cap and hooked it over the window latch so the moving air would dry it.

Jimmy fell asleep, and Jane watched him for a while. It was about two and a half hours from the East Syracuse station to Buffalo—about 150 miles of thruway. The flat, straight highway was monotonous in the dark, and Jane's exertion in the fight made her welcome the sleep that finally took her.

She woke as the bus slowed a bit to drift through the toll-booth at exit 50. The lights of the little outpost shone through the windshield and the window beside her, and then she sat up. She studied Jimmy's face as the bus passed through the dim light. He looked calm, relaxed, and untroubled. A terrible thought occurred to her, so she wetted her index finger and held it beneath his nostrils for a second to feel his breath. He was okay, just in a peaceful sleep. She looked at the highway signs. Even at almost midnight, the bus might take a while to get to the station, so she let him sleep. As she surveyed the bus, she and the driver seemed to be the only ones awake.

Riding with the sleeping Jimmy gave Jane a chance to consider what to do. There could be a cop or two in the Buffalo bus station. Sometimes police departments placed cops in airports and stations to watch for people who in-terested them—organized crime figures, parole violators, or fugitives. They were usually old-timers because experienced cops had long memories. She would have to watch for them. Where should he turn himself in? The trip to Akron or Bata-via was too long and complicated to be practical unless they could find a taxi at the station.

There were several police stations in downtown Buffalo, and at least one sheriff's station. They would probably put Jimmy in the Erie County Holding Center at the foot of Delaware Avenue, or if there was no room, put him in a station holding cell overnight and then take him to the Erie County Correctional Facility in Alden. Any police station would transport him where he needed to go. The one near the lower end of Franklin might be the closest, and that would matter if she and Jimmy were on foot.

One of the things that had been bothering Jane for the past few days was that she always felt a step behind. She had spent years learning to do something risky and diffi-cult, and what she knew should have made this easier than it was. Now she was about to do something she knew was wrong—walk her friend into a bus station, one of the most common places to find people who were running away from something. And instead of doing it during the day, when Jimmy would have been surrounded by hundreds of respectable travelers, she was going to take him in at midnight, when there would be no more than the dozen hollow-eyed, weary people who were on this bus, and maybe a few others waiting for the next one. And she was going in with both of them wearing clothes they'd worn to jump a train and fight off muggers in an alley.

Jane had survived so many trips with runners by keeping the odds in her favor. She'd taught them to look like everybody else, to change anything that was distinctive, to travel without being noticed. She'd told them to avoid confrontations, controversy, and even speech, if possible.

The bus turned onto Ellicott Street. She took a deep breath, let it out, and shook Jimmy gently. "We're in Buffalo."

He sat up straight, stretched, and looked around him. There were still some passengers asleep nearby, but others sat in the dark interior of the bus, their eyes now open and unblinking so they looked like wary night creatures.

Through the windshield Jane could see the low, lighted building, the roof beside it to shelter passengers from weather, and the buses in a row. Just beyond the station was an office building like a box with rows of lighted windows. The bus pulled into the entrance to the lot, came around the building, and slid into a space in front.

Jane waited for the first few passengers to file out the door at the front, then stood and picked up her backpack. She glanced out the window from her new, higher angle, and saw a sight that made her freeze where she stood.

Through the bus window she saw an elderly female figure wearing a light raincoat over a flowered dress, and high-heeled shoes. The woman stood, unmoving, with both hands in front of her holding the strap of her purse. She was facing

Jane's window, and her eyes seemed to bore into Jane, to demand her attention. A casual observer who saw the woman would have passed on to more interesting sights, but Jane recognized the woman. She was Alma Rivers, clan mother of the Snipe clan, Jane's father's clan. Alma's expression was solemn and her gaze grew more intense. As Jane stood and looked down at her through the window, her head moved, slightly but perceptibly, from side to side: *No.*

Jane whispered to Jimmy, "Get down and stay on the bus." He nodded and slumped down across the seat.

Jane moved to the open door of the bus, went down the steps, and watched Alma's eyes as she walked toward the station. Alma moved her gaze toward the interior of the station.

As Jane walked to the station entrance, she could see through the glass what Alma had been trying to warn her about. Sitting in a row in the blue plastic molded seats were three men in their thirties, watching the line of people waiting beside the bus to retrieve their luggage from the compartment in the bus's side.

Jane veered and moved along behind their row to avoid giving them an easy look at her, while giving herself a chance to study them. One was light blond with a fleshy face, and the other two were darker and leaner. None of them had baggage of any kind, none of them had the edges of tickets visible in any pockets, and none had anything in either hand. All of them were wearing thin, loose jackets that might have been chosen to hide weapons.

Jane reached the ticket window. "When does the bus out there leave for Erie?"

"About five more minutes."

"Two tickets, please." She handed him two fifty-dollar bills, and looked up at the glass over the window to study the three men in the reflection.

She took the tickets and change, and walked behind the three men to the doors. A line was forming at the door of the bus, and Jane joined it. She glanced over at the area near the doors where Alma Rivers stood. She was still there, unmoving, still watching Jane. When their eyes met, Alma nodded once, turned, and walked around the corner of the building—maybe to the parking lot, maybe to the street. All Jane knew was that she was gone.

The bus driver began taking tickets. "Thank you, welcome aboard," he said as each person handed him a ticket. "Thank you, welcome aboard."

Jane handed him her two tickets. "One is for my husband, asleep in the back of the bus."

"Thank you, welcome aboard."

Jane climbed the steps, made her way down the aisle to the seat where Jimmy waited, and sat down. In a very short time, the driver had admitted the line of passengers and come in to sit down behind the wheel. The bus backed up, then turned and drove out again. As it made the first turn toward the Niagara section of the thruway, she put her face close to Jimmy's and whispered.

"Did you see her?"

"Yes," he said. "At first I thought it must be a hallucination from getting bopped on the head, but I could tell you were seeing her too."

"She was there to warn us to keep going."

"Why?"

"I'm not sure. There were three guys sitting in the station watching for something—I think she thought they were there for you."

"Police?"

"They didn't look like police to me, and I don't think Alma thought so either."

"How did she even know we were coming in on a bus, or when?"

Jane shrugged. "I can't guess what they know or how they know it. Maybe they've been waiting at the airport, the bus station, the train station, and your mother's house for days, watching to be sure you make it back safely. Maybe they know people so well they can predict what we're going to do."

"What do you think we should do now?" he asked.

"We're doing it," she said. "We've got another three-hour ride. Sleep as much as you can to get your strength back."

Jimmy sat back and closed his eyes, and the sound of the bus rolling through the night lulled him back to sleep.

When they reached Erie a little after three, Jane got off the bus, went to the ticket booth, and then returned. "We'll have to wait for a few hours to catch the next bus to Cleveland. It leaves at eight." They bought snacks and water from vending machines. Jane whispered, "We can relax a little bit. Just crossing a state line still makes your face a bit less familiar, unless you were a movie star before your troubles started. Just look normal."

"How do I do that?"

"Make up a little story and live it. You and I are from Rochester. We live in an apartment on Maplewood Avenue, near the Genesee River. We've been married for, say, eight years. We're comfortable together, but we're past the stage where we have our hands all over each other in public. We took the bus because it's a cheap, easy way to visit my mother in Cleveland. You also want to see the Indians play while we're there."

Jimmy sat for a few seconds. "You're right. When I think about how that guy feels, I forget to be nervous, and I don't wonder what to do, because I know what he'd do. Right now he'd go get a newspaper and read it while you take a turn sleeping."

"I'll keep my eyes open until you get back with your paper."

When he came back from the newspaper vending machine, he sat down on one of the long, pew-like benches, and

Jane fell asleep beside him with her head on her backpack. They stayed that way until it was time to catch their next bus.

They got off the bus in Cleveland at around nine thirty in the morning. The station was a 1930s futuristic building, all rounded corners with a tall vertical sign like the marquee on a theater. They walked along Chester Street for a couple of blocks and came to a street with a sign that had an arrow and the words ROCK AND ROLL HALL OF FAME.

Jimmy looked at it, then looked at Jane.

She shrugged. "It gives us a destination. And it raises the odds that there will be food in the area."

They followed the arrows and walked a few blocks before they saw it. There were rows of man-high guitars painted in bright colors, and then a plaza up a wide set of steps. The building itself was a glass pyramid with concrete boxlike structures beside and above it. But what caught Jane's attention was a roofed area at the margin with a pay phone. "Wait for me," she said, and walked to it.

She put in a coin and dialed Carey's cell number, then put in more coins when the operator told her to.

"Hello."

"Hi, Doctor McKinnon," she said. "I love you."

"Hold on." She could hear him walking from a place where there were noises in the background to a smaller, quieter space, then closing the door. "Hi. I've been worried."

"Sorry. You got my message about ditching my cell phone, right?"

"Yes."

"I had started to suspect somebody was using the GPS to follow me. What's going on there?"

Carey said, "Ellen Dickerson called. She's been trying to reach you, but couldn't, of course. She has something to tell you, and I've got her number here."

Jane took out her pencil and the bus ticket stub. "Okay, go ahead."

He read the number and she wrote it down and repeated it back to him. Then she said, "How are you holding up?"

"If I complain, is there anything you can do to make it better?"

"At the moment, honestly, no. Maybe before too long." Jane stared ahead at the Rock and Roll Hall of Fame, behind its sculptures of enormous guitars.

"Look, I don't want to fight with you about it. Just do what you have to and get back here," he said.

"I love you."

"That's twice. It just reminds me of how stupid it is to be apart."

"I know it's stupid," she said. "But if you understood what I'm doing, you would know that anyone would do the same. Even logical, sensible you. When it's done, we can have a nice, dull time. I promise."

He laughed. "Actually, that sounds really good."

"It does to me, too. I've got to go. Be good."

"You too."

She hung up and stood still for a few breaths, looking out past the museum at the lake. Then she fished in her pack for more coins, put one into the phone, and dialed Ellen Dickerson's number.

Ellen's voice said, "Sge-no."

Jane answered in Seneca. "Does everybody who calls you speak Onondawaga?"

"I thought it would be you," Ellen said.

"I heard there was a problem."

"We've been worried. You can't bring him in yet. There are men who are getting themselves into the jails around here—minor infractions, the kind that will get them thirty days or sixty days. A couple of Haudenosaunee boys were in jail this week. They're good boys, a Mohawk and a Tuscarora, who were picked up after a burglary. They had nothing to do with it, so they were let go. But they said some men are waiting in jail for Jimmy when he comes in."

"Do the police know?" Jane said.

"We're having some people go talk to them, but even if the police believe them, fixing it isn't easy and will take time. For now, you're going to have to keep him away from here."

"I'll do my best," said Jane.

"We know you will," said Ellen. "Alma said you looked thin. Are you getting enough to eat?"

"Sure," she said. "I've just been getting a lot of exercise."

"To be honest, she said you looked like a stray cat. Go have lunch. And call me again when you can."

"I will."

Jane heard Ellen Dickerson hang up. She put the receiver back on the hook and walked over to sit on the steps in front of the museum with Jimmy.

"You look as though you got bad news. Is your husband mad?"

"Yes. He knows this has to be done, but he's not clear on why I should be the one to do it, and he worries." She knew she had made things sound better than they were.

"So what's wrong?"

"There are men getting themselves arrested and put into the Erie County jail system, so they'll be there when you arrive."

"Are you sure?"

"The story came from some Haudenosaunee boys who were in jail. Rumors go around in jails quickly because people don't have much to do, and gossip gives them relief from thinking about their own problems. It's always hard to tell what's true—the place is full of liars—but I think we should give people time to check this one out. If it were true, who would these men be—friends or relatives of Nick Bauermeister?"

"I don't know anything about him, so I don't have a theory. He was just a nasty drunk, a bully that I ran into one night." Jimmy sat for a moment, looking out toward the city. "So what am I supposed to do?"

"Just stick with me for a while, until it's safe to go back. I'll keep you out of sight until they give us the word."

Jimmy leaned forward and turned to look into her face. "Janie, last night I asked you a question, and you brushed me off. You know you can trust me. Whatever you tell me, I'll never tell anybody else."

Jane looked down at her feet for a few seconds, then sighed. "I'm an old friend of yours, somebody you played with as a kid. And how many of us are there? Maybe ten thousand Senecas, in five reservations in New York and Ontario, or near them, and maybe a couple thousand left in Oklahoma and Ohio and Missouri. We're about the size of one small town. You and I are probably related to each other in a hundred ways by now. You can trust me too."

"I'm not questioning that you care about what happens to me. You've already done more for me than I've ever done for anybody. But if you'll be open with me, it will help. What's going on? I got in trouble and ran, and within two days the clan mothers went straight to you. Last night three men clubbed me to the ground, and you nearly killed them, but there isn't a mark on you. Now you tell me how it feels to be in jail, and say you'll make me invisible for a while. So who are you?"

She put her hands between her knees, and shrugged. "Right now I'm exactly what I seem to be—Mrs. Carey McKinnon, the wife of a Buffalo surgeon, who lives a quiet life in a nice old house in Amherst. But for a long time, maybe fifteen years, I was a guide."

"What kind of guide?"

"People came to me who had pretty much used up their lives. They had good reason to believe that they were going to be murdered, and had no way out. I took them to other places where nobody knew them, made them into new people, and taught them how to be those new people."

He stared at her in shock for a few seconds. Finally he said, "How did you get involved in that?"

"I didn't exactly get involved. When somebody is in danger and you know how to help him, you do, that's all. When I was in college I spent three summers working for a skip tracer, so I learned how to find people. Then one night I was at a party and learned a friend of mine was in trouble. When I thought about it, I realized that I didn't just know how to find people. I knew how to lose people too. So I helped him disappear that night. But a number of our friends were at the party too, and knew what I'd done. A year later, one of them knew somebody else who needed that kind of help, and brought her to me. Then there were others, and the ones I helped told others. Pretty soon it was strangers. Over the next fifteen years I invented a lot of people."

"You were in jail. So I guess you got caught."

She shook her head. "No. Not for that reason, and not under my name. I just got myself sent to jail a couple of times because there were women in there that I had to get to."

"How did you learn to fight like that?"

"It's not about fighting. It's about running. If I'm cornered I fight dirty. Strike first without warning, use any weapon I have, hurt them as badly as I can, and then run."

"There's more to it than that. You have some kind of training."

"Years ago, there was a man I had to keep hidden for a very long time—more than eight months. Every day I taught him and tested him, making him learn to be a new person and forget the old person's tastes, habits, and attitudes. You can only do that for seven or eight hours a day. In return, he spent another seven or eight hours a day teaching me what he knew—aikido. Over the years, I learned more, and

I practice. And I stay in the best physical condition I can: I do tai chi to maintain my flexibility, balance, and tone, and I run every day." She paused, and thought about the long months of recovery after she was captured. "Unless I'm really sick, and can't get out of bed."

Jimmy said, "The clan mothers knew about all this?"

"I have no idea how they found out—who would have told them, or how long ago it was. They knew about me in the way they know other secrets. They keep things to themselves until they decide it's time not to."

Jimmy was silent, looking down at the white pavement in front of the steps.

Jane said, "What I've told you would get some very nice people, including me, into terrible trouble—jail for a few of them, death for nearly all of the others—if the wrong person found out and made the right connections. These are people who had someone really scary after them at the beginning. They're okay now, but that kind of trouble doesn't ever really go away. It just waits. I'm trusting you with our secret because your knowing will make it easier for me to help you."

"I'll never tell anybody," he said. "I promise."

"Then you can be one of my runners."

"Runners?"

"My clients. What I do is help people stay alive. I don't help them get revenge, or bring them justice, or something. I teach them to run and hide. Are you interested in that?"

"I've tried fighting, and that hasn't worked out too well."

"Then we'd better get started."

8

Jane bought a *Cleveland Plain Dealer* at a vending machine and then walked with Jimmy to a coffee shop a couple of blocks up from the lake. She scanned a page of ads. "Here," she said. "Here's the kind of thing we want. 'Suites by the day, week, or month. One or two bedroom, kitchen-slash-sitting room.'" She circled the ad with her pencil, then three others. "Any of these in this column would work. Apartments can require a background investigation, deposits, and sometimes references. Hotels only require a credit card that isn't rejected when they test run it for a hundred bucks to be sure it's valid. And once you're there, everybody's a stranger." She turned a page, then another.

"That's not enough?"

"We'll also need a car." She started circling ads again. "It has to be used, for sale by owner. A person sells his car because he wants to get more than he can get on a trade-in. He knows he might get a bad check, so what he really wants is cash, and that's good for us." She crossed off a few ads. "No antiques, no convertibles, no conversation pieces.

When you're doing this, look for low-end models from good manufacturers. You want the car that nobody remembers, the kind you'd find easy to lose in a parking lot. You're not going to try to drive it for a hundred thousand miles. It just has to run okay, and have some working life left."

"What about leasing a car, or renting one?"

"Neither option is good for you right now. Rentals are fine if you have a credit card in another name, need a car for a day or two, and can return it to the same place—or get someone else to. It's expensive after a few days, and the company can locate the car if they feel the need. A lease is a bank loan, and it triggers a credit check."

"What else do we need?"

"The rest are incidentals. If we get a place to stay and a car, everything else is easy."

They caught a cab at the Rock and Roll Hall of Fame and took it to the most promising of the extended-stay hotels. Jane rented a two-bedroom suite and came outside to bring Jimmy in. He walked around in the suite, looked in the bedrooms, and examined the main room, which was a living room with a one-wall kitchen consisting of a counter, sink, refrigerator, and stove. "How did you rent it?"

"A credit card."

"Whose?"

"Mine." She held it up so he could read it.

"Who's Diane Kazanian?"

"She's me. Years ago two women I had helped decided to send me a present. They worked in the county clerk's office in Cook County, Illinois. They added fifty birth certificates to the files there, and sent fifty certified copies to me. They were for men, women, and children, aged from about five years to seventy. One of them said Diane Kazanian and was about my age. I used the birth certificate to apply for a driver's license, took the tests, and got one. Then I used the license and the birth certificate as ID to start a small bank account. I bought some magazine subscriptions with checks, sent away for some things from big stores and paid for them, and then started getting offers for credit cards. I bought things with the cards, and paid the bills. The address is a mailbox rental in Chicago, which I pay to forward everything to another one nearer to home that's in the name of a corporation I formed. After a few years, Diane had a good credit record, a passport, a library card, and a few other things."

"Have you done that a lot?"

"Enough. For about ten years, I'd receive a batch of birth certificates every year. Most of them I've never used. But I keep growing identities, and use them in rotation so they all stay fresh."

"I can't believe you do this stuff," said Jimmy. "Where did you even learn how?"

"Some of it came from that first summer job skip tracing. I studied the methods that you can use to follow trails of people who don't want to be found. If you're the one who's running, you have to understand the risk that each thing you do carries with it."

"But aren't you ever afraid the banks will figure out there's something wrong with this new customer and call the police?"

"Banks have the biggest apparatus for detecting fraud, but they're only interested in protecting their profits, not enforcing laws. What they want is for you to deposit money so they can use it, and borrow money, so they can charge you interest. They sincerely don't care if you're an ax murderer. If you are, they don't want to know about it, and make an effort not to find out. Go online sometime and look at the list of banks with branches in the Cayman Islands. There has never been a reason for any foreigner to put money in the Cayman Islands except to hide it from their home governments. But every single major bank in the US or Europe that you can name has branches there. If your bank isn't on the list, then it's an error in the list. They're not there for the convenience of vacationers withdrawing a little cash for a dinner on the beach. It's big-time tax evasion, money laundering, profits from drugs, extortion, embezzling, kidnapping. Give banks a way to mind their own business, and they will."

Jimmy said, "Okay, so if I don't have to worry about banks, who do I have to worry about?"

"Remember that guy who was chasing us on foot?"

"How could I forget him? Sergeant Isaac Lloyd, New York State police."

"That's who you worry about—a dedicated police officer who has reason to believe you've committed a serious crime. This one went after us alone and on foot because he realized that was the way we were traveling, so it was probably the only way to follow us. He's trouble. Anybody like him is trouble."

"Let's hope there aren't any others."

"Let's do everything the right way, so he has no trail to follow."

She stood up and walked across the room to pick up her backpack. "Right now I'm going to get cleaned up and then leave you alone to do the same while I go out for a while."

"Where are you going?"

"To find us a car. It's just like renting this suite. You stay invisible." Jane disappeared into the bathroom and in a moment he heard the water running in the shower.

Twenty minutes later, Jane emerged from the bathroom wearing fresh, clean clothes—a black blouse, a pair of gray pants, and flat shoes—and carrying a small black purse. Her hair was shiny and clean, and she wore makeup. Jimmy looked up from the television set. "You still clean up nice."

"Thank you," she said. "When I go out the door, lock it. If there's a knock, don't open it. It'll probably be housekeeping, and all they can want is to turn down the sheets. We can do that ourselves. Just stay where you are, be nice and quiet, and don't talk to anyone. And this may take a while. I have the other key, so don't worry about letting me in." She picked up the newspaper classified ads, took the single page of used car ads out, folded it, and put it in her purse.

"Okay. Good luck."

She went downstairs and through the lobby. It was still midafternoon, so she used a pay phone to call three of the numbers in the car ads to make appointments to see the cars. As she stepped out of the hotel she looked to her left and saw that there were three cabs waiting down the drive for passengers, so she raised her hand and one pulled to the curb to pick her up. She gave the driver the address of the first and most likely car for sale, and sat quietly while he drove there.

When she arrived in her cab, she paid the driver and said thanks. She watched him drive off, and then she went to the door of the house and rang the bell.

The door opened and a young, trim black woman wearing the pants and blouse from a business suit and an apron stood in the doorway. When she saw Jane she took off the apron, tossed it onto the table by the door, and came out. "I'll bet you're Diane Kazanian."

"Yes," said Jane. They shook hands.

"I'm Tyler Winters."

"I hope I'm not interrupting dinner."

"No," she said. "I just got home from work a little while ago, and I thought I'd get it into the oven before my husband comes home. I'm free for a while. Ready to see the car?" She reached onto the table and pressed a remote control unit, so the garage door rolled upward.

"Sure," said Jane. As they walked to the garage she said, "Is the car yours?"

"Not exactly," Tyler Winters said. "It's my mom's. I'm just selling it for her."

Jane smiled. "I thought not. You seem more like the BMW type."

The woman laughed. "You got me. I have a Three Series, but I've been driving mom's car for a few days so I could leave it in the company lot with a sign on it. How do you do that—guess the car?"

"I don't know," Jane said. "It's just a knack I guess."

"Well, you don't strike me as the type for a six-year-old Chevy Malibu either."

"Normally I wouldn't seek it out," said Jane. "But right now for work I need a small, reliable car that doesn't catch the eye. I don't want the car somebody would pick out in a parking lot to rob. I'm in pharmaceutical sales, and it's much safer not to drive *that* car."

"Then I think you've come to the right place." She led Jane to the garage. The Chevy Malibu was a nondescript gray with cloth seats and the standard interior, but it was clean and shiny, without any nicks or dents, and the tires looked nearly new. Jane leaned close to the window. The interior was spotless. She said, "What's the mileage?"

Tyler handed her the key. "You have to turn it on to read it."

Jane sat in the driver's seat and turned the key, then said, "One hundred and two thousand, two oh three."

"Would you like to drive it?"

"Love to."

Jane waited for her to get into the passenger seat, and then tested the headlights while it was still in the garage and she could see the two bright spots on the garage wall, backed out, and drove it up the street. "Your mother took great care of it."

"Yes," said Tyler. "My husband helped her, but she's always been careful with things. This is just like the car I learned to drive on, and she kept that one for twelve years. We couldn't talk her into letting us buy her a new one until I volunteered to sell the old one for her."

"She drives a hard bargain," said Jane.

"She sure does. But she's getting old, and I'd just feel better if she had something new instead of waiting for some part to go."

"Your ad said four thousand."

"I'm willing to bargain a little, but that's what my husband thinks is fair."

"I'll take it."

"Really?"

"I like it," said Jane. "And I think your husband is probably right about the price. Now what? Should we go see your mother to have her sign it over?"

Tyler said, "Uh, this is kind of awkward, but—"

"You want cash?"

"I'm sorry," Tyler said. "But we don't know you, and—"

"I brought cash. I assumed nobody wants to take a personal check from somebody who just arrived in town and answered an ad."

"Great," said Tyler. "My mother has already signed the pink slip, and a bill of sale. I just have to fill in the amount and hand it over. You can take the car right away."

Ten minutes later, Jane had a car with the appropriate papers, traceable with great difficulty to a woman named Kazanian, whose last address was in Illinois, but who had no physical residence on earth. Jane drove her car out onto the street again, and made a few stops at stores. By the time she returned to the hotel she was very pleased with her purchases.

When she opened the door of the hotel suite, Jimmy stood and went outside to help her bring in four grocery bags and a few bags from clothing stores. They loaded the food into the refrigerator, and then opened the clothing bags.

Jimmy looked at the clothes she had bought him. He held up a sport jacket, and then looked at a pair of shoes, a pair of dress slacks, and a pile of shirts in their packages. "Thanks so much. These are really nice, but you know, I don't usually wear stuff like this."

"I can't think of a better reason to start," Jane said. "So now you do."

"Why?"

"For a lot of reasons," she said. "One I just told you. The people who are searching for you are looking for a guy who wears T-shirts in the summer, sweat shirts and puffy jackets in the winter, hoodies in the spring and fall. He goes to places where that's what everybody is wearing."

"I guess that makes sense, sort of."

"Yes. So now you stay out of those places. You're a guy who goes to a job every day and comes home to his wife and kids in the evening. Maybe you're a lawyer or business-man. You're local. That's important. And when you travel, you dress the way that kind of guy dresses for travel. Think polo shirts, light sport jackets, khaki pants, walking shoes."

"I don't know if I can carry that off."

"You'll learn."

"Aren't these clothes kind of expensive?"

"Not as much as you'd expect, but they do look that way. What that accomplishes is that people who see you will make a series of assumptions, based on very little evidence. They'll think you're financially solvent. You proba-bly don't steal hubcaps off cars for a living. You're probably not physically dangerous. You're not crazy in any way that matters to anybody. The police, who are the ones we're con-cerned about right now, are not looking for a man dressed like you. Most of the time they're only looking at people dressed the way you used to. And in these clothes you'll be easily accepted into the kinds of places where the police aren't looking anyway."

"A safe car, a safe place to sleep, clothes that will help us hide. That's a lot to accomplish in one shopping trip. Thank you."

"You're forgetting the food," she said. "I did that too. Let's make some dinner."

9

Dan Crane knocked on the door of Chelsea's house. Knocking on her door always struck him as a stupid formality, a bit of the past blocking his progress in the present. He was a believer in the present. He was busy, in a hurry much of the time, scrambling to get things done. When he'd already come off the highway and driven up a hundred-yard gravel driveway with his Range Rover kicking up dust to get here, then stepped up on the creaking wooden porch, she should know he was here and have the door open by now.

As he thought it, the door swung open. Chelsea stood behind the closed screen door and smiled. "Hi, Dan. I didn't know you were coming. I look awful."

Crane detected a hint of a complaint. She didn't look awful. She looked amazing. She was suggesting that he should have called her ahead of time to ask her permission to come and see her. "I'm sorry," he said. "I happened to be driving past, so I thought I'd see how you were." Crane swung his arm around his body from behind his back and held out the small bouquet of flowers. "I'd better leave these with you. I look like a sissy carrying them around."

Her bright blue eyes widened, and her smile placed two dimples in the smooth white skin of her cheeks. "Are those for me?"

"I happened to be driving by a florist's shop that was having a sale."

"Really," she said as she unhooked the hook-and-eye on the screen door to open it. "You happened to be in a florist's shop and they fell into your hands. Then, when you drove off you happened to be going by here."

He stepped inside and she kissed him on the cheek. It was only after that half second that he felt in retrospect the damp, pillowy lips on his cheek and a slight brush of her skin, but she had already withdrawn. His cheek was bereft, feeling where her lips had been.

She was moving away through the little dining room into the kitchen. He followed at a distance, watching the movement of her body in the shorts and the halter top, and hearing the whisper of her bare feet on the floor. She opened a kitchen cupboard, leaned forward over the counter, and stretched upward as far as she could to reach a vase on the top shelf, and he could see a few inches of bare back and the thin white elastic band at the top of the pink imitation silk of her panties. She snagged the vase, a blue-and-yellow glass vessel that nearly matched the small bunch of blue lilies and yellow daffodils. He retreated a few paces.

She came back into the living room, the smile still glowing. "This is just so thoughtful, Dan."

"It's nothing. Pretty flowers seem to need a pretty lady to make them complete."

Chelsea looked up and studied him for the hundredth time. He was kind of handsome, if you were a little ways off or the light was dim. He was tall, with square shoulders and a slim waist, and she liked that. He had a grown-up haircut without any hair over his collar or greased and sticking up straight in bristles or anything like that. But up close, he seemed a little bit more ordinary. He was quite a bit older, at least forty, and you could see the difference in the texture of his skin. You could notice things, like when he said something he thought was clever there was a thing with his mouth that wasn't quite right. It looked a little like a sneer. She wished, if only for his own sake, that he would stop that. She was ashamed of herself for having such shallow thoughts about a man who was always kind to her.

She overcompensated for what she'd been thinking about him. "Thanks so much, Dan. Since Nick died, you've been just great. You've turned out to be practically the only one of his friends who didn't disappear as soon as the funeral was over."

"Nick was a good guy," Crane said. "But he's gone now. We've lost him forever. The person who deserves the attention is you."

He watched her closely. Her eyes lowered, and she seemed to blush. He had never believed that women actually did that. In his life he had never seen any evidence that women were any more delicate or sensitive than, say, dogs or cows. But here it was. She was a princess who wore cut-off shorts and bare feet.

Chelsea set the vase on the table in the dining room, then frowned and moved it to the mantel, where the mirror doubled the colorful petals of the flowers. "Do you like it better there?"

He started to answer, but only got in "Sure" before she spoke over him. "I do too. The mantel is a good place to see them when you come in. It's sort of the center of the house—at least visually."

Crane said, "I was just thinking. It's eleven thirty. Maybe you and I could go to an early lunch, and get in somewhere before everybody else shows up and there's a big wait."

She held her hands out from her sides in a gesture that seemed to say, "Can't you see the way I'm dressed?" What she said aloud was, "That's so sweet. But I've got so many chores to do that I really don't have time for anything today."

She saw his face go dead, as though something living behind the face had been injured and contracted. "Okay," he said. "Another time." His voice was hollow and emotionless. He took two steps toward the door.

"Dan," she said carefully. "It's only been a short time. A few weeks. And it isn't as though he had some long disease so I had time to get used to the idea. Or even that he died in some accident, the kind that happens all the time. A guy stood out there in front of this house and shot him right here. When I came out of the bedroom he was lying just about where you're standing now, and his head looked like it had exploded. I'm just not ready yet to do things for fun."

Crane became solicitous. "I understand. Believe me. It was just a thought. When you feel ready, you should start going out again and seeing people. When you do, if you want company I'll be here."

"I know you will," Chelsea said. She took another step in his direction and then stopped. She had wanted to herd him out the door by occupying the space as he gave it up, so he couldn't come back into the center of the room. But she also didn't want him to think that she was coming closer to hug him.

He waited.

"Well," she said. "I'd better get back to work."

He relented. "Me too. I'll talk to you soon."

"Bye." She sensed that she had said it too soon. It would have been more graceful if she had waited until he was out the door, and then she could have said it and shut the door. This way she had to stand in silence while he left.

He opened the door, went out to the porch, and closed the screen door gently so its spring wouldn't snap it back and slam it, the way they always did—the way they were supposed to. Slamming shut kept out the flies. As he went down the porch steps, she thought it was just like him. He had to control everything, including things that were none of his business and took care of themselves.

Chelsea stepped backward to stand far back in the living room where he couldn't see her to watch him climb into his Range Rover, back it up a couple of times to turn it around, and lumber down the gravel driveway to the highway. That car was a mistake too. It was a big, fat boxy thing. She had looked the model up on the computer and seen that it had cost him more than a hundred thousand dollars. For a lot less money he could have bought something a woman could enjoy riding up to a restaurant or a fancy party in—a normal car she could get into without climbing steps in heels, or having them catch on something and make her fall flat. He acted as though he was thoughtful, but he just wasn't. When he turned onto the highway and sped away toward the west, she felt the tension go out of her neck and shoulders.

DANIEL CRANE DROVE ALONG THE flat, straight highway past a sign that said BUFFALO 20 MILES. All along here the older homes were set far back from the road at the ends of long gravel driveways like Chelsea's. They had been farms a generation ago, with crops between the road and the house. Usually there were vegetables planted there because they were easier to hoe, weed, watch, and pick if they were close to the house. A lot of these houses had even had rough, heavy wooden tables that stayed at the ends of their driveways all year, some with roofs over them so they could be used as roadside vegetable stands. But the big tractor-cultivated cash crops and the dairy pastures were all on the back hundred acres. Most of those back hundreds had been sold off long ago and turned into suburban tracts, with new streets running through them.

He had grown up going past those places and thinking what relics they were. What prosperous people around here had been doing for some time was to buy a place like that, drive a bulldozer through the old farmhouse, and build a much bigger house surrounded by the tall, old hardwood trees that had once shaded the farmhouse. They paved the gravel drive, put a rail fence or a stone wall or a hedge along the highway, and they had themselves a nice two- or three-acre estate. That was what he had done. Or the last owner before him had anyway, and it was the same thing. Now he lived in a neighborhood full of doctors and lawyers, all of their houses secluded on woodsy lots. Sometimes as he passed, he saw the kids walking the hundred yards or so down those long driveways to get to the end so the school bus could pick them up. They looked pretty cold sometimes in the winter, but it was worth a little discomfort to live in a house like that.

As Crane drove around Western New York, he looked for neighborhoods with plenty of big, new houses set far apart. Behind them they had pools and tennis courts, and the best of them had horses grazing on pastures that were relics of the farming days. Lately whenever he went through an area with old farmhouses like Chelsea's, he knew that the next time he passed through, the developers would have begun their transformation, tearing them down to build houses for the upwardly mobile. He would have made a good land developer himself, but what he did produced more money.

The center of his empire was a storage facility he had built not far from here. The land was a twenty-acre remnant of one of those old farms. He had taken out a loan against it, poured a long, narrow slab of concrete, and then erected what amounted to a connected series of ten-by-fifteen-foot enclosures made of cinderblock with a roof of corrugated steel and an aluminum garage door on each one. A year later he'd poured the next long, narrow slab of concrete and built the next set of storage bays. Two years later, he'd built three more rows. Now he always had a new set of bays under construction, barely able to build them fast enough. He was rich.

As he drove on, he still could hardly get over the sting of this morning's conversation with Chelsea. She was putting him off, keeping him at a distance.

Chelsea couldn't be actually unkind to him. He had been far too generous and steadfast for that. But she wasn't responding the way he had hoped and expected. He wondered for a moment. Had her boyfriend Nick told her something about him? He followed the question up and down all avenues in rapid succession.

Nick had been stupid and he had been overconfident. His fight in a bar with that Indian had been just like him—a man revealing his whole nature in one performance, like a character in an opera. But Nick had not been naïve enough to let Chelsea know that the work he did for Crane was not just renting storage space to people who had bought so much crap that they couldn't keep it all in their houses. Most of the money Nick brought home had come from the other parts of Crane's business. Chelsea had liked Nick, but if Nick had told her he was a thief she would have thrown him out. Nick couldn't have told her anything about Dan Crane. Was there any other way she could have found out? Had Nick inadvertently left something lying around that she could have interpreted as evidence that Crane was paying him to commit break-ins? No again. She would have left. And she certainly wouldn't have let Crane inside her house.

Chelsea could only believe that Crane was what she could see—a nice guy a few years older who had been her boyfriend's boss and patron. Nick had been dead almost two months. By now it must have crossed Chelsea's mind that she no longer had a boyfriend, and that she would have to find another one. Crane was rich, fairly good-looking, and successful. Nick had been what? A big lout. A dolt. A man who had probably been manipulated and used by everyone he met. Nick had been so greedy, and so lazy, that it was impossible not to know what inducements would beguile him. Crane had turned him into a thief by simply offering to include him on a crew he was sending to clear out one of those newly built houses set back from the road. Being a burglar had sounded easy, so Nick had jumped on the truck.

It occurred to Crane that almost the same crew was out right now doing another break-in. He searched his mind to see if he could detect any regret at not having Nick alive to work this trip. No, he felt no regret. The men who were left would just have to work a little faster and lift a little more weight into the truck. He wasn't sorry he had shot Nick. He had done it because he had wanted Chelsea, but there had been many other good reasons to get rid of him. Having a stupid man know his secrets was too risky.

Crane pushed Nick to the back of his mind for a moment, and went over the details of today's trip. They would probably be loading up the truck right now. They would haul the merchandise to the storage facility, and put it all into J-17. He had already rented that bay to a fictitious customer who had paid in cash for the first six months. The guys would close the bay, slide the bolt into the receptacle, put the standard padlock on the bolt, and leave. The rental agreement was on the books already, and the rental money was in the safe. Anybody looking for stolen items today would have 164 identical bays to search, and 106 empty ones with padlocks on them. He looked at his watch again. He would check with his spies after five. He always sent two, and made sure neither knew about the other. He asked enough questions to pick it up if someone were diverting merchandise instead of turning it all in to him.

After he killed Nick he had considered starting a rumor that the reason Nick was gone was that he had pocketed a valuable ring from a burglary. After thinking more about it, Crane had decided that he would benefit more from taking revenge on Nick's killer, that Indian who had decked Nick in the bar fight. Scaring his employees would have been good, but risky. He had to believe that building their loyalty would be better.

He ran through other topics to keep his mind from returning to Chelsea Schnell. Did he need anything at the supermarket? Had he let any bills go too long without paying them? Did he have clothes ready at the cleaners'? He knew that thinking about Chelsea was a waste of time. Thinking about her was not going to solve any problems, but he couldn't get her out of his mind. As he drove, he relived the short visit he had made to her house.

He had knocked on her door, and there she was, behind the screen door. Her image had been slightly unclear, because the screen was like a veil between her and him. What, exactly, had her expression been? Had she been pleased to see him, or only surprised, but not really pleased? Teeth. He clearly recalled seeing the row of small, perfect white teeth as she'd appeared behind the screen door.

A smile. She had been glad. That moment was the one that mattered most, he decided. His appearing at her door unexpectedly had made her smile. She hadn't had time to overcome some other reaction, hide it, and paste a fake smile on her face. The smile had been genuine, a sincere reflexive impulse from nervous system to facial muscle, without delay or disguise. She had been pleased to see him.

Anything after that could have been thought out, a conscious decision. She had taken the flowers, and walked away from him to the kitchen. She was easily old enough and experienced enough to know he would be watching her, his eyes naturally taking in the shine of her golden hair, the graceful white shoulders, the narrow waist, the rounded hips and bottom. She had walked very appealingly, swaying a little from side to side. Could that have been anything but intentional? Women, alone among all creatures, practiced their walks. And then, when she had leaned herself against the counter her ass had been pushed outward, her lower back and midriff bared by the stretch to reach up into the cupboard. The pose had shown him parts of her ivory skin that most people never saw. Could any of that not have been choreographed? She had been trying to entice him.

He considered the possibilities. Maybe she was simply one of those women who wanted all men to see how beautiful she was, and found it pleasant to know they were feeling the pain and sadness of not being able to touch her. But Chelsea wasn't flirting with all men. She wasn't even going out anywhere to be where men could see her. She wasn't going to work or visiting or shopping. She was only displaying herself to Dan Crane. So why was she doing that? She pointed out today that Nick had only been dead a few weeks, and that explained why she didn't want to go out with another man. Maybe she didn't want people—other women, really—to be critical of her for getting over Nick too quickly. Or maybe she really didn't feel any interest in other men yet. That couldn't be right, though. If she felt that way, she wouldn't be flirting with him. She seemed to draw him in, then push him away. She had used the flowers as an excuse to say nice things about him and kiss him, and then shut him down when he had asked her to have a simple lunch in a public place.

Another idea began to form in his mind. What had she shown that she liked? She had liked Nick Bauermeister. Who was he? He was a big, muscular, dumb guy who had the manners of an ape and treated her as though he owned her and she wasn't especially valuable. In the few times when he had seen them together, Nick had paid no attention to her for long periods, talking mostly to the other guys. On one night he remembered her reminding Nick that she had to work the next morning, and asking if he could please take her home so she could get some sleep. He had laughed, told her to go get him another beer, and slapped her on the ass when she had left to get it. Crane had heard somewhere that women loved men who had confidence and took charge. They pretended that men who were concerned about their preferences, and sensitive, and asked permission for everything, were the only ones who were behaving acceptably. But they never fell in love with them. They practically stood in line to throw themselves at men like Nick.

Crane drove to his storage facility, stopped at the gate, pressed the button and took a ticket, then pulled the Range Rover forward as the barrier rose to admit him. He parked between the two electric golf carts plugged in and charging beside the office, and stepped to the door. The office was the only two-story building on the property. The bottom level held special storage bays like closets, where customers stored things they were especially worried about. Two men occupied the office twenty-four hours a day, so there was an added layer of protection. He opened the door and climbed the staircase. One of the things he liked about the storage business was that it didn't require many people. He had only a dozen men working for him. All of them worked on his break-in crews, and also worked shifts here, renting out storage bays and watching the place. He didn't have a secretary or bookkeeper, salespeople, or any other office workers. He handled his own books, and let his ads and website do his selling. Whoever was on duty answered the phone.

He reached the second floor, where the office was. He could see Harriman was the one sitting at the desk watching the long, narrow storage buildings through the office windows. There were also eight television screens showing what the security cameras aimed up and down the drives between the storage buildings could see, but those were most useful for looking closely at things too far from the windows. Harriman had heard Crane climbing the stairs, and now he glanced over his shoulder to see him. "Hey, Dan."

"Hi. Anything up?"

"My friend Carl is in the Erie County lockup for ninety days. He had his girlfriend in court to say he beat her again."

"Carl. Which one is he?"

"Carl Ralston. The biker. You remember the big guy, a little overweight, with the tattoos up both arms?"

"Uh, yeah," said Crane. "Will he actually do it?"

Harriman said, "I'm thinking Carl Ralston is the most likely to succeed. He's been in jail a few times, and he knows the routines. Like when the guards are likely to toss a guy's cell to look for stuff, and where the blind spots of the cameras are."

Crane shrugged. "It doesn't add up to much unless he's willing to actually kill the guy who shot Nick."

"If he gets a decent chance at him, he'll do it. He's not going to shank him in front of a guard, but he's killed people before. He's one of the few guys around who will get a benefit for doing it. The bikers he hangs out with will respect him for it. Respect matters to bikers."

"I suppose it would," said Crane. "And you told him what it pays?"

"I told him twenty-five thousand." Harriman suddenly looked worried. "That was right, wasn't it? I really don't want to wait until he's done it and then tell him different."

"No, no. Don't worry. Twenty-five is right. And even if it wasn't, I'd cover for you just so you wouldn't need to get word to him now while he's inside. Any communication between you and him could bring attention to us. You did your job. Now let him do his."

"I will," said Harriman.

"Good. Are the guys back from Orchard Park yet?"

"They got back a while ago. They went out again to re-paint the sides of the truck so it won't say Sears on it."

"All of them went?" asked Crane.

"No. Steel and Slawicky stayed back to do the inventory and put the stuff in storage."

"Maybe I'll go down and take a look." Crane took off his sport coat and hung it on a wooden hanger, then put it in the closet, rolled up the sleeves of his dress shirt, and walked to the stairs. He descended to the first floor and walked past the small-size units in the hallway. They looked like narrow closet doors, but they were deep enough to hold most things that were really valuable, and they had built-in four-button locks that made customers feel safe leaving things they might not want to entrust to a garage door with a padlock on it.

He went out the door and walked down the long road-way between two storage buildings, past bay after bay. He could see J-17 from a few hundred feet away. The roll-down door was open a couple of feet from the bottom so there was air inside, but no passerby could see anything that was going on in there. He approved of that precaution. In the summer those bays could get pretty hot, and with this humidity, they could be awfully uncomfortable.

When he reached the bay, he pulled up the door and watched the two men spin toward him. Steel was taller than Crane, thin and dark with close-set dark eyes, and Slawicky was wider and older, with thick, muscular arms. He had blond hair and a small, round nose. Crane said, "Sorry. I didn't mean to startle you." He had, actually. If they were hiding something from him, he wanted to know.

"No problem," said Steel, but he looked a little sheepish because he had jumped.

"Right," said Slawicky. "Harriman would have called us if he'd seen a customer or a cop heading down here."

Crane wondered. Had Harriman called them to let them know that the boss was on his way out to the bay? Possibly. If he had a chance he would check Harriman's phone for recently called numbers. He stepped closer. "What did we get?" He realized he had said it in a way they would resent. "I really mean what did *you* get? I was driving around wasting my morning while you guys did all the work."

Slawicky waved toward a coffee table a few feet away, where small objects were piled in neat rows. "The best stuff is on the table."

Crane picked up a stack of money with a thick rubber band around it. He read the slip of paper under the band. "Three thousand four hundred and sixty. Not too bad. It pays for expenses, anyway." He set the money on the table and turned his attention to a jewelry box that was made to look like a hardcover book. He opened it and lifted a thick chain necklace, bounced it up and down on his palm to feel the weight, then looked at it more closely. "Feels like gold."

"We haven't tested it yet."

"I'll bet I'm right." He picked up a tennis bracelet studded with small diamonds. "This is all pretty good stuff. Assuming the diamonds are real, this would be about five grand new."

"That's about what I figured," said Steel. "There are a couple of pairs of diamond earrings too, and an emerald ring."

"What else have you got?"

Slawicky said, "The furniture is all good—all new and high-end. We also got a couple of Apple laptops, both over there."

Crane said, "That could be really good. Salamone's got people who might be able to hack their way in and see if anything on their hard drives leads anywhere. They might be able to do some online banking or something."

"That pillowcase over there is full of financial stuff we found in the little home office they had. We took it without looking too closely, but there's a tax return, and that will have social security numbers and all that. We also brought the paintings and sculptures because they looked real."

"Salamone's people will have to decide about that stuff. They don't usually want anything that's one of a kind, but maybe they can sell it in another country or something. Good job, you guys. And you didn't have any trouble?"

"No," said Slawicky. "It was the usual thing. We backed the truck into the driveway all the way to the house, opened the cargo bay, and brought big cardboard boxes down the ramp and into the house on a dolly, like we were delivering a refrigerator, stove, washer and dryer. Everybody worked fast, wore gloves and hats, and cleared the place. If anybody saw anything, they don't know what they saw."

"Great," said Crane. "I'll leave you guys alone, and go do some work in the office."

The others didn't offer any more information, and as he walked back to the office neither of them ran after Crane to tell him anything he needed to hear privately. He would see each of them alone over the next day or two.

Crane climbed back up to the second floor and into the office, and went to sit at his desk. He was still thinking about Chelsea. She was always in the back of his mind the way there were always a few programs running on a computer behind what he saw on the screen. He had thought of a few theories about her, but he had made no progress figuring out what she wanted. The one idea he'd had that seemed promising was to remember everything he could about her relationship with Nick Bauermeister. Thinking about her with Nick wasn't pleasant for him, but whatever Nick had done, she must have liked it.

"Car coming in," said Harriman. He was looking out the front window toward the street.

Crane raised his eyes to the color security monitor for the camera at the gate and saw the dark gray Mercedes stopped at the front gate. The driver reached out his window and took a ticket from the machine, the barrier went up, and the car glided into the lot. Crane knew the car, which had always seemed a little eerie to him. The color was exactly the dark gray color of the road, so it was practically invisible except for the chrome parts. Crane saw that the driver's arm still hung out the open window, and the hand released the ticket to flutter to the pavement. The car pulled up to the building and parked directly behind Crane's Range Rover, blocking him in.

Crane said, "You can go down and help Steel and Slawicky for a bit."

Harriman got up and went down the stairs. Crane could hear him open the side door, and he looked up at the monitor to watch him start walking along the drive between two long rows of storage bays.

Crane waited. He always felt a twinge of fear when Salamone showed up this way. Some time ago Crane had begun to think that the last sounds he would hear on earth might be the footsteps of Salamone and a couple of his guys on the stairs. The idea had bothered him for such a long time that he had tried several ways of lessening the anxiety. He had tried talking to Salamone on the telephone so he wouldn't have a reason to drive all the way out here in person. But Salamone wouldn't talk to him on the telephone. He said he liked to be able to look into a man's face while he talked business, but Crane suspected it was because so many men of Salamone's acquaintance had been the victims of wiretaps.

He had also tried keeping a short-barreled shotgun in the coat closet behind his desk. The shotgun hadn't been a good idea. Salamone came in one rainy day, took off his coat, and opened the closet door to hang it up. He said, "What's the shotgun for?"

Crane said, "Protection. People know we have duplicate keys to all the bays, and we take in cash and checks. I don't want some holdup jerk to come in and kill one of my guys so he can steal some customer's stamp collection."

"If your guy is smart enough to give him the keys, nobody gets killed. Get rid of the shotgun. If your place gets robbed, we'll get it all back. I promise."

Crane knew that Salamone was telling the truth, that it had been the truth for over a hundred years, and that it would still be true after they were both gone and forgotten. Salamone wasn't just some guy. He was speaking as a member and representative of the organization, which in Western New York was called the Arm.

Crane listened to the footsteps coming up the stairs. As always, the first one to appear was Cantorese, the big man. He was about six feet three and fat. It was a hot, humid day, and he was wearing a loose Hawaiian shirt that hung down over his belt and covered the gun at the back of his pants. His small eyes were already scanning everything in sight, and then settled on Crane and never left him. He stepped aside from the landing and stopped to Crane's right. The etiquette of these meetings was that one didn't greet Cantorese. He was there, and you could nod to him or—if you were, for some strange reason, happy to see him—you could smile. He didn't care what you thought, so either was wasted.

The second man up was Salamone. He was about fifty years old, but his body seemed younger. He had good posture and was light on his feet. Today he looked as though he had been golfing. He wore a dark blue polo shirt and a pair of well-tailored black pants, with a pair of rubber-soled walking shoes.

Behind him was Pistore, who trailed behind Salamone by five or six steps and half turned to look over his shoulder occasionally. It was clear to Crane that if something had been happening behind the three men, it was Pistore's job to take care of it. Crane had, a couple of times, caught sight of guns on Pistore. Today he didn't have a sports jacket, but he carried a thin nylon windbreaker over his left arm, undoubtedly to conceal something lethal.

Salamone reached the office and stepped up to Crane. "Danny boy." He gave Crane a quick hug and a pat on the back, then held him at arm's length and stared into his eyes for a half second, then released him. He went to sit behind Crane's desk.

When Salamone was settled, Pistore returned to the top of the stairwell and leaned against the wall. From there he could see the bottom of the stairs, the big paved aisles between storage buildings, and Daniel Crane. Pistore was a generation younger than the other men, so he seemed to do most of the chores. Crane knew that if death were to come, he would probably be the one to administer it.

Salamone sat back in Crane's leather desk chair looking contented. Crane knew that the hug Salamone sometimes gave other men had nothing to do with friendship. He had been checking to see if Crane had microphones or wires on his body. Salamone was the conduit for Crane's stolen goods, but Crane couldn't know all of the other businesses that Salamone had going. For many years he had run the network of barbershops, bars, gas stations, and convenience stores where people bought each week's football betting slips in this area. On Mondays, Salamone drove around to those businesses and picked up his profits. He also had some kind of deal with the people who stole luggage at the airport, and some share of an auto parts business. But he could be doing almost anything.

Salamone leaned forward. "Well, Danny, what have you got to tell me?"

"I've got your percentage for the storage business," Crane said. "It was pretty good last month. People paint and remodel during the summer, or go on vacations, so they seem to store things more often." He went to the safe in the corner of the room. It was left unlocked during the day, so he just opened the door and took out a stack of bills he had placed there. He set it on his desk in front of Salamone.

Salamone pursed his lips and gave a silent whistle to show he was impressed. "How much is that?"

"Six thousand, seven hundred forty-five. Ten percent."

Salamone nodded, then held it up to hand it to Cantorese, who made the money disappear under his voluminous shirt. Salamone said, "I've got something for you, too. It's the money for the last load of stuff we sold. Pistore, give him his money."

Pistore stepped up to the unoccupied desk where Harriman had sat, spread his windbreaker on the surface, and unzipped the pockets. Out of each pocket he took a stack of bills with a rubber band around it. When the stacks were all on the desk, he stepped back and put on his windbreaker.

Salamone said, "It's twenty-two thousand. Are you pleased?"

"It's hard not to be," said Crane.

"How are we doing so far this month?"

"It looks good again. We got another load in this morning, just like the last few. Summer has always been good for us. Vacations, like I said. And people open a lot of windows and forget to close one when they go somewhere. It's also when there's a lot of remodeling and construction and stuff, so nobody notices one more truck parked by a house."

Salamone smiled and nodded, then reverted to his serious expression. "Danny, you kind of skipped over something that I've been wondering about. You told me how good last month was, but you lost a guy last month, that guy Nick."

"Well, yeah," said Crane. "I didn't think you'd be interested in that."

"He got shot to death. Sure I'm interested. Who killed him?"

"Nick said he got drunk in a bar, and got into a fight with some Indian. The guy knocked him cold. The cops were pressing charges for assault."

"So who killed him?"

"The Indian, I guess."

"No, he didn't. Guys kill people for reasons. They kill for money, or over a girl, or something like that. Nobody beats some stranger up in a bar and then comes back and kills him too. Winning a fight is kind of a one-act deal." He paused. "So I'm asking you, Danny. Who killed him?"

"The police think—"

"I'll ask one more time. Who killed him?"

"I did."

Salamone grinned and looked at Cantorese and Pistore. "See?" He tapped his index finger on his temple.

The others said nothing, and showed neither surprise nor disapproval.

Salamone turned to Crane again. "You did the right thing by being honest with me. I want to make that clear to you. Pistore, give him the rest of his money."

Pistore reached into another pocket in his jacket and put another stack of bills on the desk.

Salamone said, "You're honest with us, so we're honest with you. Tell me why you killed him."

Crane's mind raced. He wanted to tell Salamone that Nick had diverted some money from a robbery, or a piece of jewelry, but he knew Salamone would want to know which piece, and he couldn't remember the pieces he had given Salamone to sell last month. He could see Salamone's face darkening. Time was going by, and then gone. "I wanted his girlfriend."

Salamone kept his eyes on Crane as he said, "You can go back to the car and wait for me." Pistore and Cantorese went down the stairs. It seemed to take a long time. When he heard the door downstairs close, Salamone said, "So where is the girlfriend? Did you get her?"

"Not exactly. Not yet."

"Why not? Did she get you to kill him and then change her mind about you?"

"No," said Crane. "It's not like that. She didn't know about it. I never told her I was going to do it. I never even told her I wanted her."

Salamone rested his elbow on Crane's desk and leaned his chin on the palm of his hand. "So how is she supposed to know?"

"I plan to tell her," he said. "I just think I need to give her some time."

"For what?"

"To get used to the fact that Nick is dead."

"Is she a little slow or something? I read in the paper that she was right there when the bullet went through the bastard's head. The blood must have sprayed the walls."

"She just thinks of me as a friend—somebody she knew through Nick, who has been nice to her since he died. She isn't ready to start dating again."

Salamone rolled his eyes. "If people waited until they were ready for things, not a goddamn thing would ever happen. Things get sprung on them, and they either keep up or get trampled. You'd better move quick, or somebody else is going to get in there ahead of you. Right now she's alone and she's going to be receptive. Make sure it's to you."

"You think so?"

"Show me a guy who waits around until she's all ready, and I'll show you a guy who's going to be on the guest list for her wedding—way at the back with the groom's third cousins."

"I'm going to have to think about it."

"Here's a start. She's probably short on money. Nick won't be bringing any pay home this month. Even if you didn't give a shit about her you should be generous to her just because he worked for you. That will keep the other guys on your crew thinking you take care of your people. If you don't care about them, they won't care about you. And women can't help loving money, just the way men do. Giving her money when she's broke is an easy way to show her you're desirable. That's better than being hung like a horse, and even if you are, the money is a lot easier to show without risking embarrassment."

"I guess you're right. I'll do it today. I'll pay her rent, and give her some spending money."

"A good start," said Salamone. He stared at Crane for a few seconds, and then sighed. "I'm afraid there's one more thing we have to talk about."

"What's that?"

"I heard that guys were checking themselves into the Erie County jail to wait for this Indian. You know anything about that?"

"Well, I did ask my guys if they knew a couple of friends we could pay to make sure the Indian didn't get off. They got four of them to get arrested for small things—probation violation, domestic abuse, that kind of thing."

Salamone stared at him, and he could feel the eyes were seeing through his skin and into his innards. "You know that I like you, Danny," he said. "Not personally, of course. That's a different thing, and I have a very big family for that. But you're a good earner. Every month, I get a shipment from you that's full of good things to resell, and I get an honest percentage of the storage business. You've made me a lot of money, and I haven't had to spend much time worrying that you'll do something stupid and put me in danger."

Crane said, "I try to be smart."

"I've appreciated that. You run your business right. No outsiders who aren't in on things and might ask questions, and not much chance of strangers noticing what you do. You do your own books and pay taxes and all that. We could go on forever and die rich old men. You want that, right?"

"Yes," Crane said. "That's exactly what I want."

"That's the way to be," said Salamone. "When this business gets big enough and you've diversified your investments and set aside money for trouble, you could stop doing burglaries and just collect your rent. So here we are. And this is what gets me. You're like forty years old, and I've got to explain the way the world works, and our place in it."

"You don't really," said Crane. "I don't need—"

"Yes you do," Salamone snapped. "So here it is. You know that the little bit of power I have on this earth isn't from me, or from the handful of guys like Pistore and Cantorese who work for me. It comes from people up above me, the people I work for. Most of the power that matters belongs to Mr. Malconi."

"I know who he is," said Crane.

"See, that's exactly my point. You do, and you don't. He's the guy you've seen in the papers. The don, the capo, the boss of the Arm. They keep showing that one picture of him from his last indictment twenty years ago, outside the courthouse, with the two FBI guys holding his arms. The wind blew his hair straight up, so he looks like an old man with a porcupine sitting on his head. That's who you know, but that's not him."

"I'm not sure I understand."

"Mr. Malconi is the man who is at the top of the pyramid. Below him are a couple of underbosses, and then there

are about a hundred guys just like me, who have a few businesses that he allows to operate, and that he protects. We
can each pay ten or twenty guys like Pistore and Cantorese,
and we send a percentage of our profits up the line to Mr.
Malconi. I send him a part of what you give me, for in-
stance. Once in a great while, Mr. Malconi will pass down
an order to those hundred guys like me, and we each pass
down the order to our ten best guys, so in an hour or two,
there are a thousand guys following that order. If the order
was about trouble, he would also call the bosses of nearby
places—Rochester, Cleveland, Toronto, or Pittsburgh, or
even Boston or New York."

"I guess what I meant before was that I don't know why
you're telling me this," said Crane.

"To help you," said Salamone. "I don't ever want to
drive up to this place and find a hundred-gallon drum with
two hundred pounds of unidentifiable goo in it that used to
be you. Am I getting through to you?"

Crane was wide-eyed. "Have I done something that
would make him want me dead?"

"I sincerely hope not. What I'm trying to do is explain
to you some things that I had assumed you had learned.
You're a good businessman and a competent burglar. Those
are really good things to be, both at once. What you're not
is *un uomo duro*, a hard guy. It's not what you've done, and
you weren't brought up to it. You should be glad, and stay
away from that stuff. Know your place in the universe, and
accept it."

Crane was sweating, and his mouth was dry. "Are you
saying I shouldn't have killed Nick Bauermeister?"

"You wanted the girl, and so you thought with your
dick instead of your brain. You're human. All I'm saying is
that you should have gone about it the right way. If I were
in that situation, I wouldn't just go out at night with a rifle,
shoot him, and expect to forget it. I wouldn't do it and then

tell Mr. Malconi, 'By the way, I killed a guy on my crew.' I would go to Mr. Malconi first, explain my problem, and ask his permission to kill the guy. That way, I keep Mr. Malconi convinced I'm not suddenly becoming a crazy, unreliable man. I give Mr. Malconi a chance to make sure that he, and anybody he's worried about, has an alibi, and can't be connected to it through me. It also gives him a chance to make sure I don't get in the way of anything else his people are doing. Or, if I'm really lucky, he might say, 'This Salamone is a good man, but he's no killer. I'll tell him to sit tight, and I'll have somebody else do it—somebody who's used to doing that kind of thing and isn't going to screw up and get us all in trouble.'"

"Mr. Malconi wouldn't have done that for me," said Crane. "He doesn't even know I exist."

Salamone looked at Crane again. His face seemed to express simple curiosity, as though he were seeing a rare creature for the first time. "You're not getting this. You killed somebody, which is the kind of behavior that causes trouble, gets you noticed, and poses a risk to everybody who deals with you. I'm letting that slide because it's love, and I'm a sucker for that. But now you want to kill another person, this Indian. Call it off."

"I can't do that," said Crane. "It's too late. I've hired three guys to get arrested, add another offense to their records, and then wait around for a month or more for the Indian to get caught."

Salamone shrugged cheerfully. "I didn't say you couldn't pay them what you offered. In fact, I'd like you to do that, to tie up the loose ends. You don't want guys like that thinking you stiffed them. If you pay them, they'll be happy that they didn't have to do anything to earn it."

"I really don't know how to pull this off," Crane said. "How can I have a secret conversation with them now that they're in jail?"

"I'll tell you what. And I don't know why I'm doing this, except that I feel sorry for you. Get me the names and the lockups where they've been sent, and I'll send somebody." He paused. "Get them to me today, because I don't want to lose you. The jails are just one of those areas that Mr. Malconi controls. If somebody gets killed in there, it better be something he set up, not you."

"What can I do to make things right?" Crane's throat was dry, and his voice came out in a raspy croak.

"Nothing. Not a goddamn thing. Once you give me those names and locations, I'll get it called off. And I'll take care of this problem with the Indian too."

"I thought you didn't want the Indian killed. And how can you even do it if even the police can't find him?"

Salamone stood up, looked at his watch, and walked to the stairway, then stopped at the top. "It's not your place to know any of that. Get me those names in the next hour. Then the thing in the jail will get called off, the Indian will go to wherever Indians go when they die, and you will owe me big."

10

Jane drove the Chevrolet Malibu past the Legacy Village shopping mall in Lyndhurst in the eastern part of Cleveland, turned off the highway at the next street, and parked. She went into a drugstore and bought three prepaid cell phones and three cards worth three hundred minutes each. She paid in cash for them and walked away. The precautions she had used in the days when she had been taking people out of the world had all come back. She had fallen into old patterns again without effort. One day she had been searching for Jimmy, and the next she had been trying to make sure nobody else found him.

She kept the car she was using away from the security cameras installed outside stores by parking on the residential streets nearby and walking the rest of the way. Today she wore her hair loose so her face would be covered most of the time, and wore an oversize pair of sunglasses that would have disguised her by themselves. She stepped into the parking lot, attached herself to a gaggle of shoppers, and walked into the main entrance of the mall with them. Once she was inside she slipped into the first men's clothing store where she wanted to shop.

Jane was being extremely careful for the moment. She had told Jimmy to stay within the hotel grounds. "It's only temporary," she said. "For now, we'll keep you in the suite most of the time. You can go down to the pool and swim or work out in the fitness center on the second floor as long as you do it early in the morning before people get up. In a few days, when I know more about what's going on, we may be able to loosen up a bit."

Jimmy said, "It's okay. I guess this will get me used to jail."

"If we do everything right, maybe we can put that off for a long time." She patted him on the shoulder. "I wish I could say you'd never have to go, but I think you will be charged, and you'll have to be there until your trial."

"I know," he said. "I'm going to be considered a flight risk. That's my fault."

Jane said nothing. He had been sensible during the past few days at the hotel. He had gotten up at four each morning and gone down to the fitness center to exercise, and then out to the pool to swim. Then he'd come back and cooked himself some breakfast and read the newspaper that the hotel management left at their door overnight, and watched television or read the magazines she had brought him until evening, helped with dinner, and then gone to bed. Jane was glad that he was sane enough to do what he was told.

Jane had talked to Jimmy many times about the murder. Could he remember ever meeting a man named Walter Slawicky? Had there been a man with that name in the army, or at a construction job that he had forgotten until now? Could there have been someone else with that surname—a woman, or an elderly person? Had there been anyone with Nick Bauermeister the night of the fight? Had Jimmy ever owned a rifle like the one that had killed Bauermeister? She had tried every avenue she could think of to try to stimulate his memory, but gotten nowhere. Jimmy's predicament seemed inexplicable. And the idea that anyone would get himself sent to jail to do Jimmy harm didn't make sense either.

She walked into their hotel suite, opened the door, and found Jimmy working at the long counter that held their kitchen appliances. He looked up. "I'm making us some dinner. I figured we should have the fish you bought today while it's still fresh."

"I'll look forward to it."

He said, "In case you're worried, I also washed all the silverware and plates the hotel provided. I set the dishwasher on the nuclear fusion setting. No offense to the hotel."

"Nope," she said. "I'll never tell them." She set her bag on the couch, went to the dishwasher, and opened it. She touched one of the dishes. "It's certainly hot enough. Besides, we're probably immune to microbes after all that time living in the woods and sleeping on dirt."

"What's in the bags?"

"This one has phones. I bought us some throwaway prepaid phones and three hundred minutes. You get one and I get one, and we'll use them to talk to each other, if we need to." She reached into the bag and pulled one out. "See? They're small, light, and simple. You can call or text, but don't sign on to the Web. I'm setting them to vibrate, so the ring won't get us noticed, and programming them so we can call each other by hitting one button. For now, we'd better call only each other."

"Right." He picked one of them up and looked at it.

"Oh, yeah," she said. "There's already one exception to the no-calls rule. I'm calling Ellen Dickerson right now."

"I'll hold the fish while you do that, and then cook it after you get back."

Jane dialed the number as she was walking into her bedroom. The familiar voice came on. "Sge-no."

"Hi," said Jane. "You must have been waiting by the phone."

"No, it waits by me. I have a cell phone like everybody else. Are you both okay?"

"Yes," said Jane. She felt slightly uncomfortable not telling her that Jimmy had been hit over the head a few days ago, but he seemed to have recovered.

"Are you eating?"

"Yes. Jimmy is in the kitchen right now with the makings of a fish dinner, which we'll have as soon as I hang up. Thank you for asking. The thing that's been bothering me most is what you said before—that men are getting themselves into the jail to harm Jimmy. That isn't something that happens very often. Have you found out anything more?"

"We still don't know very much. I told you about the two young men who heard the rumors while they were in the county jail. We don't have anybody in there now. We seldom do. Normally that would be a good thing. It still would be if we didn't have to worry about Jimmy."

"It's a good thing now, too," said Jane. "We don't want anybody getting killed trying to pry into jail gossip. If there really were men in there waiting to harm Jimmy, they're still there. Judges tend to sentence people to jail for thirty, sixty, or ninety days. If they're awaiting trial for something serious, it might be a bit longer, but long sentences get served in a prison."

"That's what I've heard," said Ellen. "I'm not an expert."

"I am, unfortunately."

"I'm sorry about that, but what you know seems to be what's keeping Jimmy safe, so it's what we need right now. Is there any kind of help we can give you? Send you money or something?"

"No, thanks," said Jane. "I brought some with me, and we're trying to live modestly. The best thing we can do is keep this small, quiet, and simple. Anything you can find out about people searching for Jimmy, or meaning to harm him, is important."

"Is there something we should watch for?"

"Anything. Any strangers who seem to be interested in Jimmy or his case. I know you're already helping Jimmy's mother, and that will help him through this."

"I'll call you as soon as we find out anything at all. What number can I use to reach you?"

"If you get the answer, here's the number." Jane read it off the display on her phone. "But it would be best if you had someone else call from their phone. Jimmy's case seems to be attracting attention from so many unusual sources that I'm getting nervous. Some of the police agencies who are likely to be looking for him are capable of getting phone records, so the fewer calls between us the better. I'll get in touch with one of the other clan mothers if I have a question, so you won't have lots of calls from one city."

"We'll be waiting," said Ellen Dickerson. "Your clan is proud of you, Janie, and so are the others. We all wish you and Jimmy all the strength and courage you need."

"I'll tell him."

"Good-bye."

Jane tossed the phone on the bed and sat still for a moment, then stood and went back into the living room and on to the counter and stood beside Jimmy. "No news, really," she said. "The mothers wish us strength and courage."

He set the fish in the hot pan and it began to sizzle. "We'll have more of both after we eat this."

When they had finished their dinner, Jane said, "Nia:wen."

Jimmy also said, "Nia:wen."

They both looked at each other for a moment. The word *nia:wen* meant "thanks." In English it sounded so small and simple, but in Seneca it conveyed something big and fundamental—thanks to the person who obtained and cooked the food, to the plants and animals that gave up their lives to provide them with sustenance, and to the ordered universe beginning with the earth and water and moving outward into the air and sky and the things beyond the stars, and to the Creator.

Jane had cooked for her husband, Carey, for seven years already, and every evening after dinner, she had said it quietly to herself: "Nia:wen." She was usually the only one who said it, alone in the kitchen, and although her husband was included among all the things she was giving thanks for, he seldom heard her say it. But she had just said it aloud in front of Jimmy, because it was the normal thing for two Seneca people to do.

They cleared the table and went to work loading the dishwasher and cleaning the kitchen area. Jimmy said, "I'll bet you're getting ready to leave for home."

"You'd lose," she said.

"Why? You've got me pretty well set up here—a comfortable long-term hotel, a car, new clothes, and everything. Nobody knows I'm here. I'll pay you back for all that stuff as soon as I can, by the way. But I can drive you to the airport in about half an hour, and you could be in Buffalo an hour or two after that."

"I'm not ready to leave," she said. "You would have to show your face whenever you bought groceries, went to a restaurant, or answered the door. And things happen. If you made a driving mistake or somebody else did, you'd have to show your license and registration, and maybe fill out a police report."

"I suppose you're right," he said. "Believe me, I'm delighted that you're around. I just thought it was getting to be too much to ask. In fact, it was too much a while ago."

"Until I figure out who's after you, the best thing we can do is keep you out of sight. Be patient."

"You sound as though you heard something bad from Ellen Dickerson that you don't want to tell me."

"No," she said. "She's heard nothing new. But we don't need anything new. From the beginning, it's seemed to me that there's something odd that we aren't understanding. We have one man who was willing to go to the police and lie about selling you the weapon in a homicide. Why would he be willing to take that risk? And now there are some who were getting themselves sent to jail to wait for you—who are they? The only plan they could have is to kill you. I think we need to be prepared to hold out for a while before we walk into the middle of that."

"What does the delay do for us?"

"The same thing staying ahead of the dogs does for a rabbit. He gets to stay alive for another day."

The next day Jane went out again, and returned just before noon with several more shopping bags. After she put away the food she'd bought, there were still several others.

"What's that?" asked Jimmy.

"I'm going to teach you more about being hard to find. This is your next lesson. People looking for fugitives do it with photographs and descriptions and lists of habits. So change everything about yourself that you can change." She took out a box with a picture of a beautiful woman flipping her shiny light brown hair.

"Hair dye?"

"Afraid so," Jane said. "I picked a shade that's not ridiculously light, but it's lighter than your hair or mine. Our black hair is on one end of the spectrum, and platinum blond is on the other. If you're trying to blend into the crowd, the place you want to be is the middle. This is something I've had lots of runners do, because it's easy. The best way to use dye is to do it right away, so you don't meet people while your hair is black and then switch to light brown. It makes them wonder about you, and wondering is the worst response you're likely to get. They'll think about you and talk about you." She set the box aside. "Whether you do it or not is up to you. You have time to think about it, and if you want to, I can apply it for you. I'm pretty good."

"Thank you," he said. "I'm persuaded."

"While we're at it, I should warn you that anytime you use something like hair dye, make sure that there's nothing left of the packaging, or the chemicals, or the receipt from the store. I've already bought the coloring this time and paid for it in cash, so you don't have to worry about the security cameras in the store. But you don't want to leave anything that will tip off the chasers about changes to your appearance."

The next thing she brought out was a pair of glasses. "Try these on."

"My eyes are two of the few things I have that are perfect." He took the glasses.

"As you can see, the lenses are just clear plastic. I also got aviator sunglasses and photosensitive glasses that darken in sunlight, and some with a dark brown tint. Sunglasses are a good thing to wear whenever you're outdoors."

He put on the glasses, went to the bathroom mirror, and studied himself, turning his head from side to side. "It's a different feeling."

"It's better than I'd hoped," said Jane. "You look good, but what's especially good is you don't look like you."

"I guess I can get used to them." He took them off and set them on the coffee table.

"That's the right idea," Jane said. "Everything you can change should be changed. If you were fat, I'd try to get you to lose weight. If you were thin, I'd try to get you into body building. You're muscular, so I'm weaning you away from T-shirts and into business casual clothes. If you were illiterate I'd try to get you to carry a book with you. These mechanical changes are easy and they're quick. But they're only the start."

He studied her for a moment. "Are you sure you didn't hear something bad from Ellen that you're not telling me?"

"I didn't."

"Then this is about the guy who's framing me. He's probably the one who did the shooting, and there's a record of him buying the right kind of rifle, so he decided that saying he sold it to me would get him off."

"All very good thinking, except that he didn't do the shooting. He will have an absolutely ironclad alibi, which is why he could put himself forward like that. I think he's doing a favor for whoever really did it, and so are the men who went to jail to kill you. Is any of this normal? No."

"But you're starting to sound as though I'm going to have to stay away from home for a really long time."

"I'm not sure," said Jane. "Maybe you won't have to. I'm teaching you how to stay free for a short time, but the principles are the same, if you have to keep it up."

Jane handed him the next bag. "Now that I'm sure about your sizes, I bought you more clothes. I'm aiming for the look I told you about before—upscale and professional. You have to be able to walk in a crowd on the street and never be one of the first men a cop looks at. Clothes can help accomplish that. From now on, you don't wear sneakers unless you're jogging. No knit caps unless you're in the woods or it's snowing. No sweatshirts unless they have the name of some university. You get the idea?"

"Sure." He looked into the bag and pulled out some of the clothes. "Pretty nice. Maybe I should start dressing like this anyway."

"That should be enough to think about for now," she said. "If things ever got really awful and we had to give you a permanent new identity, there would be a lot more to learn. We can do a little more later. Right now, I'm tired. I think I'll go take an afternoon nap."

"Thanks, Jane," he said. "I haven't spent any time with you for at least twenty years, but you've turned out to be about the best friend I have."

"I'm trying to be," she said. She went across the room to avoid his stare, but still felt that he hadn't looked away. She said, "See you later," went into her bedroom, and closed the door.

They didn't start again until after dinner that night and the kitchen was clean. Jane said, "Time for the next lesson." They went to sit on the living room couch.

"What's this lesson about?"

She said, "When professionals are searching for a fugitive, one of the most effective ways they do it is to keep his family and friends under surveillance—if necessary, for long periods of time. They check the mail before it's delivered, record and trace their phone calls, and watch their houses. Sometimes there are private detective types searching, and they'll do the illegal stuff—install hidden microphones, hack into their e-mail, and so on. The minute a runner contacts a relative or a friend, he's given up his location. So the best advice is to let those relationships go."

"Let them go? You mean give up your family?"

"Yes," said Jane. "If you go back to the past, the ones waiting for you there are the chasers."

"What kind of choice is that?"

"Not a very good one," she said. "The only things it's an improvement on are going to jail and dying."

"How can anybody give up his family?"

"It's all part of one process. You learn to forget everything about the past, and concentrate on inventing a future for yourself. Changing identities is an interesting opportunity for some people, like being reborn a new person. Once you've lived to about our age, the idea of making some different choices has its attractions. Did you always want to be something different—an artist, a musician, a teacher? Once your old life is obliterated or becomes too dangerous to live, you've got to be somebody, so why not that?"

"I suppose," he said. "If you can't be who you are, you have to be somebody else. I'm not in that position."

"No," said Jane. "But play along. It's an exercise."

"Okay," Jimmy said. "If I had to give up my regular life, I suppose I'd like to try being an architect. I've been doing construction for years, and I've got some ideas I'd like to try out."

"Usually I would recommend a profession that's not even remotely related to your last one, but for the moment, architecture is fine," she said. "First thing we'd have to do is get you into architecture school. School is a good choice. The people who look for fugitives don't usually have a good ready-made way of searching campuses for people living under new names. School also takes time, so your trail gets cold."

"How would I get into architecture school?"

"Fraud and chicanery," she said. "Also some forgery. I'm experienced at getting people into places where they wouldn't normally belong, and I have good relationships with some people who can produce just about anything on paper. But you really would have to get through the school yourself and learn how to be an architect. You can't fake that."

"Of course," he said. "I would want to be a real architect."

She smiled. "Great. You're getting it already. Being a successful runner isn't about pretending to be somebody. It's about really becoming somebody. You don't assume an identity because it hides your real identity. The new person becomes your only identity, and you live the life of that person."

"Interesting," he said. "But right now I'm not at that stage yet."

"Okay," she said. "Let's do an exercise that could help in your present situation. You ought to start thinking about possible problems."

"Like what?"

"Suppose I've gone back to my house in Amherst to get something. You're still here at this hotel in Cleveland. Think about what you do if everything suddenly goes wrong. You hear and feel heavy male footsteps coming up the hallway. There's a loud knock on the door. You know that there's no reason why five men would come to your door unless they were after you. What are your plans? Do you plan to fight, or run? If you run, what do you have time to take with you, and where are you heading? When you get there, who will you be? The same person you've always been, or a new person? What's his name?"

"I haven't thought about any of that."

"That's what we're doing now. There's the knock. What do you do?"

"Go out the window, I guess."

"We're on the second floor, about thirty feet from the ground. If you jump, you'll probably break a leg. Want to go back in time and do something first?"

"I'd like to have a rope, a nylon rope hidden close to the window, so I could just go out the window and down."

"Good idea. Let's think about the rope some more. How long does it take to tie a knot?"

"I could tie a slip knot ahead of time and just loop it over something solid like the bed frame, and then go."

"Fine. Once you're out and on the ground, what next?"

"I check to see if there are police cars near my car, or blocking the exit from the parking lot."

"Smart. This time it's clear. Somebody recognized you and called the police, so the police don't even know you have a car. Did you remember to bring the key?"

"I sure hope so."

"Let's assume you did. You drive off. Do you have some cash? Do you have a name or anything memorized that you could say to anyone who asks who you are?"

"Not at the moment."

"Exactly," Jane said. "Think about all of the things you'd like to have with you if you went out that window. We can collect them. But where would you put them?"

"What do you think?" he asked.

"What we're talking about is a bug out kit. If you were a woman, I would tell you to put together a kit in a purse that you use for nothing else. For a man, the best thing is not to have a briefcase or backpack or anything. Instead, you want to look as though you're carrying nothing. There are sports jackets designed for travel. They're lightweight and have five or six hidden zippered pockets to foil a pickpocket. You buy one, not too snug. In the hidden pockets you put cash, some form of identification you can use if you have to lie to someone, a duplicate car key, and whatever else would be useful. Then you hang the coat in the closet, always in the same spot, where you can reach it in the dark if you're sleepy, distracted, or looking in the other direction. Practice finding and putting it on a hundred times or so. Keep thinking about ways to improve or update it."

"And that's all I take when I go?"

Jane nodded. "It's a way. There are other ways. Some people have a second kit in another location so they just have to get out and go to it. You might even want one in another town."

"Do you do this?"

She looked at him out of the corner of her eye. "This isn't about me. It's about you."

"You told me that for years you made people disappear. There must be a lot more people after you than there are after me."

She hesitated. "Yes. I do things like this. I was at it for years. It wasn't very long before what I worried about wasn't just that the police would arrest me for carrying false identification or something. There were people who would do anything to catch me alive and make me tell them where runners had gone and what their new names were. There were others who would be satisfied to just kill me on sight. Many of those people are still out there, so I've had to keep making arrangements and contingency plans."

"What about your husband?"

"I make arrangements for him too."

"I mean he's all established, and he's a doctor and everything. After all those years of work, would he just run off with you and live in hiding like this forever?"

Jane looked at Jimmy, feeling stung, and thought about how disastrous it would be if she allowed her anger to fill the air between them. She took a couple of deep breaths, then said, "If the danger were only to me, I wouldn't ask him to run. I would just go, and hope we could get back in touch later. I believe in preparing for the worst, and what I consider the worst is something that would hit him, too."

"But would he go with you, and give up the life he built?"

"That would be up to him."

"You're ducking my question."

Jane controlled her irritation. "I'm answering as well as I can. He's always been a very bright and sensible man. He loves me, and he wouldn't want to lose me. If I said we needed to go, I think by now he'd believe me. So I think he would go if I asked. But nobody knows how anyone will react. There are moments when saving your life means immediately doing the same things that you would do if you had an hour to think about them first. So nobody knows how it will go until it happens."

"Okay," said Jimmy. "I just wondered."

"That's fine," said Jane. "I guess the bigger answer to your question is that I believe the things I'm telling you will make you safer. Some are things I've taught other runners to do, and those people are nearly all well and living new lives. I do the same things for myself." She stood and picked up her coat on the way to the door. "Now I'll give you a chance to think about what we've said so far. I've got to go out for a bit, but I'll be back." She had talked her way out the door before he had a chance to reply.

She went down the back stairs, along the lower hall, and out the side door of the hotel. As she walked she came close to the car and glanced at the windows and tires as she passed, then continued out to the street. She walked past a row of fast-food restaurants and an open field, and on for about a mile. The night air and the solitude gave her a chance to cool down and think.

There must be a reason she had been stung by Jimmy's questions. Maybe it was that he had discovered the uncertainty she had always lived with and hidden from everyone. It was humiliating to admit that the uncertainty existed, and maybe more so because Jimmy was an old acquaintance, almost a member of the family. She had wanted him to think of her as invulnerable rather than weak and plagued with marital problems. She hadn't been able to ignore him or throw him off the scent. He was wondering what she had always wondered, and he had a relative's prying persistence. His sincerity was disarming, and it had made her try to answer questions she would have cut off if anyone else had asked. Tonight was a bad time for her to have this conversation, because Carey was angry with her, and she had already been in a bad mood about it.

She had never admitted it aloud to anybody, but being married to somebody who wasn't Seneca was difficult. She loved Carey and knew him well, and she thought hard about everything she heard him say or saw him do. She believed that he loved her just as much, and thought as hard about her. But over the past year something disturbing had come to her.

A year ago she had lived through a series of terrible trials. When she had reached her worst point, when she was in fiery, throbbing pain from the burns, and weak from the gunshot wound, surrounded alone by cruel enemies and preparing herself for death, she had thought about Carey, and the thought of him had not helped her. He was something good that she'd had while she was strong and happy, not a weapon she still possessed that could strengthen her when she was in a battle for her life. Thinking about Carey had only made her wish to live and get back to him, not to stay strong and live up to the promises she had made to her runners. Thinking about Carey had made her weak, the way thinking about food makes a starving person weak.

As she had endured the ordeal, she kept digging into the back of her mind, searching for something that would help her in those last days of life. What she'd found were her ancestors, the Seneca warriors who had fought the wars of the forests. The men who had gone off in small parties to raid the countries of enemies would sometimes find themselves in trouble. As they were returning home along the trails they might be overtaken by a party of enemies so large that they could never hope to fight them off. Sometimes one warrior would run for a time with the others, then come to a strategic point, often one with the high wall of a cliff on one side and a ravine on the other. He would stop there and turn to block the trail while his friends and companions continued on to escape. The lone warrior would stand on that spot and fight. As the enemies arrived, he would kill as many as he could with arrows, then fight hand to hand for as long as he could raise a war club or thrust a knife. His intention was to fight until he was killed, but sometimes the enemies would overwhelm him and take him captive.

Jane knew that captive warriors had been tormented—beaten, then cut, mutilated, flayed, then burned. A warrior was expected to remain strong and unyielding through all of it, to display such incredible bravery that his captors would be shocked and fear the next Seneca warriors who came their way. Even after the warrior knew he was too deeply wounded and crippled to save himself, he would still look for a chance to strike, grab one of the captors, and kill him before his own death came.

In Jane's mind the stories about captured warriors were distilled into a vision of a single warrior. His solitude was part of his torment, just as it was part of hers. She thought about the warrior and pictured him among his enemies until she could almost see him with her eyes open. She honored him for his courage and his pride, and tried to behave the way he had. When she began to feel the weakness coming on her, feel herself becoming too tired to struggle, too hopeless to remain silent through the pain, she used the warrior's image to fight it. She thought about the old Seneca warrior at the darkest time, concentrating hard and continuously. She knew that he had been one of her ancestors. He would have recognized her face, her hair, her skin, and the language she spoke, and understood her and known her in spite of the blue eyes she'd inherited from her mother. And during her ordeal she became, for a brief time, like that warrior. She had watched until her chance had come, until the two men guarding her had fallen asleep. Because of that she was alive tonight, walking along a highway outside Cleveland, and they and their friends were dead.

A part of what was bothering her now was that she could have told Jimmy about all this, but she'd had a year and still hadn't told her husband, Carey. She had been afraid he would never understand, and might say something that would stay between them forever. What she feared was a rejection of the part of her that was Seneca. She was a modern, educated woman, and sometimes it seemed to her that it was easiest for Carey to assume that was all she was— that she was just like everybody else they had known at Cornell, or even the women they met at cocktail parties and hospital benefits. Right now she resented him for that, even while she admitted to herself that the real reason he didn't know things was that she hadn't been able to tell him.

She turned around after a few miles and walked back toward the hotel. She considered calling Carey, but first she analyzed why she wanted to call. She was feeling guilty for having thoughts about him that weren't fair. She was afraid that she was being drawn too much into the Seneca world and a culture that he could never share. She was afraid the balance that sustained her was being disrupted. Even that thought was a problem—the Haudenosaunee peoples' belief that all things needed to be kept in balance. And she was lonely for Carey, but also irritated at him for not seeing that she loved him too much to leave him unless she had to.

As she walked on, she decided that none of the reasons for calling Carey was the right one. She had told him last time not to expect a call. And she had told Jimmy that getting in touch with people at home was dangerous. It went for her too. A small risk was still a risk. There was no reason for Carey to listen to her saying over and over that she loved him and would come home when she could. If she said those words enough times on long-distance calls, they began to feel like lies.

She stopped in a diner and had a cup of coffee, and then let the waitress refill it while she sat thinking about her life and her marriage until she realized that she had been there too long. She got up and continued the walk to the hotel.

When Jane reached the parking lot of the hotel she stayed outside it until she had walked the perimeter, keeping her path out of the overhead lights that shone down to protect the parked cars. She studied the Chevy Malibu again to be sure nobody was watching it, either from another parked car or from the sort of van that the police used for surveillance. By then she was near the dark side of the building, so she walked along the brick wall. She looked at her watch. She had been gone more than three hours. It was late enough now to be sure the hotel's side entrance was locked, so she went on to the main entrance.

Through the double glass doors she could see the night desk clerk. He was occupied, talking with two men who looked like business travelers who had just driven from the airport and not brought their luggage from the car yet. They were leaning on the long counter, the three of them all close and preoccupied. As Jane walked by, something unusual happened. One of the two men came around and joined the desk clerk behind the counter. He turned the screen of the computer so his companion could see it too, and they began to scroll down a page that was a series of divided sections.

Jane stood at the elevator and pretended to hit the button, but kept watching the men without seeming to. As she watched, the man behind the counter raised his right hand and pointed a finger at one of the lines of text. As he did, his sport jacket rode up and she could see the gun under it. Jane pressed the button and the elevator door opened, she stepped inside, and the door slid shut.

11

In the elevator Jane pressed the key on her phone. "We've got to get out. Pack whatever you can in the next three minutes and then start wiping fingerprints off every surface we touched. I'll be there in a minute."

As soon as the elevator door opened she was out and running along the fourth floor hallway. Before she reached the door of their suite she had her key card out, and when she reached the door she stuck the card in the reader and opened the door just far enough to slip inside, then set the deadbolt.

Jimmy was stuffing his new clothes into his backpack. Jane stepped past him into her room, rolled her clothes and placed them in her backpack, then went into the bathroom and swept the cosmetics and soaps into a plastic bag. After she put the bag into her backpack she took a hand towel and began wiping every surface. She stepped to the door, saw Jimmy wiping doorknobs and counters with a napkin from the coffee service, and tossed him a hand towel. "Use this. While you're at it, check the window for watchers or suspicious cars, but don't get spotted."

Jimmy stepped to the window and looked out the lower right corner for a few seconds. "I don't see anybody out there. There's nobody near our car."

"Good. Keep wiping. Anything either of us may have touched." She put all of the dishes from the cupboards into the dishwasher, added soap, and started it. She picked up the magazines from the coffee table and put them in a trash bag, then swept everything from the refrigerator into the bag after them.

Jimmy had completed his circuit of the suite, so Jane said, "All right. Go down the stairs."

Jimmy went while Jane stayed a few seconds to wipe off the door and its inner and outer handles, and let it swing shut. She slipped into the stairwell just as she heard the elevator bell ring.

At the bottom of the stairwell, Jane edged past Jimmy, slipped out the door, and moved to the small enclosure where the garbage dumpsters were hidden from view. She emptied the bag of trash into a dumpster, then crumpled the bag, tossed it in too, and walked with Jimmy to the Chevrolet Malibu. She set her backpack on the backseat, and got into the driver's seat. Jimmy sat beside her.

She started the car and backed out of the space, then headed toward the exit from the parking lot. "If they're going to take us, it will be in the next few seconds, before we hit the street." She drove at a moderate, unhurried speed to the exit, signaled, looked both ways, and pulled out into the traffic on the highway. She matched her speed to the other cars, and eased the Malibu into the stream of cars in the left lane. For a few seconds, she kept glancing at the side mirrors for any sign that they were being followed. Then she turned to Jimmy. "How's your mom?"

"Oh, no," he said. "Somebody traced the call?"

"I'm not absolutely positive what happened," she said. "I would have liked a chance to get a better look at what the men I saw in the lobby were doing, but I didn't think it was a good idea to stick around. They looked like plainclothes police officers of some kind. I saw the guns but not the badges, so I can't swear to that. They were with the desk clerk looking at the guest list on his computer. What I'm hoping is that they'll go through it all, not figure out that you were staying in a room registered in a woman's name, and move on to the next hotel. When you called your mother you were in the hotel?"

"Yes," he said. "Jane, I'm really sorry. I thought that if I was using a throwaway phone, nobody could trace it to me."

"That's right," she said. "But if they were monitoring your mother's calls, they would know she got a call from a number that was pinging off a particular tower outside Cleveland. That's what they wait for."

"I can't believe I was too stupid to think of that," said Jimmy. "I'm ashamed of myself for putting you in danger along with me."

"I don't want to go on and on about this," Jane said. "But you've got to listen to whatever I tell you and take it seriously. I'm willing to take some of the blame for this, because I didn't explain why we can't call home, just told you not to. And if we're in trouble, then the person who will suffer most for it isn't me."

"I'm so sorry. I just thought—"

She interrupted. "It was a mistake. But this is a special situation, where we can't make mistakes. None. I know my way, and you don't, so pay attention—all the time."

"I'm sorry," he said.

Jane drove on in silence, checking the side mirrors frequently in case she'd missed something earlier. There were still no cars staying too long back there, but she knew she had to take more precautions to be sure. "Take the battery out of your phone and toss it out the window. Then the phone."

Jimmy took the battery out, dropped it on the road, and then the cell phone.

When she reached a small plaza she pulled over and said, "You drive for a while." When they had changed places, she said, "Go up there to the right and get on the eastbound ramp for the interstate."

Jimmy put the car in gear and drove. As Jimmy pulled onto the interstate ramp, Jane leaned back in her seat and let her muscles relax.

Jimmy had been watching her. "What's the plan?"

She said, "If anybody was tracking your phone's GPS, they'll go where the last pings were going."

"Is that why we're going east?"

"Partly."

"What are the other reasons?"

"One is that we've already come west, so if someone is following at a distance, or has just decided to, he'll assume we're still going in the same direction, because that's what people do. I've also found over the years that people who run away tend to favor places to the south and west, where it's warm, a little bit exotic, and living isn't hard work. Hardly anybody wants to go where it's cold in the winter. Right now I'm taking every choice that makes finding us less likely, even if it's only a tiny bit less likely. Advantages add up."

"That sounds smart."

Jane sat in silence. She decided that her inability to get through to him must have been caused by the lifelong relationship between them. When they were children they had been equals. Or maybe the advantage had been a bit on Jimmy's side. They had been comfortable playing together, partly because she was a girl who didn't like sitting still. She was physical and energetic, and that helped Jimmy accept her. She liked to run and climb and explore. Jimmy was handsome, strong, and athletic, and Jane—if she remembered it right—had been tall and bony and unattractive. The first time anyone had said she was beautiful was in college, and she'd thought they were being sarcastic.

Now, over twenty years later, Jimmy was about the same, but Jane was different. He seemed to be having trouble accepting the fact that she knew so much that he didn't. If he wasn't going to take what she said seriously, they were both in trouble.

If he had been a stranger, a person who needed her help and came to her to ask for it, she would have spoken harshly when he'd ignored her orders. She might even have picked up her backpack, said, "This is as far as I go. You're on your own," and left. She would never be able to do that to Jimmy, but that wasn't the problem. Maybe the problem was that he knew it. She looked at Jimmy. "Just keep driving east. When you get tired, wake me up and I'll take over." She leaned back, closed her eyes, and waited for the gentle rocking and the quiet hiss of the tires on the road to put her to sleep.

Jane woke when the car lurched hard to the side and skidded, throwing her forward against the restraint of her seat belt. She clutched the armrest but the car fishtailed as Jimmy struggled to keep the wheels headed forward, then hit the brakes. She saw a set of taillights to the left, and then a series of them flashing past to the right. Jimmy shouted, "That guy tried to hit me!"

"Pull to the right, away from him." She punched the emergency blinker switch on the dashboard so it began to tick and flash, lowered her window, and stretched her arm out to signal to the cars coming up, half leaning out to look into their headlights. "Go now!"

Jimmy moved over one lane and kept going. Jane kept her arm out the window as she watched for an opening, then said, "Now!" Jimmy made it to the right lane. "Take the next exit, and get there as fast as you can."

As he reached the exit a few seconds later and guided the car to the ramp, Jane held on to the back of her seat and stared out the rear window of the car. "He doesn't seem to have made it over to the exit, but he'll take the next one."

"He was actually trying to hit me," Jimmy said. "It was as though he wanted to slam us into the rail." He stopped at the bottom of the ramp and then pulled cautiously into the traffic moving to his right on the road.

"Pull into that lot up there—the hotel—and around the building to the back."

Jimmy pulled off the road and into the large parking lot that surrounded a twenty-story hotel. He drove up an aisle filled with cars and around the building, then pulled into one of the empty spaces at the rear of the building where their car could not be seen from the street.

"Leave the motor running. This will only take a minute." Jane got out and walked around the car, and then knelt beside the driver's side door. After a few seconds she swung the door open and Jimmy got out.

"You didn't find anything, right?" Jimmy said. "The SUV didn't actually hit us, but he would have if I hadn't seen him in time."

"The driver wasn't trying to smash into us." Jane pointed at the bottom of the door just above the rocker panel. There was a small round hole punched in the sheet metal of the door. "That's a bullet hole. There's another one here. The shooter in the passenger seat must not have been prepared for you to drop back so suddenly. When you stomped on the brake he had to take his shot after he was ahead of you with his arm trailing out the window."

"Why would cops shoot at me?"

"They weren't the police. Cops give you a chance to let them take you the easy way. They don't just open up on a car going seventy in traffic. I also think the shots weren't loud enough, so the gun must have had a suppressor. The police don't use them."

"I don't get this."

"I don't either. But from the look of the holes, I'd guess he could have been aiming for your left front tire to get us to pull over. He could also have been aiming at you." She sat in the driver's seat. "Get in. They'll be taking the next exit about now. We'd better be gone before they get back here."

Jimmy got in, and Jane backed out of the space and drove around the big building. "We'll change course and stay off the interstate. While you're watching for the black SUV, also watch for a sign that says Route Eleven. It'll be one of those white state highway signs."

"Okay."

Jane drove aggressively, not breaking any laws except the speed limit, but changing lanes frequently to avoid being trapped behind slow cars and trucks.

Jimmy said, "What kind of person would be coming after me with a gun with a silencer? Who even *has* a silencer?"

"Last time I looked it up there were thirty-nine states where it was legal to own one, and Ohio was one of them. You pay a two hundred dollar transfer tax to the ATF, and wait for them to process your application. If you're somebody who can legally own a handgun, eventually you'll get your silencer." She kept her eyes on the road, trying to use each moment to get as far as she could from the highway exit they'd taken.

She looked into the rearview mirror and said, "If I were you, I wouldn't be thinking about hardware. I'd be trying to bring back anything I could about Nick Bauermeister, or his lawyers, his friends, family, or anything else that would tell us why somebody in another state would be looking for you."

"I don't know. I told you I didn't kill him. I don't know anything about him except that he was a drunk taking a swing at me in a bar. Maybe he had a relative or friend who's a badass and doesn't trust the police to get me."

"This isn't one man," Jane said. "I saw two men at the hotel, and just now there were a driver and a shooter. The only way anybody could have found us in Ohio was by looking at your mother's phone record. That narrows things down."

"I thought you said it wasn't the police."

"Now I'm sure it isn't. But there could be somebody who works for some police agency who's doing a favor, or somebody in the phone company. There are also data brokers you can reach online who might get a list of calls made to your mother's phone. Nick Bauermeister's angry cousin isn't likely to have done these things. Angry amateurs lose control and try to strangle you in court. They don't hire pairs of killers to hunt you down two states away."

"There's the sign for Route Eleven up ahead."

"I see it. Hold on." Jane sped to the intersection and turned right without signaling, then accelerated away from the intersection down Route 11 to the south. She glanced in the rearview mirrors frequently as she drove.

Jimmy said, "Do you think the guys in that SUV could have caught up with us this quickly?"

"No, but I'm sure they could dial a cell phone this quickly to tell their friends where we're likely to be. If you don't mind, take a look behind us and memorize the cars. We'll be away from the city lights in a few minutes, so study the way their headlights look, too. If anybody stays with us too long, or adjusts his speed just to keep us in sight, tell me."

"Headlights? Just two lights."

"They're all different. Brightness, height from the ground, and so on. Look especially at SUVs, since that's what just tried to force us off the road."

Jimmy turned around in his seat and stared for a few minutes. "We've got a few candidates, but nothing conclusive.

Two SUVs. One black, like the one on the interstate, and the other light gray. There's a white pickup. Looks like a Ford 250 with big tires, a yellow VW, a little red Fiat, and a—nope, that one dropped out at the Walmart."

"Good. That's what I see, too. The VW and the Fiat are almost certainly harmless."

"Agreed."

"The white pickup we should keep an eye on, but usually what we have to fear from those guys is that they'll drive so aggressively that they'll kill us by accident. By the way, it's a good idea to look for women."

"You mean woman drivers?"

"Anywhere in the vehicle. There are a lot of bad things to be said about women, but they don't get into this kind of work much. If you see a woman in any of the cars, we can pretty safely take it off the list."

"That leaves the two SUVs."

"Watch them for signs that we have a problem."

"I'm watching. What am I looking for?"

"Signs that they're trying to deceive us. Sometimes two cars will follow you by taking turns. One drops so far behind that you forget it exists, while the other keeps you in sight. Then they switch, so you don't start wondering about the one you can see. When you see the first one again, you think it's new. Sometimes a follower will get ahead of you for a while so you think you're following them. Nobody who tries to fool you has a nice reason for it."

Jimmy looked at her for a moment, then out the back window. "Did you know these things by instinct when you started, or have they all happened to you?"

"I've spent a lot of years helping people who are running away. All of them have someone chasing them. The important thing is to learn to trust yourself. If you look at anything—a car, a house, a person—and it seems a little off, avoid it. Simple."

Jimmy stared out the rear window. "I brought this on by making that call home to my mother. I'm regretting it every minute. But I'm not sure I'll see the next mistake before I make it."

"That's what I'm here for," Jane said. "The trick is to be alert. Always look for a way to improve the odds in your favor."

"Those two SUVs are still back there."

"I know," she said. "I don't like it either."

Jane drove on. Route 11 became less heavily traveled as the hour grew late. The road moved away from the city into a rural landscape, and then narrowed to two lanes. When they went through a town it was always small, with darkened business signs and traffic signals that blinked yellow over deserted intersections. As they passed one that looked no different from the others, things changed abruptly.

A pair of black SUVs similar to the one that had attacked them on the interstate pulled into the road a few hundred yards ahead. One came from a driveway to Jane's right that ran like a bridge over a small stream in a ditch beside the road. The other emerged from the lot in front of a gas station on the left. They met like doors closing across the road.

"Trouble," she said. She hit her high beam headlights, bathing the two cars in light, and steered her car toward the spot just behind the car that had come over the ditch.

"There's a ditch on that side," Jimmy said. When nothing changed he said, "Jane. A ditch."

"I see it."

She held the wheel in both hands, still steering straight at the rear of the car blocking the right lane. "Make sure your seat belt is tight, but keep your head low. Remember the other one shot at us."

Jimmy slumped lower, so he could barely see over the dashboard.

Jane sped up slightly, aiming her car at the SUV on the right. She could see a head in the front side window turned toward her. The man in the driver's seat had the best view, and he was getting frightened. His eyes were open wide and he gripped the steering wheel tightly. Jane altered her aim slightly, just enough so her car would look to him like a projectile streaking straight for him.

Finally, he panicked. He threw his transmission into reverse and backed up quickly. He seemed to have forgotten how narrow the driveway was. His left set of tires found their way onto the driveway, but the right set slipped off into the ditch, and the vehicle tipped onto its side.

Jane swerved, but not toward the space that had opened between the two SUVs. She aimed at the remaining vehicle and sped up again. She adjusted her aim to be sure that if she hit anything, it would be the passenger door.

The driver blocking the left lane pulled forward to block the space that had opened up in the middle of the road.

Jane saw a wash of white light projected onto her dashboard from behind, and didn't have to look into the rearview mirror to know that the SUV that had been following her for miles was coming up fast behind her.

In another second she was at the roadblock, flashing past with two wheels on the road and the other two on the pavement of the gas station behind the left SUV. She narrowly missed the first gas pump and adjusted her trajectory to make it back onto the road to avoid the telephone pole at the end of the lot.

The black SUV that had been following her shot past in the space between the two other black SUVs that had formed the roadblock, and began to gain on her.

Jimmy turned around in his seat to watch the vehicle behind. "I can't believe this. Who the heck are these guys?"

"I can't tell. They don't seem to be good at stopping people without killing them."

Jane was driving hard now, accelerating steadily, trying to hug the inside of each curve and straighten to aim at the next one. Jimmy looked at the speedometer and watched the needle climb over ninety-five miles an hour, a hundred, and still move higher. The broken white lines on the pavement streaked toward them like tracer rounds.

"You're going too fast. What if a cop sees us?"

"What if two carloads of armed thugs catch up with us on a deserted highway?"

"Can we ditch the car somewhere and slip off on foot?"

Jane kept glancing in the mirrors, her hands gripping the steering wheel to keep the car from spinning out. "If I see the right place, we can try. I haven't seen one yet. We'd have to get far enough ahead so they can't see us bail out, and if I can accomplish that, we're better off in the car."

"But you're going—"

"Jimmy." She said it quietly, but he understood that she didn't intend to argue. The car was going so fast that when she reached a slight rise, the car rose on its springs to be nearly airborne at the crest, and then burrowed downward into the shallow trough beyond it. Jimmy gripped the armrest, his teeth clenched so his jaw muscles bulged whenever he felt a bounce or a rocking of the car, but he was clearly determined not to remind her that what she was doing was dangerous.

Jane glanced in the mirror again. She reached a long, straight stretch, and kept her eyes on the mirror for a long time.

Jimmy turned in his seat and looked. "I don't see them anymore."

"Neither do I. Keep watching, in case one of them is crazy enough to follow us without headlights."

She kept going, but she let up on the gas pedal a bit. They hurtled through the night for another ten minutes before she lowered her speed again, this time to only ten miles

an hour over the speed limit. "Okay," she said. "We're looking for Route Twenty-two now. There should be signs."

"Who do you think those guys are?"

"Enemies. Watch for the signs for Route Twenty-two."

"Where will that take us?"

"Away from them."

12

This is pitiful," said Teddy Mangeoli. "Dreadful. I've never been so embarrassed in my life. What am I going to say?"

"I'm sorry, Teddy," said Donato. "I'm sorry. I sent six really good men. The idea was to avoid shooting up the whole city and making a lot of trouble for everybody, right?"

"Right," said Mangeoli. "Was that too tall an order? Six picked men can't go to a hotel where we know some guy is staying, and put him down quietly? This was a favor for a very important and respected man, a near neighbor we might need on our side someday soon."

"It wasn't too tall an order. We just didn't know some crucial things, and it made all the difference. Nobody mentioned that the guy had a girlfriend with him in the hotel. She happened to go down to the lobby while Santoro and Molinaro were talking to the desk clerk, and made them somehow. By the time Santoro and Molinaro got upstairs to take the guy out, the guy and the girlfriend were out and driving away in a car."

"Michael. My very good friend. Take a step back from all these details. Think about the magnitude of what's happened to us. Our thing here in Cleveland was a force for a hundred years, an organization to be admired and feared. This was where Big Joe Lonardo put together the corn syrup monopoly. He dominated the corn liquor business during Prohibition."

"And lost it in the corn syrup wars."

"I'm talking about the size, strength, and importance of the Cleveland organization. Hell, the Statler Hotel was where the first national sit-down took place in 1928."

"Well, it never actually took place," said Donato. "Everybody got arrested before it got started."

"That doesn't matter. They all came, didn't they? The most powerful, important men in La Cosa Nostra. They came here from New York, Chicago, Florida, everywhere. And in those days, you couldn't just hop on a plane. You had to be sincere enough to spend a couple of days on a train. The point is the Cleveland organization was respected. Now we can't take out one Indian from Buffalo and his girlfriend. We can't do a simple favor for a very important ally. We're a sad, diminished thing. We've got more guys in jail than on the street."

"This isn't just some unsuspecting dope. The guys said they tried to force him to pull over on the interstate, but he outmaneuvered them. Our guys followed the car to Route Eleven, then called ahead to set up a roadblock. The car blew right through before they were ready. This guy was going a hundred and ten. You can't stop somebody like that quietly. It's like flagging down a suicide bomber."

"You're not getting my point," said Teddy Mangeoli. "Once there was Big Joe Lonardo, then Big Ange Lonardo. Then Big Al Polizzi. Have you ever heard anybody call me Big Teddy Mangeoli?"

"Those were big guys, that's all. You're like, five foot six."

"Eight. Five foot eight. Jesus."

"It doesn't mean those guys were more important. It was descriptive."

Teddy Mangeoli held him in his stare for a moment, and then walked across the carpeted office. He was usually happy when he was in this room. He loved being in charge of a bank, and he loved being its biggest shareholder. This morning the luxury of the office seemed to him to be an indictment. The man he was going to call was the head of the Arm in Buffalo. Just the sound of it made his spine tingle— the Arm. Lorenzo Malconi was from another generation, when men were a scarier species. Malconi had gotten where he was because he had burned some powder and he had dug some graves.

When Teddy Mangeoli got to the cabinet, he turned to Donato. "Give me some time alone. I don't need anybody to watch me grovel." He picked up the receiver of the special telephone that was swept by the security people every day, and dialed. He fought the feeling of shame and dread that seemed to double with each ring.

IN BUFFALO, ANDY SPATO PICKED up the telephone and said, "Malconi residence." He listened for a moment, then said, "One moment please." Then he walked out through the sliding glass door into the garden.

"Mr. Malconi?" Andy Spato stood holding the telephone with his big hand over the receiver. "It's Teddy Mangeoli in Cleveland. Would you like me to have him call back?"

The old man opened his eyes, but didn't move his head even a centimeter. He was tentatively ready for a disappointment or a new chore. Being a boss looked like being a king, but it sometimes felt like being everybody's servant.

You couldn't just say you didn't care what anybody's problem was. He held out his hand.

Spato handed him the phone and backed away, his eyes still on Mr. Malconi, waiting for a nod from him. That was usually the signal that he was dismissed. When he saw the old man nod, he spun on his heel and stepped back toward the house. He went inside and closed the sliding glass door.

He took a last look at the old man sitting on the chaise longue in the garden with his feet up, wearing his comfortable old sport coat with the elbow patches and his leather driving slippers. For the hundredth time, Spato thought about how much like a kind elderly gentleman he looked. Spato could almost imagine a half dozen little grandchildren gathering around him to listen to a story. The truth was that he was probably surrounded by the ghosts of a few dozen people waiting for him to die so they could tear his soul to shreds. Spato went into the kitchen and poured himself a cup of coffee. He had promised himself he'd have one while the old man had his afternoon nap.

In the garden, Mr. Malconi spoke into the phone. "Hello, Teddy."

"Don Lorenzo, I'm calling you with a very difficult and humiliating piece of news."

"What is it?"

"I would have come in person, but it would have taken longer, and I was sure you would want to know right away. It pains me to tell you that the small favor you asked was bungled."

"Bungled?"

"Botched. Fumbled. I can't think of any other way to say it. My guys failed you."

"Should I be listening for a knock on my door, Teddy?"

"Oh, no, Don Lorenzo. Nothing like that. Six men were sent to look at the hotel registers in the Cleveland area where that phone call originated—three teams of two men.

The target apparently had a girlfriend with him, and she accidentally saw one of the teams by the hotel computer. She and the target drove off at over a hundred miles an hour. Our guys had big-ass SUVs, and you know how bad those are for that kind of driving. They're heavy, and have a high center of gravity. Mario Andretti couldn't hold one of those fat pigs on a winding road at over a hundred. As it was, one of the SUVs had to be towed out of a ditch."

"Anybody hurt?"

"No, thank God," said Teddy Mangeoli. "It's a blessing things weren't worse."

"Driving into a ditch at a hundred miles an hour?" said Mr. Malconi. "It's a miracle."

Teddy Mangeoli felt a wave of heat wash over him. That wasn't what he had meant, and it sounded impossible, but it was too late to correct the impression. He could only hope that Mr. Malconi didn't consider it a lie. "Anyway, the guy and his girlfriend are gone. We failed you, and I'm very sorry."

"Do you know which direction they were going?"

"South on Route Eleven, toward West Virginia and Maryland."

"Do they know who was looking for them?"

"I don't see how they could," said Teddy Mangeoli. "My guys were in identical black Escalades. Since we knew this target was a wanted man, I thought that might make our teams look like feds coming to arrest him. You remember when the FBI raided Danny Spoccato's office in Newark? Big black SUVs. I saw it on the television news over and over. Now the Escalades are back where they came from, and the guys never got close enough to get identified."

"Where did they come from?"

"A friend of ours has a Cadillac dealership."

"A friend of ours?" *A friend of mine* was just a friend. *A friend of ours* was a member of La Cosa Nostra.

"Yes. Mike Donato."

"Do you think he might be able to get me a deal on a new CTS-V sedan?"

"I'll have one sent to you tomorrow. What color do you like?"

"They have a really deep black, but I like a nice dark gray, you know—conservative, like a good suit," said Mr. Malconi. "But I wasn't asking for a present."

"It's as good as done. It's the least I can do to show you my regard. I know it doesn't make up for the mistake."

Mr. Malconi said, "Forget that other thing. It's just a small favor for a friend of a friend. I'll make another phone call or two to the people who live where the happy couple are headed. Somebody will see them at the right time and place, and that will be the end of it. These things can sometimes take a week or two. It's not unusual."

"Again, Don Lorenzo, I apologize."

"Don't give it another thought. I'll talk to you after my new Cadillac arrives."

The two men hung up. Teddy Mangeoli walked stiffly to his desk and sat down on the top of it, his mind churning. He had made mistakes, and sounded as though he was making excuses and lying. He had missed a chance to build a relationship with a man who had been a power practically since the beginning of time. What the hell had he been thinking? He should have sent a hundred men to the hotel district after this fugitive. It had been a huge opportunity, and he had left it to underlings.

Mike Donato opened the door a crack, only an eye visible. When he saw that Teddy Mangeoli had finished his call, he came in and shut the thick office door. "How did it go?"

"Rotten. I'm sure he thinks we're stupid and worthless. I kind of misspoke and gave him the impression that one of the SUVs was driven into a ditch at a hundred miles an hour and nobody was hurt, so he thinks I'm a liar too."

"I saw the one that they rolled over this morning, and it looks like hell. It will cost thousands of dollars to restore that paint job."

"That reminds me. I told him we'd send him a new Caddy tomorrow. A CTS-V. Get somebody to drive it to Buffalo. And he's particular about the color. He wants a nice dark gray, like a conservative suit."

"He means Phantom Gray Metallic," said Donato. "A new CTS-V. Those things start at sixty-four thousand bucks, and go up from there. I don't even have Phantom Gray Metallic on the lot right now. And how the hell am I going to get one there tomorrow?"

"Honestly, I don't know," said Teddy. "If you have to get the right one from another dealer in Cincinnati or Columbus or someplace, do it. If you don't have anybody to drive it to Buffalo, do it yourself. If you screw this up, we're not going to get another chance with him."

IN THE GARDEN BEHIND THE big brick house on Middlesex in Buffalo, Lorenzo Malconi closed his eyes again. He never really slept in the afternoon, but pretending to nap made people underestimate him and gave him a chance to think. Teddy Mangeoli was in a position that wasn't warranted by his talents or his character. The next strong wind would blow him away like a brown leaf off a tree. But Lorenzo Malconi had never been an impatient man, and at this stage of his life he valued cunning above audacity. He would not be the one to send Teddy Mangeoli to the undertakers. Instead, he might be the one who waited until somebody else did, and then administer justice on the culprit and exert his moral authority over both families. That would depend on who moved first.

13

They were in Cleveland," said Mr. Malconi.

"They?" said Salamone. "I thought he was alone."

"No. He made a phone call to his mother that came from the hotel district just outside of Cleveland. Some men went to check whether the guy was staying in one of them. He had come with a girlfriend, and she had done the registering, so it took a while to find the right room. By the time the guys got there, he and his girlfriend had slipped out."

"So they got away?"

"I know," said Mr. Malconi. "I was a little surprised myself. It sounded to me like the Indian drove fast, and none of them had the balls to drive as fast as he did. It stands to reason that Teddy's guys weren't anxious to die to please me, but I like to see men who don't give up that easy."

"Should I be getting my crew to start looking?"

"No, no," said Malconi. "Teddy says the guy and his girlfriend were heading south out of Ohio toward West Virginia or Maryland, and I called some friends of ours down there just before you called me. I think we'll hear some good news before too long. They can operate better than we can on their own ground, and we won't waste our guys' time on the Indian when they could be up here earning money."

"I understand. Thank you for doing me the honor of telling me this. We'll just sit tight until you tell us different."

"You know," said Mr. Malconi. "There is one thing you can do for me while you're waiting. This guy Crane considers you his partner, right?"

"A silent partner," said Salamone. "I get ten percent."

"I'd like you to get a storage unit for me. Make that two, but not next to each other. Put them in names like Smith and Brown. Not the same name. And make sure that I have the only keys to the locks."

"Of course, Mr. Malconi. I'll do that today."

"Good," said Malconi. "When you bring me the keys, maybe I'll know more about your problem." He hung up.

Salamone stood for a moment looking at his cell phone's display to be sure the call had ended, and he hadn't just lost the signal for a moment. He didn't want the old man listening to his conversations for the rest of the day.

He shook his head. It was always risky to call Mr. Malconi. And expensive. Every time the old man talked to anybody about anything, he exacted some kind of payment, like a tax. If Mr. Malconi knew you had the owner of a prosthetics factory on the hook, he would want a free leg or something. Salamone thought about the two storage bays. He could only hope the old man didn't do anything strange with them. Salamone didn't want to have a bunch of drugs in them, or a cache of explosives. Malconi's business dealings could include anything.

JANE AND JIMMY HAD BEEN driving eastward all day through the rural countryside of Upstate New York on Route 20. They passed through small towns where traffic signals impeded their progress, and they ate in small diners. Between towns they stopped at roadside stands and bought fruit and snacks. They avoided taverns, because they all had television sets mounted in the corners and above the bar, where people intending to watch some game might instead see a mug shot of the man being sought for the murder of Nick Bauermeister. Their progress was slow, but a car following them on Route 20 would be easy to spot.

Once when Jimmy was taking his turn to drive, he said, "I'm getting a little tired of small-town America. Can we switch to the thruway for a couple of hours?"

"It's better to stay off any road with tolls," Jane said.

"Are we out of money?"

"No. It's not the tolls that bother me. It's the booths. They all have cameras mounted on them, and the police have been using them more and more often to see if a car with a license plate they're looking for has gone through."

"Do you think they know this car or its license number?"

Jane shrugged. "Can't tell. The people who chased us out of Cleveland saw it. If all they need to do is get you into a jail, they might pass that information to the New York State police through some innocent-looking intermediary."

"Slow back roads it is, then," said Jimmy. "I'm always shocked by how far you think ahead."

"It's not clairvoyance. It's avoiding situations that might increase the risks. If you don't want to be found, you stay away from cameras, particularly ones operated by police agencies. You try to be sure as few people see your face as possible. None of these precautions is hard. They're just inconvenient."

"The hard things are more than inconvenient. It's hard not to be able to go home, and not to be able to check up on my mother, to be sure she has what she needs. Half the time her car isn't working right."

"You're luckier than most people in that way. Your mother is surrounded by people who care about her. There are probably four hundred people on the reservation who would love to drive her wherever she wants—one a day for a year and a month."

"But none of them is me."

"I think you'll be back before long."

He smiled. "Where are we going?"

"I'll know when we get there. We're just passing through New York State on the way, because as soon as you cross a state line, you're no longer at the top of the list of fugitives. You're somebody else's problem."

In the evening Jane rented a motel room near Saratoga Springs, and the next morning after breakfast they crossed into Vermont. In the afternoon they drove through miles of hills covered with thick, old-growth forests, and then crossed the Connecticut river into Lebanon, New Hampshire.

Jane drove north through Lebanon. There were restaurants, a couple of plazas full of huge discount stores, a few hotels, a sign for a hospital that was back from the road at the end of a driveway that wound out of sight among the trees. Next the road narrowed again and they passed rows of clapboard houses, most of them white, built with steep, smooth gray roofs designed to make the deep snows of the winter slide off them. And then they were in Hanover. As they drove past small stores selling clothing, food, furniture, and housewares, they reached the center of the small town and were surrounded by the lawns and the white spires and redbrick buildings of Dartmouth College.

"Dartmouth," said Jimmy. "We'd better get out of here before somebody notices I don't fit in."

"We look perfect," Jane said. "The place was started as a school for Indians. Thayendanegea's sons were among their first graduates. It must have been in the seventeen seventies or so."

"Oh, yeah. I forgot you went to Cornell. You and Thay-endanegea are Ivy Leaguers. Is this where they taught him to call himself Joseph Brant?"

"No," said Jane. "After his father died, his mother mar-ried a Mohawk named Brant. She had the same clan name as I was given—Owandah. That's why I was curious about her when I was a kid. What do you think of the town?"

"It's pretty nice. Not big, but nice. I'll bet it's a bear in the winter, though."

"Is there some part of Haudenosaunee country that's not a bear in the winter? Some tropical island in the middle of Lake Ontario?"

"Not that I know of, but I can dream."

"You remember I said I'd know the right place when I saw it?"

"Sure. Is this it?"

"I think so. It's hundreds of miles from the last place anybody saw you, and it's not on any of the usual routes people use to get anywhere. It's a college town, so maybe half the town is made up of strangers from all over the world. Most of them won't even arrive until early fall. It's got everything necessary for a comfortable life, but it's too small to attract creeps. It's hard to rob somebody you'll see again in the next week." Jane turned onto Wheelock Street and kept going slowly, looking at the buildings and the peo-ple walking on the sidewalks.

Jimmy said, "It seems pleasant enough. How long do you want to stay here?"

"That's the next thing I have to tell you," said Jane. "Not long. I'm leaving you here on your own for a while."

"You are?"

"Somebody has to go back and find out why people you don't know are chasing you. There isn't any way for you to go with me. You'd be recognized."

Jimmy said, "No. Please don't do that. At least one of the guys in Avon killed Nick Bauermeister. And one of the guys in Cleveland fired two rounds into our car."

"You see the problem?" she said. "The number seems to be growing. I don't know why. And one of these times they're going to succeed in killing us."

They stayed at a Marriott hotel in Lebanon near the hospital for the next two nights while Jane found an apartment to rent. She picked one that was on the lower floor of a house near the downtown section of Hanover on Chambers Street and rented it as Mr. and Mrs. Dennis Kaplan. She filled out the application, paid the deposit and a month's rent with her Melissa Kaplan credit card. She listed her husband's profession as "disabled veteran" so nobody would wonder why he never went out to work, and hers as "sales" to explain why she was going to be away most of the time. It took less than a half hour before she received the call telling her that the application had been approved. She bought a bed, a dresser, a couch, and a laptop computer. Then she set up an Internet account under Melissa Kaplan's name. The next day she bought a set of dishes, a table and chairs, filled the refrigerator with groceries, and spent the night on the new couch.

In the morning while they were having breakfast she said to Jimmy, "Today is the day."

"Are you—"

"Sure? Yes."

"What time is your flight?"

"No time. I'm taking the Greyhound bus to Boston. The bus stop is at Wheelock and Main, within walking distance from here. Then I'll fly from Boston to Buffalo, and arrive tonight."

"I could drive you to the Boston airport. In fact, I could drive you to Buffalo."

"Not a good idea. I've got everything worked out."

"What's everything?"

She opened her purse and began taking things out. "Here's some cash. It's nearly five thousand dollars. Pay for things with it—food and so on." She put a thick pile of hundred dollar bills on the table. "The rent, electricity, water, and gas are all paid for a month. If a bill comes due, write in the number of this credit card and sign Melissa Kaplan's name. Try to keep your fingerprints off things like that. There's a box of thin disposable rubber gloves in that drawer, and you can use them for handling mail. That reminds me. Don't write letters to anyone, or use your phone to call any number but my cell."

"I won't," he said. "I'm stupid, but I learn."

"Just remember all the things I've taught you about staying invisible. If you have to go out, do it mostly at night in the car. I've filled the tank with gas so you'll be able to wait awhile before it's empty again. Keep the tank at least half full in case you have to get out quickly. Don't start conversations with people, but if they speak to you, smile and answer in a friendly way. After that, don't linger. Have your fake life story ready, and rehearse it when you're alone. You know what it has to be—dull, average-guy stuff. Nothing anybody can use as an interesting story about a guy she met at the Laundromat. Wear the clothes I bought you when you go out. Look clean and neat. Before you leave, take a look out the window to see what other men have on that day. Right now the men I saw on the street are wearing polo shirts, shorts, sneakers, baseball caps. Keep the other stuff for evenings or cooler weather."

Jane looked up at the ceiling. "What else? Be observant, but don't seem to be staring at people. There's no reason to believe anybody knows you're here, so you don't need to look too hard. The main thing is to remember that every contact is a risk. Minimize risk. Anything I'm forgetting to say? Any questions for me?"

"You know I feel terrible about this, right? The idea that you're doing something dangerous for me makes me sick."

"I know that," she said. "If it helps, I'm not going back to fight any battles. I'm going because if I can find out what we're running from it will give me a way keep us both safe." She patted his shoulder and lifted her backpack as she headed for the door. "I'll be back as soon as I can. If you have to get out in the meantime, do it fast, and then call me later." The door opened and closed, and Jane was gone

IT WAS AFTER NINE AT night when Dr. Carey McKinnon drove along the highway toward home. Even after dark he would be able to see the house in the next mile, he knew, because he'd been using this route since he was a small child. The McKinnon house was an old one, built along the side of a minor Seneca trail. In 1726 the French had built Fort Niagara about twenty miles from here to control the place where the river flowed into Lake Ontario, and when the British and Iroquois took it in 1759, a McKinnon had been at the nineteen-day siege.

A few months later the former soldier built his two-story log-and-mortar house and began to farm and trade with the Senecas. Later he sheathed the house in fieldstones, and expanded the structure beyond the simple rectangle it had been. The house today still stood on a remnant of his farm, and it had been expanded periodically over the next two centuries. Most of the trees in the ten acres around the house had been alive at the time the house was built, all of them now three or four feet thick and very tall—white oak, black walnut, sycamore, bitternut hickory, sugar maple, chestnut. The next few generations of McKinnons had been doctors, and the farming they did on the side became less and less important. If Carey had been the sort of fool whose pride in his family depended on their long tenure in the area, marrying a Seneca woman was the perfect cure for that folly. How long had Jane's family been here? Ten thousand years? Twenty? He missed her, and it seemed that almost any thought he had led him back to her. Worse than missing her was thinking about the way they had parted. Worse than that was the worry.

This time when the big stone house came into view, there were lights on in the first-floor windows. He searched his memory, trying not to leap to conclusions, but he remembered turning off the last light when he had left for the hospital before dawn. His foot involuntarily stepped harder on the gas pedal, and the BMW took the turn into his driveway a bit faster than he had intended. He pulled around the house, craning his neck to see into the lighted windows, but all he saw from the car was ceilings. He drove into the garage that had once been the old carriage house, and then trotted to the kitchen door. It was unlocked.

He swung the door open and saw her standing on the other side of the big old kitchen, a figure in black. The doctor in him took note that she seemed thin. She said, "Pretty fast driving, Doc. If you roll your car when your wife is away, who will call the ambulance?"

He crossed the kitchen and held her in his arms. "I must have been showing off for you."

"It's not necessary," she said. "I'm already sufficiently seduced. You've got me on your hands for life." They shared a long, slow kiss, until Jane gently separated herself from him and held him at arm's length. "You don't seem that mad at me anymore."

"You don't seem that mad at me, either."

"I'm quietly holding a grudge. It's late, and I'll bet you're starving. I made us some dinner."

"I thought I smelled something good."

"The meat will take a couple more minutes. Go sit down so I don't burn you, and I'll bring it in."

Carey went to the dining room sideboard and opened a bottle of Bordeaux he had bought and set aside for a time when Jane was home, took glasses from the shelf, and filled them while Jane brought in their plates. "Rack of lamb," said Carey. "My favorite."

"I may not get a high grade for attendance, but I've learned a few things you like." She set the plates across from each other at the far end of the long antique table.

"To you," he said. "My eyes don't want to stop looking at you, so I probably won't be able to eat this beautiful meal and I'll starve to death."

"To both of us," she said. "And if I know you, somehow you'll manage."

Carey had come home later than usual this evening, because when Jane was away he took longer with his evening rounds to visit his surgical patients, so they were both very hungry. They ate and drank their wine with little conversation at first, and then Carey said, "I was really worried about you."

"I'm sorry."

"And I kept wishing that I hadn't reacted the way I did before you left," Carey said. "I know it's bad enough to have to do something difficult, without having your family criticizing you for doing it."

"It's okay," she said. "It's just a bad situation. Nobody asked to be in it—not you, or me, or Jimmy. We'll just have to get through it."

When they were finished, Jane said, "Nia:wen." She sat still and watched him.

Carey repeated, "Nia:wen."

He stood and began to clear the table and she joined him. When they met a few minutes later with their hands free of dishes, they kissed again and held each other.

Jane said softly, "How much wine is left?"

"Not enough to drown a hummingbird."

"So at least it's not a safety hazard. Bring some cognac and glasses and I'll meet you upstairs."

After a few minutes Carey came upstairs carrying the two small snifters and the bottle, and walked down the hallway into the master bedroom, where Jane stood waiting for him, naked. "Oh, there you are," she said.

Carey put the two glasses on his dresser, poured a splash of cognac into each, and handed her one. "This is a nice surprise. With all these lights on, I assumed you'd be dressed more formally."

She shrugged and took a sip of her cognac. "It would be kind of silly to hide anything from you, Dr. McKinnon. There's nothing new to see, but I know how much you like to verify that for yourself."

"Yes, you're a very practical girl," he said. He set his glass on the dresser, scooped Jane up, carried her to the bed. The cover had been pulled back, and he set her gently on the sheets. In a few seconds he was undressed too, and they were together on the bed. It felt wrong.

Their talk had been false, a way to gloss over the distance that had grown between them, and they both knew it. Their movements were awkward. Too much time had passed while Jane was away and they were resenting each other, so they both felt clumsy and uncertain, as though they were strangers.

Jane sat up and held Carey's face in her hands so they had to look into each other's eyes. "I love you," she said. "I'm not going to let things turn sad because we can't put our problems out of our minds for a while. We're going to fight some more about this another time. Not tonight. And we'll still love each other just as much at the end of that fight too. Right now, be with me."

"I am," he said. "I love you." He put his arms around her and held her.

They caressed each other slowly and gently, a lavish, leisurely expenditure of time, savoring the fact that she was at home with him tonight and not somewhere else that neither of them wanted to think about. They didn't speak, only touched and kissed, feeling the understanding that they loved each other deeply and permanently—that for him, she was the one woman who would stand in his life for all women, and in her life, he would stand for all men.

They were grateful to and for each other, and as their pulses and breathing sped up and their skin temperatures rose with the excitement, each of them tried to give the other more pleasure, to cause it and feel it and observe it at the same time. They began to express their own love and receive the other's love at the same instant, and to increase the pleasure and increase it until the strain of containing it overwhelmed them.

They lay motionless on the bed for a few seconds, and then Jane got up and turned off the big light on the ceiling, so there was only the moonlight through the window. "I'm not in the mood for the glare anymore."

"If I can't see you I'll find you by touch."

"Or I'll find you." Jane leaned over him and kissed him softly, her lips lingering on his, barely touching. They lay close for a time, not talking or needing to talk.

Then they touched again, neither of them really knowing who had moved a hand first and initiated the touch, but both knowing instantly that this touch was different, and responding to it before it was over, prolonging and intensifying the touch. They were more uninhibited this time, less aware of themselves and their own bodies but more aware of each other, and when it ended it left them tired and at peace. Carey got up and opened the window, and they lay back together on the bed, feeling the cool, soothing air of the night drifting over their bodies. And then Jane fell asleep.

She was still lying on the bed beside Carey and she knew they had both been sleeping, and that she was still asleep, when she heard the faint sound of a person climbing the stairs to the second floor. The feet were silent, but a few of the steps of the staircase creaked faintly when a person stepped on them. She had trained herself to hear the sounds. In the silence that followed, Jane could feel someone coming along the hallway toward her.

The woman appeared in the doorway, and Jane sat up on the bed to look at her. The woman wore a deerskin dress with leggings and moccasins. Her shining black hair was long, combed and straight, and Jane could see that its weight made it swing a little each time she moved her head. As the woman stepped into the bedroom, the silver-blue light from the moon shone on her and Jane could see that her dress, leggings, and moccasins were decorated with dyed porcupine quills sewn like embroidery in the shapes of wildflowers. Jane knew she was from the old time.

The woman spoke in Seneca. "Owandah. Or maybe I should call you Onyo:ah." This was Jane's secret name, a nickname her father had given her when she was little.

Jane pulled the bed sheet up to her neck.

"Don't bother hiding yourself," said the woman. "You've been doing what you should be doing." She looked at Carey. "Your husband is good and he's strong. You're a good match."

"You know the name my father gave me." *Onyo:ah* was a call used in the peach-pit game. It meant that five of the six peach pits in a player's throw had landed with the black, burned side up, and only one was on the unburned side— literally "one white." If all six had been black, the player would have been allowed to take five score counters. With one white, he could take only one counter. Her father had explained to her that Onyo:ah meant the player was winning, but by slow, gradual steps, the way people did in life.

The game was played at Midwinter and Green Corn to celebrate the triumph of life over winter. But it was first played just after the beginning of time by Hawenneyu the Creator and Hanegoategah the Destroyer, the twin gods who transformed the dirt on the great turtle's back into a world. The twins' grandmother proposed that she and the destroyer play the game against Hawenneyu the Creator to decide who would have dominion over the earth. When she rolled the pits from the bowl, she got no points. When Hawenneyu cast the pits, he won.

"Of course I know your name. I'm in your mind. Maybe I'm one of the four messengers, a *hatioyake:ono*, a sky dweller. Maybe I'm just a side of you—a part that you need and miss."

"Why are you here?"

The woman shrugged, and the fringe on her shirt swung, then settled. "You called me."

"Who are you?"

"Just a woman like you. I'm from the dark times, when no village was at peace with another. If a man met a stranger in the forest, the wisest thing to do was try to kill him, and if you were a woman, the wisest thing to do was run. Villages were built in high places, or on peninsulas jutting out into lakes, surrounded by palisades of tree trunks set into the ground and sharpened on top. I lived less than an hour's walk from this spot. I was working at the edge of a field outside the village planting corn, beans, and squash with my sisters and cousins when I saw a warrior moving among the trees. He was a stranger who had come with eight friends to catch someone off guard and kill him. Our eyes met, and I turned to run. He tried to keep me from giving the alarm, but I got out a scream before the war club he swung hit my head."

The woman half turned and pulled her hair aside, and Jane could see a huge gash where the bone of her skull had been shattered. The back of her beautiful dress was reddish brown where the blood had poured out and run down it. "All of the women heard me, and began running and shouting, so the warriors from the village came and chased down the man and his friends, and killed them all. I was nineteen."

"It's terrible and sad," said Jane. "Nineteen is so young."

The woman shrugged. "Everybody dies. The part that hurt me most was that I had a young baby, a beautiful boy. I took him everywhere, and right then he was hanging in his cradleboard from a branch of a tree. When the wind blew, it rocked him back and forth. When I saw the killer, I ran away from my baby to distract the killer from him. After the fighting was over, two of my sisters came back and got him from the tree."

"What happened to him?"

"He lived to be a man. He was a famous runner and good fighter, and the men all listened to him respectfully in council. He fathered seven children by two wives, and died in a fight against the Cat People on an island in the Niagara River when he was over fifty. He's satisfied with his life. My sisters and the other women of the clan did a good job raising him without me."

"There must be a reason why you're the one who's here."

"I told you why. You chose me."

"Why would I do that?"

"Maybe your mind chose me because I'm from the time when things were in chaos, before the great peace. My times are the reason why the Senecas and the other longhouse nations hate discord and anarchy. We lived it. We died of it. You live a violent life. You've killed people, and that's not an easy thing for a woman. Killing strains against our nature. Maybe it's making you sick. You know *sken:nen* means peace, but the same word means health."

"I've only tried to keep people from being killed," said Jane. "I taught them to evade, to run, to start new lives. How could anyone—man or woman—not do that much?"

"If that's not what's wrong, then maybe something is missing from your life."

Jane sighed. "I wanted a baby."

"You still do."

"I suppose I do, but Carey and I have tried for years and it hasn't happened, so I'm training myself not to keep longing for what I can't have."

"Now you're setting a snare, trying to trip me up so I'll accidentally tell you whether you'll have a baby or not. I'm sorry, but I come from you. I know exactly what you know, and no more. Maybe I know a few things that you saw or heard but have forgotten. But you haven't seen the future, so I haven't either."

"Admit that you were sent to me."

"I was sent to you," said the woman.

"By the good brother or the evil one?"

"You know better than to ask that. Which is God—birth and growth, or death and decay? They seem to fight, but they don't."

"Are either of them real?"

"If there's a creator, he created your parents and grand-parents, your mind, your memory, this dream, and sent me to guide you. If there is no creator, and your subconscious mind put me together out of memories and imagination because your mind needs me, then your brain sent me to guide you. Tell me which it is."

"I can't."

"Then neither can I," said the woman. "And my time will be up soon. This is your last REM cycle for the night, and it should be thirty minutes, or forty. The best thing you have in your life is Carey. It's not always in your power to make him happy, but it is in your power to make him know that you love him."

"Am I making him jealous by worrying about Jimmy?"

"He's not jealous," said the woman. "Maybe you think he should be."

"I'm not interested in Jimmy that way. But being around him makes me—I don't know—miss something."

"Jimmy looks like a Seneca and speaks Seneca with you as your father did, so it's natural to feel the connection. You think that you were supposed to marry a man like Jimmy but didn't, so you feel guilty, and now you feel guilty for feeling guilty because that's not fair to Carey. I can tell you that you were right to pick the man who didn't just give you a faint friendly feeling. Instead you took the one who gave you a trembling in your stomach and weak knees."

"If I stay home with my husband, what will happen to Jimmy?"

"You won't do that. Being Jimmy's guide is something the clan mothers require of you—that life demands of you. But you've got to do whatever you're going to do soon. Time isn't helping you."

"That's your advice? Hurry up?" said Jane.

"Jimmy's enemies are getting more powerful, so you have to be quick. Follow the poisoned stream to where the spring seeps out of the ground. Find out everything you can and then do what you have to. But you have to act soon. Jimmy won't see the man in the forest before he swings the club. You might."

Jane woke while the sky was just lightening from black to blue gray. The stars outside the window were still bright and glowing, but she could see the leaves of the old walnut tree on the far side of the carriage house. She sat up, still naked, slid out from under the sheet, and looked down at Carey sprawled beside her. He always slept with an innocent, peaceful look on his face, especially after a night like last night. He undoubtedly had disturbing dreams sometimes, but white people didn't study their dreams, or make much of them.

She got up and walked quietly out of the room, passed the master bathroom, and continued down the hall to one of the bathrooms attached to guest rooms and turned on the shower. The warm water felt good.

A few minutes later she saw through the glass door of the shower that he had appeared. "Dr. M.," she said. "To what do I owe this pleasure?"

He opened the shower door and stepped in with her. "I woke up alone and came looking for you. You're home now, but you won't be soon." He sidestepped past her, ducked under the shower and got wet, then scrubbed himself with soap.

She was very still. "You know that?"

"Since I saw you in the kitchen last night I've been listening for you to say this was over—that Jimmy Sanders was safe and you were home for good. You haven't said it, so it isn't over."

She hugged him, feeling the water spraying her back. "I'm sorry, Carey. I don't have a choice right now."

"I know you think that," he said. "I was here for the beginning, the day they asked you to take this on. I didn't like it, and I still don't like it. Last night wasn't the time for the argument. Is this the time?"

"I don't think so." She turned off the shower, took his hand, and stepped out of the stall with him. She tossed him a bath towel, took one herself, and led him into the guest room. They made love gently and then passionately, and lay lazily on the bed. After a time she could tell he was looking at her.

He leaned over her and kissed her. "You're leaving right away, aren't you?"

"As soon as I check the refrigerator to see what you ought to have but didn't buy for yourself, and go to the grocery store. But when I get back, we'll spend about three days just going from room to room doing this."

14

Jane spent the morning preparing to leave home. She packed the clothes that she would need in a small suitcase and included her empty backpack inside, two more packets of identification and credit cards, and more cash. She walked to the nearest grocery store, which was only about a half mile down the road, bought food for Carey, and walked back. She left a bottle of eighteen-year-old Macallan single malt scotch on the kitchen table with a crystal glass to hold down her note to him. All it said was: "There are still fourteen more rooms in this house." That would give him something to think about.

She said quietly to the empty house in Seneca, "Thank you for visiting me in my dream, grandmother. I'll name you Keha kah je: sta e." It was literally *my black eyes.*

Jane went outside, locked the door, and walked down the road to the bus stop to catch the bus to the station at Sheridan Drive and Getzville Road. She caught the rural service bus to Lockport, took another to Batavia, but got off at the Pembroke exit of the thruway. She took out her copy of the service order Ray Snow had given her when she'd left her car with him. She dialed the number she found on it and heard, "Snow's auto."

"Hi, Ray. This is Jane Whitefield."

"Hey, Janie. Are you coming back for your car?"

"Well, I'm making my way there. I've gotten as far as the Pembroke rest stop on the thruway. I took a Greyhound."

"Get yourself a cup of coffee. I'll be there in fifteen or twenty minutes."

"See you then."

Twenty minutes later, she saw her white Volvo S60 coast along the exit ramp into the parking lot, and then glide up to the building. Jane tossed her suitcase on the backseat, sat down beside Ray, and fastened her seat belt. Ray smiled. "How was your hike?"

"Tiring. Thanks so much for picking me up, Ray."

"No big deal. We do this all the time for our customers, and most of them don't have such nice cars." He drove toward the ramp back onto the thruway.

"I'm glad you like it. It's about six years old."

"Mechanics like a car that's been cared for, and I like them better if they didn't just come off the lot. I buy a few used ones now and then and fix them up for resale. If you ever want to get rid of this one, don't trade it in. I'll give you a better deal."

Jane looked at him through the corner of her eye. "Do you happen to have any cars you've fixed up at the shop right now?"

"A couple."

"I'm wondering if you have one I could rent for a while."

"So you found Jimmy."

"If you knew something like that, then sometime you might get asked about it under oath. You'd have to tell the truth. Fortunately I don't know who you're talking about. But what about the car?"

"Sure. I'll rent you one."

"I've got to be clear about this. I might not be able to return it in mint condition or right away. But I'll pay for anything that happens to it."

"Fine," he said. He looked at her thoughtfully for a moment, then returned his eyes to the road ahead.

They drove up to Snow's garage and he parked Jane's car in a row of other cars of various makes and models. He walked over to a Ford Mustang that was red with black stripes running along the hood, roof, and trunk. "I put a five-liter Racing Crate Mustang Boss 302 V8 in there. It's supposed to deliver four hundred forty-four horsepower, but I brought everything else up a notch too, so it should be faster than that."

"I was thinking of something quieter, a little less vivid."

"I've got that too," Ray said. He stepped up to a small navy blue car and patted it on the trunk. "This VW Passat is a good, reliable car, and one you can hardly see if you're standing beside it. I haven't done anything but a tune-up, because it runs great and doesn't have dents or scratches. That's not the kind of car that interests me much."

"That's perfect. Dull is good."

"Hold on a second." He went into the shop and opened a drawer behind the back counter, then came back with the keys. He handed them to her.

"What about my Volvo? Can I pay now for the work you did?"

"No. It'll be easier to handle everything at once when you come back. Besides, I heard something when we were driving on the thruway a few minutes ago—a little faint whine. It could just be a fan belt, or it could be a transmission problem. I'll have to keep it to check it out. That VW is your free loaner until your car is ready."

"Gee, Ray. You're such a lousy liar I'll trust you forever."

"Thanks. By the way, the car came from Pennsylvania. The old license plate is still in the trunk, and it's current.

Maybe you'll find a use for it. Say hi for me to, uh, any old friends you happen to meet." He took Jane's suitcase out of the backseat of the Volvo and put it in the backseat of the Volkswagen.

"I'll do that." Jane got in and backed the VW out of its space. She could already hear the smoothness of the engine. She drove down the road a few miles to the thruway, and then east to Rochester and stopped at the Hyatt Regency hotel on East Main Street adjacent to the Convention Center. The hotel was large, fairly new, and had been renovated within the past couple of years. She checked in and gave the desk clerk a credit card in the name of Janet Eisen.

Jane had built Janet Eisen over a period of six years, beginning with a birth certificate that had been inserted into the records of the county clerk's office in Chicago. She had gotten an Illinois driver's license, a diploma from a long-defunct local parochial high school, St. Luc's. In time Janet Eisen had submitted her resume to a few online employment agencies. The resume listed a BA degree from North Ohio Business and Technical School, an entity that had gone bankrupt in the 1990s, but had a ghostly afterlife due to the efforts of a man who sold artfully concocted academic transcripts. Janet Eisen had also applied for everything she could get without much risk or effort—library cards, gym memberships, magazine subscriptions, frequent flyer programs—so within a year or two she had been firmly established in an online existence. Jane had even inserted a few articles about her in online publications so anyone checking her name on Google would find her. Jane had hired her to work in Mc-Shaller, Inc., the consulting business Jane had incorporated fifteen years ago. Jane used the business to run credit checks and buy information, but it also allowed the fictitious Janet Eisen to give imaginary people jobs, employment histories, and glowing recommendations.

Jane didn't have a clear idea of who might be searching for Jimmy—or for her—or what resources they might use. Today she was making sure that if someone searched, she would be in a spot that was far down the list of likely hiding places. This hotel was big and full of business people just like Janet Eisen who were in Rochester for conferences, business meetings, and sales visits to local companies. As soon as Jane had checked in at the hotel she walked down Main to the convention center and registered for the convention that was starting that day. It was a convention for the medical information storage and transcription industry, and would last a week. She paid a two-hundred-dollar fee, accepted a folder full of information about meetings and presentations, and a map of booths in the Convention Center. While she waited, her name badge was printed and inserted in a plastic case that hung from a lanyard. She put it around her neck so she looked like everyone else, then walked back to the hotel with a few of the women from the convention.

She went to the hotel business center and signed on to a computer using the account of McShaller Systems, her consulting corporation. She read the *Buffalo News*, the *Rochester Democrat and Chronicle*, the *Livingston County News*. She scanned every article about Jimmy Sanders or Nick Bauermeister. They all had the same things to say about the case: Bauermeister had died of a single rifle shot fired through the front window of the house he shared with his girlfriend, Chelsea Schnell, age twenty-three. Police had interviewed neighbors, friends, employers, co-workers, and then begun seeking Jimmy Sanders for an interview because he'd had a fight with Bauermeister and been charged with assault. They had left messages, but had not connected with him yet when a man came forward claiming to have sold a .30-06 rifle and a box of ammunition to Jimmy at a garage sale a couple of weeks before the murder.

Jane wrote down the name of the girlfriend and then looked up the address. She wrote down the name of the supposed gun seller, Walter Slawicky. The Livingston County paper, which was published in Geneseo, had seen fit to include a few details that the big-city papers had left out, including Nick Bauermeister's employer, a storage company called Box Farm Personal Storage on Telephone Road near Avon. On the computer Jane ranged further in space and time, searching for the names of Bauermeister, his girlfriend, his employer, and the gun seller in any context, asking the engine to search the past five years up to the present day. Whenever she found anything she printed the page.

When Jane had exhausted her search, she tried to assess what she had. The most interesting person to look at first would be the man she knew was lying to connect Jimmy with the crime. She found Walter Slawicky's address online. He lived on Iroquois Road in Caledonia. She looked at views of the house from street level and from above, then signed out.

Jane went back upstairs to her room, plugged her cell phone in to charge, set the alarm on it, and lay on the bed. She was asleep in a few minutes, still tired from the late night with Carey. At ten the alarm went off. She got up, dressed in a pair of black jeans, black running shoes, and a black pullover sweater. She took out a black baseball cap, but didn't put it on yet. She wore a light gray hooded sweatshirt to counteract the unrelieved black, then took the stairs to the garage and got into her Passat.

The drive from Rochester down Interstate 390 to Caledonia was easy and fast at night. Her car was small, dark, and nondescript, so she felt confident leaving it parked along the street in Caledonia where there were a few restaurants still open. The line of other cars at the curb would camouflage hers, and she expected to be gone before the bars closed. She took off her hoodie, put on her baseball cap, and got out to walk.

Slawicky's house was on the opposite side of the street, but Jane approached it by staying along the side where the shadows were deepest and hurrying past any building that cast light on the sidewalks. When she found the address she could see that the house had lights on. Someone must be at home. She crossed the street.

As she approached the house she looked carefully in all directions to be sure there wasn't anyone on the street and nobody standing at windows to notice her. She slipped into the yard, then moved along the tall, untrimmed hedge at the border of the property, letting it hide her silhouette.

The house was an old one, probably from the late nineteenth or early twentieth century, with a sagging covered porch and tall, narrow windows that looked cloudy as though they hadn't been washed recently, and wispy whitish curtains behind them.

When Jane was as far back in the side yard as the first window, she glided silently to the side of the house and looked in. The window showed her a small dining room with an old table that had a number of rings in its finish from years of wet glasses, and a vase in the center with dusty silk roses in it—a faded red and a white that was now yellowish. A still-folded newspaper and pieces of junk mail were strewn around on the surface. She saw no signs of a recent female presence, and no female belongings. She was fairly sure no man would buy fake roses for his house. This looked like a house Slawicky had inherited from elderly relatives and never cleaned.

Through a wide opening beyond the dining room table she could see a darkened living room where the changing glow of a television set was visible on the ceiling. She moved into the deeper darkness away from the dining room window and toward the living room. She picked a window on the television's side where she would not have its glare in her eyes. What she had to minimize now was motion. If

Slawicky's eye caught movement he would be unable to keep from turning to look. She slowly moved her face close to the side of the house and brought only her left eye near the corner of the window.

There he was in a chair in front of the television set. He was about forty-five to fifty years old, and his hair on top was retreating to the back of his skull. He was broad, and wore a light blue T-shirt that rose above his pants to reveal a round, hairy belly. There was a bottle of beer in his right hand and occasionally he lifted it to drink, but his eyes remained aimed at the television set, the pupils barely moving. When he drank, the pressure of the bottle to his mouth made his small round nose bob up and down.

The furnishings in the living room were consistent with everything Jane had seen so far. The couch was swaybacked and the arms had ladders of frayed fabric where people had leaned on them. The chair where Slawicky sat matched the couch, and both looked as though they had been bought by an earlier generation, and inherited with the house. The chair was aimed precisely at the television screen. Jane caught a reflection in the dark window across from the television set, and decided get a better look from another angle.

She moved around to the opposite window where she could see the television set. It was well over five feet wide, a plasma high-definition screen of the sort that she'd seen in stores for around four thousand dollars. In the two corners at that end of the room were pairs of detached speakers, two tall and two short. She had no idea of what those had cost, only that it was more than most people would have paid to hear every whisper of the inane commentary on televised games.

Jane moved along the driveway to the garage. The big door was closed, but she could see there was a man-size door on the side, so she tried the knob. It was locked, so she took out her pocketknife, inserted the blade into the space between door and jamb by the strike plate, pushed to depress the plunger, then pulled the door open. Inside she could see the sleek, rounded, gleaming shape of a Porsche. She stepped in and read the letters across the back: Carrera. She moved along the car, and noticed that there was a slight cloudy residue on the rear side window where the dealer's sticker had been poorly scraped off. The car was new. It had to cost around eighty-five thousand.

Jane slipped out and relocked the door. As she stood there she saw a car slowing down and moving to the right slightly as it passed the driveway, as though the driver were planning to park. She moved around the garage to the back, and saw something else that didn't belong, a lump under a tarp. She lifted it. This time it was a Jet Ski, bright and gleaming. She had no idea what those cost, since she detested them. She covered the Jet Ski again and moved along the side of the garage to watch the street.

She caught the shape of a man moving from the street into the far side of the yard where she had entered, and, as Jane had done, stepping along the high unruly hedge to keep his silhouette shaded by its dark opaque shape. Jane prepared to run. The man was on the side of the yard she had come from, and that put him between her and her car. If she went, she would have to go left for a distance, sneak across the road into one of the yards, and run along the backs of the houses and out to the street where her car was parked.

She pulled her black baseball cap down tight on her head with the brim low on her forehead to shield her eyes from moonlight and the faint light pollution from neon signs and distant streetlamps. She judged where the new man must be and stared to the side of that spot until she saw him move into it. He stood perfectly still for a minute or more, and then began to move again.

Jane stayed still. This man was trouble. He knew how to move in the dark without being easily detected. He took a few silent steps, then stopped and waited. He knew that if someone had heard him or sensed movement, then he must wait until the opponent's mind had determined that there was nothing there—the impression must have been false or self-generated or unthreatening, because there had not been another to make into a pattern.

He stepped away from the hedge to the side of the house. As he did, the light from the dining room window illuminated him for a second. He was tall, thin, almost stork-like, with very short blond hair. *Hello, Ike.* It was the man who had been tracking her and Jimmy in Allegheny, Technical Sergeant Isaac Lloyd, State Police Bureau of Criminal Investigation. He didn't stop at the window for long, because in a moment Jane saw him appear at the rear corner of the house. She pulled back her head and crouched on the opposite side of the garage as he kept coming. She heard him open the smaller door of the garage and step inside.

Jane stood and moved quietly up the driveway, across the street into the yard of the house opposite Slawicky's. She walked along behind it to the street, stayed low as she came around the trunk of her car and into the driver's seat, slipped the key in, and started the engine.

As she drove along Iroquois Street away from Caledonia, she thought about her visit to Slawicky's. Apparently what Sergeant Lloyd had been doing since he had lost the trail of Jimmy Sanders in the Alleghenies was looking more closely at the people who had some connection to the murder. Walter Slawicky, the man who had come forward to report that he'd sold Jimmy the murder weapon, seemed to have caught his attention. Sergeant Lloyd had just seen what she had—that the man who had implicated Jimmy Sanders in the murder seemed to have come into some money.

15

Chelsea Schnell sat in the passenger seat of the Range Rover beside Daniel Crane, looking out the windshield most of the time but taking an occasional glance at him when she was sure her eyes wouldn't meet his. He had taken her to the Escarpment tonight. It was even better than she had imagined it would be. The restaurant was built on a flat limestone shelf high above the Niagara Gorge in Lewiston. After the river washed over the falls, it ran onward through another seven miles of rapids and swift water to Lake Ontario. The river had dug a steep canyon there, three hundred feet below the restaurant's patio, where she and Dan had sat for dinner on this warm summer evening. They had arrived at seven, when there was still plenty of daylight, and finished by candlelight three hours later.

The quality of the food and wine had taken her off guard. She had only agreed to go with him because he had kept asking and asking, and she had run out of excuses. She hadn't had the mental and emotional energy to brush him off again. Each of his previous invitations had been to very nice places, but when he had offered the Escarpment, she had finally given in. She had always wished that Nick would take her to a place like the Escarpment just once. No, she admitted to herself, just once wouldn't have been what she wanted. Once she'd been there, she would have wanted to come on special times, maybe birthdays or anniversaries. The thought of an anniversary made her feel lonely and bereft, so she decided to distract herself.

She said, "That was such a wonderful restaurant, Dan. Thank you so much for taking me."

"You're welcome," he said. "It was my pleasure."

She waited a few seconds, but he didn't add anything, so she spoke again. "You were right that I should get out of the house once in a while."

"I knew you would like it," he said. "You know another place that's really nice? There's a great restaurant—and I mean great—right outside of Rochester, in Pittsford. It's been written up in a lot of food magazines. It's where famous people go when they come to Rochester."

"What's it called?" *What famous people ever went to Rochester?*

"It's called the Old Canal Inn. It's built on the site of an eighteenth-century hotel. The road and the hotel were there before the Erie Canal, but I guess they want people to know it's beside the canal. I'll take you there."

"I wasn't hinting to make you treat me again. I was just curious," she said. "After the meal we had tonight, I can't even think about food again for a few days."

"I liked the Escarpment too," said Crane. "I've always liked it, but tonight it was at its best. It's such a beautiful view anyway, but having you across the table made it even more beautiful." He watched her for a reaction, but didn't detect one, so he persisted. "I meant that, you know."

Chelsea could feel herself getting panicky. He was trying to be nice, but being with him made the interior of the car seem suddenly smaller. She felt an impulse to open the car door and get out, but the car was moving. She held her discomfort in check. "You shouldn't be such a kiss ass. People will think you're trying to make fools of them."

"Me?" said Crane. "I'd never do that to you. I do think you're beautiful. I'm sure you can see that for yourself in the mirror every day, but it doesn't hurt you to know that other people appreciate you." He grinned. "You're raising the property values around here, so it's good for everybody."

"Always glad to help the real estate people," she said. "Let's talk about something else. You've been careful all through dinner not to talk about work. So tell me about your day at work. How was it?"

"Good," he said. "Business is always good. Whenever the economy starts looking up, people buy too much and don't have anyplace to put the excess but storage. When the economy goes down again, they lose their big fancy homes and have to put *all* of it in storage."

"So they have to come to you no matter what."

"The smart ones don't, but they don't matter. There are so few of them that they're not a big share of the market. How about your job? Are you back at work yet?"

"Not yet," she said. "I was thinking of going back this week, but my mother asked me to go on a little trip with her, so I told the bank I wasn't ready. She was going to fly to Denver to help my cousin Amelia with her new baby, and she wanted me to go with her. At the last minute I couldn't face it. I realized it would have been the same thing that kept me from going back to work—lots of questions about Nick and the investigation and what I feel, and people saying it's too bad we weren't married, because then there would be insurance. It would be even worse in Denver. I'd edge out Amelia and her baby for attention and everybody would feel bad for me instead of good for her. I'd rather be around people who have gotten tired of talking about it."

"It's not that we're tired of talking about it. We just—"

"I am," she said. "I should probably be ashamed of that, but it's how I feel. I don't want to go through the whole story over and over again for a bunch of new people, and relive everything to catch them up."

"I understand," said Crane. "You can visit your Denver relatives another time after it's all over."

She glared at him, coiling herself for a fight. Nick's murder wasn't ever going to be over. Death wasn't a temporary setback. Her life had been marked forever. Saying that sometime it was all going to fade away was stupid. As the seconds passed she watched his face. He was trying so hard, and he had just made a small mistake trying to comfort her. He didn't deserve a hysterical tirade from the same woman he had just bought the most expensive dinner in Western New York and tried to flatter and distract for over three hours. "It's true," she said. "Denver will still be there when I'm ready." She noticed that he didn't make the turn at Telephone Road. "I think you just went past my turn."

"Don't worry," he said. "We'll get you there. Just a brief detour." He kept driving, his eyes on the road. He seemed to be speeding up.

Chelsea didn't like the way he avoided looking at her, and she didn't like it that he had not asked if she minded taking a detour. She felt manipulated and trapped. But she was determined to remain silent, and give him enough time to realize she was irritated. Maybe then he would get around to discussing why she felt that way. The silence went on, and she began to suspect that she was more uncomfortable with silence than he was. "So what's with the detour?"

"I just have to stop at my place for a minute before I swing back your way. I left some papers at home that have to be in the office in the morning, and that's in the direction of your place, so I can drop them off on my way home from there. I'm sorry to do this, but it's payroll stuff, and it'll save me a long trip later."

She ran his excuse through her mind and listened to the tone of his voice for evidence that he was lying to get her alone in a place where he could make an unwelcome move that would only cause them both embarrassment. She couldn't detect anything. In penance for her suspicion she was inclined to be agreeable about this. He could just as easily have made whatever misguided advance he'd wanted at her house. She lived there alone now, and was always alone when he came to visit or pick her up.

Crane turned a corner onto a knot of smaller roads, and she knew that they were in the space somewhere between the Country Club of Buffalo and the Park Country Club because she'd once worked a night job for a caterer, but she had lost her sense of exact location from being turned around a couple of times. The houses were all big now, most of them long and low, with huge lawns and tall trees, all at the ends of long driveways marked by rural mailboxes on posts, but then curving up to modern houses.

Chelsea had always hated the mailbox where she and Nick had lived, because it epitomized for her the fact that she and Nick lived out in the sticks. She had to trudge all the way down the gravel drive in rain or snow to retrieve a few bills and a pile of garish ads for things she wouldn't buy in a million years. But in this neighborhood, the mailboxes at the ends of long driveways symbolized the ownership of a big house on a vast piece of land.

Daniel Crane drove along the road, and then turned right into one of the driveways. The surface looked like cobblestones, but she knew that the stones must be some modern imitation, partly because every stone was identical and perfectly level. As he drove along the driveway's big curve, she caught herself trying to look ahead of the sweeping headlights to see what came next. First thick shrubbery for privacy from the road, then neat plantings of bright dahlias, hydrangeas, and rock roses, then the trunks of tall pine trees, and then a lawn like a golf course. The house itself was one story, a sprawling, plain dark brown building that she only now realized was natural wood. There was a narrow opening between wings of the house, and through it she could see a Japanese garden that seemed to be surrounded by glass.

Crane stopped the SUV in front of the entrance, where she could see the garden beyond the opening by the dim light coming from the house's interior through the glass wall. "Just give me a few minutes." He undid his seat belt and let it retract.

"Beautiful house," Chelsea said.

He turned to look at her. "Want to take a look inside? I feel weird leaving you sitting out here alone."

She hesitated, thinking about sitting here alone in the dark while he went inside. "Sure," she said. She unlatched her seat belt and put her hand on the door handle, but he was there opening the door before she could go anywhere, offering her his hand.

She was glad she'd taken it when she stepped to the pavement. Her high heels were uncertain and a little wobbly on the stone driveway. She followed him as he opened the front door and punched in the alarm code on the keypad on the wall. He flipped a few switches and various parts of the house lit up.

The right side of the living room was the glass wall she had glimpsed from the front. The light out there was from small spotlights along the edge of the roof, and it showed her a big boulder with water trickling from a natural depression at the top, down its side into a tiny pond and recycling to flow down continuously. There was a bed of fine gravel raked into patterns to circle dark volcanic-looking boulders in a seemingly random arrangement, with a few twisted evergreen shrubs. A simple wooden bench beside the garden was where she could imagine herself sitting on a warm day reading.

Recessed lights in the living room ceiling lit floor-to-ceiling bookcases built into one wall filled with books and the occasional small sculpture or ceramic. Others threw softer beams of light on a semicircular arc of couches arranged as a conversation area around a low, round table.

But Crane was already across the room and disappearing under an arch into a wide gallery. "Make yourself at home," he called over his shoulder. Chelsea lost sight of him, but had the impression that he turned to the right somewhere on his walk, and then had the sense that his office must overlook the Japanese garden from the side.

She walked across the living room, looked through a matching arch that seemed to end in the kitchen, where she could see gleaming stainless steel, and a couple of unlit rooms that opened on either side of that gallery.

Chelsea stood still and stared at everything, shocked. The house looked like it belonged to a celebrity who had incredibly sophisticated taste. The pictures on the white walls were mostly not of anything, just beautiful colors smeared or dribbled or painted on in stripes with so many layers that they seemed to be deep enough to fall into. There were smaller ones, drawings or watercolors, mostly of girls, a few of them just girls' faces or girls not naked. She loved this house. It looked like something in a magazine.

She walked along the bookcases identifying tall art books, architecture books, thick collections of essays about opera, classical music, or philosophy. She had never imagined Dan Crane was interested in any of these topics. She had an urge to take some of the books down and look at them, but she could see that they had been arranged so precisely that he would know if she disturbed one, and might not like it.

She heard a door closing somewhere in the distance, and then Dan's shoes on the hardwood floor. She looked toward the arch and saw him reappear, carrying a half-inch-thin soft leather briefcase. "This house is gorgeous, Daniel."

He tossed his briefcase on the nearest couch and said, "Come on. I'll give you a quick tour."

"Can we start in the kitchen?"

He looked surprised. "Sure. This way."

The kitchen was exactly as she had guessed—huge and airy, with granite counters, a big island with sinks and overhead ventilation hood. There was a Sub-Zero refrigerator, a nine-burner stove, a double oven. Everything was gleaming and spotless. She was sure Dan Crane never cooked here, but someone certainly could. He led her out and opened a door on the corridor, and she saw a big television screen and some identical leather chairs with end tables beside each of them. "Screening room."

As she went with him from room to room she couldn't help wondering what it would be like to live here. The woman who had this house would live with Daniel Crane, of course, and that wasn't something that appealed to her at first thought, but tonight she had begun to think that she had judged him too soon. She had been aware from the beginning that he had money. He owned the company where Nick had worked, so obviously he'd have more money than Nick. What she hadn't known before was that he had such good taste, such a rich imagination, such an appreciation for beauty. He had a lively inner life that she had never suspected.

As she watched him on the tour she reflected that he was better looking than he had been before. She thought it might be because he had confidence tonight. He knew he had impressed her with the restaurant, and when he was here on his home ground he seemed masterful. He stood straighter and spoke with an ease that even made its way into his voice.

He stopped in the living room in front of a section of white wall and said, "Something from the bar?" He pressed a spot and a section of the white surface slid upward to reveal a granite bar with a sink, cabinets where glasses of various shapes and sizes were displayed, and rows of liquor bottles. He reached for a short, round bottle and said, "This is a really nice cognac. Perfect for sipping while we complete the tour."

"None for me," she said. "I've already had more wine than I ever drink. That will just put me to sleep."

"You're probably right," he said. "And I'm going to be driving, so I'd better skip it too. A soft drink then." He opened a cabinet that had no glass in front, and revealed that it was a small refrigerator. "Ginger ale?"

"Is it diet?"

He took out a can and looked at it. "It says it is." He popped it and poured a glass for her and another for himself. He left the bar open and led her onward. There was an office in the place where she had guessed it must be, big and neat with a desk that showed a reflection, and a big sliding glass door to the Japanese garden. They passed three bedroom suites, all of them perfectly furnished and untouched. "There's another one with Japanese watercolors that overlooks the garden," he said, "and two others I made into a den and a pool room."

That was the last thing that she heard him say before she became aware of the sun. It wasn't shining directly on her, or making her hot. Its light just invaded her sleep until she was forced to open her eyes. She stared at the scene in front of her, trying to make sense of it. Nothing seemed all right. Where was the yellow color of her bedroom wall? And her dresser was missing. It should be right here, where she could see it when she was lying in bed on her left side, like this. She rolled and sat up.

She had moved too fast. Her head felt tender and bloated, not quite a headache but not normal either. She looked at the room and realized she had seen this room before, but couldn't quite place it. She exerted greater effort and realized she must be in Daniel Crane's bedroom. She was in his bed, naked. And now she admitted to herself that she could feel that she'd had sex. How could she have done that?

She tried to bring the answer out of her memory, but her mind was sluggish, like a heavy thing that she wasn't strong enough to move. She would push it, and it seemed to be going in the right direction, returning to the dinner, the view of the deep chasm with the river at the bottom, the ride. She remembered coming into the house, some vague flashes of rooms, although in no particular order. She recalled that she had felt the effect of the wine, but that had just been a buzz. She hadn't had the spins or even felt dizzy. And then she brought back the secret bar in the wall and the cognac. Had she had too much of that? She couldn't remember.

Chelsea thought harder. She felt bad, frightened by the idea that she couldn't remember. The word *rape* floated to the surface of her mind. Had Dan Crane drugged her? She got up from the bed and looked down at her body, then stood in front of the full-length mirror. There were no marks or scratches. But would there be? This was terrible. She panicked. She wanted to run.

She whirled, looking for her clothes. There, on the chair. Her underwear was on top, and under it, her dress—not tossed carelessly, but laid over the back of the chair to keep it from being wrinkled. She sucked in a breath. That was the way she would have left her clothes. When she had undressed in front of a man before, she had found she liked to face away from him. It made her less self-conscious and aware that he would be staring at her, and she knew that her back and bottom were pretty. She came closer and noticed the shoes. She would have stepped out of them while she was facing away from the man and left them exactly that way, with the toes pointed toward the chair. If a man had taken them off, he would have left them with the toes pointed outward, away from the chair. She looked at the clothes again. No matter who had taken them off her, the dress would have been first, and the underwear last, on top. But if he had put her dress there, would he have done it exactly the way she did? It seemed impossible. She must have done it herself. She must have done this, decided on her own to have sex with Daniel Crane.

Where was he? She realized that in the past five seconds she had begun to smell coffee. She picked up her clothes and hurried into the bathroom, shut the door, and locked it.

She turned on the shower and let it run. The water was already hot. Of course he would have one of those water heater systems that circulated hot water all the time. She stepped into the stream, letting the hot water wash over her. She scrubbed herself hard, soaping up and rinsing the lather off over and over, trying to feel clean but not feeling satisfied. She kept thinking that the water would wake her up and clear her mind, but she didn't feel any effect.

She still didn't remember anything that had gone on during the second half of her tour of the house. She must have been so completely drunk that she'd paid no attention to anything that he had said, and her eyes must have been closing half the time and unfocused the rest, so her subconscious mind had simply not bothered to retain the fragmentary information. How horrible and humiliating to have been so drunk. But if she had been so drunk, why had he had sex with her? Couldn't he tell? Had she even been conscious?

She had to think about this carefully. Accusing somebody of a crime as serious as rape was a big deal. The evidence she had found so far was that she didn't remember being with him, but that didn't mean rape. She hadn't been handled roughly, or there would be marks on her, and there weren't any. Her clothes had been laid out the way she would have left them.

Chelsea worked hard, and reconstructed what she could of the sequence of her thoughts from last night. She had been thinking about Dan, and his house, and his tastes, and how much better he had looked in his own place. She had been gazing at him through wine goggles. How did she get in his bed? She was pretty sure she must have invited herself. Maybe when they visited this bedroom suite on the grand tour.

She turned off the water in the shower and took one of the oversized thick, soft towels from the rack. As she dried herself, she looked around. The master bathroom was a bit larger than her bedroom at the house where she'd lived with Nick, and it was covered floor to ceiling in beautiful marble, with two sinks that looked like ceramic bowls. The shower was big enough for six people, with four dish-size shower heads on the ceiling and others spraying from the walls. Everything matched and looked as though it had been hand polished a moment ago.

Dan had a lot of money, and he was generous with it, and good at thinking of tasteful ways of spending it. She searched further in her memory. Had she gone to bed with him because she was attracted to his money? No, she decided. What might have happened was that he was a trusted friend, she was grateful for the good time he had given her, and the wine had swept away her restraint and inhibitions. She had observed that when a person was drunk he did what he'd wanted to do all along. But he went further than he would at other times, didn't wait, or consider, or speak quietly, or think about consequences.

With that word a horrible thought came to her, but she pushed it away. She had not been careful last night, but she definitely wasn't pregnant. She had not made any plans to ever have sex with anyone after Nick had died, but she had not stopped taking her pills. She hadn't made any changes to any part of her life, because change would have taken energy and thought, and she'd been too busy grieving.

She supposed that wasn't entirely true. Without knowing it, she must have been thinking about Dan Crane. She used Dan's hair dryer and the brush from her purse to dry and brush her hair, dressed in the clothes from last night, and looked in the mirror. The damage was done. She had thrown herself at Dan Crane. Now she would have to carry herself as well as she could and see if there was anything in that relationship to salvage, or if she had to break it off and refuse to see him ever again. She put on her makeup, taking special care to get it exactly right.

She opened the bathroom door and stepped into the bedroom. On the table by the window were a tray with a coffee pitcher and a small glass of orange juice, and a couple of small pastries on a plate. But beside them, dwarfing the tray, was a glass vase with a dozen long-stemmed yellow roses. How had he gone to a florist already? She looked around for a clock, but there was none, so she took her cell phone out of her purse. Ten fifteen. Of course. He hadn't gone, he had simply made a phone call and they'd been delivered. She saw there was a little envelope. She plucked it out of the flowers, opened it, her chest feeling hollow with dread, and read the card.

"Good morning, Chelsea. I hope you'll join me for breakfast at Semel's." Not so bad. No gushing, and no humiliating references to the sex. She put the note in her purse and prepared for the next challenge. She would have to see him and talk to him. She stepped out of the bedroom.

He was sitting on the bench in the Japanese garden drinking coffee and reading the newspaper. There was Dan Crane under glass, still unaware of her watching. He was hers to study, like a rare specimen sitting motionless in a terrarium. He looked slim but strong, and the way the sunlight filtered through the overhead bough of a pine tree and fell on his head and shoulders made him seem contemplative, sensitive.

She decided that when the time came, she would have to go out with him again. Next time she would avoid alcohol and keep her eyes wide open. After that she would figure out what she had done to herself—something bad, or something good. She walked to the sliding glass door and opened it.

16

It was late—nearly morning—and Jane lay in a clump of maple saplings near the back of the large plot of weedy land around the small old farmhouse near Avon. The only sounds were the breezes rustling the leaves of the tall maples that shaded her thicket. She had spent the night making visits to some places she'd thought might help her understand Jimmy Sanders's problem.

When she left Slawicky's, she had driven to the bar in Akron where Jimmy and Nick Bauermeister had fought. She had stayed outside to watch the door and the parking lot for a couple of hours to get a sense of what sort of place it was and what its patrons were like. Both the bar and its customers had seemed pretty ordinary. It was just a typical Western New York place that drew a steady stream of locals who drank beer and sat around talking. There was no band, no pickup scene, no bouncers, nobody hanging around the lot outside. When it was very late she had driven to this small farmhouse, the address of the victim and the scene of his death.

When Jane arrived, she had parked in the lot of a closed gas station and walked the rest of the way. The house was set far back from the road in the middle of an expanse that had once been a farmer's field, so it would have been risky to bring a car. Instead she moved across the field in her black clothes, hip-deep in brush and weeds, no more visible than a shadow, and then stopped at the back of the house. She'd looked in the windows, one by one, and found that nobody was inside. Nick Bauermeister's girlfriend, Chelsea Schnell, had left a few dim lights burning—a table lamp in the bedroom beside her undisturbed bed, another in the living room, and a small fluorescent over the stove in the kitchen.

The house was still fully furnished, so Chelsea hadn't moved out yet. Jane went around to the front of the house and stepped up on the porch to examine the windows. It didn't take long to find the one the bullet had passed through into Nick Bauermeister. The outer frame of it had been spackled to fill nail holes where a piece of plywood must have been nailed to cover the window until it had been replaced. She looked closer and saw the glazing compound around the edges of the big pane was fresh and white. She could see that the wall of the living room across from her looked different, probably a new coat of paint that didn't quite match the color of the rest, so that must have been the place where the bullet and blood spatter had ended up.

Jane left the porch and went around the house looking for the best way in. At the side was an old-fashioned cellar entrance, a concrete frame covered by a pair of wooden doors at a thirty-degree angle from the house to the ground. There were a hasp and padlock to keep it closed, but Jane took out her pocketknife and removed the screws holding the hasp. She went down the steps, avoiding a rattrap on the fourth step, then closed the doors and waited for her eyes to adjust to seeing in the moonlight that the small cobwebbed cellar windows admitted. Then Jane carefully headed for the wooden steps leading upstairs into the kitchen, watching her feet to keep from stepping on anything in the near darkness.

The kitchen was small and neat, without much space for clutter or adornment. She opened the refrigerator door to verify that the girlfriend was still living here, and saw women's food—yogurt, carrot sticks, celery sticks, a lot of vegetables in one drawer, boxes of vegetarian burgers and breakfast sausages in another, and premade diet meals in the freezer.

Jane moved through the house, not looking for anything, but looking at everything. The newspapers had said the girl was twenty-three, but none had carried a picture of her. In the bedroom Jane found framed photographs on the low woman's dresser. One was a blond, blue-eyed girl about the right age with a woman about forty-five to fifty who resembled her. Jane studied the photograph, then moved to the next one.

This time the girl was with a young man. He was more than a foot taller than she was, and broad shouldered with a small head. The word that came into Jane's mind was "lout." He was beefy, but the arm muscles showing were not defined. He had a quarter inch of blond hair, small, pale close-set eyes, and a smile that was crooked, as though the smile was about to become a smirk. The eyes had an opaque quality that Jane had seen in people who weren't very bright but prided themselves on their cunning.

Nicholas Bauermeister had not been a very attractive man, but Jane was aware that there were certain young women who found his type very male, and therefore, appealing. Jane had never been one of them, but so far there was no indication that Bauermeister had ever done anything that would have made his murder deserved or even likely.

Jane looked in the closet at Chelsea's clothes. She was a size four. She didn't have bad taste, but the clothes were inexpensive, mostly from discount chains. She had a collection of sneakers and flip-flops, all well-worn, and three pairs of high heels that she hadn't worn much, and some bad-weather boots. There was another bedroom that had an old, swaybacked bed with a clean cover, and a closet full of male clothes. Nick's clothes were big—size thirteen boots and sneakers, double-X shirts, and jeans with a thirty-five-inch inseam. He had a few pairs of cargo shorts, but no sport coats or dress shoes.

Jane worked as efficiently as she could, touching little, moving nothing, and searching a whole room before going on to the next. She found that Chelsea kept a shoebox filled with the upper parts of bills she had paid and other business mail. One piece was a set of bank statements dated two weeks ago. Since banks predated everything, these had probably just arrived. Chelsea had just under two thousand dollars in her checking account, and a bit under five thousand in a savings account. Nick had about nine thousand in checking, and no savings.

In a drawer near the kitchen door Jane found a flashlight. She turned it on and went down the steps to the basement. It took only a few minutes of searching to find the first surprise, a large battered toolbox under a workbench. She opened it and found a black cloth bag with handles like a satchel. Inside were an eighteen-inch crowbar, a center hole punch, a pair of wire cutters, long-handled bolt cutters, a headband with a light on it, a small bright LED flashlight, a couple of hacksaw blades with tape wrapped around one end to form a handle, and a piece of sheet metal cut with a hook on the end to make a slim-jim for opening a car door lock. The last object in the box was a small white cloth bag. Jane touched it and recognized the feel. She opened it and found a pair of thin leather gloves, a pullover ski mask, and a Glock 19 pistol. Jane ejected the magazine, found it was loaded, and pushed it back in.

Nicholas Bauermeister had been a thief.

Jane returned the objects to the cloth bag, and then the toolbox, and put the box back under the bench. How had the police missed Bauermeister's burglary kit? They had come to the house in response to Chelsea's call that he had been murdered, and that made the whole house a crime scene, not just the living room and the field in front of the house. It was true that they hadn't come to investigate the victim, but when police had control of a victim's house they usually tried to figure out who he had been and what could have brought him the kind of enemies who shot people to death. Jane supposed that the local police in this peaceful rural area had very little experience with homicides.

Jane searched harder now, examining every part of the basement for anything else that might be hidden. She checked the oil furnace, then tugged on the aluminum air ducts to see if one made a suspicious rattle or had a joint that came apart easily. That was one of her favorite hiding places in the old house where she had grown up. Nothing.

She used the flashlight to take a panoramic view of the basement. There were the standard sewer pipes, a water heater and copper pipes, the work bench, the washer and dryer, a couple of stationary tubs. There was an old refrigerator in the corner. She opened it, found about a case of Molson's Golden, and a few diet colas. She lifted each to be sure none was heavier or lighter than the others. She opened the freezer, but found it empty.

In another corner of the basement were a snow blower and a double stack of twenty-five pound bags of rock salt. Nick Bauermeister had undoubtedly used the salt to melt ice on the steps and the blower to clear the long driveway in the winter. As she moved the flashlight beam again she noticed something and brought it back. The top two bags and the bottom two bags were identical, but the two in the middle seemed thinner.

She came closer, removed the top two bags, and examined the middle pair. As soon as she touched the first bag she knew she had something. The seam of the bag facing the wall was just folded over. The two bags had been opened from the bottom. She opened the first bag and felt inside, then pulled out a clear plastic Ziploc bag. Inside were a ring with a diamond of at least three carats, five pairs of stud earrings with colored stones, and a woman's Cartier tank watch with a sapphire on the stem. The next bag had three men's watches—two Rolexes and a Tag Heuer. There were a few other bags that held only one or two items—a spectacular cocktail ring, a necklace, or a pin. She laid them out and took pictures with her phone's camera, and then put them back in the salt bag. The next salt bag had some odd things—about twenty gold coins in the small cardboard coin holders with plastic windows that collectors used, and a fancy pocketknife with a handle of inlaid opal, onyx, and coral. There was a set of heavy gold cuff links and tie tack with blue stones she guessed were lapis lazuli. She photographed these too and returned them to the salt bag.

She tried to interpret what she had just found. What it looked like to her was not the proceeds of one burglary. The trove seemed to be small, choice items from a number of burglaries. But a professional burglar wouldn't hold on to a cache of distinctive traceable jewelry for very long. If the pieces were insured, then the insurance company would have pictures. A pro would want to move the jewels quickly, usually to a fence who would break them up, reset them, and melt the original settings down. The fence would at least sell them in another part of the country. Burglars didn't want to build up collections of stolen jewelry. What they wanted was cash.

Bauermeister's hoard brought to mind one of the hazards of holding on to loot. It made the burglar a potential robbery victim. But the one who had killed Bauermeister hadn't come after the jewels. He had simply shot him and left without ever coming inside. Maybe Bauermeister had been working with a partner, or even a crew, and had gotten into the habit of pocketing an especially valuable item now and again. That might make a colleague kill him. It was true that nobody had come for these hidden jewels, but if there were a colleague Bauermeister had cheated, maybe he didn't know about these items. Maybe he had caught Bauermeister stealing something else.

Theories kept occurring to Jane as she searched the basement, but she couldn't find evidence to make her settle on one theory, and she found nothing else. It was very late, and she had been in the house too long. She went up the steps to the kitchen and returned the flashlight to its drawer, then went through the darkened basement to the cellar door, climbed out, and closed the doors. She put the hasp and padlock back, then reinserted the screws and tightened them with her pocketknife.

She stepped to the garage and opened the door. There were two vehicles inside, a small old Mazda and a newer black Dodge pickup. Jane did a quick search of the Mazda and found little except the sorts of things Chelsea might be expected to have left—gum, hairbrush, bottled water, hand lotion, sunscreen, pens, receipts, a yoga mat. Chelsea was apparently a woman who used her car as a big purse. There was nothing in it to tell Jane anything about Nick Bauermeister.

The pickup was next. The flatbed was empty; the glove compartment held only the manual, registration, insurance receipt, and a pocketknife. On the floor was a bar for locking the steering wheel that had its key in it. She popped the hood and searched for hiding places, looked beneath the truck and under the seats, but found nothing.

She searched the garage, but found nothing else that was of interest. There could be more, she thought. But then she realized where it might be, if there was anything. Nick Bau-ermeister had worked at a storage facility.

Jane left the garage, closed the door, and made her way across the dark field and along the road to the gas station to retrieve her car. She got in and drove along Telephone Road, then stopped after a mile, checked her printed sheets to be sure she had remembered the address correctly, and went on.

When she reached Box Farm Personal Storage it was after 4:00 AM. As she drove by she studied the complex. A seven-foot chain link fence with four strands of barbed wire strung along the top enclosed it. Inside were four long, low buildings, each consisting of nothing but a double row of storage bays, one after another. There was also a two-story building, which seemed to have smaller storage bays on the ground floor and an office with big windows on the second floor. In one of them she could see a man sitting at a desk. She caught a glimpse of a row of television monitors on the wall above him. That meant there were security cameras mounted on the eaves of the buildings or on the light poles above the parking lot.

She passed without stopping. When she reached the out-skirts of the town of Akron she found an empty carport in a large apartment complex, parked her car inside, and went to sleep.

At six the sun woke her, and she drove to the business section, where she found a diner that seemed to have the right number of customers. She took a booth near the back, sat where she could face the rear wall, and ate breakfast while she thought about what she had seen during the night. At seven she drove back past Chelsea Schnell's small farm-house. As Jane drove past she saw that the same lights were on in the windows, and nothing else had changed, so she drove another half mile and parked her car off the road. She walked back and stationed herself in a thicket of saplings beneath the tall maples at the rear of the field behind the house.

The car that brought Chelsea Schnell home at noon was a new Range Rover. As it turned off the highway onto the long gravel drive to the house, Jane studied what she could see of the driver. He was a man in his early forties. He drove up to the front porch and got out to let Chelsea out of the passenger side. She was wearing a fancy black dress and high heels that seemed wrong for this time of day. She took a set of keys from her purse and unlocked the door, and the man followed her in.

Jane moved in closer until she could read the license plate, then moved in close enough to take a picture with her phone. She put it away, and then moved to the side of the house, where she couldn't be as easily seen from the street, and then to the back. As she ducked to cross under one of the rear windows, she heard voices. She stopped to keep from making noise or having one of them look out the window and see her. The voices stopped, and then she heard something else. There was a squeaky sound, slow at first, and then a bit louder. Could it be?

She moved her body close to the wall, slowly raised herself, put one eye to the corner of the window then away almost instantly, and ducked down. She had seen enough to know that it was time to go. Neither of the people inside the bedroom would be looking out the window very soon, because they were on the bed having sex.

Jane made her way to the back, where there were trees and bushes to hide her. She walked a course parallel to the road, and didn't alter it until she came to her car. As she left, she looked at her watch. It was half past noon.

Jane drove to Interstate 390, took it north to the Rochester Inner Loop and got off on Main, then drove to her hotel and parked in the underground garage. She put the lanyard that held her badge for the medical records management convention around her neck, carried her folder under her arm, and took the elevator upstairs to the lobby, where there were dozens of other men and women with convention badges coming in or out of the hotel restaurants and the business center. She took a second elevator to her floor, went into her room, hung the PLEASE DO NOT DISTURB sign on the door latch, closed the door, and bolted it.

It was strange to be in this room. All of this time she had been within seventy miles of her home and her husband, but she was in hiding. She couldn't do the things she needed to and then go home and sleep in her own bed. She couldn't risk leading someone back to the McKinnon house. Those things had all been clear from the beginning. But what bothered her at that moment was that she couldn't be there because Carey would ask her questions, and she would have to lie to him, have to avoid letting him see her come and go, and argue with him about what she was doing. If she argued this time she couldn't say that what she'd been doing was legal, or that it was safe, or that it was nearly over. It was none of those things.

She took off her clothes, showered, and then went to bed. She slept from two o'clock until nine in the evening, and got up still thinking about what she had learned during the night and morning. She wondered how Jimmy was doing, and whether he was still safely hidden. She knew she had to trust him, to assume that he had the sense to follow her instructions long enough for her to find out what was going on.

At ten she was dressed in a black shirt and black jeans and ready to go out in the dark again. She went down to the garage, retrieved her car, and drove to the Tonawanda Reservation. She pulled over to the side of the road near Ellen Dickerson's house and walked along the shoulder. She listened to the sound of her feet crunching the first sycamore leaves to fall to the ground. It was still summer, but the sycamores always seemed to drop a few green leaves bigger than the spread of a big man's hand about now, reminders that summer was not permanent, and someday winter would come back. Jane felt an increasing sense of reluctance and trepidation at dropping in like this at the home of the clan mother of the Wolf clan. What she was doing felt presumptuous.

She stepped up the four steps to the wooden porch and the front door opened. Ellen Dickerson was standing in the doorway wearing blue jeans and a loose shirt with the light behind her and her face in shadow. "Hello, Jane." There was no surprise in her voice, no real emotion except patience.

Seeing her there already waiting made Jane pause for a second before she came forward the rest of the way. Maybe it had been a coincidence. Maybe Ellen had seen the light from Jane's car and wondered who had come, or heard her walking on the crisp dry leaves. Maybe she had heard her feet on the porch and already been near the door. "Hello, Ellen," she said. "I'm sorry to come without calling."

"We've been waiting." She came out onto the porch and closed her front door behind her, leaving them both in shadow. She stood by the railing and stared up the road into the darkness beyond Jane's car, then in the other direction. When she was satisfied, she said, "Come in. We'll talk."

They went inside, and Jane followed her through the small, neat living room into the kitchen. Ellen was as tall as Jane and a bit broader, with a face that had obviously been striking and beautiful when it was young, and had aged without softening. Her face had a way of making anyone in her presence try to read what she was feeling and fail. Her expression was calm, dignified, attentive, motherly at the same time—but not the doting sort of mother, the stern sort. Her piercing black eyes had a clarity and intensity that must have made some people want to look away, but made Jane want to look into them more deeply.

Ellen said, "Things aren't going as well as you'd like."

"No," said Jane. "I still haven't been able to do what you asked."

"Tell me what you can."

Jane said carefully, "Jimmy is living in a small town in another state. He has what he needs to live comfortably for a while."

"Thank you, Jane. That's what we'd hoped you would do."

"But it isn't what you asked. It's only a way of delaying what's going to happen, not preventing it. Jimmy is still in danger."

"From whom?"

"That's where the problem begins," Jane said. "There are so many people involved in this that I'm not sure yet what really happened."

"We know about the men who are waiting for Jimmy in jail."

"Yes," Jane said. "They could be some of Nick Bauermeister's friends or relatives. But Jimmy and I were being hunted and chased in Cleveland by men who looked and acted like something else. One of them fired a gun into the side of our car. The man who lied about selling Jimmy the murder weapon has got at least a hundred thousand dollars' worth of new toys—TV, car, and Jet Ski, at least." Jane went on with her recitation. She had seen the girl the newspapers referred to as the murder victim's fiancée having sex with an older man in the bed she must have shared with the victim. And the murdered man had been a burglar, had probably been stealing from his partners, and hidden the loot he'd kept from them in his basement. "These are all people who benefited from the death of Nick Bauermeister or had motives not to want him around."

Ellen Dickerson nodded slowly. "Greed, jealousy, revenge. Sometimes people are a disappointing bunch."

"Yes," said Jane.

"We need to clear our minds." Ellen stood and went to a kitchen cabinet, opened the door, and took down a big coffee can. "Come on out in the back."

She took Jane out onto the wooden deck in back of the house, which overlooked a path into the woods. She opened the can and poured a pile of tobacco onto a small rustic table that had been covered with a piece of sheet metal. Jane recognized it as *oyenkwa:onwe*, "the real tobacco," which was greenish and dried to almost a powder. It didn't look much like the tobacco sold in stores.

Ellen whispered for about thirty seconds. Jane could tell that they were Seneca words, but did not listen to them because she was aware that they were not addressed to her. Ellen knew things that were the property of secret societies, so Jane kept her distance and didn't try to hear any of it. Ellen lit the tobacco with a match, and the smoke began to rise straight up in the windless air. She said in Seneca loud enough for Jane to hear, "We burn oyenkwa:onwe to give thanks for keeping both of our children safe and out of the hands of enemies. We ask for clear minds to help us find a way through this trouble."

It was simple and clear and it reminded Jane of things she had always loved. Senecas weren't in the habit of praying to ask for gifts. They gave thanks. When they did make a request, it was almost always to be better—more worthy, more able, braver, wiser. She silently added the strength of her mind to the prayer, willing the fire to send the stream of tobacco smoke upward to the sky.

After a few minutes the tobacco burned out and Jane followed Ellen to the door. She felt almost reluctant to leave the quiet, private space, the platform surrounded by tall, thick-trunked trees with the patch of deep, starlit sky above. It occurred to Jane that there never seemed to be anywhere in Western New York where the sky was as full of stars as over the reservation. She saw Ellen watching her.

Ellen said, "It was nice of you to come and fill us in."

"It may be a while before I can do it again."

"We'll understand."

Jane said, "I think I'm going to have to get a lawyer involved now. Jimmy won't ever be safe until the law is satisfied."

Ellen said, "The clan mothers aren't opposed to lawyers. Ely Parker learned to be a lawyer to help save the reservation. He and Mr. Martindale are two of the reasons that there is a reservation."

Jane nodded. The Mr. Martindale Ellen was talking about was the attorney who had engineered the clan mothers' twenty-five-year strategy of delaying tactics and lawsuits that had secured the reservation title in the 1850s. And the Tonawanda Seneca chief Ely S. Parker was also the Union general who wrote the terms of the Confederate surrender at Appomattox in 1865. A few generations were an eyeblink to the clan mothers. "This lawyer is a friend of mine."

"We trust your judgment."

"The lawyer is—"

"We trust your judgment." Her voice was still soft, still patient.

"Thanks. I'd better be going," Jane said.

Ellen enveloped her in a hug that reminded her of the hugs she had received as a child, a strong and protective embrace that seemed to cover her entirely for a moment. Ellen released her, reached into the pocket of her jeans, and pulled out two soft deer-leather pouches. "Take this tobacco. One is for Jimmy, and the other for you. It wouldn't hurt to toss a little on the road before you go."

"Thank you," said Jane. She took them, went out the door and into the night. Somehow the night felt a little different from the way it had before. Now the darkness was a covering, a thing that had protected her in the past, and was protecting her again. She reached Ray Snow's Volkswagen Passat and remembered what Ellen had said. She sprinkled a pinch on each of the car's tires, and then tossed another into the air above the road in front of the Passat. "It's me," she said. "Onyo:ah. You know what I'm trying to do. Thanks for letting Jimmy and me get this far alive."

17

The next morning Jane drove to a shopping mall in Batavia and parked near the street far from the stores, where mall security cameras might pick her up. She dialed the cell phone number of her old college friend Allison.

"Hello?" Jane could hear the familiar melodious voice, almost see the blond hair and the long, graceful neck. Allison didn't look or sound like a trial lawyer.

"Hi, Allison. It's me."

"I didn't expect to hear your voice. I see you have another new number."

"Nearly every week."

"I suppose that makes sense. If this is your phone call to your attorney, tell me where they're holding you. They don't have to let these calls go on and—"

"It's not," Jane interrupted. "I'm not the one in trouble."

"That's a relief," said Allison. "Who is?"

"A guy I grew up with. He's an Indian like me."

"If he got caught, he's not much like you. What's his name?"

"James Sanders. Goes by Jimmy. About two months ago a drunk took a swing at him in a bar in Akron, New York. He dropped the drunk and went home. The police got a complaint from the drunk, whose name was Nick Bauermeister, and arrested Jimmy. No big deal, until about a month later, when Bauermeister was murdered. He was shot with a rifle through the front window of his house."

"What's the evidence against your friend?"

"A man came forward to tell the police he'd had a garage sale and sold Jimmy a rifle of the right caliber and some ammo before the murder."

"A selfless act, since he was admitting to an illegal transaction. He sold it to Jimmy, not just to some guy who looked a bit like him?"

"He supposedly picked Jimmy's picture out of a stack and said he was the one. I went to see who this witness was last night and noticed he has a brand-new Porsche, a new Jet Ski, and a giant new television set. His house is a teardown, but he seems to have had a shot of money recently."

"What's the victim's name again?"

"Nick Bauermeister. I guess that's probably Nicholas."

"Got it. And where are they holding your friend Jimmy?"

"They're not. They're hunting for him."

"Here we go again. You're hiding him. I'll need to talk to him before he turns himself in."

"I'll arrange that when I can. Should I keep using this number?"

"Yes. Can't you bring him to see me, or take me to him?"

"I'm sorry, Allison. The problem is that he can't turn himself in just yet. There are people trying to kill him. I don't know who they are yet, but I've actually seen some of them. And I have reliable information that there are also some who have gotten themselves sent to jail to wait for him."

Allison sighed. "I knew this couldn't be a simple case of getting a false charge dismissed."

"No," Jane said. "And this time it's not me just asking for a quick favor. It's a real case, and I expect to pay your exorbitant fees, including the billable time for this call. If I know you, it'll be the best money I ever spent."

"We'll talk money later," said Allison.

"As long as you don't try to weasel out of your paycheck when the time comes."

"Can I get Karen Alvarez involved in this? She's great on murder."

"I'd love to have her. She knows how to keep a secret."

"That and obfuscate. It's what we do all day. Let me start nosing around this case without letting anybody know I've been retained and see what I can find out, and what ideas Karen has. Did you say the murder was in Akron? Is that Monroe County?"

"The murder was in Avon. That's in Erie County."

"Okay. Anything else?"

"Thanks, Allison. And give my regards to Karen."

"I'm about to go down to her office now. Go do whatever it is you need to do. If anything goes wrong, call me and I'll be there as soon as I can to bail you out."

"What could go wrong?"

"Just make sure he has my number and knows enough to tell the police he won't talk until I get there."

"I will. And thanks again."

"Don't mention it. And I really mean don't. Bye."

Jane thought about Allison. She had been one of Jane's friends at Cornell nearly twenty years ago. She was beautiful in the conventional ways—very blond, very white complexion, with blue eyes. Those qualities had made it easy to dismiss her at first. But she had also been quick-witted, with a ferocious critical intelligence that made her one of Jane's favorites. She had been one of the inner circle at the party on the night when Jane realized that a male friend of theirs who was about to go to prison had another option.

Years later, Allison had become a lawyer in New York City, and she had called Jane. She said, "Remember the night when you helped John?"

"Yes," Jane said.

"I have a client who's in the same position. He's innocent. He's out on bail during the trial. Sometime tomorrow when the jury comes in, he's going to jail, and I think this judge will give him a life sentence. Do you think you can still do what you did that time?"

"Are you sure that's what he needs?" Jane asked.

"He needs to be left alone, and given a chance to live a life. That's not what's going to happen if he's still here when the verdict comes in."

"I'll be there tonight," Jane said.

"What time?" Allison said. "I'll meet your plane."

"Don't," said Jane. "Be somewhere far from the airport, and be sure there are lots of other people who will remember they were with you. Just give me his address and phone number."

Allison's client had been gone for fifteen years now. Jane heard from him by mail about once a year, but he'd never tried to get in touch with Allison again. There was a chance that even now some law enforcement agency might be waiting for him to make that mistake. Their friend John, the first one Jane had taken out, had been gone for nearly twenty.

Karen Alvarez was a partner in Allison's firm. A year ago when Jane had needed to pretend to be a lawyer in order to sneak James Shelby out of the Clara Shortridge Foltz criminal courthouse in Los Angeles, Karen Alvarez had let her use her identity. Both women were tall and thin, with long black hair and olive skin, and Jane had impersonated her easily. Jane had succeeded in getting Shelby out and into a car, but Jane had not made it far from the courthouse. The memory of it made Jane's thigh hurt again where the bullet had passed near the bone.

Jane took out the pages she had copied in the business center, and took another look. This time what caught her eye was the name of the man who owned Box Farm Personal Storage—Daniel Crane. She took out her phone, went to Google, and typed in the name with her thumb. She found one in Williamsville, New York, then used her corporation's subscription service to run a quick background check on him. It took her several minutes of staring at a little wheel spinning at the top of her phone's screen before things began to appear. She read the new information, turned off the phone, plugged it into the car's electrical outlet to recharge, and drove.

The house was technically in Williamsville, but the distinctions were a bit vague. Williamsville was surrounded by Amherst, and that was where she and Carey lived, but their house was not near his. She found the proper number on the rural mailbox, drove on, and parked about a quarter mile farther down the road, then walked back.

When she returned to the address, she avoided the curving cobbled driveway and took a shortcut through the brush and trees that hid the house from the road. When she reached the edge of the stand of trees she saw that the garage beside the house was open. One of the cars inside was a black Corvette. The other was a Range Rover.

Jane moved closer and compared the Range Rover's license plate with the picture on her cell phone. They were the same. Daniel Crane had to be the man she had seen at Chelsea Schnell's house. The man this girl had been sleeping with was her dead boyfriend's boss. Jane thought about the revelation without drawing any conclusion yet. People who weren't supposed to fall in love often did.

Jane walked around outside of the house, staying in the trees, away from the margin of light that spilled outward from the big windows. The house was big and modern, and everything she could see through the glass looked expensive. It made sense that a man who was collecting hundreds of dollars a month for each empty ten-by-fifteen-foot space of a large complex would have plenty of money. He didn't have to be much of a salesman—the real salesmen had been the ones who had sold the customers more stuff than they had room for.

Jane watched the house all night, and then returned the next day and the next. The neighborhood was an easy one for watching because the houses were so far apart. Down the road was a small, modern commercial district. She found that she could park at any of three medical and dental buildings where each doctor's staff would assume she had an appointment with another doctor, in the lots of two nearby golf courses where she could approach Crane's house without crossing a road, or at a mini-mall that contained a supermarket and a couple of restaurants.

She studied Crane's routines. Every morning, Crane drove off in the Range Rover around eight. Every afternoon around four he returned, showered and changed, and went to take Chelsea Schnell somewhere for dinner. One night he returned alone, and the others he brought her home with him. Chelsea Schnell was always dressed up in the evening, but beginning the second night she brought with her a small overnight bag and changed into jeans in the morning for the trip home. Her clothes made Jane think the girl might be attracted to the man rather than his money. The clothes, both the dress-up outfits and the casual ones, were items Jane had seen hanging in Chelsea Schnell's closet on her first visit. That meant Chelsea wasn't taking money from Daniel Crane and buying things for herself.

Crane's clothes were more extravagant, but he seemed to buy them on websites. In the three days Jane watched the house, she saw the UPS truck deliver four packages and leave them on his porch. She opened all of them, found they contained clothes he had ordered online, rewrapped them, and left them on the porch.

Each day a woman about fifty years old drove up at ten and went inside to clean the house, do laundry, and sometimes drive out to perform some light grocery shopping. She spent about half her time washing the huge windows, doing a couple each day until she had done them all, then starting the next ones, in a continuous rotation. Each day she raked the small Japanese garden in the courtyard. She was always gone before Crane came home at four. Jane timed her and chose the moment when she was busy with the windows on the back wall of the house to open her car door and read the registration in her glove compartment. The car's owners were Wilfred and Verna Machak.

Jane visited the inside of the house on the second and third mornings at eight after Crane had driven off. On those mornings Chelsea Schnell left with him, having stayed the night. Jane found little in the house that surprised her. She confirmed that the two had slept together by the state of the bed in the master bedroom, the only one that had been touched. She could see that they had been drinking, at least moderately, from the champagne flutes left in the bedroom one morning and cognac snifters the next. She noticed that although Chelsea Schnell had now slept in the house at least three times in a short period, she had not left any of her belongings anywhere in the house. It was possible that she was very well organized, or that she was being careful not to scare Crane off. It was also possible that Chelsea wasn't yet sure she really wanted Crane, and was trying to avoid having to gather toothbrushes and panties when she left for the last time.

On the fourth evening at sunset Jane drove to the reservation to visit Mattie Sanders, Jimmy's mother. Jane parked at the old cemetery by the council house and walked. It was a windless evening and Jane could hear the chirps of sparrows and the warbling of robins competing with the crickets as she walked. She was aware of the sounds her feet made as she went, and found herself treading carefully along the shoulder of the road to avoid frightening the animals into silence. She turned off the road onto a trail through the woods to the smaller road that led to Mattie's house, but stopped to watch the road through the trees and to study every building, every parked car. She was searching for the presence of strangers—anyone who might be watching the Sanders house or the approaches to it.

All the way to Mattie's house she watched and studied, and when she arrived she had still seen nothing. It was almost as disturbing as it would have been to see something. It would have been reassuring to see signs that the state police were watching Mattie, but if they had been, they weren't tonight. Someone must have been monitoring Mattie's telephone, or the false cops would have had no way to find her and Jimmy in Cleveland. As Jane walked, the birds went to their nests and night fell.

When Jane stepped onto the front porch and knocked, Mattie opened the front door a few inches. "Janie," she said. "Come on in."

Jane entered and Mattie closed the door and then hugged her. "I'm so pleased to see you're back," she said.

Mattie was being scrupulously patient, but Jane knew she must be going mad with worry. "He's fine," she whispered in Mattie's ear. Then she added, "Let's go out for a walk."

Mattie nodded and led her to the back door through the small, neat kitchen. She looked out for a few seconds, stepped out, locked the door, and headed into the woods. They moved along in silence for a few minutes, hearing only the crickets raising the volume now that it was fully dark. Jane remembered this path from her childhood, but it was the first time she'd been in this section of woods since the fall when she'd left for college. She stopped for a few seconds and listened, but heard no change in the frequency of the crickets. She said softly, "Jimmy is well and safe. I left him with new clothes, plenty of cash, and a reliable used car in a nice small town a long way from here. He knows what he has to do to stay hidden while I look into things here."

Mattie eyed her. "Ellen Dickerson told me you said he was okay a couple of days ago, but I didn't know how much confidence to put in that. Things could have changed."

"He would call me if they did."

"You're not going to say exactly where he is?"

Jane said, "I want you to be able to take a lie detector test and say you don't know. And the time may come when somebody asks you under oath."

Mattie smiled sadly, and her beautiful brown skin seemed to tighten. "And if I get tempted to go see my son, I can't lead anybody to him."

Jane frowned. "I'm sorry. But there are easy ways for anybody to track your car, or use the GPS on your cell phone, or half a dozen other things to track you. I can't even be sure I know all the ways, so I can't warn you about them."

"I found a little gadget stuck to the bottom of my gas tank with a magnet two days ago."

"What did you do with it?"

"I left it there," said Mattie. "If I threw it away, I figure they'll do something else next time that I don't know about. And I don't care if they track me to the market. If I want to sneak off, I'll get rid of it then."

"That's right," said Jane. "Maybe we should wait a few days until the battery gets weak and watch your car to see who comes to replace it. To tell you the truth, one of the reasons I came by was to see who was watching you these days."

They walked along for a few more paces, and then Jane took Mattie's hand and put a stack of bills into it. "Another reason was to give you this."

"What's the money for?"

"We needed to be sure you're provided for."

"I'm fine."

"It's important that I be able to tell Jimmy that I saw you and made sure. What he's doing isn't easy, and it helps if he's not trying to check on you himself."

"That phone call."

"Yes," said Jane. "He didn't know what a bad idea it was. I'm hoping he won't make a mistake like that again. Somebody was monitoring your phone, so they got his number and the cell tower where his signal was picked up and transmitted."

"The police?"

"I think they were something else. They shot at us, and police wouldn't do that at first sight." The two women walked for a time, and then Jane said, "We should probably get back to your house. My nights are kind of busy right now. It's when I can see people, but they can't see me."

"All right," said Mattie. "It was really sweet of you to check on me and let me know what's happening—that he's all right."

"I wish—" She stopped and stood perfectly still. "Hear it?"

Mattie was still too. "Cars."

"They sound like they're heading up your road."

"Police?"

"I don't think they'd come to ask questions at night without calling, and this sounds like two or three cars."

"Who, then?"

"I'm wondering if the people who have been trying to kill Jimmy got tired of waiting for him to come to them," Jane said. "Where's your car?"

"It's beside the house. Didn't you see it?"

"I came through the woods from the cemetery by the council house."

"The car's on the other side, up the driveway."

"You have the keys with you?"

Mattie held them up. "My house key is on the same ring."

"This is going to be tricky. Give them to me, and you take these." She handed Mattie her keys and took Mattie's. "Stay in the woods off the trail for a few minutes, until you hear the cars leaving. Then go through the woods to the council house cemetery. You'll find a blue VW Passat parked there. Take it. Drive to Rochester. There's a big Hyatt Hotel on East Main Street by the Convention Center. Drive into the underground garage, take a ticket from the machine, and park. I'll meet you there as soon as I can."

"But what if it's only the police?"

"If it is the police, I'll see them and come back here for you. If I don't come back right away, go. Do you have your cell phone with you?"

"No. It's in the kitchen."

"Good. Leave it."

Jane took a step off the path, but Mattie stopped her. "Are you sure you want to do this?"

"Yes," said Jane. "Positive. Listen for the cars, and I'll see you later in Rochester."

"See you."

Jane melted into the woods. She moved swiftly at first, gliding between the tall trees toward the house. When she reached a thicket of saplings growing beside a stand of oaks, she crouched in the thicket and watched.

There were three cars, all of them big and dark, two of them SUVs with tinted side windows. A black sedan stopped just ahead of the intersection of Mattie's road and Council House Road, where it could guard the crossroads without drawing much attention. The other two stopped at the Sanders house, one across the driveway, and the other in front of Mattie's front door.

The doors of the two vehicles opened and six men poured out, moving quickly onto the porch. All were wearing street clothes, and none displayed badges or identification. They didn't call out or knock, just kicked in Mattie's front door and stormed into the house, spreading immediately from room to room as they filled the building from bottom to top like a flood. The first man through each doorway had a pistol drawn.

Jane advanced to the rear of the house and then slipped around the corner to the garage side just before two men opened the back door and stepped onto the back porch. Jane dropped to her hands and knees to cross under the side windows and crawled to the front of Mattie's brown Toyota Camry. She stayed low to slide into the driver's seat with the keys already in her hand. She started the engine and slammed the door as she swung backward onto the front lawn.

The SUV in front of the driveway moved to block her in, but she drove across the lawn into the small garden Mattie kept, cutting through a row of squash and beans and onto the road.

The sound of her engine drew the attention of the men in the house, and she heard two shots, then one more, but didn't hear or feel anything hit the car. Jane accelerated toward the intersection where she could see the big black car waiting. The driver started his engine and turned his headlights on, throwing a glare into Jane's eyes as she approached.

Jane switched on her high beams as the other driver pulled his car away from the shoulder and tried to block the road. She kept speeding toward it, and she could see both men in the car duck down to prepare for the collision that was coming. She took that moment to veer to the left and off the road into a weedy field. As she bounced along she heard and felt the drag of the tall weeds against the undercarriage of the car, then accelerated up and over the shoulder onto the road again. She switched off her lights just as she heard two more shots.

Jane knew that on this dark road she would see the glow of headlights in the intersection ahead if a car were coming to the other road, and she saw nothing, so she went into the turn without hitting her brakes. She accelerated out of the turn to keep control, and pushed Mattie's Camry to higher speeds as she hurtled along in the dark. She had walked every one of these roads in childhood summers, so she drove them tonight by memory and feel and moonlight.

She knew the drivers of the two SUVs would have to wait for the six men in the house to pile into the vehicles before they attempted to pursue her. The lookout car's headlights were beginning to light up the intersection far behind her now, so she spun into the next right turn blind, then took the next left and turned her lights on. At last she had a chance to look at the dashboard, which had lit up too. Mattie's Camry had over a half tank of gas. Jane sent a silent thank-you to her. That would be enough.

At ninety miles an hour, Jane reached the Pembroke entrance to the New York State Thruway in a few minutes. She slowed, drove onto the westbound side, and stopped at the Pembroke rest stop. She coasted into the parking lot and parked between a tall pickup truck and a camper, got out, hurried to the back of the car, and went down on her side. She reached up under Mattie's car, pulled the small black box off the gas tank, and examined it. The black plastic part of the box said FASTTRACK TRANSPONDER in raised letters. Jane walked briskly toward the building, scanning the lot.

She selected a tour bus with Ontario plates at the side of the rest stop building, reloading a line of tourists, most of them elderly and all of them speaking German. She went to the left side of the bus away from the doors and stared into the bus's left side mirror. The driver wasn't in his seat.

It took less than a second to squat, attach the little black transponder to a clean spot under the bus's chassis so its magnet held it there, stand, and keep walking. She stepped into the building and stopped in the ladies' room. When she came outside, the bus had already moved down the entrance ramp. She could see it far ahead, diminishing into the distance, probably toward a hotel so the tourists could go to sleep and get up early to visit Niagara Falls.

Jane returned to Mattie's Camry, pulled out onto the thruway and took the exit at Depew, went on the cloverleaf over the thruway to the eastbound side, and drove toward Rochester. She took exit 46, I-390 to Rochester. All the time while she was driving she watched to be sure she had not been followed. She got off I-390 at the Greater Rochester International Airport, parked Mattie's Camry in the long-term lot, walked to the terminal, and took a cab to the Hyatt Hotel on Main Street in Rochester.

At the hotel Jane went to her room, retrieved her small suitcase, wiped everything for prints, and stopped at the front desk to check out. Then she walked across the lobby to the elevator, took it to the first level of the underground garage, and found the Volkswagen Passat with Mattie sitting behind the wheel looking uncomfortable. When Mattie saw Jane walking toward her she smiled, opened the door, and got out. "You'd better drive. I don't even know where we're going."

"Happy to," Jane said. She reached inside, popped the trunk open, put her suitcase inside, and then closed the trunk and sat behind the wheel. She backed out, drove to I-390, and turned south.

"They weren't police, huh?" Mattie said.

"No," said Jane. "I'm pretty sure they were men who wanted to kidnap you to force Jimmy to come back."

"Where are we going?"

"Hanover, New Hampshire."

"What's there?"

"Jimmy."

18

Jane drove along Route 20 to the east, going steadily
through small towns where the high school, town hall,
and public library were yards from each other, all of them
dark. There were long stretches of open farmland. She had
been this way dozens of times, and each part was familiar to
her, as were the many places where she could turn down a
barely marked cross street and disappear. Mattie was silent
for a time, and Jane concentrated on being sure that nobody was following. Then Mattie seemed to decide she had
waited long enough to talk.

"Where did you leave my car?"

"The long-term parking lot at the Rochester airport."
She reached into her pocket. "Here are your keys, while I'm
thinking about it." She placed them in Mattie's hand.

"Why the airport?"

"A few reasons," Jane said. "People fly out of an airport
and sometimes don't come back for a month or two, so your
car won't get towed before then. If the police find it, or the
men who were trying to kidnap you find it, they'll come to

the conclusion that you drove it there and left town. They'll waste valuable time finding out which flight you might have taken, and where it was going. The longer it takes for them to find the car, the more flights will have left Rochester. If they're persistent, they'll get lists of people on each of those flights, but they won't see your name. They'll try to figure out which names might be ones you could have used. You wouldn't pretend to be George, but you might have been Nancy or Maria. Or since you probably didn't plan this far in advance, they'll try to investigate people who flew standby. If they're imaginative, they'll think of all kinds of other things to look for. All of it will keep them occupied. It will give them false hopes that will only result in disappointment and frustration and fatigue."

"Goodness."

"The best, of course, would be if the men who were after you would decide to sit in the parking lot and wait for you to come back, while the police did the same thing. They could hardly help bumping heads, and I know which heads I'd bet on."

"You're really good at this, aren't you?"

"I hope so," said Jane. She'd said too much. She prepared herself for the next few questions, dreading the prospect of lying to Mattie Sanders.

"Would you mind if I drove for a while?" Mattie said. "This much inactivity begins to get to me after a while. It makes me anxious. You could even get some sleep."

"A good offer," said Jane. "I'll take it. Just stay on Route 20. It goes all the way to Kenmore Square in Boston."

"We're not going there, are we?"

"No. If you see Interstate Ninety-One north, take it. That should be in three hundred miles or so, and I'd better be up long before then."

Jane pulled off the highway onto the shoulder and they traded places. She lay back in the passenger seat while Mattie adjusted the seat and mirrors, then pulled out onto the road. Jane pretended to be asleep for a few minutes while she watched the speedometer and the road with one eye. When she was satisfied that Mattie was still a competent driver, real sleep overtook her.

She woke when it was still dark, but she could tell that it would be morning before long. The window beside her felt cold, and there was a fog that had gathered in the bottoms of the valleys and put rainbow auras around the streetlamps they passed. There were already a few delivery trucks out unloading supplies of various sorts, and lights in a few house windows. She stretched, rubbed her eyes, and said, "How are you doing, Mattie?"

"Fine. It's been a nice, easy trip with so little traffic."

"I'm feeling rested. I'm ready to take over when you feel like it."

"I'd like to stop for breakfast somewhere."

They stopped at a diner in the next town. There were a surprising number of customers, most of them men who wore jeans or work uniforms, and sat at the counter. Jane and Mattie sat in a booth and ordered fried eggs, hash browns, and toast, but ate mostly in silence because they didn't want to attract attention. After about twenty minutes a pair of police officers came in, a man and woman who were both about thirty years old and were hard to see as anything but a couple. Jane and Mattie finished their food, paid in cash, and went back to their car. This time Jane took the wheel.

They crossed the Hudson into Massachusetts in the morning sunshine and drove north up Interstate 93 into New Hampshire, and then switched to Interstate 89 just north of Manchester. The rolling mountains of New Hampshire made Jane think of huge sleeping prehistoric creatures, their big rounded bodies covered over the centuries of sleep with windblown leaves, then humus, then trees. The fog had burned off while Jane and Mattie were still in New York State, and now the sky was a fresh, robin's egg blue with small puffs of white cloud in rows like the letters of an unknown language. Every ten minutes Jane and Mattie seemed to cross a bridge over a dark river that ran out of the forest. There were several with signs that said, BRIDGE FREEZES BEFORE THE ROAD, a warning that this was a different sort of country in the winter, and soon there were signs in swampy places that said MOOSE CROSSING.

Every town had its eighteenth-century churches and cemeteries, and a few had outlying margins of malls and discount stores and fast-food outlets. But most of the route was forest, and from the road Jane could see deep into shady spaces between white pine, maple, white oak and hickory, beech and birch trees. They got off at exit 18, and drove into Hanover on Route 120 past the hospital, into the center of town, and found themselves on the Dartmouth campus. There was no clear separation between the town and the college, only the realization at some point that the buildings had gotten bigger and fancier. In the center was a vast expanse of grass leading to a long brick building with a white steeple.

When they reached the apartment house where Jimmy Sanders was staying Jane parked the car and knocked on the door. She saw no movement, only felt a vague impression that the curtain had been disturbed. The door opened and Jimmy was visible a few feet back from the open door, where he would not be seen from the street.

When Mattie stepped in, she and Jimmy stood in silence and hugged each other for a few seconds while Jane closed the door and slipped the bolt. Jimmy said, "What are you doing here, Mom?" Then he turned to Jane. "This can't be safe."

Mattie said, "Safer than home. A bunch of men came to get me."

"Came to get you?"

"Bad men. Jane thinks they've gotten tired of waiting for you to come home, so they decided to grab me and see if they could get you to come back."

Jimmy looked at Jane, his eyes troubled.

Jane said, "They were in three cars—one lookout car with two men to control the street, one SUV to block the driveway, and another SUV to take her away. Six men rushed the house with guns drawn. The only thing to do was get her out of there. I should have done it before. Your mother is the most obvious way to get to you."

"I can't believe this," said Jimmy. "Two months ago I had no enemies, and my mother was as safe as anybody could be, surrounded by a couple hundred families, nearly all relatives—brothers and sisters, practically."

Jane stepped to the refrigerator, opened it, and then closed it again. "You two can catch each other up on things," she said. "I'm going out to stock up on groceries. When I come back I'll make us some dinner and tell you what I've learned so far."

She saw Jimmy's keys on the kitchen counter, took them, and put the Passat's keys in their place, then went out the front door. She drove back out on Route 120, filled Jimmy's Chevrolet Malibu with gas, then stopped at the Co-op. She bought lots of fresh meat, fish, vegetables, and fruit, and then filled her cart the rest of the way with a hoard of canned and frozen food so Jimmy and Mattie would not have to go out for a while.

When she returned she could see that mother and son had been talking. As she and Mattie worked together to make a dinner of chicken and vegetables and corn soup, Mattie seemed to be studying her whenever she wasn't looking. Finally, while they were setting the table, Jane said, "So Jimmy told you about me."

"Yes," said Mattie. "Why didn't you? I can keep a secret."

"I don't have only one secret."

"I don't understand."

Jane said, "Over the years I've taken a lot of people out of lives that had gotten too dangerous. Who every one of those people used to be, who he is now, and where he lives, are all secrets. I may have made those secrets, but they don't belong to me. Because I know them, I have a responsibility to keep myself from getting discovered and caught." She held Mattie with her strange blue eyes. "Otherwise, there won't be any more."

"Any more what? People like Jimmy?"

She nodded. "If my own secret gets out, I'll be useless to those people—the ones yet to come, the ones who may already be trying to find the way to me. There will be people who are running for their lives and need a door out of the world. The door won't be there anymore."

Mattie said, "He told me the clan mothers knew. I'd cut my throat before I told anyone else."

"So would they," said Jane. "Let's hope nobody has to."

They served the food, sat at the table, and ate together. When they had finished they said, "Nia:wen," and Mattie and Jimmy stood to begin clearing the table.

"Sit," said Jane. "I've learned some things, and you should know them too."

They resumed their places, and Jane began to talk. She told them about Chelsea Schnell and the small house where Nick Bauermeister had been shot, about Bauermeister's burglary kit and his cache of jewelry inside the salt sacks. She told them about Chelsea's relationship with her dead boyfriend's boss, Daniel Crane. She told them about the witness who said he'd sold Jimmy the murder weapon and his sudden show of wealth. Finally she told them she had retained Allison the lawyer and her partner Karen Alvarez. When she had finished, she smiled. "Dah-ne-hoh." It was what Seneca storytellers said at the end of a story, and it meant "I have spoken."

Mattie and Jimmy looked at her, then at each other, and then at Jane again. "Isn't all that enough to get me off?" said Jimmy.

"Allison didn't say it was," Jane said. "And she's the expert. A lot of people whose cases had what any sensible person would call reasonable doubt are sitting in prisons."

"Well sure, but—"

"The victim was a burglar, but that doesn't mean it was okay to kill him. His girlfriend is having an affair with his boss. That doesn't prove that she or he wanted him dead, and certainly not that either of them killed him. If it came out, they would probably say they were comforting each other for their mutual loss. And it might be true. The witness who says he sold you the rifle has come up with money for new things, but nobody has demanded to know where he got it, and he seems to be a convincing liar. I wouldn't want to go to court with that. Do you?"

"I guess not," said Jimmy.

"Of course not," Mattie said to him.

Jane said quietly, "And we still don't know who these other people are who are so interested in getting rid of you. Until we know, I don't think you can turn yourself in."

Mattie said, "So what do we do now?"

Jane shrugged. "Jimmy has learned a lot about how to keep from being noticed. For the moment, the one who goes out and shops, or shows a face to the world, has to be you. And you shouldn't do it very often."

"Is that enough?" said Mattie. "Just sit here and hide?"

"For the moment. Keep to yourselves, live quietly, and let Jimmy stay out of sight most of the time. You've got gas in the car, a pantry full of food, and some money for when it runs out. Tomorrow I'm going to pay the rent that comes due next week, and the utility bills."

"Where are you going?"

"Back to where the murder happened," Jane said. "It's the only place I can find anything out." She got up and carried some dishes to the sink, and the others joined her. In a few minutes, they had loaded and started the dishwasher, and they could hear the water rushing into it. She reached into her pocket and pulled out one of the small leather pouches. "Ellen Dickerson sent you this." She handed Jimmy the pouch.

He looked inside, then poured a little tobacco out into his hand and looked at it, and then returned it to the pouch. "That was nice of her. Maybe we should burn some before you go."

"She gave me some too," Jane said. "I put a little on my tires before I left her house."

"You really did that?" said Jimmy.

Jane said, "It didn't hurt to remind myself that we have friends and relatives, and they're in this too."

"And maybe friends who aren't people?"

Jane shrugged. "I'll take the help."

The next morning when Mattie got up, she walked quietly and carefully from the spare room into the living room to keep from waking Jane. She looked at the couch and saw that the blanket was neatly folded and the pillow was on top of it. She looked at the spot where Jane had left the keys to the Passat. They were gone, replaced by the keys to the Chevrolet Malibu.

19

Jane reached Western New York in the dark. It had been a seven-hour drive, but she had stopped for meals and breaks, and then had taken time to sleep for two hours at a rest stop. The urgency she had been feeling since the night the ancient woman had come to her in her dream seemed to burn in her until she had worn herself out. Now she was feeling stronger.

There was a hotel on Niagara Falls Boulevard that she had driven past many times and felt curious about, so she checked in and got a room on the third floor. She ordered a late dinner from room service, showered, and changed into dark-colored clothes and running shoes.

Her mind kept returning to Walter Slawicky. When she had stared into his windows and watched him, he struck her as a person who had decayed along with the old house where he lived. He looked slovenly, even physically dirty. He had clearly been spending money lately, and that might mean he had done a service for someone. All she really knew was that he was a liar. He had not sold Jimmy Sanders a rifle and ammunition.

Jane decided to see what else she could learn about him. She drove east to his house in Caledonia, parked on the next street parallel to Iroquois Street, and walked up the sidewalk intending to turn at the corner toward his street. When she reached the cross street she saw a car she had seen before. It was parked on the right side, facing Slawicky's street, no more than a hundred and fifty feet from Slawicky's house, but far enough from the corner so it could not be seen from Slawicky's. As she came up on the parked car she peered in the side windows.

It was a plain-wrap police car, the one she had seen Sergeant Isaac Lloyd park the first time she'd been to Slawicky's. She could see the police radio under the dashboard, the Remington 870 shotgun upright in the rack, the police flashers on the shelf at the back window. If Isaac Lloyd was here, she was going to miss tonight's chance to find out more about the witness. She stopped and prepared to go back the way she'd come.

Then it occurred to her that leaving might be a mistake. This could be an opportunity to learn what the state police were doing. She crouched and put her ear to the car window to see if she could hear anything, but the police radio was turned off.

She walked to Iroquois Street, then trotted across it to Slawicky's next-door neighbor's house on the right. She kept going until she reached the side of the house, and then moved more slowly beside the clapboards to the back, went low, and leaned out enough to look across the backyard into Slawicky's.

Slawicky had made another new purchase. Parked on the lawn behind his garage was a motor home. It had the round-cornered silhouette of the newer RVs, but it was one of the small models that looked like a little bus. Jane ran her eyes along its contours, and then focused and stared. What her eyes had at first accepted as a deeper shadow began to move and assume a recognizable shape. It was a man on his hands and knees, crawling along the ground beside the vehicle, looking under it. As she watched, the man made it to the space just behind the front wheels, fiddled with something in his jacket pocket, and then reached under. He turned on a flashlight.

Jane stared at the cone-shaped area lit by the beam. What had aroused his curiosity was a spot underneath the parked motor home. It didn't look green like the rest of the lawn. It seemed to be a patch of bare earth about four feet on a side. It had some light brown substance sprinkled over it—mulch, maybe, with white specks of chemical fertilizer that were picked up by the beam of the flashlight.

As the flashlight played over the patch, its glow illuminated the bottom of the vehicle, the grass, and the face of Sergeant Isaac Lloyd. Then the light went off, and Jane pulled her head back. Ike would get up now and move to something else. She didn't dare put her head out again for fear of being seen, but she listened hard, ready to run if she heard him coming in her direction.

She heard nothing at first. It worried her because she knew he was good at moving quietly.

When she heard footsteps they were louder than they should have been, and they seemed to be coming from the wrong spot. Her ears placed them at the far side of Slawicky's yard, by the hedge. They sped up, breaking into a run—two or three men at once. She heard a harsh, popping sound, then two more. Somebody was firing a gun with a silencer.

She looked out from behind the neighbor's house and saw three men firing at Ike Lloyd. She saw Lloyd sheltering at the back of the motor home, and saw him reach into his jacket for a gun. He aimed, then fired at one of his assailants, but missed. The shooter made it to the house while the others spread out. The pop of the next silenced pistol came from a different angle, and Lloyd spun and went down. He was hit. He rose to a sitting position and clutched his thigh with his left hand, but he leaned close to the big vehicle and raised his gun arm again.

Jane had no weapon, nothing she could use to help him. She pivoted and sprinted along the side of the neighbor's house and across Iroquois Street. In a few more seconds she was beside the plain black police car. She took out her pocketknife without opening it, gripped the handle with the rounded brass end protruding below her fist, and hammered the side window. It shattered, throwing little glittering cubes of broken glass onto the driver's seat. She grasped the inner door handle, swung it open, tugged the shotgun up and out of its rack, pumped it once, and ran with it.

As she dashed across the street she saw a flash of sparks spew from the muzzle of a silencer, and stopped. She raised the shotgun to her shoulder and fired. The report of the shotgun was like a thunderclap, and the kick rocked her back. She ducked low and ran the rest of the way across the street, pumped the shotgun again and moved across the front of the neighbor's yard to the porch of Slawicky's house. She went to her belly and searched for her next target.

She could see that the man she had just shot was lying on his back, face to the sky, with his arms apart. In the dark she couldn't see him very well, but she could detect no movement from him. The police load was usually number four buckshot, but she had been no more than forty feet away. He was probably severely wounded, or even dead. She couldn't see the other two men, so she rose to a crouch and ran around to the back of Slawicky's house.

Jane leaned out from the corner of the house in time to see the other two men begin to move. One of them ran toward the front of the motor home, and the other toward the back. Jane aimed and fired at the one heading for the front, and he dived face forward, lay on his belly, and slithered backward to withdraw. The other man changed his course to get behind the motor home.

Jane braced the shotgun's barrel against the clapboards at the corner of the house in case the others appeared again, took out her cell phone, and dialed 911.

"Town of Caledonia. What's your emergency?"

"A state police officer has been shot. He's in the back-yard of the house at ninety-six ninety-two Iroquois Street, and there are two men shooting at him. Another is lying in the yard."

"Give me your name, please."

"Get cops and an ambulance here now."

"Officers are on the way. Your name—"

Jane turned off the phone and waited there, where she could keep the two healthy shooters from getting near Ike Lloyd. After a minute or two, she heard lots of rustling sounds as the men moved across the yard and back toward the street. She advanced to the rear wall of the garage, closer to the wounded man.

She called, "Sergeant Lloyd." After a pause, she said, "Ike."

"Who are you?"

"The lady who borrowed your shotgun. They're clearing off. I called nine one one and they said cops are on the way. Can you hold out until they get here?"

"I think so."

"Use your belt as a tourniquet. I'll leave your shotgun in your car."

"Wait," he called. "Don't move. Do not leave the scene. We're going to need—"

Jane turned and ran along the side of the house. She was across the road and at the black police car in ten seconds. She wiped the shotgun off with her sleeve and set it on the floor of the backseat, and then ran again. She was in the Passat and driving toward the west with her window open when she heard the sirens approach. She pulled over, turned off her lights, and ducked down while their lights appeared and flashed past. Then she sat up, turned on her lights, and drove.

When she reached her hotel in Rochester she went to her room and showered, then picked up her clothes. She was sure a short-barreled twelve gauge shotgun must leave plenty of burned powder on the shooter, so she put all of her clothes in the bathtub, scrubbed them with soap, and rinsed them off with the shower, then soaked them in the tub and hung them up to dry before she went to sleep.

Her sleep was dark and dreamless, and she awoke in the late afternoon feeling alert. She went to a Laundromat, washed, dried, and folded her clothes, stopped in a restaurant for an early dinner, and then turned on the television set in her room at six to see the local news.

After the station's logo she saw the word BREAKING. A girl who looked barely out of high school was sitting in as a newsreader with the veteran anchor, Don Hennick, who must have been nearly eighty. She introduced herself as Kimberly Wachtman and said, "We have live, breaking news at this hour." Don Hennick said, "A state police officer has been shot in Caledonia. An accident in Cheektowaga holds up a train, and the Bisons win three in a row. We'll be back in sixty seconds."

There was a commercial for a supermarket chain in which a husband, who appeared to have been stunned by high voltage, walked in an endless aisle unable to find what he wanted, only to be saved by his wife, and then a commercial during which a pair of loathsome fast-talking car salesmen tried to talk an innocent young couple into buying an inferior car until they escaped to a neighboring lot, where the really good cars were sold by a handsome man. Next there was a series of rapid-fire pitches for five of the network's new shows.

The news returned with "live breaking news!" Kimberly said, "A state police officer has been shot. We go live to Brenda Sturridge at the scene in Caledonia."

Brenda Sturridge was a familiar face to Jane, a forty-five-year-old blonde holding a microphone on the sidewalk in front of Walter Slawicky's house. Behind her, police officers and technicians were moving around, ducking under the yellow CRIME SCENE tape to go back and forth to their vehicles. "Yes, Kimberly and Don, I'm at the house now. Caledonia police have not yet finished their investigation, but they've told me that a state police officer was in the yard of the house behind me on the ninety-two hundred block of Iroquois Street. They say he was watching the house of a witness in an ongoing investigation when he was ambushed by gunmen, shot, and wounded. The police will not elaborate further on the case, but said the officer was able to administer first aid to himself, which may have saved his life. They refuse to speculate on the motives for the shooting, but the investigation continues. Brenda Sturridge, Western New York News. Back to you, Don and Kimberly."

The image of the old man and the young woman in the studio returned. "Now we go live to Amy Norris at Buffalo General Hospital for more," said Don as Kimberly looked serious beside him.

This time the scene was outside a rear entrance of the big brick hospital building. Amy Norris was a tall, thin black woman who looked like a fashion model. "I'm outside the hospital where the state police officer has been taken. Hospital spokesmen have stated he's in stable condition. He sustained a bullet wound in his right thigh, but they predict he will make a full recovery. He has been identified as Sergeant Isaac Lloyd, age forty-one. The state police headquarters revealed today that he is an eighteen-year veteran with the force, with citations for outstanding merit and valor. The state police spokesman declined to comment on the incident, or on the case Sergeant Lloyd had been assigned to. Amy Norris, Western New York News."

Jane watched the image change to Don and Kimberly in the studio again. Don said, "An illegal U-turn over a set of railroad tracks has ended in tragedy today." Jane turned off the television set.

She left the hotel and drove to the store where Carey's nurses often bought their work gear. She went inside, selected a package that contained two sets of light blue scrubs, a package of surgical masks, a box of thin latex gloves, and a cap like the ones surgeons wore. She found a bag with a shoulder strap, took all her selections to the counter, and paid for them in cash.

IKE LLOYD LAY IN HIS hospital bed, his right leg throbbing. All day there had been a little nurse who had been very gentle, very solicitous of his well-being and comfort. All she had really been able to do for him was come in every three hours or so and give him another shot of painkiller, but she had smiled and spoken softly. Each time she left he fell asleep again, a strange dreamy sleep, very colorful and vivid.

Whenever Lloyd awoke, he fought to bring his dreams back. Most of them started well—running the marathon in New York City last year, or walking through the woods around Salamanca, or sitting in an Adirondack guide boat fishing on Tupper Lake. In one dream he had actually been having sex with Molly. He had hated to let that one go, and had struggled to stay asleep until the pain in his leg had grown too sharp. That one had probably been triggered by her visit to his hospital room, and then missing her after she'd gone home. He had called her to tell her about it, and she had laughed and told him he was still too weak to have that kind of dream.

All the other dreams but that one seemed to shade off into a second part. It got dark. Men had shot him, but in the dream their pistols had thrown flames. Next he would feel the stab of pain as the fire tore through the muscle of his leg. He supposed that these sensations were triggered when his medicine wore off and the pain woke him.

The leg was worse than painful; it was damaged. He had always been a runner. He loved running, and had been a habitual runner, for over thirty years. If last night had left him permanently crippled, it would turn that pleasure into agony and sorrow. When he'd been a kid he'd hated school until he discovered that his running didn't have to be just a way to forget the fact that other kids had friends, money, and nice clothes. He got to run on the cross-country team in the fall and the track team in the spring. Running had given him an identity and acceptance.

Ike had been a farm boy whose family lived on somebody else's farm and worked for next week's groceries while they tried to make this week's last. They were lucky if there was enough money left over to put gas in his father's old Ford pickup. The Lloyds were backwoods people who had come up from Pennsylvania when Ike was about ten. Through his childhood he and his father had hunted. The Lloyds had been meat hunters, and they'd weighed the cost of each shot against the value it could bring the family.

One of the memories that reappeared in his sleep tonight was a day when his father had wounded a deer. His father walked with a limp because of something that had happened in the army, so Ike had been the one to run after the deer. His concern had been to keep the deer from running all day in pain and then coming to rest in a secluded copse somewhere deep in the woods to bleed out, so its death and suffering would be completely wasted. Ike had run through the forest tracking the buck until he caught up with it, shot it through the head, hung the carcass, dressed it, and brought it home. Ike's father had cut the meat, then preserved it in the farm freezer. Ike remembered his mother defrosting pieces of the venison all the next winter, and each time they had it, his father would repeat the story of Ike running it down to prevent the sin of wasting a life.

Ike was beginning to feel fully awake again when the night nurse came in. This one was much taller—maybe five nine or ten, and thin, with olive skin but bright blue eyes. She wore a cap on her head that covered her hair and a white surgical mask over her nose and mouth.

At first he'd thought she must be one of the surgeons who had taken care of his bullet wound, but she was a nurse all right, because she fussed with things—moving the rolling stand so his call button was about seven feet from him and he couldn't even reach the damned thing, opening a drawer on the other side and putting his stuff—wallet, watch, phone—into a plastic bag in the bottom drawer of the built-in dresser in his open closet. He didn't exactly mind that part. He had thought Molly would take all that with her when she'd left tonight to go put the kids to sleep. And he didn't really care where the nurses put things. They'd sort it all out another day when he was released.

"Did the other girl go home?"

"You mean the nurse?" the new one said.

"Yes. I guess I shouldn't have said 'girl.' I'm not a jerk. I'm just kind of lazy headed right now. Drugs and all that."

The new nurse said, "It's okay. Everybody knows you're the good guy, Ike. I guess her shift ended. But you'll probably see her again tomorrow."

"Did you come to give me another shot?"

"No. I came to talk to you a little. But I'll leave soon, and when I do we can ring for the next one."

He said, "Are you afraid of getting me sick?"

"You mean the mask? No, it's not to protect you from my germs. It's to protect me."

"Oh," he said. "You called me Ike. Who are you?"

"You don't recognize my voice? I'm the woman who borrowed your shotgun last night."

"What?"

"I shot the man who was coming around the RV to get you in a crossfire. I hit him in the chest. I think I hit one of the others too, but not very seriously. I didn't go after him or his friend because it seemed more important to call for help to get you taken to a hospital."

He rolled and lunged for the call button, but it was out of his reach.

"Don't do that," she said. "You'll only hurt yourself."

"What do you want?"

"Information. I watched the local news this evening, and they told the story of what happened, sort of. A couple of things were missing."

"What were they?"

"One was me."

"You want publicity?"

"No. If keeping me out of the story was your idea, thank you. The other thing that was missing was the man I shot."

"You must know that the local news isn't going to know everything, or get everything they hear straight."

"No, Ike. Too much time has passed for them not to have noticed a dead or wounded man. The police have had control of the scene for almost twenty-four hours."

"Have I been here that long?"

"Approximately. But so far the news people haven't mentioned a man or a body. That struck me as odd."

"Maybe he got away."

"I hit him in the center of his chest from closer than forty feet. When I last saw him he was lying on his back with his arms splayed out. Your ammo is number four buckshot, right?"

"Why do you care? If he's alive he can't find you."

"I want to know who he is and what those men were doing at Slawicky's."

"I don't know, and I don't know why he's missing," said Lloyd. "I saw him go down, and I'm pretty sure I saw blood after he was lying there. But from that moment on, I was only worrying about the other two, and I think shock was setting in. If you hadn't reminded me to use my belt, I might have bled out."

"You're welcome. I have some things to tell you too."

He sighed. "You must know that I'm not on the case anymore."

"You're the only one that I can tell. Nick Bauermeister was a thief—a burglar, to be precise. I found his break-in kit, mask, and a loaded gun in a toolbox under the workbench in his basement. He was storing bags of salt for winter, and the ones in the center of the pile all have jewelry in them. His girlfriend, Chelsea Schnell, is having an affair with his boss, Daniel Crane. And Walter Slawicky never sold a rifle to Jimmy Sanders. He lied to the police about that. I think somebody paid him."

Lloyd said, "I saw the new Porsche in his garage, and of course it was hard to miss the motor home. He doesn't seem to have a job."

"That's what I thought," she said. "I've got to go now. Sorry I had to move your phone and call button."

"What has this got to do with you? Who are you?"

"Why do you care? Do you want to send me a thank-you note?"

"I'm officially ordering you to tell me your name."

"Thanks, Ike. Get well. When I'm gone, if you want the nurse, just pull the blood pressure clip off your finger. It sets off an alarm at the desk, and they'll come to reset it." She opened the door and stepped out into the hallway.

The beep-beep tone went off at the nurse's station and when the nurse got up and hurried toward Ike Lloyd's room, she didn't see the woman in scrubs who strode past her station behind her and kept going to the elevator.

Jane descended to the ground floor and walked outside through the door where the garbage was taken from the cafeteria kitchen to the dumpsters. She went past the enclosure where the big air-conditioning condensers and heating plant were. She didn't remove her mask and cap until she was far from the hospital's security cameras and enveloped in darkness once again.

20

Jane changed her clothes in her car. It was still dark when she drove to Avon and along Telephone Road. As she passed the long driveway to Chelsea Schnell's, she took time to study the house. There were no signs that anything had changed. Sometime soon, she hoped, Ike Lloyd would repeat what she'd told him to the police officers who had taken over Jimmy's case. They would obtain a search warrant for the little house, and find the gun, tools, and stolen jewelry. He could be calling them now. How long would it take to obtain a warrant?

Jane looked at her watch. It was 5:00 AM. She parked her Passat in the row of cars at the gas station down the road and walked back along the deserted stretch of Telephone Road to the house. If she was going to take another look, this had to be it.

This time she walked into the field by the house to the back where the stand of maple trees and the high thickets would hide her if the police came earlier than she had anticipated.

She walked to the rear of the house, climbed up onto the back porch, went to the kitchen window, and studied the room in the light thrown by the fluorescent above the stove. There were no dishes out, and the coffee pot was disassembled on the counter. She moved to the garage and saw through the side door that Chelsea's car was parked there, went to the bedroom window and moved her eye to the corner, then pulled back.

The bed was smooth, the bedspread pulled straight and tight, and the pillows arranged neatly in a double row— bright decorative ones in front, and white pillows behind. Nobody was home and nobody had slept here.

Jane moved to the sloped cellar door, unscrewed and removed the hasp and its padlock, and went down the steps. She had not expected to enter the house, but she still had the small LED flashlight she'd brought with her to the hospital. She picked up a rag to open Nick Bauermeister's toolbox and checked to be sure that the tools, mask, and gun were still there, then touched the middle bags of salt to verify that the jewelry was still there too. Finally she climbed the wooden steps to the kitchen.

Something had changed. The small kitchen was still neat and orderly, but it was stuffy. The air had stayed in the same place for too long because the doors and windows had been closed. She stepped to the refrigerator and tugged it open. A sour smell hit her, and seemed to be coming from the open milk carton on the top shelf. She peered through the glass tops of two drawers at the bottom and saw one full of lettuce with faint brownish streaks and leaves with curling edges. There were tomatoes with skin that had begun to pucker slightly. She closed the refrigerator and moved to the living room.

There were plants in pots lined up on a windowsill. They looked limp. Jane touched the soil in a couple of them, and they were dry. Chelsea had not been home in a while. Jane pulled her hand back into her sleeve and picked up the telephone. There was still a dial tone.

She went to Chelsea's bedroom and checked the closet and dresser. She thought there were a few articles of clothing missing since her last visit, but most of them were still there. She moved the chair to the closet, stood on it, opened the small attic access door, and used her flashlight to look, but all she saw was a layer of pink insulation that had been installed long after the house was built.

She closed it carefully and went through the house again, looking under pieces of furniture and in the usual hiding places—the freezer, inside pots and pans, taped to the undersides of drawers, behind the plates of switches that didn't seem to operate anything, and behind heating grates. As she searched, part of her was listening for the sound of police cars, and as long as she heard nothing, she kept searching. At last, she ran out of places to look.

Jane went down to the basement, up to the cellar door, and out. The sun was bright and glaring. She replaced the hasp and padlock and went across the field to the gas station and retrieved her car. As she drove along the road, there was a steady stream of cars going in both directions, people taking their kids to school or going to work, but no police cars. She looked at her watch. It was nearly eight already. Daniel Crane would be leaving for work.

DANIEL CRANE DROVE TOWARD HIS storage business, but he didn't feel right about leaving home. Maybe he didn't really have to go in today. He took out his phone and called the office.

Thompson picked up. "Storage."

"Box Farm Personal Storage," Crane said. "I've told you guys about eighty times."

"Sorry Dan. I was on my way downstairs, and Harriman was on the phone at my desk so I had to run over here to get it, and I was afraid the caller would give up."

"Okay," said Crane. "Four words. Box Farm Personal Storage. I don't know how I can build the business if you guys don't sound professional."

"Sorry. I'll be more careful."

"What I called for was to see if Mr. Salamone let anybody know when he's coming today."

"I haven't heard. Let me check." Crane could hear the rubbing sound of a hand covering the phone, and a faint voice calling across the room. "Nope. He hasn't called or anything. Nobody's called and asked for you yet, either."

"Okay," said Crane. "I'll see you in a little while." He hung up, then pressed the phone number of the office again.

"Box Farm Personal Storage."

"Very good," Crane said. "That wasn't so hard, was it?" He hung up again and slid the phone into his jacket pocket.

He had hoped Salamone might have called to tell him when he was coming, or even better, that he wasn't coming. Salamone had already missed making his usual rounds yesterday, and of course, he hadn't called. Why should he? Making people wait and not showing up was a way of keeping them off balance. They had to think about you on that day, and each day after that until you finally appeared.

Crane had wanted to stay home with Chelsea this morning. He'd had trouble with her last night, and he really wanted to see what her state of mind was going to be today.

They had gone out to dinner and a play in downtown Buffalo, and he had expected that afterward she would be bright and cheerful and talkative. The play had been a revival of O'Neill's *The Emperor Jones*. To him it had been a little stagey and dull, but Chelsea had watched it intently, so he had assumed she'd liked it. She had been quiet on the drive home, but not sullen or withdrawn.

After he pulled the Range Rover into the garage and got out, she had just sat there for a minute. At first he thought she was being a grand lady and waiting for him to walk around the car and open her door for her. That would have been okay—*was* okay in his mind when he'd come to her door. To him it had been a sign that she was feeling comfortable with him, relishing the fact that he loved her—happy that he was attentive enough to sense what she wanted.

That hadn't been it. When he had swung her door open she simply sat there looking straight ahead.

"Honey?" he'd said. "Chelsea?"

She had reacted only after he said her name, and then it was as though he'd nudged her from a reverie. She'd looked at him and then got out. As he followed her to the front door he said, "Are you all right?"

She had not answered at first, but then she said, "Yes." But she had sounded too firm, too assertive.

When he opened the door she went in ahead of him and kept walking, never stopping on her way across the living room and through the gallery toward his bedroom—their bedroom. When he finished locking the door and turning up the lights he looked again and his last sight before she disappeared through the arch to the gallery was her reaching up to grasp the zipper at the back of her dress. When she did that the dress was pulled tighter across her bottom and waist. Her thin, graceful fingers tugged down the zipper a few inches and he saw the bare white skin below her neck for an instant.

He felt his pulse quicken. She was going to the bedroom taking her dress off. Chelsea didn't usually initiate sex; she acquiesced to it. Crane began to feel good. Maybe his life was about to get even better. He tried to keep his anticipation in control. It was late, and she just might be tired. In a minute she might come back out wearing flannel pajamas and fuzzy slippers and say good-night. He considered. How did he want her to see him when she returned?

He wanted to look confident and relaxed. He opened the bar hidden on the left wall and poured himself a cognac, and set a second glass next to his, with the bottle beside it as an invitation. She had turned down drinks lately. She'd said something about alcohol not agreeing with her. It had occurred to him that it might have been a reaction to the powder he had put in her drink the night they'd first had sex. He hadn't mentioned that to her, of course. He sipped his cognac and waited, trying not to picture her in the bedroom naked, waiting for him to join her. The house was silent, and he thought he could hear his own heartbeat. Was the cognac a bad idea? He took a cocktail glass off the shelf and poured her a diet ginger ale.

He heard the bedroom door close, and then the flap of rubber on the tile floor of the gallery, and then turned to look at her.

She was wearing the tank top and shorts she'd often worn when he had visited her at her house, and a pair of flip-flops. He tried to stifle his disappointment. *Okay. She looks beautiful, and in that outfit she must feel comfortable.*

She didn't. She looked anxious and miserable. Then he noticed the strap on her shoulder. What was that?

"Hi, baby," he said, and forced a smile. "Have a ginger ale?" He held it up.

"I—" she said, then paused, like a stutterer who had to start over. "Sure." She stepped closer and took it, then stepped away with it. She slipped the strap off her shoulder and set her overnight bag on the floor. "I need to talk to you."

"Okay," he said. His mouth was suddenly dry. He sipped his cognac. "Come and sit down."

She looked undecided, and he realized that she had made some plan that had not included sitting down. But she turned and walked with him to the semicircular couch coiled around the big polished walnut coffee table. Her

262

expression was serious, troubled. Could she be breaking up with him?

As though she were answering, she said, "This isn't working out."

He felt an emptiness in his stomach. He watched her, silent.

She began again. "You've been really kind and generous, and a true friend. You were the only one of Nick's friends who even kept in touch with me. Nobody else gave a crap. Their girlfriends, who were always chatty and supposedly my friends, didn't bother to call after the funeral. I would have thought you'd be the least likely to care, because you were the boss and older and everything. I'll always be grateful that you were there for me."

Maybe this wasn't as bad as he had first feared. He knew he was walking along the edge of a precipice, but what she'd said made him decide to be bold and honest. "I did it because I love you." He watched her face, hoping it would show something—if not joy, at least pleasure, however mild. Even surprise would give him a foothold he might be able to use, a chance to save himself. But her head gave a tiny involuntary shake, like a shiver.

Chelsea said, "This is my fault. I didn't intend it, but I guess I've been leading you on. I wanted to give us both a chance to see if we could be happy together, but I should have been smarter about this."

"You did nothing wrong," he said. "Don't think of it that way." He swallowed hard, then stood. "Jesus, my throat is dry." He went to the bar, reached into the refrigerator and got another ginger ale, and poured it in a glass. While he was there he reached under the bar to the cardboard box there and took one of the little brown envelopes. As he walked back to the couch he palmed it and held it in his left hand.

He sat down and drank, looking at her and noting the position of her glass.

Chelsea had gathered her thoughts while he'd been away. "This is the time to be open and honest. I went out with you because you're such a great guy, and I felt safe with you. I felt I could talk to you about anything, but that you wouldn't make me relive Nick's murder. The first night we went out, I enjoyed it and forgot how sad I was for a while. I was distracted, and I was drinking, and I guess that one night I got carried away."

Crane realized Chelsea was being absolutely sincere. She had actually remembered none of that night—passing out, his carrying her to the bedroom, moving her this way and that as he'd stripped her, the sex. The powder was magical. It had absolutely erased her memory. He had never used GHB before that night, but it had lived up to its reputation completely.

He could see she was blushing, and that it embarrassed her to look at him, but she wanted to be sure she was getting through to him. If she couldn't see his hurt, then she couldn't be sure he was hearing her.

She said, "The next morning I realized I had passed out at some point and a lot was a blank. I must have thrown myself at you, and so we'd had sex. I decided that since I'd done that, I owed it to you, and to me—I'm not saying I was being unselfish—to try to see if this was what we both really wanted, or just a drunken mistake."

"It wasn't a mistake," Crane said. "I know this has been awkward for you, so soon after Nick died. But we hardly ever get to choose when it's time for things in our lives, good or bad, to happen."

Chelsea reached out and touched his hand, and he took it as permission to come closer on the couch. "It was good. It was," she said. "But it's still a mistake, and I'm so, so sorry."

She began to cry. She bent her head down and he hugged her. He could feel her sobbing, and he could tell her tears were making the shoulder of his sport coat wet. While he held her with his hands behind her back, he tore off the end of the envelope, transferred the envelope from his left hand to his right, and poured the envelope into her ginger ale, trying to make his gesture quick and measure the dose by eye. Was that too much? He slipped the empty envelope into his coat pocket and brought his hand up to pat her tenderly. He stayed there, could have stayed there forever holding her, but after another minute or two she straightened, her head came up, and he had to release her.

He handed her the silk handkerchief from the breast pocket of his sport coat. She wiped her nose and dabbed at her eyes. The black eyeliner smeared on it, and she cried some more. "I'm ruining this."

"Keep it." While she was occupied with staring at his handkerchief, he watched the last of the white powder dissolve in her ginger ale.

She pivoted to face the coffee table, picked up the ginger ale, took a few swallows, and set it down. She seemed to collect herself. "I made a mistake. You're a wonderful man, but I'm not in love with you."

"I think you are, deep down. Whenever you're not thinking, brooding over things, everything is fine. Maybe this was too soon to start a new relationship and you weren't ready, as you say. Maybe we need to step back and take things more slowly. We can still see each other, and over time—"

She was already shaking her head impatiently. "I've got to be totally honest. If I thought that could be the problem, then I'd leave things the way they are, keep my mouth shut, and wait. That's what I wanted to do, but I can't. This has got to be over before the future can start."

He took a drink of his ginger ale, trying to get her to feel thirsty.

It worked. She took another long draft of her ginger ale, stood, carried it to the bar, and set her glass on the granite surface. "I need to go home."

"Please don't go back to that empty house now. It's late. We don't have to talk about this anymore. I can sleep in one of the guest rooms, and in the morning I'll drive you back there."

"I know it's not fair to drag you out to drive me at this hour. I'll call a cab."

"No," he said. He stood up from the couch. "Of course I'll drive you home if that's what you want. Just give me a minute to pull myself together." He walked to the arch leading to the gallery and headed for the bedroom.

In the bedroom he checked the spots where she had always put her things on overnight stays. She had left nothing. It occurred to him that while he'd been standing at the bar imagining her hanging up her dress and brushing out her long blond hair in front of the mirror, she had been feverishly stuffing the dress into her overnight bag and gathering her other belongings as fast as she could.

He went into the bathroom and pissed, brushed his teeth to get rid of the smell of cognac on his breath, combed his hair, went to his closet, hung up his sport coat and returned his tie to the rack, and then took out a windbreaker. He put it on and walked slowly back up the gallery to the living room.

She was sitting on the couch again, so he could only see the back of her head, but it looked odd. She was slouching, leaning her head back against the top of the couch as though she were studying the ceiling. As he came around to the front of the couch he saw that her eyes were closed and her mouth open. He glanced in the direction of the bar and realized that while she was waiting she must have downed the last of the ginger ale.

The powder seemed to have taken her much more quickly than it had the first time. He touched her neck. Her pulse was slow, but strong. He was still a little worried. He had ordered the powder from an online pharmacy in

Mexico. He didn't know what sort of regulation there was in another country, how strong the powder was, or even if it was the same strength all the way through. But it was too late to undo this, and she had been fine the first time.

He began by taking her overnight bag into the bedroom, then unpacking it. He laid the dress she'd worn across the top of the chair and her shoes on the floor as though she had stepped out of them. He went into the bathroom and put her toothbrush and toothpaste, mouthwash, hairbrush, makeup case, and deodorant out on the counter by the second sink. He ran water over the toothbrush and shook it a bit to make it seem used. He even ran the fresh bar of soap under the faucet for a second and put it back on the soap dish.

He went into the bedroom, opened the covers on the bed to bare the sheets, and then returned to the living room to pick her up off the couch and carry her back to place her on the bed. Her shorts and tank top came off much more easily than the dress had last time. She had done much of his work for him.

This morning as he drove toward his storage facility, he remembered the rest. He went over each detail. He had started to pull the covers over her sleeping form, but he had made the mistake of letting his eyes linger too long on her. He was hoping she would believe she'd relented during the part of the evening she wouldn't remember, and if that had happened, they probably would have had make up sex. He felt a little guilty, but then assured himself that he had the right, after all he'd done for her. He also knew that this might very well be the last time.

Now he wished that he could still be at home to try to guide her to the proper interpretation of what she would see when she woke up. He had planned to be there. He had called to give Verna Machak the day off so she wouldn't be in the way, but a few minutes later he'd remembered that

Salamone hadn't come to the storage office on his usual day, so he probably would come today.

JANE DROVE PAST DAVID CRANE'S house at eight fifteen, and on to the plaza to park her car. She returned on foot and went through the little woods to watch the house. The Range Rover was gone, and she knew it would be at least two hours before the housekeeper, Mrs. Machak, arrived. She moved to the house and walked slowly and quietly, checking windows to see if the girl Chelsea was still there.

Jane moved from window to window, but the house appeared to be empty. There were a few rooms that she suspected only opened onto the central Japanese garden and the broad hallway with the pillars. She moved into the garden and looked. There was an empty office, a living room, and a couple of rooms that had no obvious purpose. She followed the wall and realized she had misinterpreted the structure of the building. It seemed to fold twice, to wrap itself around the garden, giving the illusion that the garden was completely surrounded.

She saw that there was a louvered window in the pantry beside the kitchen. She touched it, wiggled one of the louvers a little, and saw what she had been hoping for. The sheets of glass were tempered—maybe even unbreakable—but they were mounted in an aluminum framework that opened and closed with a crank. She took out her pocket-knife and used its blade to bend the frames holding the first two louvers, then slipped the first one out. She removed the next and the next the same way. Soon she had all eight out and piled neatly on the ground beside her.

Jane hoisted herself up and slithered in the window, stopped and listened for a minute, pulled herself through and listened again, and then moved out of the kitchen. She looked for the bedrooms first. People who had something to hide seemed to be most comfortable keeping it close to them while they slept. The row of bedrooms was where she had thought it would be, off the gallery on the right side where there was a view of the garden, but the windows were shielded by the protruding front wing.

There were a couple of model bedrooms that looked as though nobody ever stepped inside except to dust. Then she reached the master suite. She slipped inside and saw the girl. She was lying on the bed, fast asleep, so Jane backed out and closed the door to keep any noise from reaching her.

She went to the office she'd seen from the outside, closed the door, and began to search the drawers of the big desk. It was an impressive piece of furniture, the top of it made from two pieces of a large tree with a subtle pattern of whorls. In the inside top drawer she found a Kimber .45 caliber pistol. She checked the magazine and found it loaded.

Seeing the gun reminded her of the one she'd found in Nick Bauermeister's toolbox. It made her shift her search to places that might hold stolen jewelry. She didn't find any, or anything else that looked as though it had been hidden. The filing cabinets were full of file folders that contained Crane's personal financial records, mostly monthly broker-age reports. Other drawers seemed to be duplicates of the financial records of the Box Farm Personal Storage Company—property taxes, business taxes, and other dull paper. She moved out of the office and worked her way through the house, listening for sounds that would mean Chelsea was awake.

When she finished her first circuit of the rooms it was still only nine, and she had at least an hour before Mrs. Machak would show up. She thought about the pistol. It had been a promising find, but plenty of people owned handguns. They were legal and common. Nick Bauermeister had been killed with a rifle, so the gun proved nothing. She turned her attention to finding a hiding place that was long and narrow, but she was beginning to feel discouraged. The murder weapon was probably either destroyed or still in the possession of the shooter.

She moved along the gallery and heard something. The sound was a loud electronic beep, unchanging and harsh. "Bee bee bee bee bee bee . . ." An alarm system?

She ran toward it, hoping to be able to turn it off. Usually home systems gave the user thirty or forty seconds to disarm them before a telephone signal went to the security company or the police station. She reached the place where it was loudest, swung the door open, and found herself in the master bedroom again. She saw what it was—not an alarm system, an alarm *clock*.

The digital clock was beside the king-size bed on an end table. The alarm was one of those that got louder each minute or two, and by now it was painful to hear. It began to make a different noise, like a howl, as some car alarms did, just when Jane reached it and hit the button.

The girl had not awakened. She was still lying motionless in the bed, her head no more than three feet from the deafening alarm clock. Jane looked closely at her. She was sprawled on her back with one arm a little behind her. She seemed to be lying on it. Jane saw a small downy feather from a pillow clinging to the bedspread. She picked it up and held it beneath Chelsea's nose. The thin filaments of white barely moved, then were still for a count of five, six, seven, then moved again. The girl was barely breathing. *Drugs?*

The girl was in trouble. Jane shook her shoulder. No reaction. She shook her harder, then rolled her onto her side and pulled the arm out from under her. It was cool, and looked white as though she had been in the same position for hours. Jane got onto the bed, straddled her, and pulled her up by the shoulders. She held her and moved her hips back so she could keep her upright, then put two big pillows behind her. She patted the girl's face once, twice, then harder. "Chelsea. Chelsea, wake up."

The girl's eyes fluttered but didn't stay open. "No," she croaked. "No."

"You took something," Jane said. "What was it?"

The girl's eyes opened, but they were opaque, glassy, with no understanding. They closed again.

Jane let her lean back and hurried into the bathroom. What was it? There were no bottles or plastic bags on any of the counters. She ran back and scanned the tops of the dressers, the nightstands, then looked at the floors, and ran her hands over the bedcovers to feel for a pill bottle.

She remembered seeing a bar in the living room. There had been glasses—dirty ones left on the counter for the housekeeper to wash. She hurried into the living room and over to the bar. She sniffed the two glasses, but smelled nothing. There was also a cognac glass. She went around the granite bar and looked closely at the bottles, which seemed unremarkable, and the sink. There was no residue she could detect. When she turned to look over the bar at the room, something caught her eye. There was a shelf just below the bar for shakers, blenders, peelers, corkscrews, and other equipment, but there was also a small, plain cardboard box, and beside it the torn-off top of a little envelope. It was at most a quarter inch wide and an inch long, but the trace of white powder beside it attracted her attention. Sugar?

She knelt to look closer. The small, brown cardboard box was open at the top. Inside was a pile of identical tan paper envelopes, about an inch and a half long and less than an inch wide. She turned the small cardboard box. There was a very pretty, colorful stamp with several unfamiliar birds on it, and MEXICO CONSERVA across the bottom.

She plucked one of the envelopes out and examined them. There was a tiny pencil scribble on the side of each one: GAMMA-HYDROXYBUTYRATE.

Great. He gave her a date-rape drug. She pocketed a handful of the envelopes and ran into the bedroom. Chelsea was in exactly the same position she'd propped her in. She looked at her watch. It was after ten. Where was Mrs. Machak? Would she be here in a few seconds? A few minutes? Would she even know what to do?

Jane snatched up the telephone in the room and dialed 911.

"Nine one one, what is your emergency?"

"The address is 84792 Landover Road. There is a young woman in the master bedroom who seems to have ingested GHB. She's in a semicomatose state."

"Your name, please?"

"Mrs. Verna Machak. I'm the housekeeper."

"Do you know how she came to take the drug, Mrs. Machak?"

"I have no idea. I just came in and found her. Is the ambulance on the way?"

"Of course. Are you in the room with her?"

"No. I've got to get back there now." Jane hung up and ran to the bedroom. "Chelsea. The ambulance is coming." She knew she should get out of the house as quickly as she could, but she noticed again the clothes lying on the chair. Aware that what she was about to do was foolish, she ignored the dress, snatched up the shorts and tank top, pulled the tank top down over Chelsea's head and put her arms through, then pulled back the covers and slid Chelsea's underwear over her ankles and up over her hips, and then the shorts. People with drug overdoses didn't have much dignity to preserve, but the change made Jane feel better.

Jane pulled the covers up over the unconscious girl, took one of the small envelopes out of her pocket and tossed it on the bed beside her. Then she hurried to the front door, unlocked it and opened it wide, and ran to the kitchen.

She climbed out the louvered window, devoted a few seconds to sliding the eight glass strips back into their frame, and trotted along the back of the house to the side. She could see that the driveway was still clear, so she dashed across it into the stand of big trees. She waited until she could hear the wail of the ambulance before she jogged down the road to her car.

21

Chelsea stood at the hospital entrance, staring out the glass at the circular driveway, hoping to spot the lights of her taxi as it drove in. It was night again, and she had spent the whole day in the hospital, being examined and medicated and questioned over and over by a steady stream of strangers. Now she was desperate to get away from this place.

She was wearing the same shorts and tank top she'd had on when the ambulance had brought her here in the morning, but a few minutes ago she had gone into the hospital gift shop and bought a blue sweatshirt that said UNIVERSITY AT BUFFALO MEDICAL SCHOOL. She had felt chilled, and also had a psychological urge to bundle herself up. The sweatshirt had been the only piece of clothing for sale that was for adults. It had occurred to her that if they'd sold pajamas to replace the gowns they gave you, the store would have gotten rich.

Today had been one of the worst days of her life. Everything said or done to her for the whole day since she had awakened to the sight of doctors had been prying and horrible. Anybody who had walked into her room had felt free to ask her all about the most personal aspects of her life—things that nobody had ever asked her, even her mother. And because she had been delivered to the hospital unconscious and helpless, they all acted as though she had to answer every question. The second policewoman had been the worst, because she kept asking a question and then supplying her own answer to it, so Chelsea had to keep correcting her answers.

Finally, a little while ago, she had pressed her own question—when am I free to leave? She had asked it so many times in so many ways that she was sure the hospital staff had simply run out of ways of evading her. At last she had made them come in with a set of papers for her to sign in a dozen places. Even then she'd had to wait until an orderly arrived with a wheelchair to wheel her out to the door.

She had gone to the volunteer at the information desk to ask her for help getting a taxi. The volunteer was an older woman with white hair and a blue rinse who kept looking at her in a disapproving way. She had demanded to know why Chelsea didn't have a family member or a friend to drive her home.

Chelsea said, "Because I don't. I choose not to." The woman had reluctantly lifted the telephone receiver and set it on the counter where Chelsea could reach it.

Chelsea dialed the operator and asked for the number of a taxi company. That had triggered a cheerful female machine voice that was more human than the old lady in front of her, reciting a phone number. Chelsea dialed it and said she wanted a cab to take her from the hospital to Avon right away.

The man with a foreign accent sounded as though he was on a speakerphone in the middle of a hurricane. She'd told him what she wanted again, but she wasn't sure that he had understood her, and now, as time went on, she wasn't sure whether what he'd said to her was yes.

Chelsea had been waiting for a long time, watching through the glass for a cab to come up into the circular driveway. She was aware that the woman at the information desk was staring at her and feeling delighted that the cab had not come. Chelsea raised her eyes to focus on the reflection of the woman in the glass, and verified that she was staring.

Chelsea pushed open the glass door and stepped out into the night air. It tasted fresh, and it was much warmer than the air-conditioned hospital had been. She wondered whether she had needed the sweatshirt or not, but admitted to herself that part of the reason she had bought it was that she had felt vulnerable and half-undressed in the shorts, tank top, and flip-flops.

She was glad to be outside. She walked out farther from the entrance and along the circular drive to the street. She couldn't see a taxicab waiting where she might have missed it. She hadn't had much hope for that anyway. When a cab came to a hospital it must pull up close to the entrance, and not make sick people walk far. She noticed a bus stop on the street only a few yards past the circle, though. That would be her last resort if she couldn't get a cab, she decided. Then she remembered that she hadn't seen a bus go by on the street in all the time she'd been waiting. Maybe they didn't run this late. Maybe she should just call another cab company.

Chelsea turned and started back up the sidewalk toward the hospital entrance. It occurred to her that at this hour the emergency room probably had the most patients. She could go to that entrance and wait. Somebody might show up in a taxi too hurt or intoxicated to drive, or about to give birth. The cab driver would be delighted to get another passenger to take away from here.

There was the sound of tires squealing as a vehicle pulled onto the traffic circle behind her. She turned to look over her shoulder, but the vehicle wasn't a cab. It was a big red pickup truck, and it skidded to a stop beside her.

"Chelsea!"

She stopped and stared at the truck's open side window. The driver was Dave Wilkins, one of the men who had worked with Nick, and beside him was another, Ron Gerard.

Wilkins smiled. "Come on. Get in."

"What are you two doing here?" Chelsea said.

Gerard leaned toward her across Wilkins. "We came to see you."

Wilkins pushed him back. "Shut up," he hissed.

Chelsea knew she hadn't been meant to hear that. "It's almost midnight. Visiting hours end at nine."

Wilkins said, "We just heard they'd taken you to the hospital, so we figured you'd be in the emergency room. It took a while to find out you weren't, and then find out you'd been admitted, and then that you'd just left. You're lucky we found you. Come on. We'll give you a ride back."

"Back where?"

Gerard leaned across Wilkins again. "To Dan's."

"I don't want to go to Dan's house," she said.

Wilkins elbowed Gerard. "To your house, then. Whatever."

Chelsea hadn't had time to sort out all of her impressions, but if these men knew she'd been taken from Dan Crane's house, then Crane must have told them—sent them to get her. The policewomen had told her Dan Crane had been arrested. What could he want now? She felt a deep uneasiness growing in her. "No, thanks. I've already called somebody. They'll be here in a minute."

The two men both swiveled their heads to look around them. There were no other cars in the circle or near it. The only other person seemed to be a lone woman in blue scrubs walking up the sidewalk toward the hospital entrance carrying a black canvas shoulder bag.

"Your ride doesn't seem to have made it," said Wilkins.

Gerard was impatient. "Come on, Chelsea. It's late. We drove all the way here just to give you a ride."

"He told you to come and get me, didn't he?" she said.

"Come on," said Wilkins. "Get in. We can't sit here all night. We can talk on the way."

"No, thanks," she said. She backed away from the curb and resumed her walk toward the building.

Gerard opened his door, jumped to the pavement, and hurried around the front of the truck to step in front of her. He held his arms out from his sides to block her path. "Hold it," he said.

"Leave me alone," Chelsea said.

She tried to sidestep Gerard, and then to run, but his arms encircled her from behind and lifted her off her feet. He took a step toward the truck with her.

At that moment the tall, dark-haired woman in hospital scrubs reached them. She shrugged the bag off her shoulder and delivered a fast right jab over Chelsea's shoulder into Gerard's face.

He pushed Chelsea aside and lunged toward the woman, but she had anticipated his move. She dodged his charge and delivered a practiced combination of four punches to his face and head. He kept his head low, wheeled around and tried to tackle her, but in the instant when he pushed off toward her she sidestepped, swatted his arm down and away from her, stepped into his wake, and pushed with both hands to increase his momentum and direct him onto the driveway in front of the truck.

Wilkins had begun to coast forward to keep abreast of Gerard and Chelsea. Now he jerked the truck to a stop too late to avoid hitting Gerard from the side. Gerard sprawled on the pavement, the wind knocked out of him by the grille.

Wilkins set the brake, flung open his door, and started to get out. But as he swung his legs out, the woman kicked the door so it swung into his right leg, then hit him in the face as he tried again to get out. She bent low to snatch the strap of her black bag off the ground and swung the bag at him as he cleared the car door. He caught the bag in both hands and looked elated for a moment, but she had not released the strap or stopped moving. She stepped past him, looped the strap over his head, and yanked it hard from behind. The strap choked him and pulled him backward off balance long enough for her to get her forearm around his neck and grasp her wrist with her other hand.

She squeezed hard as he bucked and struggled and clawed at her arms, but she had stopped the flow of blood through the carotid arteries to his brain, and in few more seconds he had lost consciousness. She dropped him at her feet, slipped the strap of her bag off his neck, and looked for Gerard.

Gerard, lying on the pavement in front of the truck, seemed to be catching his breath. He sat up and held his ribs where the truck had hit him. He saw the woman come toward the front of the truck and retreated across the driveway. "Stay back," he said. "I'm suing you and your hospital."

"Just go," Chelsea said. "Both of you."

Wilkins was now conscious. He sat up with difficulty, and then grasped the door handle of his truck to pull himself to his feet. He opened the door and climbed into the driver's seat.

"Hey, Chelsea," said Gerard. "You think Dan is going to let you put him in prison? See you soon."

"Shut up," Wilkins said as Gerard climbed in beside him. He put the car in gear and drove around the circle too fast, and then off down the street.

Chelsea stood on the circle looking at the street. "Oh, my God," she whispered. "Oh my God."

The woman in scrubs stepped close to her and put her arm around her. Chelsea turned to the woman. "Thank you," she said. "I don't know what would have happened if you hadn't been here. They were going to take me. I didn't want to go, but I couldn't stop them."

The woman said, "You're Chelsea Schnell." It wasn't a question.

"You know me? I don't remember you."

"I'm not surprised. My name is Jane. How are you feeling?"

"Fine," said Chelsea automatically.

"Really?"

"No. I don't feel great."

She said, "I'd better give you a ride. Let's walk. My car is down the street and around the first corner." They began to walk together down the driveway and then along the street away from the hospital.

"I assume the doctors explained what happened to you?" the woman said.

"Yes." Chelsea looked away from her, and a tear streaked down her cheek. "They said I was drugged."

"Gamma-hydroxybutyrate."

"GHB," Chelsea said. "Of course I'd heard of it. They even warned us about it in health class, but I never thought it would happen to me. And the one who did it, I never . . ." her voice trailed off.

"You didn't think he'd do that," Jane said. "Don't blame yourself for that. None of this is your fault. What he did was a crime."

"There was a female cop in there trying to get me to accuse him of rape. But when I asked her about what other evidence they've got, she went kind of vague on me. There was more of the drug in his house, and that's illegal, but it doesn't stay in your system long, so that's a problem. And it all just feels so overwhelming right now."

"I understand."

Chelsea didn't seem to hear her, just kept talking. "My boyfriend got killed right in front of me two months ago. I loved him. He wasn't perfect, but I loved him. Have you ever seen anybody shot through the head?"

"I'm afraid I have," Jane said. "It's better not to think about it all the time, so don't. Let it fade. When it comes back to you, remind yourself that it's the quickest, and one of the most painless, ways to die."

"Right now I just can't face any more of this."

"You're a strong young woman who has about eighty percent of her life ahead of her. Good things will happen."

"Would you press charges if you were me?" Chelsea asked.

Jane said, "If the police officer advised you to do it, she thinks they could get a conviction. They don't like to waste their time. But it would be an ordeal for you. I think they have his supply of GHB, and assuming the doctors have used a rape kit, there will be proof that you had sex with him. I don't know whether I would cooperate on the charges or not. I think I would, but it's up to you what you want to do. Did you love him?"

"I tried, but I couldn't feel love for him. I was grateful to him for being nice to me, and I felt so alone. But for days I've been feeling like I made a terrible mistake, and wondering how to tell him."

"What do you want to do now?"

"I want to go home, but I can't. I'm scared to death of those two guys, and I'm even more afraid of him. He's not the way he seems at all. He sent them to take me."

"Do you have relatives you can stay with?"

"My mother. But she's visiting some relatives in Denver for a couple of months to help my cousin with her baby."

"Could you join her?"

"No. The man who did this knows she's there. He could find me there in an hour."

"Do you think there's any chance he's not trying to hurt you?"

"No. I think he just tried. Those two had no other reason to bother me. I already got him in terrible trouble with the police. Now he'll think that he's going to be charged with rape, and that if I testify I'll put him away forever. I really think he'll kill me."

"If I could take you someplace far away where nobody could find you until this is all over, would you want to go?"

"If this is a joke or something, please don't say it."

"It's no joke. Would you go?"

"Yes."

"You would have to promise never to tell anyone where you went or how you got there."

"Not even my mother?"

"I'm offering you a chance to disappear for a time. I know how to do that, and I think you're right that you're in danger. But if you go with me, then the next part of your life has to be closed forever. It's as though the story of your life had two pages permanently glued together. Nobody can ever know any of it. You could call your mother before you start, but that would be the last. If things work out so you can come back, you still can't tell her where you've been."

Chelsea looked at her and walked along for a minute in silence. "I want to go."

"Think about it some more while we're driving," the woman said. "We'll stop at your house so you can take two minutes to throw some clothes into an overnight bag."

"I don't think I can," said Chelsea. "The man who did this—Dan Crane—has a bunch of other guys working for him. They could be waiting for me at my house."

"We'll look before we go in," said Jane.

They drove to Chelsea's house. Jane drove by and made sure there was no other car parked by the house or behind

it, and then parked and took Chelsea through the field behind her house. As they went up on the porch the first thing
they saw was that a window in the back door was broken so
someone could reach the dead bolt, and the door was now
closed but unlocked. "They've been here," Chelsea said.

"Get packed. I'll keep watch."

Chelsea returned in a few minutes wearing fresh clothes—
a pair of long pants and a long-sleeved pullover, and carrying an overnight bag over her shoulder.

They went out the back door and down the steps to the
field. As they were crossing the field, a pair of headlights
appeared and turned down the long driveway toward Chelsea's house. The car pulled up at the house, and three men
got out. Jane said, "The two men from the hospital must
have called and told them you were coming home."

Chelsea said, "I recognize a couple of them. That's Allen,
and that one is Gerhardt. I can't see the other one's face."

They hurried through the field in silence for a time, and
then Chelsea said, "I can't believe they're doing this. They
all worked with Nick. They were supposed to be his friends,
but now that he's dead, they've all turned on me."

When they reached the car, Jane started it and they
moved off in the opposite direction.

"Where are we going now?" asked Chelsea.

"We'll risk one more stop so I can make some arrangements. If you still want to do this when I'm ready, we'll go."

They went to Jane's hotel on Niagara Falls Boulevard,
where she used one of the computers in the hotel's business
center to make plane reservations.

She handed Chelsea a couple of pages printed from the
computer. "Here's your itinerary. You've got a plane leaving
in three hours. That sounds like a long time but it isn't, because we've got a lot to talk about before you leave."

"Like what?"

"Some of it is unpleasant, but you need to know."

They went upstairs to Jane's room. Chelsea sat at the small table while Jane changed her clothes in the bathroom, and then came back and sat in the chair across from hers. Chelsea said, "What do you have to tell me?"

"I'll start with the hard parts. Your boyfriend Nick was a thief. Hidden in your basement there is a set of burglary tools—a kit for breaking in to houses."

Chelsea laughed, sounding partly sad and partly relieved. "That? That's a mistake. He worked at one of those storage places. Sometimes people leave their stuff in storage and never come back. If they stop paying for a certain number of months, the storage people have to break in."

Jane looked at her. "How do the mask and the gun fit into that job?"

"What are you talking about? Nick didn't have a gun."

"He didn't show you a gun. He had one, and he kept it in the toolbox under the workbench. Loaded. There was a slim-jim for opening car locks, a crowbar, a set of bump keys that burglars use for opening house locks. He also hid some jewelry in the salt bags in the basement."

"For me, maybe. It was probably presents he was hiding as a surprise."

"Some was women's jewelry. But I doubt that fifteen men's watches, a dozen men's rings, and four sets of cuff links and tie clasps were for you."

Chelsea lowered her head and began to cry.

"I'm sorry," said Jane. "I had to tell you now, before we go any further with this. I took pictures of those things with my phone." She pushed the symbol to bring up her photo collection and handed it to Chelsea.

Chelsea looked at the pictures, one by one, and then handed the phone back to Jane. "Nick too." She sobbed again, and kept crying for a time. "I saw that toolbox whenever I was down there—a couple of times a week, maybe. How could I be so stupid?"

"He was in the business of looking innocent, and he was pretty good at it, apparently. It wasn't your fault."

"Maybe, but that's the second thing you've told me isn't my fault. I should be locked up for my own good. I can't seem to pick a man who isn't some kind of criminal."

Jane patted her arm gently. "There are a lot of people who go through life unguarded and without suspicion, and some of them live long and happy lives. But if I were you, I'd probably not let the next man pick me."

Chelsea gave a little smile. "That's probably not a bad idea."

"Right now it's time to concentrate on staying safe while you make plans to have a future."

"I don't know much about what I want to do. Right now I want to get somewhere far away from Daniel Crane. I want to stop the clock, to stop having things happen, you know? I want to get past the things that have already happened, but mostly, I want to get away from here."

"That's what we're about to do. Have you looked at your itinerary?"

Chelsea opened the folded papers and looked. "New York. Then Manchester, New Hampshire? What's there?"

"A very nice, kind older woman will be at the Manchester airport. She'll drive you the rest of the way. You're going to an apartment in a small town. She and her son are people I've brought there for their protection, just like you. If you go through with this, you'll have to remember that keeping their secret is part of the bargain you made. She—"

Chelsea cut her off. "I will. I promise."

"Wait. Before you promise, I have to tell you more. The woman is named Mattie Sanders. Her son is Jimmy Sanders."

Chelsea recoiled. "Is this all a trap or something? I thought you were trying to help me."

"Jimmy is as innocent as you are. He didn't kill Nick. He didn't even want to fight with him. Nick swung at him, and he defended himself. He never did anything else at the time, and never saw him again."

Chelsea looked at Jane in desperation. "Please don't be lying to me."

"I'm not. You can go now and never see me again. Or I can put you somewhere else alone, away from the Sanderses if you want. But you'd have nobody to talk to, nobody to protect you, nobody to even know it if something happened to you. I'd advise you to trust me, and to let me trust you."

Chelsea studied Jane's face for a few seconds, then sighed. "I've already trusted you enough to go this far. And you saw those men at my house. I can't stay here. There's nowhere that's safe. And I notice that you're the one in the position to help other people. Not the one who's been sleeping with a thief and then a rapist. So I guess I ought to listen to you."

"All right," said Jane. "Then let's get to the airport."

They arrived at the Buffalo airport as the sky was beginning to show signs that sunrise was not far off. Jane said, "Your flight leaves in an hour and a half. Do you think you'd like a midnight snack?"

"I think I'll call it breakfast."

Jane took Chelsea's small carry-on bag out of the trunk and they walked into the airport terminal. Most of the concessions in the building still had steel cages across their entrances, but there was one restaurant that was open, with several employees rattling pans, brewing coffee, and firing up stoves in the kitchen area.

They bought coffee and fresh muffins because those were the only things that were ready, and sat at a table together. "Don't forget to mention that Jane sent you. If you don't know at least that much, Mattie might not be comfortable with you."

"You mean she'll think you don't trust me."

"That's exactly what I mean. Tell her I'm sorry I couldn't come with you, but I'm still looking at things here." Jane detected a change in Chelsea. The girl's face was pale, her eyes widened. She hunched her shoulders and stared down at the table, then raised one hand to her brow as though she were shielding her eyes from a glare. "What is it? See somebody?"

"It's two more of the men who worked with Nick."

Jane lifted her eyes and scanned the trickle of people coming into the broad open area between the entrance and the line of airline ticket counters. The two men were in their late twenties. They didn't walk to the counters or head for the security checkpoint to reach the gates. Jane said, "Go into the ladies' room behind us and wait for me."

Jane went to stand at an electronic board that listed arrivals and departures and then to the row of ticket counters. She bought herself a ticket to Albany, the closest destination that was listed for an early morning takeoff. While she was in line she got a chance to study the two men. They had no luggage, not even a jacket that might hold a ticket. They were in fairly good condition, men who did something physical rather than mental for a living, but not something strenuous enough to give them the sinewy forearms of laborers. She didn't see anything on either of them that might be a weapon. She decided that Daniel Crane had sent them to keep Chelsea from leaving town, or at least to see it if she did. Jane paid cash for her ticket. She went into the airport store just as the clerks finished opening it and walked to the back to look at the display of scarves. A few minutes later she arrived at the ladies' room where Chelsea was waiting.

For the moment, this ladies' room was empty and they were alone. She said, "We should go through security. Once we're in there, I'm not especially concerned about those two doing you any harm."

"You can't go through security without a ticket."

Jane held up her boarding pass. "I bought a ticket to Albany." She opened the paper bag from the store and extracted a gray scarf. In answer to Chelsea's confused expression, she said, "The security area is all out in the open. Let me see what I can do about changing how we look."

She draped the scarf over Chelsea's head, and wrapped the longer side once around Chelsea's neck.

Chelsea turned to the mirror. "One of those things Muslim ladies wear?"

"A hijab. We've got to hide all that blond hair. We're within a few miles of two good-size universities and a lot of little colleges, and people from everywhere visit Niagara Falls. The TSA people have seen these before."

Jane took a black scarf out of her paper bag and made it into a hijab for herself.

"You too?" said Chelsea. "They don't know you."

"Two is better. Stay with me, and keep your face down. Don't look for those two men, just stare ahead and get through security as quickly as possible." Jane stepped out of the ladies' room with the carry-on bag over her shoulder, and Chelsea followed.

The security area took up the first part of the terminal after the ticket counters, but at this hour of the morning the crowds were very thin and the stanchions and straps were arranged to keep the route to the first checkpoint direct. First Jane, then Chelsea showed her boarding pass and driver's license to the woman at the podium. They moved to the conveyer belt where they put their shoes in plastic bins and set them with the carry-on bag on the belt, and then stepped into the x-ray machine and out the other side.

Jane and Chelsea picked up their shoes and the bag and hurried on around the corner to the first waiting area where they were shielded from the view of people outside the secure area before they put them on. Jane watched the people who walked by. "Don't take off the scarf just yet. Those two may still figure out that the place to see who's flying out is here."

"Okay."

"Tell me their names."

"Bill Thompson is the tall one and Wesley Harriman is the other one."

"And they worked with Nick. In other words they work for Dan Crane."

"Yes." Chelsea moved her eyes to the stream of people coming past, as though talking about them might make them come.

"I guess the others must have called them, and said you were probably running."

"Couldn't it just be a coincidence? There's only one airport, and one of them might be flying somewhere today, not looking for me at all."

"I'm not a big believer in coincidences. Either way, we don't want them to see you, even by accident. What I want you to do is go into the ladies' room down there by gate six. Wait until I get there or you hear the second announcement that your flight to New York is boarding."

"All right." Chelsea got up and walked off toward the ladies' room.

Jane watched the people coming out of the security area for a few minutes. Then she got up and went to gate six to wait. Most of the waiting areas were nearly empty, but gate six was full of people. There were going to be a lot of Buffalo people in New York City this morning. She kept her eyes on the concourse most of the time to be sure Thompson and Harriman didn't show up.

After about ten minutes she saw the two men come around the corner onto the concourse. She stood up and walked to the ladies' room. She had almost convinced herself that they had been fooled or given up, but they hadn't. They must have bought tickets to get this far, and in a moment they would notice that gate six was the only waiting area that was full. The New York flight was going to be the first flight out, and it was the one to watch.

Jane found Chelsea waiting for her and told her what she'd seen. "We can't let those men follow you onto a plane or even see which one you take." She took off her scarf and set it on the shelf below the mirror.

"What are we going to do?"

"First we change clothes. I saw a pair of gray pants and a blouse in your bag. Put them on, and give me what you're wearing now."

They changed clothes quickly, and then Jane retied the two hijabs, with Chelsea wearing Jane's. She put her own clothes in the trash. Next she opened her purse and took out a stack of hundred dollar bills, held it up, and put it into Chelsea's bag. She took out a credit card and handed it to Chelsea.

She looked at it. "You're Gail Stein?"

"Sometimes." She held out her boarding pass and plucked the other from Chelsea's hand. "We need a change of plans. You're going to fly to Albany. They've already checked our IDs for the last time, so you can use my boarding pass. When you get there, use some of the cash to buy your ticket to Manchester."

"What's the credit card for?"

"The unexpected. The card's limit is twelve thousand and Gail Stein pays her bills, so don't be afraid to use it if you need to."

The loudspeaker in the ceiling blared, "United flight twenty-four thirty to JFK New York City is ready for boarding at gate six." As the female voice launched into its repetition Jane said, "That's it. We'll stay here until they call for the Albany flight."

The flight to New York was announced again and again, and Jane could tell they were trying to get the missing woman passenger to show up. Finally there was a "last call" message. Jane and Chelsea waited. Now other women were coming in and out, so they pretended to be freshening their makeup. After a few minutes Jane put their scarves on again, arranging them carefully to cover their hair.

At last, they heard the call. "Flight fifty-seven eighty-two to Albany is boarding at gate number three. Flight five seven eight two is ready for boarding at gate three."

Jane took Chelsea aside. "That's your flight. Wait for them to give the final call for boarding, and then come out of here fast and straight into the line. Keep your eyes down and get into the boarding tunnel as soon as possible." She hugged her, then released her. "I'll see you soon."

"Good-bye."

Jane stepped out of the ladies' room, kept her head down, and walked quickly past gate 6. There were two airline employees stationed at the desk, and one of them typed something into her computer to make the display change to show a flight leaving for Chicago. She heard a male voice far behind her say the word "Chelsea," but the other man said something that silenced him.

Jane increased her speed, moving quickly back toward the security area. She turned the corner, stepped into the space beside the security area into the clear corridor for arriving passengers to leave the secure area, and kept going. She edged into a group who seemed to be just off one of the first flights to land, and kept with them. She knew the two men were following her at a distance, thinking she was Chelsea. They probably couldn't believe their luck. As soon as she was alone, they would move in and try to take her.

Jane reached the open part of the terminal and kept going. She stepped into another ladies' room. As soon as she was inside, she took off Chelsea's scarf and put it into her purse. She tied back her hair, retied her running shoes, and slung her purse across her chest.

She waited until she heard the announcement for the flight to Albany, and then heard it again a few minutes later. She heard the voice warn that this was the final call. After ten more minutes, she was sure the flight had left. She took two deep breaths, and then stepped out of the ladies' room.

She walked past the ticket counters and along the glass front of the terminal, and caught her own reflection. It would have been hard to look less like Chelsea Schnell than Jane did. She was taller, her hair was longer and jet black, and her skin was olive. Near the doors there was a glass panel at right angles to the others, and she saw the reflection of the two men, now waiting outside the ladies' room she had just left, watching the door and expecting the blond Chelsea to appear at any second.

In a moment Jane was out the automatic doors and making her way across the short-term lot to the Passat. As she walked, she took out her phone and called the cell phone she had left with Jimmy Sanders. She heard his "hello."

"Hi, it's me. She's on a plane to Albany, so she'll probably get to Manchester quite a bit later than we expected."

"We'll check to see what flights there are, and be there."

"Is everything still okay?" Jane asked.

"We're fine."

"Good. Try hard to stay that way. Got to go." She hung up, got into the Passat, and drove to the exit from the lot. As she paid the parking fee, she looked into the rearview mirrors and verified that no car was following her.

22

Daniel Crane sat at his desk in the storage office feeling miserable. He wasn't entirely confident in his lawyer, Richard Brannigan, now that he'd hired him, but he was supposed to be one of the best. At first he had said that Crane had done the right thing by calling him in right away, because once a suspect retained a lawyer, the cops usually didn't even bother to question him. It hadn't worked out that way this time. They had taken him and his lawyer into a little room with cameras mounted on the ceiling and fired questions at him, and each one had felt like a puncture wound.

Brannigan had kept repeating, "Don't answer that," or "My client won't answer that," until it became annoying, but the cops had not relented.

The whole thing had been a disaster. The lead cop, a burly man with a bald head and piercing eyes said, "You gave that girl GHB and raped her. Want to tell us anything about that?" Of course it was a trap to make him give specific reasons why he was innocent, so he would contradict himself. Then there was: "You know, she has permanent brain damage, and you did that to her." He was aware that it was perfectly legal for them to lie to him in an interrogation. "We're talking to every woman you ever met, and a lot of them are giving us an earful." It was all lies. Crane had never used the powder before Chelsea. They never mentioned the brain damage again, because they hadn't fooled him.

He had drugged her because he loved her, and now he had lost her. The emergency operator had told the police that Verna Machak had come into the house, seen Chelsea, and called them, and the ambulance EMTs had brought one of the envelopes of powder from his house with them to the hospital. What right had EMTs had to do that, to search his house for drugs?

The emergency room doctors had called the cops, and then told Chelsea she had been drugged. Maybe if he'd had a chance to talk to her that morning he could have explained. He could have said he used it himself to help him sleep, and that she'd accidentally drunk from his glass that night while he was getting ready to drive her home. Or something. But he couldn't stay and talk to her because he'd had to drive to Box Farm and wait for Salamone, who hadn't even shown up, and then been taken to the police station and wasted the whole day while they tried to rattle and terrify him. He had wanted to get to the hospital and talk to her alone, but the cops had kept him until late in the day and then warned him not to try to see her, and his own lawyer had repeated it, so here he was.

Now she was gone. She had checked herself out of the hospital somehow, and she wasn't at her house and she wasn't answering her cell phone. He had sent men she knew to look for her at the hospital, and others to watch the airport, and others to talk to friends of hers to get them to call when she turned up. Nobody had accomplished anything.

Thompson and Harriman had thought they'd seen her trying to fly to New York, but when they'd gotten closer, the
woman had turned out to be somebody else.

Crane looked at his watch. It was only nine in the morning, and he felt like he'd worked a whole day already. He
got up from his desk and went to stare out the window at
the complex of storage bays. He had worked and struggled
to get where he was. He had taken risks that other men
would never have been brave enough to take. And then he
had fallen in love.

He had never been able to understand women, never
known how to get women to like him. He had never understood why they ignored him and picked dumber, poorer, less
ambitious men.

He had suspected Chelsea was one of those women
he'd heard and read about who liked a bit of an edge to
her love life. Maybe she had liked a big strong dope like
Nick Bauermeister because he overpowered her. He'd heard
many women say they liked a man who was confident and
in charge. A lot of women seemed to have a fantasy about
being taken, so they didn't have to make any decisions, just
acquiesce, and let the man's desires sweep them away. He
thought about it and realized that he hadn't heard any actual
women say that in person. They had mostly been in magazine articles written by women. But they'd said it. When
he had given Chelsea the powder that first time he'd been
trying to give her that freedom from having to decide—the
freedom from fears about the propriety of having a relationship right after her boyfriend died, or her own shyness
about being with a new man.

And it had worked. She had practically forced him the
next time. After that she had been his girlfriend, as though
they'd been together for years. She had gone out with him
every evening and gotten used to coming home with him
and staying the night. And then everything had soured in

one evening. He had felt desperate, taken the last chance he had to keep her, and that desperation had wrecked everything. He had not planned to give her the powder again, and so he hadn't been prepared. He had to work quickly, to give all his attention to pouring it into her drink without getting caught, and had probably given her too much. Now she would never understand that he had only loved her too much to let her go.

He thought about killing himself. The police had been in his house, so they had probably taken his pistol out of his desk, but he had others in his personal storage space out there beyond the window in row A. They had been taken in burglaries, and he'd stored them in case he needed to have some available that weren't registered to anyone but some guy whose house had been robbed. If he shot himself in the head with one of those, what were the police going to do— dig him up and put him in jail?

But Crane knew he wasn't going to kill himself. As long as there was any chance of getting through his trouble he wouldn't quit. He didn't feel a strong enough urge.

"Cars coming in."

Crane turned to look at the monitors on the wall. "Salamone. I'll talk to him alone." He watched Thompson get up and go down the stairs.

Crane longed to go with him. The sight of Salamone's car changed everything. Crane felt as though he had fallen into ice water. He wasn't feeling dreamy and bereft anymore; he was frightened. Did Salamone know already? Crane's lungs couldn't bring in enough air, and when he tried to make them he felt dizzy. He was aware of the sound of Thompson at the bottom of the stairs, and then he heard the back door swing open and shut.

He sat down at his desk and looked at the monitors. The big car came to the gate and the driver's arm came out and took a ticket. The gate opened and the hand released the ticket to let it flutter to the ground. The car behind Sal-amone's pulled up and the driver did the same. He didn't recognize the second car, and it irritated him. It was one thing for Salamone to do that, but these were strangers, two men in a dark gray Cadillac. Behind them was a black SUV.

On the wall monitors he watched Salamone get out of his car, and then his two men. Cantorese had been driv-ing, and he eased his fat body out from behind the wheel and straightened his short legs to stand. Pistore was out in an instant, his sharp young eyes already scanning in every direction.

Salamone went to the door, and as soon as he was inside he appeared on another monitor. As he climbed the stairs he looked somber. He wore a dark suit that seemed to have been made to fit his body by a talented tailor. Crane envied him.

Crane looked ahead and Salamone appeared in front of him. Salamone said, "Daniel. Are we alone?"

The question struck Crane as insanity. Salamone was never alone. Cantorese and Pistore were at his shoulders. But Crane said, "Yes. I sent Thompson out to the units."

Salamone nodded. "We—I mean you and me—have got trouble. Bad trouble, and we're going to talk about that later. Right now, outside in that Cadillac down there, is Mr. Malconi himself. He would like two storage units. His units won't be together. And his keys will be the only keys."

Crane could tell from his measured tone that if Crane argued, he would regret it. "Sure. How about"—he looked at the clipboard with the roster of units—"C-fifteen and J-nineteen?"

"Fine. Get the locks."

Crane went to the stock room and brought out two brand-new locks, still in their boxes.

Salamone nodded. "There will be no bill, and no list anywhere with his name on it."

"Of course."

"Come with me." The two men went down the stairs.

Crane stopped at the door. "Are you sure it's okay? I mean does he mind if I see him?"

"If he minded, you wouldn't be able to get within a hundred yards of him." Salamone pushed open the door with his left hand and pushed Crane out with the right. He walked Crane to the backseat window.

The tinted window slid down. There he was, Mr. Malconi himself. His hair was surprisingly thick and healthy looking, most of it white and bristly. His face was tanned and marked with deep creases on his forehead, around his mouth and eyes, and even on his cheeks. He looked like a doll made of a dried apple. His shining black eyes were focused on Crane. "Hello, Mr. Crane."

"Hello, sir."

The old man's expression was unchanging. "Your friend Mr. Salamone says you're a smart man. Good head for business and all that. Is it true?"

"I hope so."

"I wanted to get a look at you today, and talk to you in person." He glanced at Salamone, then back at Crane. "I believe a man should take responsibility for his actions. Do you?"

"Yes," said Crane. He wondered if this man ever heard the word "no."

"Can I talk freely, or are we going to be overheard?"

Crane looked around him and saw that Salamone's two men were on the sides of the little parking area, and that two other men had gotten out of the black SUV, and were also scanning the area. How could anyone overhear? "You can talk freely."

"Good. Now, you've got yourself in trouble because you wanted one of your men's girlfriend, so you killed him. Did you ever go to Sunday school, Mr. Crane?"

"I guess so. Yes."

"Does the name Uriah the Hittite mean anything to you?"

"I don't think so."

"Just curious. It doesn't matter. We've gone to quite a bit of trouble to keep you protected so you won't be sent away and your business broken up or abandoned. Two nights ago a cop was sneaking around the house of Walter Slawicky. You know him, right?"

"Yes." Crane's mouth was dry, but he managed to say, "He went to the police for me to say that he'd sold the rifle to Jimmy Sanders."

"Sanders is the Indian you were trying to pin the shooting on, right?"

"Yes, sir."

"I think the cop was looking for the place where Slawicky hid the rifle."

"There isn't supposed to be any such place. He was supposed to take it out in a boat and drop the pieces in Lake Ontario."

The old man's eyes seemed to sharpen. "Do you know for certain that he got rid of the rifle?"

Crane paused, then said, "I don't know why he wouldn't. Having it would get him into trouble, maybe get him charged with murder."

"You don't know why he wouldn't." The old man almost smiled. "I guess you just haven't been in trouble much. When you've been in trouble you don't like it, and you think about stashing away things that you might trade to get out of it next time—information, evidence. Maybe someday the cops will have Slawicky on a big charge. If he has the weapon, maybe he can trade it, and you, for a little slack. And maybe he doesn't trust you. He knows you killed your other guy, Nick. Why not him?"

Crane stared down at his feet, and shook his head. Things just kept getting more complicated and awful.

"Okay," said the old man. "Enough about him. Time for a sad story. The other night, we had some men watching to learn more about this Slawicky—maybe see if he still has that rifle—and who shows up, but a cop? He's snooping around Slawicky's, obviously looking for something. So one of the men shoots him."

"Those were your men?"

"Not *my* men, just men. One of them, thirty-one years old with a good family, was there. He and his friends didn't know there wasn't only one cop. A second cop who had apparently been in the car took out a shotgun and shot him in the chest. He died."

"I'm sorry," said Crane. "That's terrible."

"I'm sorry too. He was a good man. He can't even be given a decent burial for a long time, because he was connected with a lot of other people the police would like to get at."

"No burial?"

"His friends picked him up so his body wouldn't be found. You're going to take a tiny part of the responsibility. He's in that SUV back there. You're going to hold on to him for a while until arrangements can be made."

"Here? In a storage space?"

The old man looked at him, the dark eyes bright like the eyes of a predatory bird. "Do you object?"

Crane said, "No. I don't object. He can go in J-nineteen."

"Go tell the guys back by the SUV. In fact, get in and show them where to go. When you're finished, come back and give Mr. Salamone the keys."

"Yes, sir." Crane began to walk. His legs felt stiff like stilts, and he had a moment when the pavement rose up in front of him and he felt faint, but then the men from the SUV got in and opened the passenger door for him. He was relieved to sit.

The driver said, "Where to?"

"You can go around this way," Crane said. He pointed at the end of the first row of storage spaces. "J is in the third row, and the bay is number nineteen."

When the SUV reached J-19, one man got out and pulled up the door of the storage bay and the other backed the SUV up into the mouth of it. Then the two men got out, opened the hatch, and pulled out a cooler of the sort that Crane had seen at chamber of commerce picnics, about five feet long, two feet wide and deep. He imagined a man crammed in there with his knees bent. Crane moved in a reflex to help carry the cooler to the back of the storage bay and set it down on the concrete surface. He could see the cover was latched and locked, and sealed with duct tape.

The driver got back in the SUV and pulled it clear, and the other man pulled the door down and slid the bolt in. Crane took one of the locks out of its box and clasped it on the bolt. The man at the door gave the lock a tug to be sure it was fully engaged, and then got in the backseat.

A WOMAN DROVE UP TO the front gate of the storage facility in a small blue car and took a ticket, then drove in through the open gate. She parked in a space close to the main building a few feet to the right of a gray Cadillac. She had a cell phone pressed against her left ear and she was talking into it. Her window was shut, so Salamone and Mr. Malconi couldn't hear anything she was saying, and she didn't look at them. All they could really see was the cell phone and her left hand.

Mr. Malconi said to Salamone, "I've got some places to be. You can handle the rest of this, right?"

"Sure," said Salamone. "I'll bring you the keys in a day or two."

"No hurry," said Mr. Malconi. "Victor isn't going anywhere, and it will take a while to make arrangements. It'll have to be a small, quiet thing. And somebody will have to think up a story for the priest."

"I understand."

Mr. Malconi's tinted window rolled up, and his face was gone. Salamone turned and walked to the door, then disappeared inside the building. The dark gray Cadillac pulled back, turned, and went out the gate, then accelerated down the road.

The woman in the dark blue Volkswagen Passat put her cell phone away, got out of her car, and went into the building. There was a stack of printed price lists for bay rentals on a table just inside, and a stack of blank contract forms beside it. She took one of each and went back out to her car carrying them, making sure that anyone watching her would know what she was doing.

A moment later, her blue car backed up, turned, and pulled out of the lot. The driver watched to be sure she wasn't being followed, but only after a few minutes did she feel satisfied that she wasn't. Coming into the storage facility had been a risk, but while she'd been sitting a few hundred yards away she'd gotten curious about the convoy of three vehicles that had arrived. Now she was glad she had taken the chance. The cell phone pictures were clear and sharp. As she drove, she wondered what was in that big box she'd seen them putting into space J-19.

23

In his dream Isaac Lloyd was running. He felt his rhythmic breathing and strong heartbeat, the pleasant pressure of his feet padding along on the deep, spongy layer of leaves and dirt on a forest path. A faint breeze cooled his face as he ran, and the canopy of the tall trees along the path let a dapple of sunlight through.

There was someone ahead on the path that he couldn't quite see, but he knew he would catch up before long. Now and then the path ahead would straighten and he would catch a glimpse of a branch just swinging back to its normal position after someone had passed.

There was a sudden flutter of birds ascending to avoid whoever had disturbed them, and then a female voice. It said, "Ike. Hey, Ike." He ran harder. As he did, he broke through the fragile barrier of sleep and moved his real leg in the realm of consciousness and felt the sharp pain.

Ike opened his eyes. He was at home, in his own bed. Remembering and feeling it was an immense pleasure. But then he saw movement near the far wall and realized the woman's voice had been real.

"Hi, Ike," she said, and stepped to the foot of his bed. She was wearing the mask, scrubs, and cap that hid her hair so well he didn't even know the color of it.

"How did you get here? They're not supposed to give anybody a state police officer's home address."

"Don't be angry. I won't be coming again. I just needed to—"

"How did you get my address?" he said.

"When I visited you in the hospital I saw it in your file on the admission papers. I went to the hospital a while ago and learned you had been sent home, so I parked near here and waited until I saw your wife drive away. I figured that in my scrubs, anyone who saw me would figure I was a nurse checking on you, so I will. How are you feeling?"

His voice was irritable. "Have you ever been shot?"

"I'm sorry to say I have," she said. "In the leg, just like you."

"When?"

"No you don't," she said. "You'll try to use that to find my name."

"Is anything you've said to me true?"

"All of it."

"Are you even real?"

"If I weren't, I'd probably say I was. That's how dreams work. But I'm here on business."

"What business?"

"I want you to look at some pictures I took and tell me if you know these men." She reached into the pocket of her scrubs, held out her cell phone where he could see it, and tapped the first picture to make it fill the screen. "That's the storage facility where Nick Bauermeister worked."

"I recognize it," said Lloyd.

She brought up the picture of the old man in the side window of the gray Cadillac, and the other man beside him. She had taken it with the phone clapped to her ear, but it was very sharp. She tapped the screen to bring up a picture of both men.

Lloyd said, "Okay. Whatever you're doing, stop it. Right now, today. I appreciate your taking out that shotgun and giving me backup the other night. But this case is not what it looked like at first. It just got a lot more complicated."

"Who are they?"

"They're men you really don't want to meet."

"You know their names. Tell me."

"The man standing beside the car is Bobby Salamone. I don't keep up with these people most of the time, because they're not involved in my usual cases. But I know who he is. He's a member of the Mafia, kind of an underboss. He's been in prison for extortion and aggravated assault and probably other things I don't remember. He's been suspected of arranging at least a couple of murders over the years, but the evidence wasn't strong enough."

"And the old man in the car?"

"He's your prize photo. Lorenzo Malconi. He looks like a sickly old man, doesn't he? I hope he is, because he can't die soon enough for me. He's Salamone's boss, the head of the Mafia in this part of the state."

She said, "What would they be doing at the storage place?"

Lloyd looked very tired and a bit distracted, and Jane recognized the look. He had tensed a muscle and reawakened the pain. "I don't have any idea. Probably nothing illegal. People like them don't do anything. They tell people to do things and take a cut."

"I saw an SUV come in with him and then I saw two men carry a big cooler into bay J-19. That's what made me come inside the gate to take these pictures."

"There's your answer. He was putting something into storage. He brought men because he's too old to carry things himself."

"Come on, Ike. You're holding out on me. Give me what you know and I'll leave."

"I told you who these men are. That's all I know without getting a warrant and taking a look in that storage bay. For obvious reasons, I can't do that now."

Jane lifted her loose scrub shirt and pulled out a manila envelope she'd had stuck in the elastic top of her pants.

"What's that?"

"It's a record of what I've been doing—copies of the pictures I've taken. There are shots of the stolen stuff hidden in Nick Bauermeister's basement, pictures of Chelsea Schnell with Daniel Crane at his house, the shots I just showed you, the two storage bays that Malconi's men visited. You can tell the cop you give them to that he doesn't have to be careful with them. No fingerprints or anything." She held up her hands to show him that she was wearing surgical gloves. "Now go back to sleep. I'll try not to bother you again." She turned to go.

"Wait."

"Wait?" she said.

"What time is it?"

"Just about nine thirty."

"In a few hours there will be search teams at Nick Bauermeister's house and Walter Slawicky's."

"Why are you telling me?"

"Because at Slawicky's, they may find the rifle." He watched her for a reaction. "That's what you wanted, wasn't it?"

"One of the things."

"It would prove Slawicky shot Bauermeister himself."

"I'm not so sure he did," said Jane. "I don't think he would have gone to the police voluntarily unless he had an unbreakable alibi. I think he just supplied the rifle and the false story about what happened to it."

"Who, then?"

"The one who gave Slawicky the money for all the cool stuff."

"Salamone or Malconi?"

"I don't know. If they're the Mafia, why would they bother with people like Slawicky? They must have people on their payroll who do that kind of work. I think it was the one who had a reason to want Nick Bauermeister dead. The one who wanted his girlfriend."

As she slipped out the door of his bedroom she heard a car pulling into the driveway. She looked out the side window of the house and saw Lloyd's wife coming to a stop in the garage. She could see bags of groceries in the back of her station wagon. In a moment she would be carrying bags through the side door into the kitchen. Jane went out the front door, moved along the front of the Lloyd house to the next yard, and then walked quickly to her car.

MORNING WAS HELL FOR DANIEL Crane. The sun was blinding, punishing. He drove to his storage business at ten because he couldn't think of a better place to go. As he drove he kept remembering things that he would have to fix as quickly as he could. There was still quite a bit of merchandise he couldn't explain stored in his bays along the J row. Every month he had stored things his crews stole in bays registered to fictitious people. Now that he was being charged with a felony, there wasn't much to stop the police from checking to see if those renters were real, or just aliases for Daniel Crane. There would then be nothing to stop them from going through the bays, maybe with a list of items that had been reported stolen in burglaries in the area. Then they would find the body in the cooler.

Crane would have to do something to be sure Slawicky had actually sunk the rifle a few miles offshore in Lake Ontario, and not kept it somewhere with Crane's fingerprints still on it. And he couldn't just ask him. If Slawicky had kept the rifle as a threat to hold over him, then asking would make him even more defensive and paranoid. For a moment Crane considered killing him, too. Jimmy Sanders was still at large, and it had been in the newspapers that Slawicky had gone to the police and given information about him. If Slawicky died now, there would be a suspect already wanted in connection with a murder. But he remembered that Salamone had warned him not to take steps like that on his own again. Maybe he would just bring the problem up with Salamone.

As he drove up to the storage facility his eyes rested on the big sign: BOX FARM PERSONAL STORAGE. He thought he'd like to change the name. When he'd thought of it, the name had sounded pleasant—an old farm with acres of storage spaces—but the words seemed creepy now, maybe a cynical, slangy way of referring to a cemetery. He knew it was too late to change it now, after years of building the business, but he wished he could.

He pulled through the gate and drove to the office, then saw the big sedan parked in his reserved space. Salamone. What was he doing here? Salamone had never come this early in the morning. Crane got out of his Range Rover, entered the building, and climbed the stairs.

He stepped into his office and found Salamone's two companions had made themselves comfortable. Cantorese was sitting behind the second desk, where the man on duty usually sat to watch the windows and monitors and answer the phone. Cantorese sat back in the chair with his feet up on the desk, so Crane could see the soles of his shoes. Part of Crane's mind noted that even the man's feet were wide, feet made to hold up a three hundred fifty pound body. Pistore was sitting in the customer chair near the desk, the first time Crane remembered seeing him seated. Neither of them reacted to the sight of Crane coming in.

Salamone was at Crane's desk. He hadn't just sat there as he often had, because that was the most comfortable chair. He had opened all the drawers and left them open, and he had moved things around on the desktop. The bay rosters, the time sheets for the men, the bills, notices, and price lists had all been combined into one pile. As Crane approached he could see that there were two sets of papers on the cleared desktop, one facing Crane and the other facing Salamone. Two of the pens that Crane usually kept in the desk were set beside the papers.

"Hi, Danny," said Salamone. He looked at his watch. It wasn't a big, heavy stupid one with lots of little dials and buttons. It was white gold or platinum, as thin as a coin with a leather strap, the sort of watch Crane imagined on the wrist of a French banker. "Run into some traffic?"

"No," Crane said. "I overslept a little."

"Bad night, huh? I can't blame you." He looked toward the counter where the coffee maker was. "Want a minute to pour yourself a cup of coffee and get up to speed?"

"I'm fine," said Crane.

"Suit yourself. We heard you had some trouble."

"I did, but it's not going to be a big problem."

"No? I heard your girlfriend went to the hospital and the police have a bunch of roofies you'd used on her. I'm glad to hear that wasn't what happened."

"It wasn't rohypnol. It was GHB. I bought it through a Mexican online site, and they must have made a mistake in the dose, or the concentration was uneven and she got a strong batch. She was still asleep when the cleaning lady came unexpectedly, found her, and got worried. I'll explain it to Chelsea, and she'll be fine with it. The stuff disappears from the bloodstream right away, and it's a natural substance, so the police can't prove anything anyway."

"I hope you're right," said Salamone. "But I do kind of wonder what you were thinking."

"I gave her some once before, and she was okay and the next day she didn't remember a thing. The other night she was acting crazy, talking about leaving me, and I figured I'd just make her forget what she'd said. She'd sleep and then wake up the next day okay."

Salamone and Cantorese met each other's eyes. Salamone shrugged. "Okay. I hope your trouble goes away. In the meantime, I've got some papers here for you to sign. Take a look." He pushed one set of papers toward Crane.

Pistore sprung up and brought his chair to Crane so he could read and sign sitting down. Crane was expected to sit, so he sat.

After a minute Crane looked up from the papers. "This says I'm selling my business to Angela Milton. I don't know anybody named Angela Milton."

"Look, Danny. You know something about business. Do you know how mortgage insurance works? The company that lends you money isn't a hundred percent sure you'll always be able to keep paying the money back. So they cut their risk by having you insure them against you not paying."

"What does that have to do with—"

"It's an analogy to your current situation. You could be right that your little girlfriend will be generous about things and shrug off the fact that you—legally, anyway—raped her. But you've opened a big box full of uncertainty here. What happens if you're wrong?"

"There's no risk," said Crane. "The drug isn't detectable. They can't prove she took it, let alone that I gave it to her."

"Mr. Malconi has an excellent team of criminal attorneys. They tell him that having her wake up with your sperm in her and claiming not to know she'd had sex with you could be a problem. The fact that there was a supply in your home of an illegal drug that causes those symptoms makes the problem worse. Mr. Malconi has decided to make sure that he's protected."

"Can't you talk to him?"

"Danny. You met Mr. Malconi yesterday. Did he strike you as a man who changes his mind about things like this?"

"But he can't just take my business because I had a problem with my girlfriend."

"This isn't just an unfortunate spat. You had her in the first place because you shot her boyfriend through the head. Then you had the idea you'd get a stranger arrested for it, and have him die in jail. You have to be fair about this, and admit to yourself that you've given Mr. Malconi reason to think you're not a hundred percent reliable. Ninety percent isn't good enough."

"Maybe I can talk to him," said Crane.

"I've talked to him on your behalf. I've said everything you could say, and more. But even I have to be careful. You're used to businessmen like you. They negotiate everything, and then if it doesn't work out they sue each other. Mr. Malconi's options are much, much wider. I've persuaded him to limit himself to creating a simple legal safeguard. Read the papers and sign them."

Crane scanned the pages. "This says I give this person my business for five million dollars."

"A fair price, right?"

"But I'm supposed to get paid for the sale at the rate of a hundred thousand a year. That's fifty years. And the money doesn't come from Angela Milton. It comes from the business—my own business. I'm supposed to run the business and pay myself?"

"She's not a businessperson, Danny. You don't want her running it."

"Who the hell is this Angela Milton?"

"Milton is her husband's last name. Her maiden name was Torturro. She's one of Mr. Malconi's brother's grandchildren."

"Jesus."

"Mr. Malconi is protecting all of us from the possibility that you have to spend some time in jail. You could get sued in a civil suit for doing harm to Miss Chelsea, and lose. This way, your business will not be taken away from you in a forced foreclosure."

"That's a very remote possibility."

"Mr. Malconi has lived to be old by protecting himself and his people from possibilities other people thought were remote."

Crane felt acid rise from his stomach to his esophagus, but he fought it back down. He knew that if he signed the contract his business would be theirs. He would have to work for the rest of his life to pay himself for the false sale. And because he could only pay himself a hundred thousand a year from the company, he would have to keep running the burglary crew to bring Salamone a supply of stolen jewelry and furnishings. "This is unfair," he muttered. "He's just taking it."

Salamone reached out and patted him on the shoulder, and then touched him on the side of his face. It was a strange gesture, almost the way a parent caressed a child's cheek. "Be glad," he said. "You could have been found hanging in one of your storage bays. He would never do that in a business he owns."

24

Jane transferred the photographs to the temporary account she'd been given at the business center in her hotel, and sent them to the e-mail address she'd found on Sergeant Isaac Lloyd's business card. Then she checked out of the hotel.

She drove to a big chain drugstore on Niagara Falls Boulevard and bought three more prepaid cell phones, loaded them with calling minutes, and put two in her backpack and one in her pocket. She dismantled the cell phone she had been using and threw the parts into two different dumpsters and a storm sewer. She knew the photographs she had sent Isaac Lloyd couldn't be used in a court, but she was showing the police where to look, so they could find the same evidence themselves.

She used a new phone to call Jimmy Sanders in Hanover, New Hampshire.

"Hello?"

"Hi. Me again. Did you have any trouble meeting her at the airport?"

"No," said Jimmy. "We found a picture of her online from a couple of years ago. She was the twenty-fifth runner-up for some beauty contest. Ow! Okay, she won. Want to talk to the ex–beauty queen?"

"Yes."

A second later Chelsea Schnell's voice came on. "Hi."

"Hi," said Jane. "I had to leave the airport in a hurry, so I didn't actually see you off. I just wanted to be sure you got there without being followed."

"Yes. I had no trouble at all. There was nobody in the Albany airport that I'd ever seen before, and I was on a plane in forty-five minutes."

"And have you managed to talk to your mother?"

"Yes. I called her in Denver as soon as we got here. Thank you for asking. She knows I'm safe and I'm not going to be in touch again for a long time. I said I needed to be away, and that there's a man who won't stop trying to stalk me. I said I wanted time to get my head straight from all the things that had happened. I didn't tell her about the hospital and the rest, because that would just make her feel worse."

"That's probably wise," Jane said. "And I take it you're getting along with everybody there."

"Mattie's been great. And the town is pretty, and relaxed, and nice."

"And Jimmy?"

"Uh-huh. Same."

"He's still right there listening?"

"Yep."

"Okay. I'll talk to you about him another time. I changed phones again. After we hang up, check the memory on that phone and get my new number."

"Okay." She paused. "And Jane?"

"What?"

"Thank you so much for saving my life."

"Right. Got to go." She thought about what she had just learned. Chelsea and Jimmy were, at the very least, flirting. People were a strange species. They could be drugged, battered, starved, everything but murdered, but something inside them was always striving to live, to struggle out of darkness toward light. They were utterly incorrigible.

THE POLICE TEAM HAD MOVED the motor home in Slawicky's yard back twenty-five feet to uncover the bare patch that Ike Lloyd had seen the night he'd been shot. Two Caledonia police officers were doing the digging, while Technical Sergeant Arthur Reid of the New York State police stood by. He made sure to stand straight, and didn't sit down or betray a lack of attention to the work so they wouldn't think he was lounging around while they labored.

What he was really thinking was that he fervently hoped Ike Lloyd hadn't taken a bullet for nothing. Ike had been a close friend of Reid's for about fifteen of his seventeen years with the state police. Ike was going to have a split decision on this case at best. He had gotten shot because once again he had a theory that he'd gone out to test alone without following the proper procedures. But he had been shot in the line of duty, so he would get another public citation for bravery, and another private reprimand for the screw-up. If the search team found something here, then maybe this wouldn't be his final reprimand.

Reid was determined to do his best to make Ike's work count. Reid was supposed to be taking over an investigation that Ike had stalled, but what he was really doing was letting his friend direct the investigation from his bed.

Reid's phone vibrated in his pocket, and he answered. "Reid."

"It's me," said Ike.

"What's up? Did the night nurse show up again?"

"This morning. She also just sent us a whole bunch of photographs with dates and times and places. I'm going to forward them to you in a minute."

"Anything we can use?"

"I'm not going to wait to study them before I e-mail them to you, but I think there's a lot."

"I'll let you know what I can make of them after I—" He stopped in midsentence, and took a breath.

"What?"

"I think they found something. Let me call you back in a minute." Reid ended the call and stepped closer to the spot where the two Caledonia cops had stopped digging. They were kneeling in the hole now, only about two feet down. His heart began to beat faster. After questioning Walter Slawicky, Reid had known that if Slawicky had buried anything, he would not have dug very deep. He just wasn't the kind of man who would spend several hours sweating to move five or six feet of earth out of a hole and then back in again.

The two cops lifted and pulled up a black polyvinyl chloride pipe about nine inches in diameter and four feet long. He was aware that some of the other cops were shaking their heads in frustration, thinking that the two diggers had just broken the house's sewer line, but not the two diggers.

As they lifted the pipe higher he could see it was capped at both ends. They set it beside the hole and climbed out onto the grass. The lead police detective stepped up and took charge, while Reid stayed back a few feet. "Okay, great work, you guys," the detective said. "It's capped at both ends, so what we want to do next is take one cap off. Jerry, can you do that for us? Then take a flashlight and look inside. Don't take anything out or touch anything inside, but I want a preview of what it is."

A technician, presumably Jerry, stepped up putting on latex gloves, then spread a tarp beside the pipe and used a tool that looked like a carpet knife to slice away the plumber's tape that had been used to seal the cap. He then unscrewed the cap. He bent forward on the tarp, pressed his forehead to it, and aimed a small flashlight into the pipe.

He sat up again and looked at the detective. "It's a rifle," he said. He leaned forward again. "And I can see a twenty-round box of ammo. Thirty-aught-six Federal Power-Shok, one eighty grain."

"Could this be the rifle?"

"We'll have to do the test and compare the ballistics. But it's hard to think of why he'd bury it if it wasn't that rifle."

"Okay, Jerry. Cap it again and take it to your lab. Prints, DNA, anything and everything, okay?" The detective turned away while the technician obeyed. He looked past the two diggers and spotted three other cops who had been standing around.

"Bill, Hank. Go to the station and read Mr. Slawicky his rights." Slawicky had been in the act of loading suitcases into his new Porsche the night after Ike Lloyd's shooting had taken place in his yard, and he had been held for questioning.

The detective saw two technicians folding the tarp and carrying the tube to their truck. He called out, "Pictures, guys. Lots of pictures."

Art Reid stepped away from the scene and took out his cell phone. He saw that he'd received an e-mail, but he knew what it was, so he didn't stop to look. He called Lloyd's number, and let it keep ringing until Lloyd's voice came on.

"Lloyd."

"Hi, Ike. They found the rifle. It was right where you thought it would be."

WALTER SLAWICKY HAD BEEN THROUGH booking and processing. When the detectives came in to talk to him he said he would wait until he had talked to his attorney, so he sat in a holding cell for an interminable period of time, just waiting. They had taken his watch, so he couldn't even measure the time. Then there was a van that took him and two other men to the county jail. The intake ritual was long and unpleasant, a lot of standing on lines painted on the floor to wait for his forms to be created, for guards to issue him clothes, for a shower, for a cell assignment. Every single thing that got done took fifty times as long as it needed to, and all the time he was watching.

Jail was a dangerous place. Slawicky had thought about this many times since he went to work for Dan Crane. He had always stayed off Crane's payroll, doing the break-ins and a few odd jobs. He never liked being an employee, and since he'd fallen off the forklift when he'd run it into the high shelf at the big box store a few years ago, he'd been on full disability. He hadn't wanted to mess that up.

He had assumed his cell would be with the two men who had been transported in the van with him. Nobody had been allowed to talk, but he had formed an opinion about them, and he didn't think they would be a problem. There had been no crazy-eyed stares, no signs of belligerence.

One of them was a young guy the cops called Oakes who kept watching everybody else for cues, probably because he thought the older guys must have been through this before. The other seemed to Slawicky to actually have been in jail a few times. He was at least fifty and the tattoos on his hands and forearms had not been done by a professional. He was called Gordon, and he had the lean look of a man who had lived a marginal life for a long time. His eyes had squint lines and his teeth and fingers were stained brown from smoking. Slawicky figured that the man's chain-smoking had probably been a reasonable decision, because he didn't seem to be likely to live much longer anyway.

The thing that first struck Slawicky about jail was that it was ugly. There were modules that looked modern, and open bay sections, but those were filled up already—maybe given to favored inmates—so he was led to a traditional block with cells and iron bars. Maybe if the DA's office scheduled a trial he would be here long enough to move. For now the guards had Slawicky in a cell alone.

Everything in the jail was made to be plain, bare, and hard. Just looking told you if you hit anything you'd just break your hand. But he needed less time than he would have expected to get used to things. He didn't miss soft furniture or any of that stuff. He had never wasted much time thinking about any furniture besides his television set. When he had worked on crews taking furniture out of houses and heard Crane say how much some of it cost, he'd seen it as wasted money.

It took Slawicky two days to run into the first of the men Dan Crane had hired to get themselves sent to jail and kill the Indian. He was Carl Ralston, the biker. Slawicky was in line waiting his turn at the cafeteria counter when he felt someone standing too close to him. Ralston was big—at least six feet three, with tattoos that showed through his shaved blond hair and on his neck. When Slawicky turned, Ralston's face was about a foot away and grinning horribly at him. It was hard to keep from flinching, but Slawicky was pretty sure he managed.

But Ralston laughed, so Slawicky did too. They side-stepped dutifully through the line, received their food, and then Slawicky followed Ralston to a table. They sat, and Ralston said, "There are five of us now."

"Us?"

"You're in here for the Indian too, right?"

Slawicky thought faster than he'd thought in years. "It's not a competition, is it?"

"No. Whoever gets the first chance at him will do it. We have it worked out that whoever else is nearby will help—block surveillance cameras, distract guards, make noise, whatever."

"He's not here yet, is he?" Slawicky asked.

"Not yet, but he could be any day."

Slawicky nodded as he considered his new situation. Crane had told him that the word had gone to the jail that the killing of Jimmy Sanders was off. Maybe the word hadn't gotten around to Ralston yet. Slawicky would certainly never have considered trying to kill Sanders, especially to save Crane. But he was a new man in a central jail. Being one of five allies who were prepared to kill somebody was a lot better than being alone in here. If Ralston and the others would help him kill Jimmy Sanders, then they'd also help him in a fight with other inmates. "You can count me in," Slawicky said. "I used to work with Nick. He didn't deserve to die."

Ralston looked at him with mild contempt. "Never met him. This isn't about Nick. It's about money."

"Well of course. But I was just saying."

Ralston watched him, but said nothing.

Slawicky said, "How do I know when it's happening?"

Ralston shrugged. "Maybe you will, and maybe you'll just hear about it after. But be ready to lend a hand."

Slawicky watched Ralston chewing his food. He wanted to ask him about what Crane had said. The killing was supposed to be off because the Italians didn't like it. He probed a little. "I heard that the Mafia has guys in here who kind of make the rules. Ever run into that?"

Ralston nodded. "I've heard that, and I've seen them around. There are a bunch of them awaiting trial for different things. They mostly hang out by themselves. I stay away from them, and you should too. You really don't want to get into trouble with those guys."

The next night Slawicky slept more soundly on his hard shelf of a bunk. At last he was protected. He was in trouble, but it probably wasn't fatal trouble. The police had found the rifle he'd buried, even though he'd parked the motor home over it. But they didn't have enough evidence to convict him of Nick's murder. There was no way. He would probably be out of here on bail before any of the stupid bastards like Ralston who had gone to jail on purpose. After he was out he would have to stay safely out of sight until the police charged Crane with the murder. But that shouldn't be hard. Crane had killed Nick, but he wasn't likely to be able to hunt down Slawicky and kill him too. He wouldn't have time, and he wasn't the man for the job.

On the third night, the man for the job arrived. His name was Angelo Boiardo, and he was in his early twenties. He had been raised in Pittsburgh, but after he'd gotten in trouble there he had been sent to Buffalo to live with an uncle. He had been working for Mr. Malconi for about four years, making himself useful, gaining knowledge and respect. At the moment he was in jail awaiting trial for carrying a concealed firearm.

His lawyer had come to the jail and told him that Mr. Salamone had personally selected him to perform a service for Mr. Malconi. Boiardo had only a vague idea what Slawicky had done to displease the old man. There was something about endangering a business by lying about throwing a gun in the lake. It didn't matter to Boiardo. If he had been expected to worry about that, he would have been told all about it.

What he was told was that at 2:39 AM, there would be a short circuit in the electronic locking system affecting his cellblock, Slawicky's cellblock, and the sliding gate between them.

Boiardo was sleek as a whippet and very quick. At 2:39 when he heard the electronic lock click and the bars begin to roll out of the way, he was already standing sideways beside the lock ready to slide his body out of his cell. He hurried down the cellblock, reached the gate when the bars had only opened a few inches, and slipped through to Slawicky's cellblock. When he reached Slawicky's cell the bars were fully open, but Slawicky was still asleep.

Boiardo produced a toothbrush handle with three blades from a safety razor embedded in the shaft like a long scalpel.

He swiftly tugged the wool blanket up over Slawicky's head with his left hand, slipped his right under the blanket, and brought it across the throat by feel. He released the toothbrush handle and held the blanket in place for a few seconds while Slawicky's heart's last beats pumped the blood in spurts from the artery and it soaked into the wool.

In three more seconds he was out again. He moved down the cellblock like a shadow to his own cellblock. A friend had kept the automatic gate from locking by placing a book between the two sides. The gate bumped the book and retracted, bumped and retracted. As soon as Boiardo passed, the man removed the book and the bars clanged shut. The two men were in their cells long before the guards came to find out why the gate had been registering an unlocked signal.

The tracing of the short circuit that had opened the locks on one circuit for a few minutes began a few hours later, but it had to be interrupted because that morning there was a general alarm and lockdown, so the electrician couldn't work. A prisoner had been found dead in his cell.

25

As Sally Schnell sat on the couch in the living room of her niece Amy's house in Aurora, Colorado, she felt unsettled and worried. She was holding little Madison, rocking the pudgy newborn and humming to soothe her, but her mind was on her own child. Maybe she had made a terrible mistake that would make Chelsea furious at her. Maybe she had done exactly the right thing, and saved Chelsea from danger. The uncertainty was terrible.

The two federal agents had come to her here in Aurora. They had arrived with no warning at all. When they rang the bell at the front door, Amy's husband, Sam, had been the one to go to the door. He had looked through the peephole first and seen two men in suits. They were both athletic looking, one of them blond and the other darker. As soon as Sam opened the door, the two held up little black wallets with their pictures on cards like licenses on one side, and gold badges on the other. When she had looked at the wallets closely a minute later, she had seen a big spread eagle on the top and DEA in the middle.

Sally had been across the room from the door and seen them and heard the blond one say, "Sir, I'm Special Agent McNally, and this is Special Agent Herrera, Drug Enforcement Administration. We're here to speak with Chelsea Schnell. Can you get her for us, please?"

Sam was so shocked that at first he was speechless. Then he had said, "What? Chelsea?"

"Yes, sir. We need to speak with her."

Sam was stunned. He had turned to look at Sally on the couch, opening the door wider so the two men were able to see into the living room. "Chelsea's mother is here, but Chelsea isn't."

Special Agent McNally said, "May we come in, please?"

There was that oh-so-careful politeness that police officers had, no matter what they were called, but this one spoke in an especially cold, no-nonsense way. The fact that they were federal instead of local seemed to make them even more cold and steely. Of course Sam let them in. Who knew what would happen if he didn't?

The two men stepped into the living room and held up their identification wallets so Sally could see them and repeated their names. Sally had been trembling so hard by then that she was afraid she'd drop the baby. She realized after a few seconds that she had been breathing through her mouth. She held little Madison up so Sam would take her.

Special Agent McNally said, "Your name, please?"

"Me?" she said. "Sally Schnell."

"And you're Chelsea Schnell's mother?"

"Yes. What's happening?"

"We're looking for Miss Schnell in connection with an investigation," said Special Agent Herrera. "Is she here?"

"No," she said. "She's not. She had planned to come, and we'd even bought tickets for both of us, but she decided she just couldn't come right now."

"So you can assure us that she's not in the house right now."

"Yes," said Sally. "She didn't come to Colorado with me. I don't know if you're aware of it or not, but only a few weeks ago her boyfriend was shot to death in front of her eyes."

"We were made aware of that, Mrs. Schnell," Special Agent McNally said. "We're very sorry for your daughter's loss."

"Yes," Special Agent Herrera said. "What we've come to talk with her about was her most recent misfortune. As I'm sure you understand, one aspect of the case falls within our area of responsibility."

"What most recent misfortune?"

Herrera looked at her, incredulous. "She hasn't told you?"

"No. What misfortune? What's happened to her?" Sally was terribly agitated now, and her hands were trembling so much that they felt useless, limp and fluttering. "Is she hurt?"

Herrera looked solemnly at McNally, who took a breath and said, "She was allegedly given a drug known for short as GHB. It's a common date-rape drug. While she was unconscious, she was allegedly sexually assaulted."

"Oh, no!" She put her hand over her mouth and a second later the two agents blurred and she knew she was crying. "Oh no no no no. Not Chelsea."

"I'm afraid so, ma'am," said Herrera. "Our agency was contacted because GHB is an illegal substance. In this case it entered the country from Mexico."

"But the man. Who?"

"A suspect has been arrested. His name is Daniel Crane, and he had been dating your daughter recently."

"That can't be. She just saw her boyfriend killed. She's been in a state of mourning. She wasn't ready to date anybody yet."

McNally spoke. "I'm sorry, ma'am. We understand your surprise, and the precise nature of the relationship will be a matter for the court, no doubt. Our specific task concerns the possession and use of illegal substances. In this case, the drug was GHB, which has a very strong but transitory effect on the victim. By the time she was tested at the hospital, the GHB had been metabolized and the tests weren't conclusive. That's why we need her cooperation."

Herrera said, "In cases that aren't mostly about narcotics offenses, we're usually a secondary resource, a source of expert consulting. But because of the kind of drug it was, the local police don't have much to charge the suspect with. So for the moment, we're the lead agency in the case. Of course we've taken steps to stop the people who sold the drug, and Mr. Crane will be charged with possession of the drug. For the more serious offenses, they'll need the help of the victim."

"You're telling me Chelsea has to be grilled and forced to relive a rape in front of a court?"

"It's more complicated than that I'm afraid," McNally said. "Stopping all illegal drugs from entering the country is impossible, but we stop some of them. This is about a victim, your daughter. She deserves some justice."

"I don't know," Sally said. All of this was confusing. But Chelsea certainly had decided what to do—go away for a while, and stay out of sight. "What if she's not up to this?"

"She might be subpoenaed to testify in a trial. No judge would be able to tell her what to say. But she would be reminded that if she doesn't cooperate, the man who raped her will pay a fine and walk away. Someone has to stand up and say, 'I did not consent to sex with this man, but the tests show he had sex with me.' Otherwise, he'll do this to other women. There will be other pointless investigations and trials until a victim has the courage to stand up."

Sally Schnell could think of nothing to say. She knew that they were right. Letting him go on doing this was terrible, a sin.

Herrera said, "She's not at her home in Avon, New York. Can you tell us why that is?"

"I can't really tell you. She didn't even tell me what had happened to her. She went away. Now I guess I know why she wanted to get away."

"Mrs. Schnell, can you tell us where she is at present?"

"She wants time to get over this, to get her head straight. That's what she said. It's what she needs, and she made me promise not to tell anyone anything for any reason. Let her come home when she's ready to face this."

Herrera and McNally looked at each other, and their expressions turned grim. McNally said, "We appreciate your position. But I'm going to ask you again. There are two very good reasons to answer. The first and most important is that we happen to know Mr. Crane has been trying hard to find Chelsea. Probably she doesn't want to hear him pleading with her not to testify. But we believe it's more serious than that. He knows that he's about to be charged with a crime that could result in a very long prison sentence."

"Oh, my God."

"Think about it. If she testifies he could spend the rest of his life in prison. If she doesn't, he'll pay a small fine and the case will be closed."

"Oh," said Sally. "I've got to call her."

"We have to ask you not to do that," said McNally.

"Why not?"

"Chelsea has a choice about whether to cooperate with the investigation—not legally, of course, but in practical terms. She has no choice about whether or not to submit to an interview. We—or our colleagues—must speak with her. And these interviews have to be conducted in person, not over the phone. Please give us her current address, and we can be on our way."

Sally hesitated. "All right. Do you carry a pad or something? I'll write it down for you."

McNally produced a small spiral notebook and a pen. She wrote and handed it back. He read aloud, "Thirteen sixty-four North Chambers Street, Hanover, New Hampshire. Is that correct?"

"Yes."

McNally looked down again at his small spiral notebook, then put it into his pocket. "Thank you, ma'am. We may be in touch later. If you get any other information, call us. Here's my card." They headed to the door.

She looked at the card and said, "What was the other reason?"

"Ma'am?"

"The other reason why I should give you her address."

Herrera said, "We're federal officers. Lying to us or not answering our questions is a crime. Both you and she could have been charged with obstruction of justice. It would be a terrible thing if the rapist went free and the rape victim and her mother went to a federal prison."

Then they were out the door. She was relieved that they had not told her the second reason until after she had decided. She would always have had to wonder if she'd done it to save her child or to save herself. This way she knew.

As the two men walked away from the house, the tall blond one turned toward his companion. "You drive. I'll make the call."

They got into their rental car and the shorter, darker man drove away from the house. The blond one dialed and waited, and then said, "Hello. This is Al Galbano, calling for Mr. Salamone."

He waited for a few seconds, watching his companion maneuver into the traffic heading for Denver.

"This is Salamone."

"Mr. Salamone, I'm calling you from Denver. Ron Pozzo and I found the cousin's house, but Chelsea never came to Denver. We talked to her mother, and got another address for her."

"You think this is the right one?"

"Yes, I do. Pozzo and I do this routine where we're special agents in the DEA. We use it to confiscate drugs and money. We usually let the drug dealer go, and charge him a fee for protection. We've got ID and badges, and we've convinced everybody so far."

Salamone laughed. "You pulled that on the girl's mother?"

"Yes. We said we were involved in her case because of the drugs. We said the guy who raped her daughter would walk away with a small fine for possession of the drug if she didn't get the girl to cooperate with us and prove he used it on her."

"Brilliant. Absolute genius. Can you give me the address?"

McNally took out the small notebook, read the address to Salamone, and then tore the sheet out of the notebook, crumpled it, and let it fly out the window. There was no sense in leaving an address like that in his notebook. Pretty soon it would be a dangerous thing to have.

26

Jane drove the Volkswagen Passat up New Hampshire Route 120 to the town of Lebanon, continued to Hanover, and turned on Wheelock Street to North Chambers Street. She drifted past the apartment at 1364, looking at the doors and in the windows. She couldn't see Jimmy, Mattie, or Chelsea, but there seemed to be no damage to glass, locks, or latches, and no signs of anyone watching the house.

She had driven for several hours, and she had been extremely careful. She had brought two people here in separate trips over a period of a few weeks and sent a third by plane. There had never been any sign of a problem, but three was a lot of trips. All the way here she watched to be sure that no other car stayed in her rearview mirror for long enough to be following her. When she left her hotel in Niagara Falls she had looked under the car with a makeup mirror to be sure nothing had been stuck to the undercarriage or in the engine compartment, and checked again after she'd made a stop in Albany. On the way she had taken exits from the thruway four times to see who came off the ramp after her, and then gotten back on. Nobody had followed.

Now Jane drove along the streets in the vicinity of the apartment. She studied the cars parked within sight of the apartment building, looking for heads inside. She searched for any van that could hold a surveillance team, and for any SUV that reminded her of the ones that had pursued her in Ohio and on the reservation, or the one that had brought the cooler to the storage facility outside Akron. She saw high school students and their parents who had come during summer to look at Dartmouth, a number of earnest-looking graduate students, and another group, mostly young men, wearing shorts, backpacks, and hiking boots, many of them carrying hiking staffs. There was an entrance to the Appalachian Trail between a store and a restaurant on Main Street, and Hanover was a good place to stop and get a good meal on the long walk from Maine to Georgia.

When Jane was satisfied, she parked on a street parallel to Chambers so she could come out the back door of the apartment and get to her car if she needed to. As she walked to the apartment she never stopped watching for any sign that she might have missed while she was in the car.

When she reached the apartment building she looked even more carefully to see if any window held a human silhouette or the glint of a lens. She saw nothing. She rang the bell and Mattie opened the door. Mattie took Jane's hand, pulled her inside, and hugged her for a moment. "It's so good to see you," she said.

Jane looked over Mattie's shoulder. Jimmy and Chelsea came out of another room together, and Jimmy was carrying the remote control from the television set. "Jane," he said. When the two stopped a few feet away, Jane noticed their shoulders were touching, and that they stayed that way.

Jane released Mattie. "Hi, everybody." She slung her backpack off her shoulder and set it by the couch, then sat down. "I made the trip again because I've done all I can back there for the moment. It's safer for all of us if I'm here."

"What does that mean?" Mattie asked.

"I've learned some things about our troubles. I've managed to get what I've found out into the hands of a state police sergeant who's been searching for Jimmy all this time. He's been in the hospital but he's sane and honest, so he'll get the information to the people who are now running the investigation of the murder."

"The state trooper we saw in the woods?" asked Jimmy. "The runner?"

"Yes. I did him a favor, so he owed me."

"He let you tell him all this stuff and walk away without having you followed or anything?" said Jimmy.

"I didn't say it was a small favor."

Chelsea said, "So where are we now?"

"I've set the dogs after the people who are responsible for this mess. Now we stay out of sight for a while and give the dogs time to work."

Mattie said, "I'll get you something to eat."

Jane said, "Thank you, Mattie." She knew that refusing food would be foolish and insulting. Jane was a traveler who had genuinely just come off the trail, and Mattie was the older woman, the hostess, so she would bring out food.

While Mattie went off to the kitchen and was out of hearing, Jane said, "Maybe I'll go help her."

"I'll do it," Chelsea said, and hurried after her.

"Okay."

Jimmy took a step in that direction.

"Not you."

Jimmy sat down in the chair across from where Jane sat on the couch.

Jane said, "Want to fill me in?"

"About what?"

"How long has she been here? A week?"

"A little longer."

"Not much. You know that she's been through a whole lot in the past couple of months. And you may recall that what the police want you for is killing her boyfriend."

"But I didn't," he said. "She knows that."

"I can see she does."

"You don't approve."

Jane shrugged. "I'm offering you the benefit of my skepticism. You'll both do what you decide to do. She's lost somebody she cared about, and afterward learned that he was a thief. The next man in her life drugged and raped her, and now he seems to be trying to find her to keep her from testifying against him. It's not hard to look good in that field."

"Do I deserve this?"

"No," Jane said. "You're a good, honest, decent man she's been cooped up with for over a week. You're also a victim of the same scheme that has hurt her." She smiled. "And I guess you're not as ugly as you used to be. She's undoubtedly missing her mother, and you've even been sharing yours with her. My point is that it wouldn't be too strange if she turned to you on the rebound just because she needs somebody who's not a monster. She doesn't deserve to be hurt again, and I don't want this to end badly for you, either."

He sighed deeply. "You're the objective observer."

A voice from behind them said, "But do we need one of those?"

They both looked to see Chelsea standing in the kitchen doorway. "I'm okay now. I have all my faculties. I like Jimmy and I can tell he likes me. For the moment that's all there is. You wanted us all to get along, and we do. Just what you wanted."

Jane said, "That's good. It's just that whatever living together in hiding is, it's not normal, and it's not permanent."

Mattie came in carrying a hot plate. Jane could see slices of roast beef, some asparagus, and a baked potato. "These are leftovers, I'm afraid, but it's what we had for dinner and it's pretty good."

"It looks better than that," Jane said. "I'll eat at the kitchen table."

While Jane ate, Mattie talked about Hanover, the stores where she had found the best food, and the way the region was in the summer, with farmers' markets along the roads to the east, and over the Vermont border to the west. The others had little to add, because they had rarely been outdoors.

As the night wore on, first Mattie got tired and went off to bed. Then Jimmy brought out a blanket and pillow and lay down on the couch.

"I guess we'll share a bed," said Chelsea. "If you don't mind."

"No, it's fine," said Jane. She glanced at Jimmy. "I guess it's time."

They said good-night to Jimmy, and went into the remaining bedroom. In a few minutes they were in the dark and in bed.

Chelsea spoke in a whisper. "I'm really grateful for everything you've done. I was in danger, and you fought for me. I needed to get away, and I needed a rest from being sad or angry or scared, and you sent me here. It's been good to be with normal people in a safe place. And I've had a lot of time to think."

"I'm glad."

"I said that so you would understand what I'm going to tell you now. I don't want to let you risk your life because of me, and then lie to you."

"About Jimmy?"

"Yes."

"You like him more than you've said."

"Much more," she said. "I heard what you said to him.

Yes, I've been through a lot, and then been locked up with an attractive man, and knowing his mother makes me see what made him such a good man. But if I hadn't been through anything, and I had met him some other way, I would still feel the same."

"I'm only interested in keeping you safe. If you both remember why you're here, then I'll be satisfied. The rest is up to you."

"Thanks," said Chelsea. "I've taken your advice, and I'm not just letting some guy pick me. I'm doing the picking. It's a good feeling." She turned away from Jane, tugged the covers up to her chin, and closed her eyes.

Jane lay in the dark, staring up toward the ceiling, where the smoke detector's tiny red light blinked once every ten seconds. There was as much to worry about as there had been when she had started. She had, for the moment, managed to keep Jimmy, Mattie, and Chelsea alive and hidden far away from the people who were hunting them. She had kept Ike Lloyd alive, barely. She had set the forces in motion, but all she could do now was wait and see if the forces accomplished what she wanted. Maybe what she'd done would be enough.

She was exhausted from the days and nights of stalking and hiding, and the long drive to New Hampshire. It was late. After a time the slow, rhythmic sound of Chelsea's breathing put Jane to sleep. She slept peacefully in an empty place, without sight or sound or thought.

"Jane." It was a whisper, but it wasn't Chelsea's voice, Mattie's, or Jimmy's. "Jane!" This time she thought she recognized it. In her dream she pulled aside the covers and got up, then put on her clothes. "Jane," the whisper came again.

Jane opened the bedroom door, walked silently past Jimmy where he lay on the couch, out the front door, and closed the door behind her. There he was. She said, "Hi, Harry. I see I'm dreaming."

Harry stood in the shadow a few feet from her at the corner of the porch, leaning against the redbrick wall. "Of course you're dreaming."

Harry Kemple was the runner she had lost. He was the only one who had been found by his pursuer and killed, and his death had been Jane's fault. Harry died about ten years ago, and he had visited her in her sleep many times since then. Harry was still wearing the bad gray-green sport coat he wore the first time she'd met him. He had made his living running a floating poker game, and the coat with elbows worn from leaning on a table and the pants with the seat shiny from sitting through the endless games were his work clothes. He had come to her in a hurry from Chicago.

Harry was alive only because at the moment when the shooters had burst in on his game and shot all of the men at the table, he had been in the bathroom. He had heard the gunshots and then the silence, opened the door a crack, and seen them. When they were gone he had come to Jane. She had taken him to the stationery store in Vancouver where Lewis Feng, a highly skilled forger, was selling identities to Chinese nationals who had fled to Canada. Feng had made a new identity for Harry. Years later, Jane had taken John Felker, another runner who needed a new identity, to see Lewis Feng. She had not known that Feng kept a written record of the identities he had sold, and that Harry's new name and address were on the list.

Within a day Feng had been tortured and killed. A day after that, John Felker had found his way to Santa Barbara, California, and cut Harry's throat. Whenever Jane saw Harry in her dreams, it was with his throat cut, and sewn back together by the undertaker or the coroner with a stitch that looked like the stitching on a baseball.

"Janie," he said. "You always look so guilty when you see me."

"I am guilty."

"Sorry my being dead makes you uncomfortable. Think how it makes me feel."

"I've never let that happen to anybody again," said Jane. "He fooled me into taking him to the same person who had made your ID. I was stupid. I'm sorry."

"What the hell." Harry shrugged, and the coat seemed to rise and fall by itself. "Love is blind and deaf and ignorant and forgetful."

"It wasn't love."

"You certainly went through all the motions. Does your husband know about John Felker?"

"He was long before Carey's time. And you know there was no John Felker. That was just a name he made up to fool me and seduce me, and eventually, kill you and me. His name was Martin. James Michael Martin. Why are you here, Harry?"

"Because you need to be reminded."

"Have I left something undone? Is there something I didn't see or remember?"

"Is there something? Yes. Think about what happened to me, not what happened to you. Tonight you told Jimmy and Chelsea not to do what you did—jump into the sack with what amounts to a stranger."

"Is that bad advice, Harry?"

"Not bad, just beside the point. What you should be remembering is what I consider the main event—my untimely death. The men who kicked down the door and killed everybody in my poker game were after Jerry Cappadocia. Mafia. The men who killed everybody, shot them through the head and chest, were hired by other guys in the Mafia."

"Of course I remember that, Harry. How could I forget?"

"The nuggets of knowledge you should have taken home are the following. They didn't mind killing six other human beings with Jerry. And it took five years for one of their hired killers, Felker—or Martin, as you prefer—to catch up with the seventh other human being, me. If it had taken five more years, they would have kept looking. If I were alive now, there would still be men out there waiting to cross me off their to-do list. They have what you might call a strong corporate memory."

"Yes," said Jane. "What I don't know is why they're involved in this at all. I'm almost certain that Daniel Crane killed Nick Bauermeister with the rifle that Walter Slawicky owned. I think he did it because he wanted Bauermeister's girlfriend."

"I've seen her. Plenty of guys would shoot somebody to get at that."

"Lovely, Harry. But why would the Mafia care about a crime of passion? Why would they go looking for Jimmy?"

"Janie, Janie, Janie. Think the way they do. What do they spend most of their time doing?"

"Getting money. Extortion. Fixing games and races. Loaning money to people for huge interest. Pumping up the price of fake stocks and then dumping them. Hijacking trucks. Taking over legitimate businesses. Laundering money. Smuggling and selling drugs. Prostitution. Gambling. Murder for hire. Stealing—"

"Yeah, yeah, yeah. One of those," said Harry. "Getting money is what they care about, so that's got to be what Crane is doing for them. That's the reason they have a stake in keeping Daniel Crane from getting caught for the murder. And now, for drugging the girl."

"You can't say what the stake is?"

"I know what you know. I'm not out there learning things anymore. I'm a leftover image stored in your brain. If I take a guess, it will be the same as yours."

"Nick Bauermeister worked for Crane. Nick Bauermeister was a burglar. Maybe that's what Crane does on the side—send out thieves and store the loot in his storage facility."

"Not bad," said Harry. "Would the Mafia take an interest in a whole storage place filled with stolen stuff—electronics, furniture, watches, and jewelry? I'm guessing they might."

"Of course they would. And that means that they still need to blame the murder on someone besides Crane," said Jane. "They need to get Jimmy."

Harry pursed his lips and squinted up at the dark sky. "I imagine they'd like to. The official story would be that the fugitive killer of Nicky B. came to a fitting end. But right this minute I think the one who's in the most danger is Chelsea Schnell." Harry turned his eyes to Jane. "Her and the one who shot one of their boys with a shotgun. But getting revenge for him would be their second choice. Take it from me, the dead are soon forgotten."

"The hell they are."

But Harry was gone. Only the plain brick wall remained.

27

In the morning Jane went for her run while it was still dark. She thought about John Felker, about her husband, and about decisions she had made years ago—some shrewd guesses and some mistakes that she regretted as much this morning as she had at the time. And then she showered and made breakfast for Mattie, Jimmy, and Chelsea. They talked about how beautiful the day was going to be.

Mattie mentioned that she had gone out alone a week ago and driven into the country for an afternoon. She had found roadside sales and swap meets along her route, where she had bought maple syrup and homemade baked goods, and seen lots of antiques and hand-sewn quilts.

Jane said, "Maybe I'll take a look around one of these days. Which way would you recommend?"

Mattie said, "I drove out on Route Four. There was a sale at Canaan, and a big antique mall place out near Grafton. And there were a few places having garage sales and things. It was fun. There were people selling just about anything you can imagine."

The talk turned to other subjects. Afterward Jane walked into the downtown section of Hanover. She was still looking around town for the kind of people who might be here to find Jimmy Sanders, but today she saw no likely suspects.

Jane returned to the apartment, turned on the laptop computer she'd left with Jimmy, and began to scan the articles in the Western New York newspapers. She checked the *Buffalo News*, the *Rochester Democrat and Chronicle*, the *Niagara Gazette*, and the *Livingston County News*. Then she found the websites of the four Buffalo local news stations and a site that reported on the city of Akron, New York.

Jimmy watched her reading for a few minutes, and then said, "What are you looking at?"

"When I was back home, I tried to get the police moving in the right direction, and looking at the right things. If something changes, I want to know."

"Couldn't you check with your BFFs, the clan mothers?"

"Not a good idea," she said. "No more phone calls until this is over."

Jimmy studied her for a moment. "You brought what sounded like good news when you came, but you seem just as worried."

She looked up from her reading. "It's not over yet."

He nodded. "You said last night that you knew more. I didn't want to ask in front of my mother and Chelsea, but did you find out who those guys in Cleveland were?"

"I have theories. When I went to watch Daniel Crane's storage facility, I saw two men there and took their pictures while I pretended to talk on my phone. Ike Lloyd told me one was named Lorenzo Malconi. He's the boss of the Buffalo family of the Mafia. The other man works for him."

"What would they have to do with Daniel Crane?"

"I don't know. They had some men with them, and they brought a big box to store in one of the storage bays. It could mean nothing. Criminals probably have things to

341

store too. But the box could be something they don't want to store on their own property, or even close to home. They had driven pretty far out in the country to store their box at Box Farm Personal Storage. As you know, that's the place where Nick Bauermeister worked, and its owner is Daniel Crane, the man who raped Chelsea. I think Daniel Crane is the one who killed Nick Bauermeister, and that they're trying to protect him."

Jimmy stared at her for a second, and then looked across the room, his eyes unfocused. "That means—"

"All it means is what we already know—that we've got to stay out of sight for a while."

"How long?"

"I've been careful to stay out of the Mafia's way in the past, and I've managed to keep them from noticing me, so far. I think they'll sniff around for a while, trying to find us. But at some point they'll reach the conclusion that it's a waste of time because it doesn't bring them more money or power, and leaving us alone won't hurt them."

"It all sounds very logical," said Jimmy. "Are they logical?"

"It's another dog and rabbit story," said Jane. "They're dogs, and we're rabbits. The dog chases the rabbit for fun. The rabbit runs just for the chance to be a rabbit again tomorrow. The rabbit almost always wins."

"Almost always."

"It's the best we can do." She went back to scrolling down through the articles posted on the Western New York websites.

The next day was Saturday. When Jane returned from her early morning run, showered, and dressed, she picked up the laptop and looked at a map of New Hampshire. She had never been on Route 4, but she could see it intersected with Interstate 89, the major roadway that she'd driven to get here.

After breakfast she said, "I'm going out for a while."

"Anywhere interesting?" asked Mattie.

"I'm just going to explore the area a little."

"I can show you some of it," Mattie said.

Jane glanced in her direction, and in the corner of her eye she saw Chelsea look up at Jimmy, and Jimmy meet her gaze. "Okay. Glad to have you."

Jane waited while Mattie went to her room and returned with her purse. "Bye, you two."

Jimmy and Chelsea said bye in chorus, as though they had practiced.

Jane and Mattie went out to the sidewalk, and Mattie sighed. "I'm so glad to get out of there for a while. Those two are so eager to be alone I can't stand it."

Jane glanced at her. "Besides being in the middle, are you okay with that?"

"It doesn't matter if I am or not. They're adults, and the universe works the way it works. I don't get a vote."

"Do you like Chelsea?"

"I think she's nice," Mattie said. "I like having her around. She's cheerful and helps with the chores, and she seems to be keeping Jimmy from getting too claustrophobic."

"Do you like her as a daughter-in-law?"

Mattie's head swiveled to look at Jane. "That's a little sudden. Especially sudden when you're talking about a girl who's been hurt so much. I'd like to get to know her better before that. Forget me. I'd like time for Jimmy to get to know her first. But I like everything I've seen so far."

"It wouldn't bother you that she's not Onondawaga?"

"She certainly isn't." Mattie walked along for a few steps. "I guess my thoughts on that subject have changed over the years. Your mother was as white and blond as Chelsea. But then I saw you come along, and watched you grow up. Is there anybody who's more Seneca than you are? You look like my great-grandmother. And you think like my great-grand*father*."

"Thank you."

Mattie laughed. "It wasn't meant as a compliment. But the fact that you think it is proves what I said."

"So you think she's helping Jimmy get through this?"

"So far. Jimmy's lonely. He's dated plenty of girls, but the relationships went only so long. He's never married, and it seems to me that at his age he's running out of chances. If it turns out he was just waiting for this one to come along, I'll be delighted. If not, she's still a nice person, and he could do worse than ending up with a nice friend."

Jane and Mattie got into the Passat, and Jane drove south out of Hanover. Jane said, "Mattie, I've got some other things we should talk over."

"All right," said Mattie.

"I no longer think that the worst thing we need to worry about is police officers coming to hold Jimmy for extradition to New York State."

"What, then?"

"I think that the men who are searching for us, and who broke into your house to kidnap you, are Mafia soldiers."

"You do?" asked Mattie. "Why? What would people like that want with us?"

"They seem to be trying to protect the man who drugged Chelsea. I think he was the one who killed her boyfriend and tried to get it blamed on Jimmy."

"So the way they'd help this man would be what?"

"First, making sure she's not around to charge him with rape and testify at his trial."

"Oh, that poor girl."

"Yes. And they still need to have someone blamed for the murder, and that means they want to find Jimmy, too."

"I guess we aren't going home anytime soon."

"I hope I'm wrong. The reason I'm telling you this is partly to get you to think differently. Trouble is not going to be police cars or police officers. And these men don't look like the gangsters on television. They could be any two or more males between twenty and fifty."

"You're not exactly narrowing it down."

"I know."

They drove onto Interstate 89 and then got off on the Route 4 exit. They rode along the curving route to Canaan and stopped at a small park across from the local market and restaurant. In the park was a gathering of tables and booths. Local artisans sold goat cheese, maple syrup and candy, handmade jewelry, herbal soaps, embroidered hangings, and knitted scarves. Jane and Mattie browsed, and then went back to the restaurant where Jane had parked the Passat, and drove on.

Their next stop was a giant parking lot that ran along in front of a row of barn-like buildings. Several of them were stores that sold antique furniture, dishes, and other household goods. Some had souvenirs and clothing. Jane moved through them with a restless, impatient eye, scanning the cases and the walls, but not seeing what she was looking for.

Outside in the lot there were rows of canvas awnings, open vans, tables and booths where people were offering all sorts of items for sale. "They've got a little of everything," Mattie said.

They went to the car, and Jane drove to the end of the lot near the open-air bazaar. She and Mattie walked from table to table, but as they went on they were attracted to separate tables. Mattie looked at milk glass vessels, but Jane was always scanning the tables and cases, studying the sellers and their vehicles for something that wasn't there.

Finally Jane gravitated to a man in his sixties with white hair and a white three-day stubble of beard who sat at a set of tables before an oversize van. On the table were duck decoys, a few knives with antler handles, some new and some used and resharpened. On one of his tables Jane spotted a worn reloading kit with a turret press, cramp dies, and decapper. On the table nearby was an old Ithaca pump shot-gun. Jane pointed to it. "Okay if I look it over?"

The man gestured and nodded, so Jane lifted it and examined the barrel and receiver for corrosion and wear. "How much?"

"A hundred."

Jane set the shotgun down again, but she didn't leave. Instead she scanned his other wares.

"Don't you want it?"

"Oh, I don't know," said Jane. "I wasn't really in the market for another shotgun. I was mostly looking for handguns."

The man looked at her with new interest. "What kind?"

"What have you got?"

The man got up from his folding lawn chair and stepped to his van, then rummaged around for a minute and came back with what looked like the center drawer of an old oak desk with the handles removed, and set it on the table in front of Jane. He had an oilcloth on it, and now he pulled the cloth aside to reveal six handguns in two rows. "I've got a few things right now, but I don't like to leave them out on the table."

He picked up a big revolver. "This one here is nice, but it might be a bit heavy for you. It's one of the last revolv-ers to be standard issue for the police. A Smith and Wesson L-frame .357 magnum. This one's got some wear on the fin-ish and a couple of dings on the grips, but it's reliable and simple."

Jane smiled. She picked it up, rotated the cylinder, swung it out, and looked into the barrel. "Not bad for thirty or forty years old."

"They don't rot," he said.

"Let's see what else you have."

He pointed at the smallest gun in the tray. "A Cobra CA380. Tiny. You could hide it anywhere—in your purse, or whatever. They sell for about six hundred, but I can give you a deal."

"They must have gone up. They used to sell for about two hundred new, and this one isn't." She smiled. "You wouldn't be making fun of me, would you?"

The man smiled. "Well, look them over. Take your time."

She examined each of the guns, then said, "Can I make you an offer?"

"I'm listening."

"I'll take this old Colt 1911 .45, the Cobra .380, and the Czech CZ 97 .45. I'll give you six hundred."

He stared at the guns. "The two .45s and the Cobra? That would be more like eight hundred."

"Seven is more like eight."

He smiled again. "Make it eight and I'll throw in two boxes of .45 ACP ammo, and most of a box of .380—maybe fifteen rounds left—and the shotgun."

"Done."

"And done," he said.

Jane reached into her pocket and pulled out hundred dollar bills one at a time while he went to his van and brought out a two-handled shopping bag with a big red Macy's star on it and placed the pistols and the boxes of ammunition inside. She handed him the eight bills. He counted them and folded them into his pocket. "You got a nice deal."

"Yes, I did," she said. "Thanks. And you don't need any paperwork, right?"

"No. Only licensed gun dealers need to do that in New Hampshire. The rest of us are free. Have a nice day."

"You too." Jane picked up the bag and the shotgun, returned to the car, locked her purchases in the trunk, and turned her head to look for Mattie. She stood by a table with sweaters and gloves pretending she hadn't been watching Jane. She stepped over to the car.

Jane drove back toward Hanover. When they reached one of the big plazas in Lebanon, Jane said, "I've got to make a stop. This wouldn't be a bad time to stock up on food. Can you get a start on the shopping and I'll meet you in the supermarket?"

"Good idea."

Jane pulled up to the market and let Mattie out, and then drove to a big discount sporting goods store she had spotted from the road. She bought three boxes of five double-aught shotgun shells, a can of Hoppe's gun oil, a can of solvent, and a gun-cleaning kit, put them in the car trunk, and went to meet Mattie.

That night after dinner, Jane brought the guns into the apartment. She spread newspapers on the kitchen table, then took each firearm apart, cleaned, and oiled it. When she was nearly finished, Chelsea walked into the kitchen.

"Oh, my God," she said. "What are you doing?"

Jane said, "Don't worry. They're just a precaution, like having a fire extinguisher or a lifeboat. A lot of really bad things would have to happen before we needed these."

"I thought you just helped people run away. That's what you said."

"True," Jane said.

"Then what's changed?"

Jane spoke quietly. "When this started, we thought that we were just hiding Jimmy so he wouldn't be arrested. I didn't want any guns because we would never use one on a policeman. Now there are other people looking for us. The main thing we're doing is still trying to avoid them, and staying out of sight."

"So why do you have guns?"

Jane sighed. "Because what these people want is to kill us. Jimmy and you in particular."

Chelsea stared at her for two breaths, and then turned away. She almost bumped into Jimmy and Mattie, who had come to the doorway when they'd heard the distress in her voice. She slipped past them, went to the bedroom she'd been sharing with Jane, and closed the door.

Jimmy followed her. After a few minutes, he reappeared. "She'll be okay."

Jane said, "Do you know how to use one of these?"

Jimmy said, "I've fired a semiauto sort of like those. I fired a Beretta M90 a few times when I was in the army."

"Good. Mattie?"

"No."

"Okay. Let me teach you. Any of these three handguns works about the same. You pull back the slide to let the first round up out of the magazine into the chamber, and release it. You push the safety off, and you can pull the trigger until the magazine is empty. These .45s hold seven rounds. If you want to reload, you press the magazine release right here, drop the magazine out, and push the bullets into it from the top. Then you push the magazine back in like this until it clicks. You cycle in the first round again. The man I got them from didn't have extra magazines, but I'll try to get some." She turned the gun around and handed it to Mattie. "It's empty."

Mattie picked it up gingerly and examined it.

Jane said, "Hold it in both hands and aim it. Get comfortable. Line things up with the sights."

Mattie and Jimmy both followed the instructions, getting as familiar as they could with the two pistols while Jane finished cleaning the compact .380.

That night after the others went to bed, Jane began her watch. She knew that if the killers found them, they would come at night.

Over the next three days Jane altered her routines. She took a nap after dinner that lasted from around eight until midnight or one. When Chelsea came in to go to bed, Jane got up. She would sit in the darkened apartment waiting and watching. Each night she took out the computer and checked the sites of the Western New York newspapers and television stations to see if anything had changed. In the tablet's dim blue light she sat and read the news. She kept the window open, listening through the screen for any sound that was out of the ordinary. Sometimes she heard owls calling to one another as they hunted above the deserted streets, or a dog bark in the distance, but otherwise the night was quiet. It wasn't until the fourth night that she found the article on the *Buffalo News* site.

COUNTY INMATE FOUND DEAD IN CELL. She scanned the text until she came to the name Walter Slawicky.

"The Erie County Sheriff's Department issued a statement today concerning the death of a Caledonia man in Erie County jail on Thursday night. Walter Slawicky, age 46, had been held in custody on suspicion of giving false evidence in a murder case, pending a bail hearing scheduled for Monday. He was found dead in his cell by guards on Friday morning.

"Slawicky had told police he had sold a rifle like the one that had killed Nicholas Bauermeister of Avon, to James Sanders of Basom, New York, shortly before the murder. Three days ago, police found the weapon buried in Mr. Slawicky's yard. Ballistic tests matched the weapon and the ammunition found with it to the bullet that killed Bauermeister. The Sheriff's Department spokesman would not speculate at this time whether the cause of Slawicky's death was suicide or homicide."

Jane found herself standing. She had to stifle the impulse to wake the others. They would want to get into the cars right away and drive toward home, but she needed time to think about the implications of Slawicky's death.

Slawicky was gone, and his claims about Jimmy discredited. That meant that the main reason the police had thought Jimmy was involved had disappeared. But he was still the one who had been in a fight with Nick Bauermeister, and he was still the one who hadn't shown up in court for the assault and battery hearing. There was almost certainly a warrant out for his arrest. If he was caught, he would probably be locked up in that same jail, if only temporarily. There was no sign yet that the men in jail waiting for him had gone anywhere. And there was no reason to believe that Daniel Crane, or the men protecting Daniel Crane, had stopped looking for him. And they were certainly still looking for Chelsea.

Jane read every version of the story on the laptop, and then clicked on every link to articles that might give her more details.

Hours later, when the others were all awake, Jane said, "I have news." She explained Slawicky's death to them, and set the computer on the table where they could read the story.

"Can we go home?" asked Mattie.

"Read the articles, and when I wake up again we can talk. There are still people looking for you. They just aren't people who want to bring anyone back home for a trial." She walked into the bedroom and closed the door.

28

Late the following night, Jane heard the sounds she had been listening for through the open window. A car passed at 3:00 AM moving slowly along the residential street. It was unusual to hear the hiss of tires at this hour on a weeknight in quiet Hanover. The Dartmouth undergraduates wouldn't be back until mid-September, and the local grown-ups weren't much for carousing. The road to the hospital was three blocks away, and the car was moving too slowly to be heading for the emergency room at 3:00. Maybe it was a police patrol she had not noticed on other nights.

Jane stepped to the wall beside the window to watch the car receding. In the moonlight she could see it was a silver SUV, not a police car. The brake lights went on. The driver didn't signal, but went into a right turn. A second person, a man, was visible in the passenger seat.

Jane picked up the laptop and looked up the state's closing hours for bars. Last call had been changed about a year ago from 1:00 to 2:00 AM. Maybe it had taken somebody a long time to drive home from a bar somewhere. Cops often spotted drunk drivers because they drove more slowly than sober ones.

Jane put the laptop in her backpack and exchanged it for the CZ 97 pistol, then moved her seat back from the window, where she could listen for more sounds from the street but remain far enough back to be invisible in the darkened room.

Five minutes later she again heard the hiss of tires on the pavement coming toward the apartment. It was the silver SUV again. The vehicle was going more slowly than five miles an hour this time, and the man beside the driver stared steadily at the apartment building. The driver nearly stopped as he leaned forward to see past his friend's head. Then he looked ahead again and sped up to the corner.

Jane stood, closed and locked the window, and went into the room she shared with Chelsea and shook her. "Get up and get dressed and ready to move. No lights. We're going to have visitors. Bring the shotgun."

She stepped to Mattie's room and shook her awake, and then went to the alcove where Jimmy slept on cushions from the couch. In about thirty seconds they had gathered in the dark kitchen. Jimmy whispered, "Are we going to fight?"

"No," said Jane as she slung her backpack over her shoulder. "We're going to run. Head for the house behind us, and make your way to my car."

She quietly opened the kitchen door and beckoned. The others slipped out past her and down the steps while Jane locked the kitchen door. Jane caught up with them and moved ahead. They filed along the side of the backyard and into the kitchen garden of the next yard. She directed the others past her and along the side of the next house toward the street.

Jane stopped and crouched to watch the building they'd just left. First one, then another, and then another silhouette, each of them bent over to keep from letting his head rise to the level of the windows, ascended to the back porch.

Jane pivoted and moved quickly after her companions. When she emerged from the yard she looked for the silver SUV she'd seen coming past the apartment, but it wasn't there. She had been hoping to find and sabotage it, but there must be a driver who was still cruising the neighborhood waiting for a pickup call. She couldn't afford to watch any longer.

She ran to the spot where she'd parked the Volkswagen Passat, and started it while the others got in. As soon as they were inside she pulled ahead, made a left turn onto Wheelock Street, and headed toward Route 120 out of town. As she passed the corner of Chambers Street where their apartment was, she saw the three men trotting out the front door of the apartment toward the waiting SUV. They must have come in quickly, seen that everyone was gone, and called for their getaway car.

"That's bad news," she muttered. She sped up and turned onto Route 120.

Jimmy said, "Where are we going?"

"I'm trying to get to Interstate 89. The main thing is to get out of sight before they pull themselves together."

"Who are they?" asked Chelsea.

Mattie said, "Could they have been the police?"

"No," Jane said. "When the police come for someone they think might resist, there are a whole bunch of them and they identify themselves."

Chelsea said, "This is my fault. They're after me."

Jane said, "That train of thought doesn't do anything for you right now. They were after all of us."

"This time it has to be about me. And—oh my God. I forgot the shotgun. You told me to bring it, and I was half-asleep, and I saw it, leaning in the corner near your side of the bed, and I just forgot."

Jane said, "It's okay. We don't need a shotgun right now. And it doesn't matter which of us they want most. They have to get all of us or they risk getting caught. Now calm down, but stay alert."

Mattie said, "There's a set of headlights way back there."

"Let's see if it's them," said Jane. She pushed down on the accelerator and added speed steadily. She kept glancing in the mirror to judge the effect on the vehicle behind them.

"They're speeding up too," said Jimmy.

Jane looked in the rearview mirror. "I see them. We'll make it to I-Eighty-nine, but we can't lose them on a six-lane highway. The road Mattie and I took on Saturday—Route Four—is the kind of road we need. That SUV has a higher center of gravity than we have, and it's far less maneuverable than this car. We've been on that road, and they probably haven't."

Jane slowed to seventy, took the ramp to the interstate, and seemed to fly onto the highway, taking a gradual swing and using the whole road to straighten out. She switched off the headlights and Chelsea gave a little shriek. Jane drove by moonlight, trying only to keep the car on the broad highway.

She saw that there was a sign ahead, so she turned the lights on again and made the exit onto Route 4. She could see there were no other cars coming so she accelerated into the left turn to the eastbound side and kept forcing the speed upward as much as she dared.

They were now at the outer edge of Lebanon, flying through intersections with red lights. Almost immediately they were past the big plazas and the darkened fast-food restaurants, and into the country. They passed big fields, then farmhouses, and in minutes they were driving through wooded areas. Through the trees to their right they could see moonlight on water, and then just trees again. The road began to rise and fall as they lost sight of the water.

Jane accelerated on curves and coasted into the straight sections, always hugging the insides of the curves and moving to the center on straight stretches to straighten the car's trajectory. She was counting on the likelihood that if a vehicle approached from the west she would see the glow of its headlights in time.

After a period, Jimmy said, "I see headlights behind us coming to that last turn, moving really fast."

Jane said, "All right. I'm going to try hard to stay ahead of them and turn off somewhere. But I think we need to prepare in case that doesn't work. Jimmy, the pistols you saw last night are in my backpack. Chelsea, hand him my pack."

Chelsea lifted the pack up from the floor to the top of her seat and Jimmy pulled it over and set it between him and his mother.

"What's next?" he said.

"Take out the .45 Colt. I've already loaded the magazine. Find it and click it into place."

"Done."

"Okay. Keep your finger along the side of the trigger guard until you're about to fire. Don't cycle the slide yet. There's a box of extra ammunition. Put it in your jacket. Mattie?"

"Yes?"

"There's also a box of .380 rounds. Take out the box and the smaller pistol, the Cobra. Do you remember how to load it?"

"Yes."

"Then now is the time. It also holds seven rounds."

"Okay."

After a couple of minutes, Mattie said, "Ready."

Jane said, "Okay. Mattie, hand me the Cobra." She held her hand over her shoulder, took the gun, and handed it, handgrips first, to Chelsea. "Hold this."

Chelsea took the pistol. Jane leaned forward and took out the CZ 97 pistol she'd been carrying and held it over her shoulder. "Mattie, take this one."

Mattie took it. "What do I do with it?"

"Here's the strategy," said Jane. "You and Jimmy are each sitting by a window in the backseat, and you each have a .45 caliber semiauto pistol. You do nothing unless the people behind us fire a gun. If they do, you charge your weapon, roll down your window, lean out just enough to aim, and fire. Try to hit the driver's side of the windshield. If you hit the car anywhere, they'll probably drop back or stop. If you hit a person, they'll turn around and head for a hospital."

"I can do that," said Jimmy.

Mattie said, "I guess I can too, if I have to."

"Let's hope you don't," said Jane. "If you do have to fire, you'll notice two problems. A .45 round is very loud— deafening in an enclosed space. It also kicks, so hold the pistol tightly, and if you can, use both hands. If you drop the gun on the road, we won't get it back."

"Okay," said Jimmy.

Jane drove on. She reached a town going eighty-five. Her headlights illuminated the sign that said CANAAN and it flashed past the window, then the restaurant on the right where she and Mattie had parked the car on Saturday, and the little town park where people had sold their food and crafts. In a few seconds they were past the town and in a few more they had passed the outlying businesses and were in woods again. Jane concentrated on holding the car on the curving, hilly road and not hitting anything.

"I see lights back there," said Jimmy. "It looks like the SUV."

"Don't do anything yet," said Jane.

They sped past a reflective sign so fast that reading it was an act of deciphering an afterimage. GRAFTON 5 MILES. Another sign. RUGGLES MINE 4 MILES.

"Chelsea," said Jane. "Take my phone."

She took it.

"Go on the Internet and find out what Ruggles Mine is."

"Okay."

Jane drove faster while Chelsea was working at it. "It's hard to get a signal," Chelsea muttered. Then, after a minute, she began to read. "Mica was first discovered in Grafton, New Hampshire, by a man named Sam Ruggles." She scanned. "The Ruggles Mine is unique because of its enormous size. The crystal formations within the Ruggles pegmatite. . . let's see. One thousand six hundred forty feet long, three hundred thirty-five feet wide, and two hundred and fifty deep." She paused. "It's also got tourmaline, amethyst—"

"Fine. Where is it?"

"There's a map, but it's just a turnoff a mile before we get to Grafton. On the right."

"Jimmy," said Jane. "Are you absolutely positive that the headlights back there are the SUV with the men who raided our apartment?"

"Yes. When it passed under the streetlights in Canaan I could see it pretty well."

"So there's zero chance it's just some kid driving too fast?"

"Zero chance."

"Then trade places with your mother so you can fire with your right hand."

After a few seconds, Jimmy said, "I'm set."

"Charge your pistol."

Jane heard the distinctive slide-snap sound.

"Okay. We've got a straight stretch ahead of us. They'll use it to try to catch up. If they get close, remember what I said. Aim for the windshield, just above the headlights. What we want to do is make them drop back and lose sight of us before we take the turnoff for the mine. I know you can do this."

"I'll do my best."

"Good. Roll your window down, and fire one round when I tell you."

Jimmy pushed the button to roll down the window, but the others only heard the first part of it, because the wind rushed into the car, blowing past their ears.

Jane focused her attention on maintaining her speed, watching the headlights in the rearview mirror, and keeping the car's trajectory straight and level. But soon the car behind them began to gain on them, its bigger, more powerful engine roaring to propel it along the straight stretch.

Jane saw the sign that said RUGGLES MINE I, and sped up, but the SUV was still coming. She shouted, "All right, Jimmy. Aim and fire."

Three or four seconds passed, the pistol flashed, and the report hammered their ears.

The headlights behind them dropped back, Jane reached a hill, and they all felt the car rise into the air an inch or two, and then slam down and bounce. Jane feathered the brakes, and moments later wrenched the steering wheel to the right, accelerating into the turn. The rear wheels of the car squealed, the car trying to spin out of control while centrifugal force threw the passengers toward the doors, their seat belts tightening on their waists to jerk their bodies to a stop and across their chests to choke their breathing. The sign for the mine road seemed to float by them as Jane completed the turn. The car shot forward up the road and then veered into the bushes on the right. Jane turned off the headlights and they were bathed in darkness.

29

Jane turned in her seat to watch Route 4. She and the others said nothing, simply waited and stared at the place where they had left the main road. After about a minute, the roadway slowly acquired definition and even faint coloration, and then brightened in the glare of the SUV's high beam headlights. The SUV flashed past, and the light vanished, leaving the road in darkness again.

Jane pulled forward out of the shelter of the bushes, bouncing a bit to get back onto the narrow pavement. She drove up over a low hill and then down the other side before she turned on her lights again.

"Can't we just turn around and go back the way we came?" asked Chelsea.

"I'm guessing we can't," said Jane. "Any minute they'll realize we're not ahead of them anymore. They'll turn around and come back this way. I just hope they'll miss this turn."

"But where are we going—to the mine?" asked Mattie.

"It sounded like a good place to get out of sight and wait until daylight, when those men will have to give up and get out of sight themselves."

As she drove, the road narrowed to a single paved lane through thick woods. The boughs of mature trees hung over the road to form a canopy between them and the sky, and bushes and saplings encroached on the margins to make the ribbon of pavement even narrower. Jane drove up the middle as quickly as she could, and reached a spot where there were a couple of buildings and a fork in the road. She stopped, backed up, and found a much smaller sign with an arrow pointing to the right onto an even smaller road with the words RUGGLES MINE. Jane got out, pulled up the stake with the sign on it, and put it into the car between her and Chelsea, then drove on.

After a few hundred feet the driving surface thinned and the hard asphalt gave way to the underlying gravel. As Jane drove on she could see in the glow of her taillights that she was kicking up dust that hung in the still night air. The only sound was the ticking of small stones kicked up against the undercarriage of the car. After another few hundred yards there was asphalt again, and she could go more quickly without worrying about spinning out on gravel. They went up hills and dipped downward at times, but she knew they were climbing gradually.

Jimmy's voice from the backseat said, "I think I saw light."

"What do you mean?" asked Chelsea.

"Back there on top of that rise, it looked like the tree-tops way back lit up for a second, then got dim again."

"Keep watching," said Jane. She accelerated, keeping the car in the center of the road and bumping up over rises and dipping down into depressions, letting the car bounce and rock as it would.

"I think they found the turn. We need a plan," Jimmy said.

"Here's what it is," Jane said. "I'll drive as close to the mine as I can. It sounded like a big, deep open-pit mine. You'll jump out, take the guns, and run. Go into the mine, whatever it consists of, and take cover. If they come after you on foot, wait until one of them is too close to miss, and shoot him. They're not here to capture you."

"What about you?" said Mattie.

"If I hide the car well enough, they might think they guessed wrong and go back toward Hanover. If they find the car, I'll try to get them to go after me."

"Can't you go with us?" said Chelsea.

Jane said, "The entrance is up ahead. I see buildings. Get ready."

The road swept downward and dissolved onto a wide, flat, empty plateau of a parking lot with two low buildings on the right side. The small, barn-like red one had a low fence in front of it and big, white cutout letters over the door that could be read in the moonlight: MINE MUSEUM. The long building beside it looked like a store. Jane stopped by the fence and stared into the dark space beyond. There was a hill with a large, cavernous opening. "There it is. Go."

Mattie, Jimmy, and Chelsea got out and ran for the opening. Jane could see the dim luminescence of a circle of moonlight far ahead of them, and realized this was not a cave, but a tunnel dug through the hillside leading to the bottom of the open-pit. Jane drove along the buildings looking ahead for some opening in the trees beyond where the road would resume, but she approached the end of the lot, and there was only a great emptiness ahead where her headlights shone into the air but hit nothing.

At the end of the parking lot she turned right into a weedy field, still searching for the mouth of a road for two hundred feet. There was nothing but brush, and then trees beyond that. She drove through the field until she reached a thicket of young trees, and pulled as far into it as she could, stopped, and turned off the headlights. She got out and looked for something to use as cover. The car was dark colored and dusty from the gravel road, but it wasn't invisible. She ran into the woods and found some broken, dead pine boughs and a floor of pine needles. She dragged the boughs out and tossed them over the car, went back a second time for more, and then went back a third time, took off her jacket, lay it down and scooped pine needles into it, then carried it back and dumped them onto the roof of the car. She went back and refilled it twice, spreading them over the trunk and roof.

As she moved farther into the woods for more boughs, she saw the lights appear. As the SUV bumped up over the last rise of the forest, its headlights shot up into the sky, and then dipped low as the vehicle coasted down the last hill into the parking lot. Jane stepped deeper into the foliage to watch.

The silver SUV moved slowly onto the flat expanse, heading along the low buildings, slowing to a stop a couple of times, once by the museum building and then at the long store building. The men seemed to be looking in the windows for signs that someone was inside. As they went on, Jane backed up inside the edge of the woods to stay out of their sight.

The SUV stopped at the end of the parking lot, its lights shining off into the empty space. From here she could see better, and she realized that ahead of the SUV the land dropped off sharply. There was only the clear black sky filled with stars, and below it, a vague dark smear of distant mountains. Then the headlights went off.

Jane lay down in the weeds as the doors of the SUV opened. The dome lights came on, and she watched four men get out. Finally she got a good look at them. They were wearing blue jeans, dark shirts, and windbreaker jackets. It occurred to her that they had probably not worn them because they'd expected to be out here in the woods, but to cover their guns. One of the men took a pistol out of the car and put it into the back of his belt, and another went to the rear hatch of the SUV, opened it, and took a rifle out of the storage space. The rifle had the distinctive shape of an AR-15 clone, with an extralong magazine extending under the receiver and a flash suppressor on the muzzle.

Jane felt the tension in her chest growing and tightening. She wished she had taken the time to bring the shotgun from the apartment herself. The four men were all standing in the glow of the SUV's dome lights. If she'd had the shotgun she would have aimed her first shot at the man with the rifle, and that might have given her time to fire again.

Jane had given the three pistols to her runners, and that left her unarmed except for her lock-blade pocketknife. She watched as the man in the back reached into the storage space again and took out flashlights. He handed them to his companions, who took them and tried them out, letting the beams dance on the ground at their feet, and then sweep the area randomly. The men began to walk toward the tunnel into the mine.

Jane moved down to the place where she had left the car. She knelt and reached up under the car to the inner side of the right wheel, got some sooty black grease on her hand, and then moved her fingers in a wavy line from her hairline to her chin, got more, and smeared it on the other side of her face, got more for her neck, and the backs of her hands. When she was painted, she moved after the men.

Jane climbed higher up the rising ground, stalking them, watching where they went. They used their flashlights, trying to keep from stumbling over stones or stepping in mud, making no attempt to remain unseen. They weren't expecting a fight. They were here for a massacre.

She watched them stop at the mouth of the tunnel and shine their flashlights into it for a minute or two. She could see a small, narrow stream of water in the tunnel, a bit of mud, a stony surface with some loose stones. Then the man with the rifle separated from the others and began to climb the hill to the right of the tunnel entrance. Jane understood. He would find a high vantage point. While the others flushed out their victims on the floor of the mine, he would take the kill shots from above. Jimmy, Mattie, and Chelsea might be able to stay hidden for a while. They might even manage to ambush one of the men entering the mine, since the men weren't expecting resistance. But they couldn't do anything to the man above with the rifle, and his weapon gave him overwhelming firepower.

The other three men entered the tunnel, but Jane concentrated on the man with the rifle. He reached the crest of the hill and moved off to the right. Jane counted to twenty and then began to move after him. She could tell by listening to his footsteps that he was walking along the rim of the open-pit mine, probably looking down for his prey as he went.

He was easy to hear in the stillness of night. His heavy feet crunched on a gravelly surface, and kicked a larger stone or two that rolled out of the way. He changed to a careful, shuffling step. Then the sounds stopped. He had found the place he'd been searching for.

Jane moved closer until she was twenty feet from him, a few feet higher and directly behind him, beside some bushes and a scraggly conifer with twisted limbs. She began to crawl toward him, very slowly, until she was within ten feet.

When she stopped she could see him clearly. He was right at the rim. He crouched, then lay on his belly and pulled back the charging lever of his rifle to seat the first round.

Jane could see the mine beyond him in the moonlight, a deep canyon at least a third of a mile long. From here the floor of the mine seemed about two hundred feet down. The long chasm was shaped roughly like a figure eight, with two round canyons connected by a narrower passage. The first section, directly below the man with the rifle, was marked by a series of cave openings, several of the largest at ground level, but the smaller ones forty or fifty feet up the opposite cliff wall.

The cliffs on the opposite side glittered in the moonlight. There were deposits of some shiny mineral that caught and amplified any glow. One of the men far below shone his flashlight up the opposite wall and made the minerals sparkle. The beam swept away, its round halo setting off bright flashes of minerals wherever it moved.

Minutes passed, and then the man with the rifle seemed to see something. He edged forward on his belly slightly and peered down.

Jane remained still and turned her attention to the area around her. In her reach were grasses, thin upright woody plants, and a gnarled tree. She wondered if the tree had dropped any limbs she could use as a club or a staff, but there was nothing lying below it. She moved her head and caught a glint of light. She reached out and touched a rock with sparkly mica flakes on the surface. It was big, about the size of a volleyball—too heavy to throw at the man from here. She pushed it back and forth to loosen it. Maybe she could—

The air below exploded with noise as gunshots echoed from one wall of the mine to the other. It sounded like five, then at least ten more shots. The man with the rifle rose to his knees. He shouldered the assault rifle and aimed downward.

Jane sprang from her hiding place and charged toward him. He seemed to hear her coming and began to spin toward her just as she reached him, but he hadn't enough time to turn before Jane dived at him and pushed. Both of her arms shot forward, the heels of both hands pounded his left shoulder at once, and he toppled.

When she skidded to a stop with her belly on the gravel, he was out over the brink and already falling, his face a mask of terror looking up at her. He shrieked, but she heard only the first second because his hand tightened spasmodically on the trigger of the rifle and it fired. The recoil of the rifle tore it from his hand and the rifle fell beside him, hurtling downward with him for second after second toward the chasm floor. When he hit, there was a terrible, hollow crack, and she knew his head had hit the rocks.

Jane lay at the edge and looked down at the rifleman's body. She squinted and moved her head a little from side to side. There seemed to be a second body lying a distance away across the mine floor, near the mouth of one of the caves. Her breath caught for a second. Had they killed Jimmy?

Far below, two men ran across the open space to the body of the rifleman. Two men. There had been three down there. As the two men reached the body, Jane saw a muzzle flash from the mouth of the cave, and the two men ducked down behind the rocks where the rifleman lay. They both fired pistols toward the cave mouth, and she heard the bullets ricochet several times in the stone cavern before the sounds faded.

Jane crawled back from the edge, stood, and found a few fist-size rocks. She threw one, then another, then another, gauging their trajectory to try to hit the two men near the dead rifleman. The first two rocks hit close to them, but as she threw the third, one of the men fired several pistol shots up at her while the other snatched up the dead man's rifle. He looked at it, then threw it down again.

She stepped back out of their view and heard a dozen pistol shots pound the edge of the cliff or fly upward, hitting nothing. The angle seemed to change, and she knew the two men were stepping back, trying to improve their angle to shoot at her.

She heard other shots coming from across the mine, and she hoped someone was hitting the two men, but didn't try to see. Instead she ran back to the gnarled pine tree behind her and squatted to pick up the volleyball-size rock. She carried it in both hands and ran along the edge of the cliff until she reached a clear space directly above the entrance to the tunnel. More shots echoed. She moved to the very edge and looked down.

The two men were backing toward the mouth of the tunnel, still firing into the entrance of the cave where Jimmy, Chelsea, and Mattie must be hiding. The men seemed to be trying to carom their shots off the walls, hoping to hit someone with a ricochet, but their main intention seemed to be keeping their opponents' heads down while they retreated.

Jane breathed deeply, watching and waiting, judging the two men's course as they backed toward the tunnel that would lead them out of the mine and up to the parking lot. *Thirty-two feet per second*, she thought. *Thirty-two, then sixty-four, then ninety-six. Now.* She dropped the heavy rock. It fell, gaining speed.

One of the men seemed to hear something, or maybe have a vague premonition. He lifted his face just as the heavy rock plummeted down from the sky, obliterated his skull, and pinned his lifeless body to the ground.

His companion spun and ran into the tunnel. Earlier Jane had looked down the tunnel when she'd seen it from the car, and she knew it was at least 150 feet long, a 20-degree upward slope on gravel and perpetually wet stone. She turned and began to run.

Jane was up and over the gentle rise at the top of the hill in seconds, and then she made her way downward quickly, sliding when she needed to, until she was just above the tunnel entrance and to the right. She looked around her for any object she might use as a weapon—a stone, a piece of wood—but she saw nothing.

Jane heard him coming. His feet slapped into a stream of water, scraped when they slipped on loose stones, and squished when he stepped in mud. His breathing was loud and rasping, the run burning his lungs and sapping his strength. Jane took out her lock-blade knife and opened the blade.

The man reached the end of the tunnel. He was big, but he was gasping for breath and walking unsteadily. He still carried his pistol in his right hand and a flashlight in his left. As he took his first step into the open, Jane sprang, landing at his back. He started to spin to bring his gun around but she thrust her knife into his back and withdrew it. He seemed to ignore the wound, maybe wasn't aware of it yet. He turned, trying to bring the gun around toward her, but she stayed behind him.

She couldn't let him pivot to face her, so she threw her left forearm around his head to cover his face and hold on, brought her knife across his throat, and stepped back. He fell before he could complete the turn, and the gun and flashlight fell beside him as he did. Jane stood still for a few seconds while the blood pooled on the carved-out rock under him and then seeped down to mix with the trickle of water that flowed into the tunnel. Then she began the walk down the tunnel into the open-pit of the mine.

When Jane approached the end of the tunnel, she stopped and called out in Seneca, "Come out now. They're all dead."

30

Beautiful summer days like today were precious, and Lorenzo Malconi knew that at his age he had probably seen most of the ones he'd see. He felt secure and content, sitting on the chaise longue with his feet up, his eyes closed behind his dark sunglasses. He knew Andy Spato was in the kitchen with Vacci drinking coffee, probably telling each other stories full of exaggerations, the way young guys did. Every thirty seconds or so, one of them would take a look through the sliding glass door at him to be sure he was okay. Knowing that made him feel safe while he was weighing options, working on plans and speculations.

Sometimes he would remind himself of things to keep his memory strong. He had never liked the feeling of suddenly realizing he had overlooked a detail or forgotten to keep track of an operation for a while. Whenever that happened, he would send somebody to invite the people involved to his house to report directly to him how things were going.

This afternoon he was thinking about the storage business outside Avon. Little Angela was now serving as the official owner for him, but of course, the business was his. There were many things an imaginative man could do with that business, more than just storing things that Daniel Crane's crew of half-wit burglars stole from suburban homes. People—customers—drove through that gate, parked inside the high fence, and went into the office. They drove vans and trucks right up to their storage bays to load or unload. What better place could there be to handle the sale and distribution of merchandise of any kind? One storage bay, ten by fifteen feet, would probably hold all the heroin ever sold in Buffalo. A few bays would hold all the cocaine. He left that idea to mature in the recesses of his brain and settled back into his chair, seeing the orange-red glow of the sun through his eyelids.

A shadow fell on Mr. Malconi, like a cloud across the sun. He was still warm, but the shadow gave him a chill. He opened his eyes, and there was a person standing at the foot of his chair, back to the sun, so at first it was only a black silhouette.

He hadn't heard the sliding door open, so he turned his head toward it. He could see Spato and Vacci through the glass. Spato was still sitting at the table, but his head was down on the tabletop, cradled in his arms, as though he were in a deep sleep. His coffee cup was on its side, and the coffee formed a pool on the kitchen table and dripped onto the floor. Vacci was lying on the floor at the other side of the room. "Spato!" Malconi shouted. "Spato! Get out here!"

"Don't bother. He's going to be asleep for a long time. So is the other one." The voice was a woman's. "There was GHB in their coffee. I knew it was good stuff because I got it from Daniel Crane's supply."

Malconi looked in her direction and started to sit up, but he could see now that she had a gun in her right hand. She held it downward with her arm straight, but all she had to do was lift it. "Who are you?" he said.

"That doesn't matter. I brought you something." She tossed a manila envelope on his lap.

He picked up the envelope and peered into the open end. There were a couple of sheets of paper printed with photographs from a computer, and he could feel some smaller stuff loose in there. He emptied it onto his lap.

There were four little plastic cards. Drivers' licenses. He picked one up, and saw the blue print across the top— Massachusetts—and the man's photograph twice, one big and one small. A little green silhouette of the state. He looked at each license. Louis Pantola, an address in Boston. Gerald Migli, Michael Tissenti, also Boston. Anthony Bollino, Newton. The names and faces meant nothing to him, but he knew exactly who they were.

He picked up the first of the printed sheets and looked at the pictures. They had been taken at night, with a couple of bright flashlights on them. One of them was a man with his head crushed and a big stone beside it. Another was lying with his body strangely twisted, as though he'd been hit by a car. The third picture was of a man who had been shot in the chest. The last one was lying facedown in a pool of blood from a wound high up on his body. "Jesus," he whispered to himself.

He put the driver's licenses and the sheets back into the envelope and looked up at the woman. He could see she was tall and thin, and she was dressed in black jeans, a black pullover, even black sneakers.

"You killed all these guys?" he asked.

"Some of them. But that's another thing that doesn't matter."

"Then what does matter?"

"It matters that you and I understand each other."

"Why would I want to understand you?"

"Because if I think you're not listening to me during the next two minutes, your life will end in that lawn chair."

"I'm listening."

"From now on, if any men like the ones in those pictures come near Jimmy Sanders or Chelsea Schnell, you will die. There will be no more warnings, no way to take anything back. Do you understand?"

"I understand."

"Then I'll leave you now."

The woman turned and opened the sliding door into his kitchen, closed it, walked past the unconscious Spato, and then disappeared into the front of the house. Mr. Malconi stood up and listened, holding his breath. He heard his front door slam. He took a deep breath and let it out. She was gone.

Mr. Malconi reached into his coat pocket, took out his cell phone, and pressed Salamone's number.

"Yes?" said Salamone.

"It's me. Get over here now. Bring Cantorese and Pistore, and at least two more guys. I'll explain when you get here."

"I'm on my way."

Mr. Malconi ended the call.

He dialed a number he knew by heart because he would never put it, or any of a few others, in a phone's memory. He stood up while it rang.

The phone rang and then he heard the voice. "This is Joe."

"Joe," he said. "This is Lorenzo Malconi. I'm calling with some very bad news."

"I know already."

"You do?"

"Yeah. It's been all over the Boston TV news yesterday and today. It was a massacre. The reporters act like they won the lottery."

Malconi said, "I'm deeply sorry. Of course I'll help the families. I'll have a man bring some money to them, and deliver it in person."

"Are you going to send some money to make up for what those four were earning for the organization?"

"You know I can't hope to make this up to you. But I'll be sending a man to you too, so you're not left with a bad feeling. I asked for a favor, and you responded like a friend. I'm sorry."

"You told me this was just some guy, and maybe his girlfriend. They had help. I want to know who."

"I don't know yet," said Malconi.

"Well, when you find out, maybe you'll send me their heads in a box," Joe said. "I'd better be going. Thanks for letting me know."

"Good-bye."

Malconi ended the connection and put the phone back in his pocket. He went to his chair and lay back in the sun, but didn't close his eyes. This time he listened to his heartbeat. It was faster than normal, but it was still strong and regular. A man his age could have a heart attack after an experience like that, but Lorenzo Malconi was not easily frightened. He began to consider his situation calmly and rationally. He thought about the strange woman with the gun. He had heard threats and ultimatums before, and he was good at detecting whether they were empty bluff or serious. This one he could not ignore. She had come here to show that she could get to him anytime she wanted and put a gun to his head.

Five minutes later, he was still thinking about what had happened to Joey Corpa's four men. The man with the crushed skull made him remember the head injuries that football players got. It was a miracle any of them had any brains left when they got to the pros. People were saying that football might be outlawed and then the families would lose the billions they made on the weekly betting slips. He knew that was a stupid worry. America loved its blood sports. Getting them to outlaw pro football would be like getting the rabble of Rome to vote to outlaw gladiators.

But maybe there was a way to pull an insurance game. If he and one of the New York families formed a clean-looking insurance company, they might be able to sell special concussion insurance to all the mothers of little football players, elementary through high school. He began to play around with names for the company. He liked the names that were midwestern cities. Maybe Topeka Mutual, or Springfield Casualty. It might be even better to use a whole state. Wisconsin seemed to be a good, trustworthy state for insurance. Wisconsin Health and Life.

He heard something and looked toward it. There was Salamone, coming out through the glass door from the kitchen. Salamone said, "What the hell happened to Spato and Vacci?"

"They're just asleep. You can have your guys put them in beds in a minute," Mr. Malconi said. "That manila envelope on the table. Take a look inside."

When Salamone took out the papers, his expression went stony, and Malconi was reminded why he liked the man. Salamone took out the four driver's licenses and fanned them like a poker hand. He put them all back into the envelope.

Malconi said, "Those are the four guys Joey Corpa sent from Boston to the address we got for Miss Chelsea. They were going to make sure she wasn't around to testify against our boy Daniel Crane."

"I see," said Salamone. "How did you get these?"

Malconi said, "Joey Corpa had a guy fly here to deliver them." There was no practical reason to tell Salamone about the woman. "The licenses have the addresses of the dead guys. You ought to send somebody to give each family some money. And some for Joey too. He took a big loss."

Salamone sighed. Every time he saw Mr. Malconi, it cost him money. "I'll do it today."

Malconi squinted up at him. "One more thing. We've gone about as far as we can for Daniel Crane. I'm tired of thinking about him."

TECH SERGEANT REID OF THE state police sat in the passenger seat of the large surveillance van as it drove toward the parking lot of Box Farm Personal Storage. He didn't like the vehicle, and he didn't like leading an operation from the rear. But in the open space in the back was his friend Tech Sergeant Ike Lloyd. Ike was belted into the bench seat, and bouncing him around too much was not a good idea while he was still recovering from his bullet wound.

Reid watched the first state police cruiser pull up to the gate and the driver pull out a ticket so the automatic gate would open. As the gate rolled aside, a trooper got out of the passenger seat and stuck a steel pipe through the chain link of the gate to keep it from closing. Then he wrapped a chain through the gate and around the steel support pole, and clapped a padlock on it to lock the gate open. The state police car pulled into the lot and parked.

The next seven cars pulled in after it and parked. Out of each car came four troopers, a few of them carrying shotguns or assault rifles. The first men into the building clambered up the stairs, and by the time the van carrying Reid and Lloyd cleared the gate, the place had been secured.

"I've got to go up and find Mr. Crane, and serve the warrant," said Reid.

"This looks like the time for it," Lloyd said. He watched Reid go inside and up the stairs. This was the first really good morning Ike Lloyd could recall having since he'd been shot. There were now teams of technicians and auditors and men from the DA's office waiting out on the road for a radio call from Reid inviting them to come in, and he judged it wouldn't be more than a few minutes before they'd get their invitation.

Reid came back and got into the van. "Crane's not here. There's a guy named Thompson who's supposed to be in charge today, so he's been served."

Reid picked up his handheld radio and said, "All right, ladies and gentlemen. You may proceed into the lot and begin your work."

Before he put his radio down, the other vehicles began to move, each one entering the lot and parking in one of the customers' spaces. Others kept going out to the ends of the rows of storage bays to begin their search and inventory. Some of the troopers in the office would be going over the list of bays and the people who had rented them, looking for familiar names or the names of people who didn't exist.

Reid said, "Ike, what were those bay numbers again?"

"J-nineteen and C-fifteen."

"Okay, let's start with J-nineteen."

A few minutes later, Ike Lloyd was standing with his crutches beside Reid while a trooper used a pair of bolt cutters to take off the lock of J-19. As soon as the lock was off, the trooper opened the hasp and raised the metal garage door. The bay was empty except for two plastic coolers, each about five feet long and two feet deep.

One of the technicians took photographs from outside the bay, then more photographs as he moved inside. After a few minutes of examining the floor and the two coolers and a period of fingerprinting, another pair of technicians arrived.

They removed the duct tape from the first of the two coolers using a pair of needle-nose pliers. They put the tape in a plastic bag to preserve any fingerprints they might have missed. Then they flipped the latches holding the cover down tight.

One technician lifted the top up on its hinges and recoiled visibly, and then recovered. There was a young man, dead, wearing a dark shirt and an open black windbreaker and jeans. The smell was the distinctive and terrible reek of a corpse.

Reid and Lloyd stepped closer. "I'm not sure who this is," said Reid. "You know him?"

Lloyd said, "Not by name. But I would say he's the missing man from my night at Slawicky's. See the holes in his shirt? Looks like number four buckshot. That's the load from the shotgun in my car."

"I think you're right," said Reid. "Double aught has only nine pellets. He's got at least a dozen holes I can see, and probably the rest were still clumped together when they hit his chest."

The technicians went to work on the second cooler, removing the tape and putting it in another evidence bag, and then flipping the latches and opening the cooler.

Lloyd and Reid stepped closer. Reid said, "Who do you suppose this is, Ike?"

"If I'm not mistaken, that's Mr. Daniel Crane himself."

31

The sounds of heavy traffic woke Mattie Sanders. She had never lived in such a noisy place. She didn't mind getting up, because she had always been an early riser. But here she was in a city where the sirens of fire trucks competed with the horns of the taxi drivers to keep a person from sleeping.

Each morning when she opened her eyes it took a few seconds to place herself on the planet. There was always a surprise that she wasn't in her house on the reservation where she had lived with Clinton Sanders until he'd died, and where she had raised their boy, Jimmy. The sounds her brain had been listening for had been the chirps and warbles of birds, maybe the distant scream of a hawk far overhead, but she heard cars instead, and her mind jumped to Hanover. But after that she had become fully awake and remembered they were in Philadelphia now.

The height of the buildings and the closeness of them made her feel uncomfortable. The hotel was cut off and in-sulated from the ground and the water. Even though it jut-ted up into the sky, the windows were all sealed and kept out the air. The only way to even tell what the weather was would be to turn on the television set and watch the news.

This morning, as she did every morning, she silently gave thanks that her son was alive, that he was well, and that they were together. She thanked the forces of the universe for sending Jane, and for the girl Chelsea. She gave thanks to the Creator for life, and to his twin brother the Destroyer for holding off her death this long.

Mattie sat up and got out of bed. She went into the bathroom and drew a hot bath. It seemed to loosen the stiffness that came on her overnight, and always made her feel good.

She dried, dressed in clean clothes, and walked out into the living room just as Jane appeared from one of the other bedrooms.

Mattie said, "Where's Chelsea?"

"When I saw her last she was in Jimmy's room helping him pack."

In her heart Mattie knew that it was the truth, but also considerably less than the truth. Chelsea must have spent the night in Jimmy's room, even if she was helping him pack now. It didn't matter. "Pack? Are we moving again?"

Jane said, "We're moving out, but not to another hiding place. It's time to go home." She went to the table by the window, picked up the laptop and refreshed its display, then handed it to Mattie. "Here. Read this. It's the *Buffalo News*. Daniel Crane is dead and the police found his fingerprints on the rifle."

JAMES SANDERS'S ATTORNEY, KAREN ALVAREZ, stood before the Honorable Mary Ann O'Riordan in the courtroom. "Your honor," she said, "I have a copy of the cell phone activity on the account of James Sanders's mother, Mrs. Mattie Sanders, for the period June sixteen through July ten of this year. It's certified by Mr. David Altner of Central Mobile Company. As you will see, Mrs. Sanders attempted to call her son eighty-nine times during the period, but a connection was never made. All of her calls went to his voice mail."

"And Mr. Sanders never thought to call her?"

"No, your honor. When Mr. Sanders's cell phone was lost, he was on a hiking trip through the forests of the Southern Tier of New York and northeastern Pennsylvania. He had no reason to think he was being sought by the police, and had often been out of touch with his mother for a few weeks."

"There were no pay phones?"

"No, your honor. He was in the forest."

"And after that?"

"When he called home, he was told that two local men, very distant relatives of his, had been in county jail and learned that there were men getting themselves sent there so they could take revenge on Mr. Sanders for the death of Nicholas Bauermeister. I have their depositions here. My client had only one way to survive, and that was to delay his surrender."

"That's an unusual defense."

"Yes, your honor. It's an unusual case. He has been cleared of any crime or infraction other than missing a court date in a case that a dozen eyewitnesses have sworn in affidavits was frivolous. He has now voluntarily turned himself in. I request that all charges be dismissed, and that he be allowed to go."

"Mr. Ferraro?" The judge stared at the assistant district attorney.

"The people concur, your honor."

The judge turned to Jimmy Sanders. "Then Mr. Sanders, the court dismisses the charge. We also advise you to answer your phone, and to call your mother more frequently. Case dismissed."

"Thank you, your honor," said Karen Alvarez.

Jimmy Sanders glanced over his shoulder to look at his mother and his girlfriend, Chelsea, standing beside her. He repeated, "Thank you, your honor," before his attorney ushered him away from the table and out of the courtroom.

THE NEXT MORNING AN EDGE of the Woods ceremony was performed on the reservation. Jimmy Sanders and his mother, Mattie, stood at the edge of the lawn near the council house beside a small fire, and they both tossed pinches of tobacco into it, so white smoke rose into the air. After a short time, a crowd of friends, relatives, and neighbors came from the council house and walked to the spot to meet them.

Although the people present were taking part in an ancient ritual, they dressed in their usual Saturday clothes, and looked like fifty members of an extended family coming together for a reunion picnic. The Edge of the Woods had once been used to honor and heal warriors returning from distant battles, or to admit important visitors into a Seneca village. It was still used to welcome people at a condolence ritual for the death of a chief and the elevation of his successor. Today the ceremony was meant to celebrate the return of a young man and his mother who had survived terrible danger and come home.

Jimmy and Mattie were symbolically returning from the woods—the dark, wild place where enemies stalked, wars were fought, and murders committed. They were being brought into the sunlit clearing, the peaceful, cleared land that had circled all Haudenosaunee villages from the beginning of civilization.

Today's was a small event, more personal than the big tribal ceremonies, but it followed the same steps. First a speaker stepped forward from the crowd. He was Jimmy's

mother's cousin, Wallace Golden, one of the Haudenosaunee league sachems. He began as the speaker always did.

"This morning we have gathered for a celebration, and
we see that the cycles of life are the same. It is our job to live
in harmony with each other and in balance with all living
things." Then he gave thanks as the Senecas always had, to
the whole universe beginning with the ground at their feet
and moving upward and outward. He thanked the earth,
the waters, the fish, the plants, the edible plants, the medici-
nal herbs, the animals, the trees, the birds, the four winds,
the thunders that bring rains, the sun, the moon, the stars,
all spirit messengers, and the Creator.

Wallace Golden went on to speak about this particular occasion. "We are thankful that our young man Jimmy
Sanders waits here at the edge of the forest, where the
cleared land begins, to be taken back in among us. We are
happy that he is cleared of all false suspicion and has come
home to us."

Wallace Golden said a few sentences recognizing that
Jimmy and Mattie's journey had been hard and dangerous.
He extended condolences for the losses and suffering that
Jimmy and his mother had needed to endure. He expressed
the hope that a return home would restore their "good
minds"—their health and well-being.

The well-wishers all greeted Jimmy and Mattie and
welcomed them home. In old times the people would have
mended their damaged clothing, given them shelter, and
tended their wounds. They still offered food. There was a
buffet of home-cooked food for everyone laid out on a row
of picnic tables, and everyone now ate and talked happily.

At the fringe of the gathering stood Mrs. Jane McKinnon, born Jane Whitefield, whose Wolf clan name was
Owandah. She chatted with a few friends and tasted several of the dishes. At a quiet moment, Jimmy Sanders approached her. "Thank you, Jane. I—"

She gave her head a little shake that an onlooker might have misinterpreted as getting her long, black hair out of her eyes. If anyone was listening, they heard her say, "It's nice to see you, Jimmy. Welcome home." Then she turned away to gather some plates and took them to the council house kitchen. She set them by the sink, where two women were already washing the first ones, when she felt a tap on her shoulder.

She turned to see Ellen Dickerson, who looked at her and walked toward the door. Jane followed her out of the kitchen and down a path that Jane wasn't sure she had ever noticed before. It was bushy where the lawn ended, but then opened up into a clear trail into the woods. She followed Ellen for a few hundred feet into a deep stand of old trees surrounding a small clearing.

Waiting for them were the clan mothers, standing in the clearing, talking quietly. When they saw Ellen and Jane arrive they all fell into silence at once, and focused on Jane. She felt it again—the strange sensation, an intimation that she was in the presence of something ancient and powerful. This was a gathering of the representatives of all the clans of her people, a direct link through a chain of women to the beginning of everything.

Jane reached into the pocket of her jeans and pulled out the strand of shell beads, the purple and white wampum they had given her to mark her appointment as the agent of their will. She held it up in front of Ellen Dickerson, mother of her own Wolf clan. "I guess it's time to give this back."

"It is," said Ellen. She took the beads and put them into her pocket. "Thank you."

The others began to hug Jane, one or two at a time, surrounding her for a moment and then stepping back.

Ellen said, "You've done everything we hoped you would. We believed there was no other way, or we would never have asked you to take such risks."

"I'm just glad everybody's safe," Jane said.

"This Edge of the Woods should have been for you, to welcome you back among us and make you whole again. We're all sorry we couldn't name you out loud without risking your secrets."

"Thank you all for understanding that," said Jane.

"The ceremony was for you too, even if we couldn't say it," said Daisy.

"We'd better get back to the party," said Alma. "People will start to wonder."

The women, one by one, kissed Jane's cheek or patted her shoulder or gave her another quick hug. Each of them turned and took a different path into the trees, so they would not all reappear at the party at once. In a moment Jane was alone.

Jane walked to Council House Road, got into the Volkswagen Passat, and drove it the last miles to Ray Snow's garage. She pulled the car into a space between a couple of the other cars he had refurbished. As she got out of the Passat, Ray Snow came out of the bay where he had a Toyota up on the lift. He was wiping his hands on a red shop rag.

"Hey, Jane. Welcome home. I finished your Volvo a week or so ago. How was the loaner?"

"It was great, Ray. But I'm afraid I drove it really hard. I'd like to pay you extra for the miles and depreciation." She handed him the keys.

"Don't worry about it," he said. "I already added enough to your Volvo's repair bill to cover anything you did to the VW."

"Please," she said.

"Not a chance. I'm already charging too much. Come on in, and I'll get your bill and the keys to your car."

He went behind his workbench where there was a counter with a computer and printer, and in seconds the printer was rolling her bill out onto the tray. "I heard Jimmy Sanders came home too."

"That's right," she said. "They had an Edge of the Woods for him today."

"Yeah," he said. "I heard that was happening, but I couldn't go on a workday, with people waiting for their cars. I'll go see him in a day or two."

"He'll be glad to see you." She took the bill, looked at it, and said, "Two hundred dollars? *Two hundred?*"

He shrugged. "I'm in a good mood."

"You're always in a good mood," she said. "I don't know what's the matter with you." She pulled a wallet out of her purse, gave him two hundreds, and took her Volvo's keys. "I'll see you, Ray."

Ray watched her get into her white Volvo and drive off. He walked to the Volkswagen Passat to see what sort of wear she had actually put on it. He opened the door, sat in the driver's seat, inserted the key, and listened to the engine while he surveyed the interior, and then looked down toward the odometer. He couldn't see the dial because there was a stack of bills propped in front of it. He took it off the dashboard and counted twenty-five hundred-dollar bills. Jane had known he wouldn't take the money before she'd even gotten out of the car, so she had left it there.

A FEW HOURS LATER, DR. Carey McKinnon walked in the kitchen door of his house carrying a bottle of champagne and a bouquet of summer flowers. He set the bottle on the counter, handed his wife the bouquet, and took her in his arms. They kissed, and they stayed that way for a long time before she pulled away.

She set the flowers on the counter. "How did you know?"

"I read the newspapers. I saw that this Crane guy was pretty much posthumously convicted of the killing."

"So you knew I'd come home."

"Not necessarily today," he said. "You may have noticed the roses I bought yesterday, or the orchids from the day before. They're in vases in the living room and dining room. It's like a funeral parlor in there."

"I saw them," she said. "It was a nice way to come home. I could tell you had been thinking about me too."

"Too?"

"Of course," she said. "And maybe that you weren't so mad at me for going away."

"I don't know. How mad did you think I was?"

"Pretty mad."

He shrugged. "If you have enough time alone with your feelings, they start to separate out like ingredients in a suspension, and you can identify their proportions. Anger wasn't the biggest part. Worrying about you was the biggest, and missing you was most of what was left." He paused. "And I guess after I thought about it for a while, I felt ashamed for pretending I didn't understand some things, when I really did."

"What things?"

"That they're your family too. They were around when you were a kid. You share a lineage and a language and a history that I don't, and they have a claim on you. I pretended to both of us that I didn't know, so I'd have a right to my irritation."

Jane hugged him, and held him to her. She said nothing about the things he understood or the ten thousand things that he didn't.

He lifted her chin and looked at her closely. "So you're done now, right?"

"Done?"

"Jimmy's safe, and the clan mothers are satisfied?"

"They said they were."

"You're home for good?"

"If I can be."

They looked into each other's eyes, and Jane could see that a hint of the sadness had returned, but he pretended he didn't know what she'd meant.

"Want to go out to dinner?" he asked. "I made reservations at the Strathmore."

"The Strathmore?" she said. "You must have amputated a few wallets while I was away."

"It's the only way I can get my patients to lose weight," he said. "While you were gone I tried to keep busy."

"What time are our reservations?"

"Seven," he said.

Her eyes widened and she gently released herself from his arms. "Then we've got to get ready right away." She walked out of the kitchen, across the dining room, into the living room. She reached the stairway and went up a few steps, then glanced over her shoulder to see him watching her, and smiled. "Too bad for you."

"I could call them and make it tomorrow night."

She took another step and looked back. "I would if I were you."